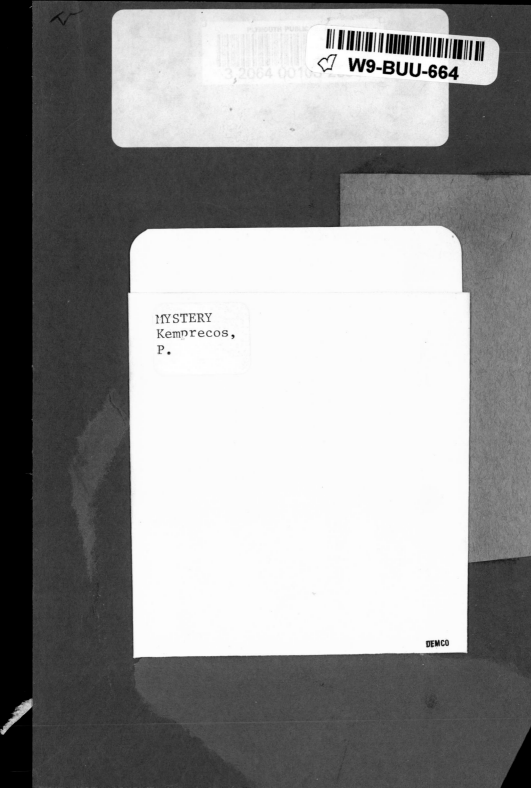

Death
in Deep Water

Death in Deep Water

Paul Kemprecos

A PERFECT CRIME BOOK

DOUBLEDAY

NEW YORK   LONDON   TORONTO   SYDNEY   AUCKLAND

A PERFECT CRIME BOOK
PUBLISHED BY DOUBLEDAY
a division of Bantam Doubleday Dell Publishing Group, Inc.
666 Fifth Avenue, New York, New York 10103

DOUBLEDAY is a trademark of Doubleday, a division of
Bantam Doubleday Dell Publishing Group, Inc.

Book design by Tasha Hall

Library of Congress Cataloging-in-Publication Data
Kemprecos, Paul.
    Death in deep water / by Paul Kemprecos.
        p.   cm.
    "A Perfect crime book."
    I. Title.
    PS3561.E4224D4   1992
    813'.54—dc20   91-46891
                                          CIP

ISBN 0-385-42379-9

1   3   5   7   9   10   8   6   4   2

First Edition

For Carol and Jeff, and for Christi

"He harms himself who does harm to another, and the evil plan is most harmful to the planner."

—HESIOD (c. 700 B.C.)

Death
in Deep Water

I

In the liquid emerald coolness, the predator waited.

Terrible in its deadly beauty, the twenty-five-foot-long body glided through the water, propelled by lazy sweeps of its spade-shaped flukes. Slowly, almost lethargically, it cruised in wide leisurely circles, steering into turns with its paddle-shaped pectoral fins, slicing the water with its tall dorsal.

The easy movements were deceiving, for no sea creature was faster, none could be more ferocious. Shaped by a harsh and demanding environment, it was a marvel of natural engineering, and except for humans, the most efficient killer on the planet. It feared nothing. Not even the savage sharks or the great leviathans who lumbered through the world's oceans were safe from its slashing teeth. The enormous energy locked in the creature's streamlined torso could send eight tons of murderous flesh hurtling toward its prey.

But for now it was tranquil.

Moving its massive round head from side to side, the predator forced air through its nasal sacs in a series of repetitive clicks that were above the human range of hearing, focusing the sound waves in a narrow directional beam that bounced off solid objects like the sonar on a submarine. The returning echoes were sonic brushstrokes that painted a sound picture of the creature's surroundings in its large and complex brain.

It was a skill developed through millions of years of evolution in the dark, deep reaches of the sea, where light never penetrates and eyes are useless.

The echoes struck a hard unbroken expanse, rebounded, ricocheted in a confusing tattoo, coming at the animal from all directions.

Then faded. The creature was silent, and in the silence, memories came to it, ghostly dreamlike recollections of endless vistas that teemed with life. But even more wonderful was the eerie music made by others of its kind, calling across the cold distances with warbled trills and trumpet blasts.

The predator felt its isolation keenly, for it was a sentient creature with a capacity for feeling and perceiving. It knew anger and frustration, happiness and sorrow, even if it couldn't put words to these emotions. Now it was hungry, not for food, but for companionship. It let out a plaintive scream, long and strident. There was no answering call.

Lonely.

The predator surfaced to breathe, sending misty exhalations from the blowhole in its head, then resumed its mindless circling. With each circuit, the animal paused at a hard transparent surface where it could see beyond its confines, then went on.

It passed again, and stopped. Something was moving on the other side of the hardness.

Curious, the animal hovered on its vertical axis, watching,

first with one black eyeball, then the other. The tail flicked, the creature shot straight up, and its huge head emerged from the water.

Yes.

The man came nearer. He looked at the animal for a very long time. Then he blew a sharp note on a whistle and signaled with his arms. The animal knew what was expected. It plummeted to the bottom, zoomed to the surface and leaped from the water, spinning high in the air, dancing on its tail in defiance of gravity.

Good.

It exulted in the chance to use its muscles, to respond, to act, to move, to be with another living being. The man slipped into the water. He swam over and stroked the shiny black-and-white skin.

Good.

The man clutched the creature's dorsal fin and pulled himself onto the animal's long back. He dug his knees into the blubbery flesh like a rodeo cowboy on a Brahma bull. Lulled by its pleasure at having company, the animal responded slowly at first. Then the great brain absorbed the significance of the pressure on its back and sides.

No.

A lightning message flashed along the spine to hundreds of nerve endings in the tail. Powerful muscles tightened under the rubbery black skin. The tail lifted, flexed, then whipped down and slapped the water like a giant flail.

Cuh-*rack!*

The ear-splitting impact echoed and reechoed. Water exploded into foamy shards.

No.

The creature hated the weight against its sensitive skin. Its mood change was electrical. The almost child-like eagerness to please vanished. Primitive reflexes took over.

The creature snapped its tail again, submerged in a shallow dive, then angled up and jumped clear of the water. The man leaned forward and gripped the slippery dorsal fin. They splashed down again as one. Tidal waves sloshed in every direction. The animal plunged deep. The man held on, desperately. The creature came up fast. It leaped from the water, higher this time, soared, then landed in a wet explosion of foam and spray.

No.

The animal rolled violently, coming down on one side, and shook the man from its back the way a cow might dislodge a tick. The man sputtered and gasped for air.

They were only a few yards apart, so close the man could see his pale, terrified face reflected in the creature's dark eye. He yelled in terror. The predator closed the space between them. It opened its mouth wide to show the long pink tongue and dagger-sharp conical teeth, then swiftly moved in on its struggling target.

2

The dusty Ford van with the avocado paint job and Rhode Island plates pulled up next to a silver BMW polished like a gravy bowl. A scruffy long-haired kid in a blue workman's uniform slithered out the passenger side and eyeballed the crowded parking lot in a quick three-hundred-sixty-degree pirouette, as graceful as Baryshnikov in his prime. Then he curled his fingers in an okay sign and two more young guys in uniforms spilled from the van. They must have figured nobody was watching them, but they were wrong. From the crest of a sand dune around a hundred feet away, where I lay belly down, the seven-by-fifty Bushnell binoculars could pick out the acne on their wise-guy faces.

It was a perfect July day. Mercury in the eighties. Not a hint of humidity or whisker of a cloud in the sky. The low thunder of breaking rollers rumbled in the distance. Black-capped laughing gulls wheeled in lazy circles overhead, their manic cackles mingling with the happy screams of kids daring the surf. People dressed for the beach threaded their way between parked cars. They lugged coolers, oversized towels, and folding chairs, and did funny little barefoot dances on the hot sunbaked blacktop.

It was hard to believe a felony was in progress.

While his buddies kept their eyes peeled, one guy slid a metal strip down into the Beemer's window. I turned to swat a greenhead fly who was sinking its fangs into my bare thigh. Missed. Looked again. The car door was open. The whole thing took about thirty seconds.

Jimmy Buffet was singing about good times and riches and son of a bitches in my head. I slipped the earphones off, stuffed my Walkman in a canvas daypack, and flicked on a Radio Shack portable CB.

"Sandman to Chowderhead. Come in, please."

A breathless voice crackled on the radio.

"This is Chowderhead."

"Stand by for instructions."

"Will do."

I swiveled the navy Boston Red Sox cap so the visor pointed backward, rapper-style, and brought a Nikon 35mm camera with a zoom lens to my eye. The letters printed on the van filled the viewfinder. ACE LOCKSMITHS. Cute cover. One of the guys was in the car. His disembodied arm handed out two tennis rackets, a duffel bag, and a camera. I banged off a half-dozen shots of the stuff moving into the van and grabbed the radio again.

"Write this down, Dougie. Man o'war with three Klingons aboard. Green Astro Ford van. Rhode Island plates. Number 896-687. Get a Federation starship in here. Pronto."

"Roger that, Sandman. Chowderhead out."

Yeow! The greenhead nailed my calf. I smashed the little bastard to a green pulp, then turned back to the parking lot. A car stereo, wires dangling, was on its way from the BMW to the van. I caught the smooth transfer on film and shook my head in admiration. These dudes were real pros.

Five minutes later they were done. They got back in the van, cruised slowly around the parking lot, and headed for the exit. Surprise! Blue and red roof lights flashed on the access road. First one police cruiser, then another swung into the lot and blocked the way. The cops hustled the guys out of the van, frisked them, and stuffed the trio into the patrol cars.

All I had to do was drop the roll of film off at the police station, tell them I'd be available to make a statement, and my job was over.

I wiped the sweat off my forehead, gulped down a swallow of lime Gatorade to replenish the moisture baked away by the summer sun, and put the camera and radio into the daypack with my Walkman and sunscreen. Then I followed the fragrant aroma of fried onion rings to a white clapboard building with a sign on it that read DOUGIE'S CLAM SHACK AND CHOWDER HOUSE.

Dougie burst out the screen door leading to the kitchen and pulled me inside. His bald head glistened with sweat and his black anarchist mustache was caked with flour.

He put his pudgy arm around me and grinned like the Big Bad Wolf. "Caught those bastards with the goods. The little pricks have been hitting my customers all summer. Friggin' cops in this town couldn't catch a cold going bare-ass in a blizzard."

"Don't be too tough on the local cops, Dougie. They haven't got the manpower to stake out every parking lot in town, especially when people don't lock up or forget to set their car alarms."

"Yeah, I guess so," he fumed. "The touristas leave their brains at home when they go on vacation. But Jeez, Soc, you'd think the town could spring one of those summer rent-a-cops you see standing on street corners hustling the babes. Sometimes I think we're supporting the LAPD from the taxes I pay. Which reminds me, pal, whadda I owe yah?"

I leaned against a pile of potato sacks and watched the

teenage kids working the fryolators at the front counter. "I dunno, Dougie. I put around ten hours into this case, not counting travel. Most of it was lying out on the dunes, so I got a great tan, but I lost fishing time on Sam's boat, and I'd like to make that up."

Dougie scratched his double chin with a batter-caked fingernail and did some mental calculations.

"How about a couple of hundred clams?"

The figure he mentioned was close to the balance on my unpaid ComElectric bill. "Sure, Dougie, that should do it," I said.

Fifteen minutes later I sat at a sticky picnic table trying to make a dent in an Everest of golden nuggets that was as high as my nose. Doug came over and patted me on the back.

"Everything okay, Soc?"

I aimed some ketchup from a plastic envelope onto the french fries and glurped most of the red stuff onto my fingers.

"Terrific, Dougie." I said, forking down a mouthful. "Tender, fresh, done to perfection. Unfortunately, these weren't the kind of clams I had in mind."

He sat next to me, frowning like a melancholy walrus. "Yeah, I know pal, you want greenbacks. Look, business has been a little off and the price of shellfish has been up near platinum, but I'll pay you in a couple of weeks. In the meantime, come by when you get hungry for the best fried seafood on Cape Cod. Bring a friend. It's on me. Okay?"

"Okay, Dougie." I munched on an onion ring. "But you might be sorry."

My name is Aristotle P. Socarides. The middle initial stands for Plato, something I don't advertise because it makes me sound like the first three chapters in a book of Greek philosophers. I live in a weatherworn boathouse on the eastery shore of Cape Cod, a seventy-mile-long arm-shaped peninsula that hooks into the Atlantic off the coast of Massachusetts. I share my lodgings, as Dr. Watson would say, with a mostly black and constantly hungry Maine coon cat named Kojak. Generations of mice who know they have nothing to fear from Kojak have transformed the walls into cooperative housing. Two noisy raccoons live under the boathouse, and from the decibel level of their frequent arguments, I'd guess their marriage is on the rocks.

The boathouse overlooks an even-tempered saltwater inlet that Samuel de Champlain mapped when he passed this way in 1606. He called it Pleasant Bay and the name stuck. Low-lying islands that were carved by glaciers in the ice age rise from the bay, and its waters are enclosed by the mainland on one side and a barrier beach a few hundred yards wide on the other. Beyond the beach is the moody Atlantic, and on clear days I swear I can see Portugal from my deck.

Elegant blue herons with necks longer than Audrey Hepburn's wade through the quiet marshes nearby, and in the warm season an intoxicating fragrance of beach plum and salt-spray rose mixes with the scents of the ocean. It's light-years away from my old life, and I prefer it that way. I quit my job as a Boston cop because I couldn't deal with the city's banana-republic politics. But you never stop being a flatfoot. An inner need to set the world in order always claws at your innards. You're like a person who can't walk by a hanging picture without straightening it. So I have my private investigator's license and take a case now and then, depending on my mood and the balance in my bank account.

Mostly I fish for cod and haddock on a line trawler owned by a fine old Yankee gentleman named Sam. He took me under his wing with no questions asked, patiently taught me the craft of fishing, and gave me work on his boat, where the clear fresh air fumigated the musty corridors of my mind.

The fishing boat is called the *Millie D.* Sam named it after his wife Mildred. He swears the trawler and the woman he adores are one and the same. Both are sturdy, broad in the beam, demand constant attention, and can handle the roughest of seas. And both are temperamental.

"Sweet as sea-clam fritters one minute, sour as rhubarb pie the next," he says. Sam's culinary appraisal aside, the *Millie D* has a definite unpredictable streak. She showed it two days after I wrapped up the Clam Shack Caper.

Sam and I had cast off from the fish pier around 4:00 A.M. and steamed east then south. Just before dawn we hove to out of sight of land off the elbow of the Cape. It was a soft day with no hard edges. The sun was bright but not blistering hot. Rolling seas nuzzled the underside of the *Millie D*'s wooden hull as gently as suckling kittens. The breeze held steady at fifteen miles per hour without the ocean-puckering gusts that often come out of the southwest in summer and kick the seas up.

I brewed a second batch of Maxwell House in the dented old pot that gives an aluminum aftertaste to our coffee and listened for a moment to the chuckling seas, convinced I was hearing what Aeschylus called "the myriad laughter of the ocean waves." Then I bent my back to the task at hand, catching fish.

Everything was going well. The long nylon trawl lines snaked from their plastic tubs and off the stern chute in a silvery blur of hooks, splashing into the chartreuse surface of the dappled sea without a single tangle or snag. No schools of hungry dogfish ate our bait. Every hook that came aboard had a wriggling silver-scaled cod on it. The cash register in Sam's head would be going *ca-ching* with every fish we caught.

By late afternoon the fish hold was filled to bursting. Smiling at our good fortune, we pulled in the last set and pointed the bow back to port. Sam was at the helm and I was coiling trawl line. Five miles from home the engine coughed like a dog with a chicken bone caught in its throat, gargled wetly, and gave up the ghost. Sam tried to get the engine going, then took his tan duck-billed cap off and crawled below to take a look.

He poked around, muttering to himself. Before long, he emerged from the engine compartment wearing war-paint streaks of grease on his long-jawed face and wagged his craggy chin sadly in a sorry-the-patient-died headshake.

"Guess we've best give the Coast Guard a call. We're not going anywhere under our own power 'less we row home."

The Coast Guard got a commercial salvage boat out to us. Five hours later we entered the darkened harbor and the *Millie D* tied up to the fish pier. I had radioed the fish dealer we'd be late. A couple of bored fish packers were on hand to unload our catch and ice it, but the trailer truck had left for the Fulton Fish Market in New York. We refrigerated our catch and crossed our fingers, hoping the high price would hold when the fish were sent out the next day.

Sam said he'd try to line up a mechanic, and I told him I would call later. Looking at water all day long had made me thirsty. I drove straight from the pier to a dark pub with a Batcave ambience. The bar used to be called the Porthole, but the hard-core drinkers who had trouble pronouncing two-syllable words slurred the name down to the 'Hole.

I sat at the bar next to a bearish charterboat skipper. "Tell me, Cap," I said, "do you think the Sophoclean definition of tragedy could be applied to a dead engine, a boatload of fish you couldn't get to market, and a hefty tow fee?"

His booze-glazed eyes squinted from a face cooked to hamburger red by too many hard days in the sun and hard nights at the 'Hole.

"I don't know what the hell you're talking about as usual, Soc, but I'll agree to anything you say if you buy me a beer."

I signaled the bartender. He slid two mugs of Bud our way and followed it with a note.

"For you, Soc. This guy has been trying to get you."

I frowned to let him know I realized it was déclassé to be called at the 'Hole. Some of the resident phonies have themselves paged so they will look important. I brightened when I read the name on the note. I went to a pay phone and charged a call to Boston on my credit card. A guttural voice answered, "Tremont Investigations."

"Hi Shaughnessy," I said. "Got your message."

"Jeezus, Soc, I've been trying to get you all day. How the hell are you?"

"Just dandy, Ed. I would have called earlier, but I was out fishing. I got in a little while ago."

"Yeah, I tried you a couple of times at home. Figured you'd show up at the 'Hole before the day was over. Listen, Soc, this is going to sound crazy, but what do you know about whales?"

I pressed the telephone tighter to my ear. The jukebox was doing a heavy riff behind "Pretty Woman" by Roy Orbison. Fueled on high test, the late-evening crowd was cranking up to a dull roar.

"There's a lot of noise at this end, Ed. I thought you said 'whales.'"

"That's right. Like *Moby Dick*. Listen, buddy, I need your help on a real weird case. You could bail me out and make a few bucks beside. Interested?"

"Hell, Ed, I'm always willing to help an old pal."

"Terrific. Look, I'd like you to see a guy named Simon Otis. Tomorrow morning in Boston. He'll give you the whole skinny. Then call me if you want to go for it." He gave me a time and place and I said I'd get back to him. The charterboat skipper whose ear I rented in exchange for a brew was trying to hit on a couple of college girls. I finished my drink and went home to call Sam.

He was about as apoplectic as his New England reserve allowed. "Every marine mechanic on the Cape is up to his eyeballs in work," Sam grumbled. "I got a fella coming from Hyannis, but he can't be here until tomorrow afternoon."

"I'll be in Boston early in the day, so I'll catch you later to see how you're doing." Sam said that would be fine.

Kojak rubbed against my leg. I fed him a can of 9-Lives Savory Seafood dinner. Then I made myself a grilled tomato-and-cheese sandwich with Velveeta and whipped up a plate of angel-hair pasta with Ragu mushroom sauce. I washed it down with a couple of cans of beer. The Gods of Olympus never had it so good.

The long day of fishing had sapped my energies. I flopped into bed, pulled the sheets over my head, and fell quickly into a deep slumber. The raccoons woke me up around 2:00 A.M. They were thumping the floorboards and screaming at each other in raccoonese. It could have been worse, I suppose; I was lucky they weren't skunks. Eventually I got back to sleep. Around seven Kojak walked on my head and woke me up.

I gave him some breakfast crunchies, drank two cups of instant coffee, showered, put on a seersucker-blue sports jacket, tan slacks, and a pair of Top-Siders, and coaxed my 1977 GMC pickup truck into life. A half hour later I parked the truck at the Burger King off the Mid-Cape Highway outside of Hyannis. I picked up a *Boston Globe* from a vending machine and settled into a window seat on the P&B commuter bus.

The ninety-minute ride to Boston gave me time to read the comics and check out baseball box scores. The Red Sox were going through their usual midseason gyrations, veering from triumph to disaster. It's like watching a plane that has lost a wing. Your heart hopes it'll come down safely even though your head knows it's going to crash. I sighed, put the paper aside, and looked out the window. The passing scenery was a blur.

What do you know about whales? Shaughnessy had asked.

It was an odd question. Coincidental, too. Two weeks ago on a fishing trip, Sam yelled and pointed off to starboard. I followed his finger and saw only the blue Atlantic. Sam has years on me, but his eye is sharper than a sea gull's on a dump run. I looked through the binoculars. A quarter of a mile away a white feathery plume erupted from the sea in a spreading umbrella.

Puff. Then another. *Puff.* The sun glinted off shiny black skin.

"Humpbacks," Sam declared. "Real pretty sight."

"Yeah, real pretty." There are loads of whales on the fishing grounds in the spring and fall. No matter how often you see them, it's always a treat.

The whales moved in slow motion across the glassy sea. One of them breached, coming nearly straight out of the water. "We're wasting our time fishing, Sam. How about turning the *Millie D* into a whalewatch boat? We could charge fifteen dollars a head and two bucks for a hot dog. I'll run the grill."

"I'll leave the whales be," Sam replied. "I've given them enough trouble for one lifetime."

My hand was on the hauler switch, ready to start the hooks coming in. I hesitated, intrigued at Sam's comment. My fishing partner is one of the gentlest men in the world.

"Sam, I can't imagine you giving *any*one or *any*thing trouble."

He scooped his pipe into a package of Edgehill and touched a match to the bowl. "It was during the war. Our side needed special oil for bombsight gears. Best oil came from blackfish—that's what we used to call the pilot whales that strand on the bayside sometimes and get their pictures on TV. The government protects them now, but in those days the feds came down the Cape and told us they needed oil. Bunch of the boys and I would get in our motorboats whooping and hollering like cowboys. We'd drive the whales onto the shallows and they'd die on the flats when the tide went out. Then we'd cut the oil melons out of their heads."

"I never thought of you as a whaler, Sam."

"Me neither, Soc. It was fun the first couple times. Chance to make big money and help the war. Not much different than catching fish, I thought." He puffed deliberately on his pipe, looking off toward the pod of humpbacks. "But one day we drove a couple dozen ashore near First Encounter Beach. I walked among them. They were making noises like children crying. The worse thing was a mother whale. She gave birth right then and there. Probably the shock of going aground. She and the calf died, a'course. I came home feeling like I had murdered somebody. Couldn't sleep that night. I talked to Millie, and she said to do what I thought was right. Figured we could beat Hitler without making life miserable for those poor critters, so I quit doing it. After a bit someone invented a way to use oil they got from the ground and they stopped going after the blackfish."

"You helped win the war, Sam. Things would have been tough if we hadn't."

"Guesso," he said. "Every once in a while, though, like when I see those humpbacks, I think back to the blackfish crying out there on the flats. It's too late now, but I wish I hadn't done it."

The moon-crater potholes on the Southeast Expressway jarred my thoughts back to the present. Minutes later I got off at South Station. The address Shaughnessy gave me was an office high rise near Rowe's Wharf, ten minutes' walk from the bus stop. The fast elevator shot to the top floor. I still had my finger on the button as the door whispered open on a red marble lobby decorated with a city photo mural covering most of one wall. The words BAY STATE INVESTMENTS were overlaid on the mural.

An attractive receptionist with a sweet smile efficiently extracted my name and buzzed somebody on an intercom, then ushered me briskly along a hushed hallway, opened a door, and quietly retreated.

I stepped inside and sank into the ankle-deep beige carpeting of a cavernous conference room. Blue light streamed through tinted floor-to-ceiling windows that overlooked the harbor and the distant twin-legged control tower at Logan Airport. Clipper ships in full sail coursed along a wallpaper sea. Hanging above the hand-buffed oak wainscoting were maps of early Boston and portraits of the stiff-collared Yankee aristocracy who ran the city before the Irish and Italians took over.

In the center of the room was a football-shaped dark mahogany table long enough to play shuffleboard on. Four men and a woman were seated at the far end. They looked at me as if I were making a Domino's pizza delivery to the bar at the Four Seasons. A silver-haired man wearing a dark pinstripe suit launched himself out of his chair and strode athletically over with his hand extended.

"Good morning, Mr. Socarides. Nice of you to come," he said. "My name is Simon Otis."

He was about six feet, an inch shorter than I am, but he had a runner's leanness that made him appear taller than he was. His grip was strong and his voice richly confident. It's always that way with people who have reversible front and back names. He indicated a leather-cushioned chair. I sat down and he took a seat opposite me.

With his mustache and natural elegance, Otis resembled an older Walter Pidgeon. I grinned at the thought and he grinned back. I was on a roll, so I grinned at the three Oriental men and a young Oriental woman who were also at the table. They were dressed in matching gray. The woman looked down at the steno pad in front of her, but the men showed off their dental work. I know when I'm outgrinned. I turned back to Otis.

"Mr. Shaughnessy spoke very highly of you," he said.

"You're in good hands if you've engaged his detective agency." The woman scribbled in the pad then leaned over and murmured to the three men who put their heads together and listened, brows furrowed.

Otis sat back in his chair and tapped the side of his long nose with a slender, well-manicured finger.

"We did substantial research before talking to Tremont Investigations. The agency has a very good reputation and extensive resources. Therefore, we were rather surprised at Mr. Shaughnessy's recommendation. Because of the peculiar nature of our problem, he said it would be best to employ one person." He paused, cocked his head slightly as if Shaughnessy's proposal still struck him as mildly preposterous. "Mr. Shaughnessy suggested that that person be you."

"It was kind of Mr. Shaughnessy to recommend me, but not surprising. We worked as partners on the Boston Police Department."

The pen flickered across the steno pad again and there was another whispered conference. I took a deep breath and let it out slowly.

"Yes," Otis said. "He mentioned that." He regarded me for a moment with pale gray eyes. "To be perfectly blunt, Mr. Socarides, I'm worried about putting this operation onto the shoulders of any one person. Particularly an individual who is an unknown quantity to us. There is a great deal at stake here."

A notepad with the company logo, a stylized BSI, lay on the table in front of me. Next to it on a marble stand was a sharply tapered black ballpoint pen in a fake brass inkwell. I took the pen and doodled on the pad as if I were writing something important, then put it down on the glossy tabletop.

"Let *me* be blunt, too, Mr. Otis. First of all, I don't take

every case thrown my way." I gestured toward the others at
the table. "And second, if you don't mind, I'd like to know
who these three gentlemen are and why they are so obviously
interested in our conversation."

The woman's hand froze in midstroke.

Otis's face flushed pink. "I'm sorry, Mr. Socarides. It was
rude of me not to introduce you. I wanted to sound you out
before we wasted time on introductions."

I sat back. "I have lots of time. Filene's Basement doesn't
close until six o'clock." I winked at the stenographer. She
looked the other way.

"Of course," Otis said. He stood up. "This is Mr.
Shimoro, Mr. Tanaka, and Mr. Mishuma." I rose and shook
hands as each man bobbed up and bowed slightly. Then I
reached over and I took the stenographer's hand. She tried to
suppress a smile by tightening her lips in a disapproving
pucker that didn't quite make it, and held on until I sat down.

The Japanese men remained inscrutable. Otis raised an
eyebrow and went on with his presentation.

"These gentlemen represent Shogun Industries, a major
Japanese conglomerate. I'm the executive liaison between
their company and ours. Bay State Investments is a real-estate development and holding company." He patted the tabletop with his palm. "We own this building and a great deal
of commercial and residential property in Boston. We have
also acquired other promising companies, including one
named Sea Amusements, which runs a marine theme park on
Cape Cod. The park is called Oceanus. Are you acquainted
with it?"

An aquarium was the last place I wanted to go after looking
codfish in the eye all day. "I've never been there, but I hear
it's got more fish than the Atlantic Ocean," I said.

He nodded. "The park was a sound investment. It has
made money and appreciated in value. Ordinarily we would

hold on to it, but BSI has been badly hurt by the real-estate slump. We invested heavily in commercial real estate. Then the bottom fell out of the market. We're faced with some unpleasant prospects. We want to cut the park loose and use the cash infusion to reconsolidate and show the stockholders and banks they have nothing to worry about. Shogun Industries has made an extremely generous offer, which we have accepted." He paused. "There is one problem, however."

Otis flipped open a leatherbound folder at his fingertips. He removed a sheaf of newspaper clippings and pushed them across the table. On top was a *Boston Herald* front page. The headline was in mile-high tabloid type:

"JAWS" KILLS
WHALE TRAINER
AT CAPE PARK

I thumbed through the pile. There were clips from the *Boston Globe*, *The New York Times*, AP, and UPI. The *Cape Cod Times* article was played across the top of the page under a banner headline:

KILLER WHALE FATALLY MAULS HANDLER AT AQUARIUM

The story had been all over radio, print, and TV, so I was familiar with the main details. A trainer at Oceanus had been found dead and the suspected instrument of his demise was a trained killer whale. The news clips featured photos of the whale, an eight-ton hunk of blubber named Rocky, and of Eddy Byron, the dead trainer. I finished going through the clips and looked up. Otis was watching patiently.

"The newsguys had a good time with this," I said.

He gathered the newspaper cuttings into a neat pile and squared the edges.

"Yes," he said. "We could have made millions of dollars in ticket sales capitalizing on the morbid fascination the public has with a killer whale who actually kills."

"Why didn't you?" I asked.

"We had more important issues to deal with." He played with his mustache. "We're in somewhat of a dilemma, Mr. Socarides. You see, Oceanus is under attack."

"Attack by whom, Mr. Otis?"

He leaned forward on his elbows and folded his hands as if they would fly away. "Environmentalists. Ecologists. Animal-rights organizations. Some people call them 'whale huggers.' Well-meaning but fuzzy-headed groups who have a rather skewered view of things. They believe it is immoral to keep dolphins and whales captive for profit. They say parks like Oceanus are 'whale jails.' "

I waited, still wondering where a private investigator fit in.

Otis went on. "They have lobbied the government for tighter regulations to the point it has become difficult to acquire permits for dolphins, virtually impossible to bring in new killer whales. The marine-park industry in this country has managed to survive, and prosper, but the incident at Oceanus changes that."

"How so, Mr. Otis?"

"The animal rightists say the whale reacted violently because it was held in captivity. There have been protests. As many as six different organizations were picketing Oceanus at one time. Even the antivivisectionists showed up, for heaven sakes! There was an attempted boycott that failed and a bomb threat that was successful. We closed the park after that."

"Bomb threats usually turn out to be hoaxes."

"Yes, we know that, but we had reason to believe this one was serious. We've lost a great deal in box-office receipts, but that's only a drop in the bucket. We could weather those losses."

"Why don't you?"

"It's much more complex. You see, the furor could torpedo our deal with Shogun. Japan is still hunting whales and is extremely sensitive to international criticism. Shogun believes acquiring Oceanus now, in the middle of this controversy, would leave them and their country open to further charges of whale exploitation and open the door to more of the kind of Japan bashing one hears out of Congress, particularly during an election year."

I looked over at the Japanese men. They were listening to the translation, dark eyes fixed on the interpreter, taking in her every word.

"Nothing is as stale as yesterday's news," I said, turning back to Otis. "The public has a short attention span. Wait long enough and people will be diverted by an air crash or a U.S. senator caught with a floozie."

"Ordinarily, I might agree with you. But we can't afford to wait. If Shogun pulls out, millions of dollars in Bay State Investments property, this very building we're sitting in, will be in jeopardy. So you see, we have to defuse the controversy as quickly as possible."

"I'm not trying to talk myself out of a job, Mr. Otis, but public relations has never been my strong point."

He chuckled dryly. "We don't need PR people. We have dozens of those. But we do require a skilled and persistent investigator for the formidable task we have in mind."

"What's that, Mr. Otis?"

He paused for dramatic effect and drummed his fingers on the table like a riverboat gambler bluffing a mark.

"We would like you to prove the killer whale is innocent."

3

Maybe it was time to see an ear doctor. My hearing failed whenever somebody said the word *whale*. First with Shaughnessy, now Otis. I straightened up in my chair, leaned forward, and resisted the urge to cup a hand behind my ear.

"Sir, could you run that by me again?"

Otis's razor-sharp eyes stared at me gravely from under thick brows. "It's really very simple. We want you to exonerate the killer whale."

"You're telling me the whale did *not* kill the trainer?"

Otis dismissed the notion with a careless wave of his hand. "I have no idea as to the animal's guilt or innocence. Nor do I care."

"I confuse easily, Mr. Otis. Could you elucidate?"

"Gladly. You see, those animal-rights groups I mentioned, and one in particular, are using the incident as a rallying cry. They want to shut down *all* marine theme parks, not just Oceanus, or tangle them in a web of regulation that would make it impossible to operate. As long as doubts about Mr.

Byron's death remain, these people can argue that the *whale*, not the trainer, was the victim. We would simply like those doubts removed."

"I'm still not sure where I fit in."

"We want the incident investigated. Quietly. Mr. Shaughnessy suggested we send in an undercover investigator to work at Oceanus. He thought your background as a diver, a fisherman, and a police officer made you the ideal candidate. We want you to join the park staff and simply keep your eyes and ears open."

Animal nuts who slap Save the Whales stickers on their bumpers give me a pain, and some of the organizations that use pictures of cute little harp seals being clubbed to death as an excuse to put their hand in someone's pocketbook are nothing but scams, in my view. At the same time I wasn't comfortable working for a client who exploited any*one* or any*thing.*

Even if the whale had bopped his trainer, there wasn't much anybody could do about it. No electric chair in the country is big enough to hold a rogue killer whale. On the other hand, there was a simple question of justice at stake. Nobody, human or not, should be tagged with a bum murder rap. I thought about Sam's World War II story again and it gave me the push I needed to make up my mind.

"Okay, Mr. Otis," I said. "I'll see what I can do."

"Splendid. Before you take the case, I should warn you. We have a time limit of one week from tomorrow. If the situation hasn't changed, Shogun will withdraw its offer."

"I'll do my best, but I can't promise anything."

Otis smiled and nodded at the Japanese men. We shook hands like pals at a drugstore cowboy reunion, and they departed with the interpreter trailing behind.

The door clicked softly shut and we were alone. Otis eyed me thoughtfully. "I hope you didn't mind those gentlemen. They asked to sit in on the interview. Since they hold the purse strings, I thought it prudent not to refuse. It was important to show them we were moving on this problem. We can talk more freely now. Do you have any questions?"

"A few. If the whale didn't kill the trainer, that narrows down the possibilities considerably. Could the trainer have been killed by accident?"

"Highly unlikely."

"That reduces the number of options even further, Mr. Otis. Are you or your company prepared to accept the possibility of foul play?"

Otis got up. He walked over to the window with his hands clasped behind his back and stared out at the harbor.

"We've considered the option that the trainer was murdered by another human," he said as coolly as if he were discussing a stock transfer.

"Why would anyone want to murder your trainer?"

"Aside from the usual reasons one has to murder another person, there are those who might like to sabotage the park, the purchase deal, or this company."

"You sound as if you have someone specific in mind."

"Oh yes," he said, turning back to me. "Mr. Shaughnessy and I have discussed some possible suspects. People who have reason to wish Oceanus ill. I suggest you give him a call."

"I'll do that."

"We hope there is a far more palatable explanation, but a murdering human is something we could live with better than a murdering whale." He gave me a wry smile. "It's an odd world we live in, isn't it? A whale who murders is a sensation. A human who murders is, as you indicated, yesterday's headline."

"Dead is dead, Mr. Otis. It doesn't matter to your trainer if the whale killed him or not."

"Quite true, Mr. Socarides, quite true. But it matters a great deal to us."

. . .

The big clocks on the Customs House tower told me I had two hours to wait for the bus back to Cape Cod. My stomach growled like a hungry puppy. A breakfast of black coffee is worse than no breakfast at all. I walked away from the harbor toward the narrow streets of the financial district. Minutes later I turned off Washington Street into an alley no wider than the cowpath it was when Sam Adams organized the Boston Tea Party a few blocks away.

The Delphi Restaurant was in an old Joe and Nemo's at the end of the alley. The walls were decorated with Aegean Islands posters and washed-out photographs of club sandwiches. A half-dozen customers sat at Formica tables reading newspapers over their coffee. Standing behind a curtain of hotpot steam was a tall man whose black curly hair rimmed a Mephistophelian face. He was arguing with a little old man who wore a double-breasted three-piece suit and a fedora. He was shouting at the customer, but the mock scowl on his mouth couldn't hide the amused gleam in his dark eyes.

He wiped his hands on a greasy apron. "I'll go over it again, my friend. The salad with the lunch special comes with one kind of dressing. *Greek* dressing. No French, no Russian, no Thousand Islands. This is a *Greek* restaurant. You want fancy, you go to Locke-Obers around the corner, but you'll pay two-ninety-five just for a lousy glass of water."

"Skip the salad," the man grumbled. "What comes with it?"

"I *told* you. Vegetables or rice. The vegetable is green peas and onions. Boiled to perfection."

"What about the rice?"

"Yeah, you can have the rice *with* gravy or the rice with no gravy."

"That's it? That's all?"

"Naw. You can have just the gravy with *no* rice. So take your pick."

"I'm picking another restaurant," the older man snapped. He slammed his tray onto the chrome-plated slider and stormed out the door. The counterman laughed and shook his head. Then he spotted me and grinned broadly. He came around the counter, pumped my hand, and put a hairy arm around my shoulder. "*Yasou*, Cousin Aristotle, what brings you to these parts?"

"*Yasou*, Cousin Nicholas. I was in town and heard the Delphi makes the best gravy with no rice in Boston."

He gave me an evil grin. "Aw, that guy. He knows damn well what the menu is. Christ, he's memorized it by heart. He's an old widow guy, kinda lonely, and a good fight over the daily special makes his day. He's probably got more money than God, but he walks over here from the backside of Beacon Hill so he can give me a hard time. Counts the beans to make sure I'm not shorting him. Sometimes I leave off the rolls just to get him going. It's a game we play. He'll be back. My day wouldn't be complete if he gave someone else an ulcer. Hey, want some chow? It's on the house."

I grabbed the abandoned tray. "Yeah, I need some Greek soul food. It's tough to get the real thing down in fish-and-chips land. Carve me off a couple of pounds of gyro. And I'll have a Coke to go with it."

"You get the *super* gyro." He used a knife that looked like a scimitar to slice thin strips expertly off a tapered hunk of spiced lamb hanging vertically in a heated spit. He placed the meat in a circular loaf of pita bread, first laying in some onions, tomatoes, and yogurt dressing. He wrapped the sandwich in waxed paper, set it on a plate, and called a dark-haired kid from the back room and asked him to take over the counter. Then he grabbed a can of Coke Classic and put it with the sandwich on my tray and ushered me to a corner table.

Nicholas gave me a run-down on his wife and kids. I listened, chewing my way through the gyro.

"So that's me, cuz," he said finally. "How's the rich branch of the Socarides family doing?"

"*They*'re doing just fine. The frozen-pizza business is competitive, but you know my mother. She's got that hardheaded Cretan stubbornness, so Parthenon Pizzas is thriving. The not-so-rich branch of the Socarides family is still fishing on Cape Cod. I guess I won't starve to death as long as I've got a taste for cod and relatives in the food business." I took another bite of gyro. I had to hold the pita bread with two hands. The hot lamb juice trickled down my chin and I wiped it away with a stiff paper napkin. "God, this is delicious, Nick. Glad to see you haven't lost your touch."

"Thanks, cousin. It's an old family recipe. Speaking of family, it looks like you might be getting some down on the Cape."

My mouth was too full to reply. I shook my head.

"I thought you knew about Uncle Constantine."

I gulped down the mouthful. "I knew Aunt Thalia died. She was a real sweetheart. I remember when they came up to visit from Florida years ago. What's that got to do with me?"

"Guess you haven't talked to your mother. Constantine's got a job on the Cape this summer."

"*Uncle* Constantine?"

Nick nodded.

Uncle Constantine's name brought back a flood of wonderful memories. He was my favorite uncle, a character out of a Kazanzakis novel, bluff and earthy, with a lusty love of life. He made his living as a sponge diver in Tarpon Springs. Once a year he and my aunt Thalia and my cousins came north to visit my family. I'd be excited for weeks ahead. Constantine would sweep into the house and pick me up with one callused hand. I thought he must be as strong as Hercules, and I probably wasn't far off the mark. He'd bring me sponges, exotic conch shells, and shark's teeth off the beaches in Florida. I still had some of them.

Best of all were his stories. How he'd fought off the hose-like tentacles of the giant octopus who chased him for miles, or escaped from the clutches of a clam big enough to swallow a man. Even then, I knew the tales were embroidered for impact, but there was nothing false about my uncle's limp, the legacy of the bends that had killed far more sponge divers than any monster of the deep.

My reaction to Nick's news was a combination of delight and confusion. "A job? At his age? The only thing he's ever done is hard-hat sponge diving."

He shrugged. "I don't know the details. I just heard it from Cousin Basil."

I looked around for the skinny hunched-over man who usually cleared the tables and swept the floor at the Delphi. "Where's Basil now?"

"He went out for an early lunch before the office crowd comes in."

"He goes *out* for lunch?"

"Yeah, he likes Thai food. I can't figure it. Anyhow, he doesn't know any more about Constantine than I told you. Give your mother a call. I'm sure she's got all the details. How's the gyro?"

I munched down the last of the pita bread and wiped the grease off my hands. "Incredible. Tasted like it came from one of those stands in the Plaka over in Athens where you can hear the bouzouki music coming out of the *tavernas*. One more bite and I would have started dancing."

Nick smiled like someone who was used to praise but never bored by it. It was nearly lunchtime. Customers were coming in, grabbing trays and cutlery and lining up at the counter. Nick's young assistant worked like a dervish, but the clattering onslaught of hungry office workers was starting to overwhelm him.

"Got to get back to work, Cousin Aristotle. Manuel looks like he needs a hand."

"Who's Manuel?"

"Kid behind the counter. He's a Brazilian. Good worker. Never complains. That's his mother at the cash register. They don't speak much English, but that's okay, I'm teaching them Greek. First time I ever heard anyone speak it with a Portuguese accent, but they're gonna be talking like they just got off the boat from Pireaus."

I got up. "Thanks for the food, Nick. I'll catch you next time I'm in Boston. Say hello to your family for me."

He slid behind the counter. "You bet, Soc. Hey, look who's back."

The elderly man who slammed out of the restaurant earlier grabbed a tray from a stack, set it on the chrome slider, and shuffled forward in line. As I walked by he said, "I'll have the special with Russian dressing."

4

The spicy taste of Nick's super gyro still clung to my mouth when the P&B bus dropped me off at the Burger King around midafternoon. I retrieved my pickup and drove across the Cape toward Hyannis, then swung east on Route 28, passing a tower of pizza, a Chinese restaurant that features black light and hula dancers for the bus tours, past motels, fast-food eateries, and T-shirt shops. Olde Cape Cod it wasn't.

The traffic-choked two-lane strip that runs along the Cape's south shore used to be the worst-case example of greed and apathy on Cape Cod. Pure Coney Island. That was before fake Colonial-style malls began to spread across the Cape like malignant toadstools. Now Route 28's antique tackiness is almost refreshing by comparison.

I left the strip at a dolphin-shaped sign with the word OCEA-NUS printed on it and drove south toward Nantucket Sound. Minutes from Route 28, a similar sign marked an entrance flanked by neatly trimmed shrubs and two jolly-looking concrete whales the size of Buicks. Four people lounged against the sculptures or sat lazily on the grass.

My arrival galvanized them. They saw me and grabbed signs made of white and colored poster board squares tacked onto lengths of wooden strapping. A goateed man and a young woman came around to my side of the truck. A couple of gray-haired women in identical purple tie-dyed shirts stood at the ready, holding their posters like Crusaders wielding two-edged swords.

The young woman smiled pleasantly, but her mouth didn't match the heated intensity of the level gaze behind her large-framed glasses.

"Sir," she said politely, "we hope you're not going to Oceanus."

I smiled back. "It was sort of on my mind."

"We would urge you not to."

The man stepped forward. "There's no point going inside, friend. The park is closed."

"Thanks for the information. I know it's closed."

One of the middle-aged women came around to my window and poked her nose close to mine. "Do you know what Oceanus is?" she said severely.

"I believe Oceanus is an aquarium, ma'am."

The woman's face turned the color of brick and her mouth twisted into an angry scowl. I felt like a kid who had just given the wrong homework answer to the meanest fourth-grade teacher in school.

"It is *not* an aquarium," she shrilled. "It is a place that keeps living, thinking creatures prisoner against their will in death tanks."

"That's right," her tie-dyed twin chimed in. "It's nothing but a *whale* jail."

The two women began to chant, *"Whale* jail, *whale* jail." The others took up the chant and all four of them marched

around the pickup, bobbing their posters in rhythm like dele-
gates at a political convention.

It gave me a chance to read the posters. Drawn on one in
Magic Marker was a skull and crossbones. In place of the eye
and nose sockets and teeth was the message WHALES DON'T
MURDER. Another poster had a crudely drawn killer whale
who stared sadly from behind bars. The message was simple:
FREE ROCKY. The remaining posters said AGGRESSION IS A DESIRE
TO BE FREE, and more simply, SHAME. Printed in the corner of
each poster-board square were the letters SOS.

"Hey, folks," I called. They ignored me, circling the truck
like a band of Apache warriors attacking a wagon train. I
raised my voice and tried again. They chanted louder and
drowned me out. So I leaned on the pickup's horn for about
ten seconds. That got their attention. They stopped chanting
and waited for me to say my piece.

I hung out the window. "I know you've got a job to do.
You've made your point and I get the message. But I'm just a
poor working slob and I've got some business to attend to, so
I'd appreciate it if you'd step aside."

Their belligerence evaporated like morning mist and they
stepped back. I put the truck into gear and drove between the
concrete whales. As I went by, the man smiled and said,
"Have a nice day."

Then they all took up the chant again.

"*Whale* jail, *whale* jail . . ."

The driveway widened into an expanse of
blacktop big enough to hold several hundred cars, but the sea
of blacktop was deserted. I parked near the main gate, got out
of the pickup, and looked around.

Oceanus had been gouged out of a pretty estuary. Tall
downy marsh grass and cattails bordered the dark banks of a
tidal creek that ran toward the sparkling waters of Nantucket

Sound, less than a quarter mile away. The air was heavy with the fecund odor of sunbaked mud. I strolled over to the gate.

The arched gateway was framed by stylized metal sculptures of dolphins and flanked by colorful killer-whale totem poles. The gate itself was locked tight. I peered through the steel bars. No one was at the ticket turnstiles. Closed signs hung over the shaded box-office windows. Overhead, blue pennants bearing pictures of killer whales in white circles snapped in the breeze. The only other noise was the occasional *clok* of a clam dropped onto the blacktop by a gull.

I walked around the complex to a smaller parking lot occupied by half a dozen cars. A metal door marked STAFF EN-TRANCE was set into the blank concrete face of a flat-roofed building. The door was locked. I pressed a button off to one side. A minute later the door was opened by a heavyset man whose graying hair was cropped to a crew cut. He wore a uniform with the word *Security* stitched on his chest.

He eyed me suspiciously.

"I'm here to see Dan Austin," I said.

"What's your name?"

"Socarides."

"Yeah. He's expecting you. Through there and turn left."

He shambled off without another word.

I walked past a pool whose concrete ledges were crowded with sun-bathing seals and sea lions that lay on their backs like giant whiskered sausages. Nearby, the tuxedoed inhabitants of the penguin rookery waddled about like playboys who'd lost their top hats after a night on the town. Eventually I came to a wide open space. Its centerpiece was an oval pool about fifty feet across ringed by bleachers on three sides. Behind the bleachers was a two-story building. I headed in that direction, walking along the perimeter of the pool.

A loud splash came from the other side and the sun glinted off the broken surface of green water. Then came a steam-valve *whoof!* of misty air. A torpedo streaked toward me in a shimmering, gunmetal blur. My eyebrows jumped to my hairline. I braced myself for the impact. At the last second the projectile swerved to a swirling halt. The water exploded at my feet and spilled over the edge in a miniature tsunami that drenched my shoes and slacks from the knees down.

"Jeezus!" I yelled.

A shiny gray head with a clown's face and a beer-bottle nose looked up at me. It was a dolphin, grinning like a used-car salesman who'd just closed a deal on a 1955 Packard. He checked me out, first with one round eye, then the other. I wrung the water ineffectually out of my slacks. They were wash-and-wear and would look good after they hung out for a few hours, but now they had more wrinkles than a box of prunes. I glowered at the dolphin.

"Thanks for the bath, baldy."

His mouth was curved up in an expression that said, "Hey dude, what's shakin'?" He let out a sharp whistle and made a sound like a rasp being drawn across the edge of a metal ruler.

My irritation evaporated. "Hey, you're one funny fish, aren't you?"

He answered with a wag of his head. I did a double take and leaned forward to make sure I wasn't talking to a man in a dolphin suit.

Someone laughed softly. I turned and saw a woman walking toward me.

"You just gave Puff the operative word," she said.

Her chestnut hair bounced playfully in slow motion against her shoulders, catching the sun in tiny red highlights. She had high cheekbones and a chin just short of stubborn. The duskiness of her complexion suggested Mediterranean love songs in her family history. She wore a sky-colored polo shirt over full breasts and her tan shorts were snug against a body that was athletic but not hard looking. The word *Ocea-*

nus was part of a stylized dolphin logo printed over the heart.
I figured her in her early thirties.

"Pardon me, I did *what?*"

Amusement gleamed in blue eyes tinged with gentian purple. "You said *fish.* That's the operative word when you phrase it in a question. Here," she said, and stood close enough for me to smell the lemon in her shampoo. "It's part of the show. A lot of kids who come with school field trips think a dolphin is no more than a very smart fish. So you explain that Puff is a warm-blooded, air-breathing mammal just like they are. Then to emphasize the point you say, 'That's right, Puff. You're not a fish, are you?' She drew the question out like somebody talking to a baby.

The dolphin waggled its head as if to say, "Hell, I'm no damned sardine."

The woman reached into a white plastic bucket she'd been carrying and pulled out a chunk of herring. She leaned over and held the fish for the dolphin. He grabbed it, not even grazing her fingertips with his sharp teeth, and smacked his reward down whole.

She turned back to me. "It makes the kids laugh and teaches them at the same time that there *is* a difference between fish and marine mammals. Puff thought you were throwing out a gag line."

I scratched my head. "First time I've ever played straight man to a f-i-s-h."

"You don't have to spell it out. It's not just the word. It's the context, the tone of your voice, and your hand motions. Here's another thing we do. We have a kid from the audience touch Puff's skin and give their impressions. Usually, they say it feels like rubber. Then we turn to the animal and say, 'That's right; you're not slimy or scaly, are you?'" She used the mother-talking-to-a-baby tone again.

The dolphin repeated its cute head maneuver. The woman rewarded it with another fish, then flicked her hand in an upward motion. The dolphin flipped onto its back. Using powerful fluttering strokes of its wide flukes, it walked backward on the surface of the water. Surf stirred up by the dolphin's jitterbug washed over the edge of the pool. The woman waved good-bye. The dolphin sank back into the water, rolled over, and waved with its right fin, then disappeared through an opening into another tank.

"You'll have to catch the show when we reopen," the woman said. She surveyed the empty rows of bleacher seats. "*If* we reopen," she added doubtfully. She rinsed her hand in the pool and dried it on her shorts. "My name is Sally Carlin. I'm the head dolphin trainer at Oceanus."

We shook hands. I was looking at her eyes. They were almond-shaped. "My name is Socarides. Most people call me Soc."

"Nice to meet you, Soc. Can I be of any help?"

"I'm looking for the manager, Dan Austin."

She pointed to a passageway. "Go through there, then climb the stairs on your right. Dan's office is on the second floor."

She looked at my soaked shoes and cuffs and shook her head.

"Sorry Puff got you wet. He likes to splash people and watch their reaction. Wait, I'll have him apologize." She blew a sharp note on the police whistle hanging from a leather thong around her neck. Seconds later the porpoise dashed back into the main pool and playfully stuck his head out of the water at our feet like a dog begging at the table.

"Shake hands with Soc and say you're sorry," Sally ordered. Puff came straight up like a missile off the launching pad. He leaped clear of the water, treading air on his tail so we were eyeball to eyeball, extended his right flipper, and whistled. I gave the fin a quick shake. He splashed back into the water and dashed around the pool.

Sally Carlin said: "You should feel flattered, Soc. Puff doesn't take so easy to strangers."

I watched the streak of silvery lightning and said, "Dolphin, drunken with the lyre, across the dark blue prows, like fire, did bound and quiver."

Sally's gaze moved from the dolphin to me. "That's very beautiful," she said.

"It's a quote from *Electra*, by Euripides. Okay, tell Puff his apology is accepted."

I said good-bye and continued around the pool, climbed an outside stairway to an office, and gave the secretary my name. She asked me to take a seat. Moments later the door behind the secretary opened, and a pale-skinned man with longish black hair and horn-rim glasses emerged. The secretary said, "Mr. Austin will see you now." I stepped through the open door into a sunlit office.

A stocky blond man got up from behind his desk and came over to shake my hand.

"I'm Dan Austin," he said. "Please have a seat." He was around forty years old, of medium height, with thinning hair combed over his balding head from a low side part. He was wearing tan slacks and a blue Oceanus polo shirt similar to the one I had seen on the dolphin trainer. It looked better on Sally Carlin.

He shut the door while I settled in a chair, and came back to his desk.

I glanced around at the framed photos and posters covering the walls, then past Austin. The office windows behind him overlooked the pool. Sally Carlin was still working with her finny friend Puff.

Austin followed my gaze. "This is a great spot," he said. "You can watch the whole show from here. I see that you've already met our head dolphin trainer."

"I met the Puff the dolphin, too."

"Oh yes, Puff is quite a character. Smart as hell." He shook his head. "Sometimes I wonder who is training whom." He tented his hands and tapped his fingertips together a few times. "Well, now to the business at hand. Otis called and asked me to cooperate fully with you."

"Mr. Otis hoped I might be able to clear up some of the questions lingering over your trainer's death."

Austin folded his arms across the chest and looked at me with unfriendly eyes.

"I'm not clear what he had in mind. After the police conducted their investigation, Otis hired a private-detective firm from Boston to poke around. They didn't turn up a damned thing new. Otis is wasting his money and your time."

"You may be right," I said, "but it never hurts to have a fresh look at a case. I'll try to be in and out of here real quick."

He unfolded his arms. "Look, I'm not trying to make your job any tougher. It's just been hell around here since Eddy's death." Austin pulled his chair close to his desk. "Okay," he said, "where should I start?"

"At the beginning. Tell me how your trainer died."

Austin looked out the window as he collected his thoughts. Sally Carlin was tossing a beach ball into the pool. The dolphin would grab the ball between its flippers, race back to Sally, and jump out of the water so she could retrieve the ball and throw it out again. Puff had his own trained human. As we watched, a guy with a physique like Conan walked over to Sally. He was wearing an Oceanus uniform. He and Sally chatted, then they strolled off together.

Austin swiveled in his chair. "What do you know about killer whales, Mr. Socarides?"

"Virtually nothing."

He pointed to the promotional pictures on the walls. In one, a black-and-white killer whale leaped like a bronco while a woman in a wet suit rode on its back cowboy-style. In another, a killer whale came straight up to take a fish from the hand of a little girl. Still another had a whale shooting out of the water like a NASA rocket. A smiling female trainer balanced on its nose, arms spread wide.

"The animal you see performing like a clown in those pictures is the biggest predator in the sea, which makes it the biggest on earth. The Romans called it sea devil. *Orcinus orca* can grow to more than thirty-one feet, weigh in at ten tons, and swim more than thirty miles an hour. It's got up to fifty teeth and knows how to use them." He let that sink in, then went on. "But the killer whale is more than just an eating machine. The brain driving all that power is one of the most highly developed on the planet. The killer whale is smart as hell, maybe more intelligent than the dolphin. It is also sociable and good-natured."

I glanced at the posters again. "You make the orca sound like a cross between Mack the Knife and someone you'd like to introduce to your unmarried daughter."

"Don't get me wrong, the whale is a killer, all right. Orca will eat anything in the sea, including its cousin the dolphin. Packs of them will bring down much bigger whales. They systematically tear them apart, usually starting at the lips."

"Are human beings normally part of their menu?"

"If you read the early literature, you'd think they were more dangerous to human beings than the great white shark."

"I hear a but in there."

"You hear right. As a general rule, orcas don't attack human beings."

"Never?"

"A couple of boats have been rammed and sunk and a surfer got chewed up by an orca in California. I think those attacks were cases of mistaken identity. I'll bet the killer

whales thought the boat was another whale, or the diver a
seal maybe. You see, all the stories had something in common."

"What was that?"

"Every one of the storytellers lived to tell the tale. Some
were thrown into the water with the whales swimming
around them, but the orcas didn't attack." He gestured toward a photo. "Look at the size and power of those babies. If
a killer whale really wants somebody for dinner, there is
nothing that can stop him."

I had to agree with him; the whales in the pictures were as
long as a bus.

"So you're saying an orca would never kill a human being?"

"Not exactly. There was a recent case in British Columbia.
Three orcas attacked and killed a trainer during a performance at a marine park. That was the first time anything like
that happened." He shrugged wearily. "I've got my doubts
about Rocky, though."

"Bounce them off me. Then maybe I'll have doubts, too."

He shook his head. "The whole damned thing just goes
against the character of the beast. It's the most ferocious
creature in the world, but it not only puts up with human
beings, it seems to *like* them. Don't ask me why. That thing
in British Columbia was a freak accident in my view. A killer
whale is not like a fish. It has a brain, and emotions, and it
can get angry and frustrated. It's not uncommon for an orca
to nip a trainer, rake him with its teeth or bump against him.
Maybe even pin the trainer to the side of the pool to show it's
irritated. We've had it happen here."

I ran my hand down my slacks to the cuffs, still damp from
Puff's practical joke. I couldn't even handle a measly little
dolphin. How was I going to deal with a critter who routinely
snacked on humpbacks? I wanted a beer, and the sooner I got

the interview over with, the quicker I could have one. I cut to the chase.

"I confuse easily, Mr. Austin. So let's put the speculation aside and start with the something everybody agrees on. We know Eddy is dead. Tell me what happened the day he died."

Austin nodded. "It was about three weeks ago. Start of the busy season. We were gearing up for a heavy schedule of shows. Eddy had been working with Rocky, our killer whale. He was having problems with the act."

"What sort of problems?"

"Rocky wouldn't allow a trainer on his back. Eddy was determined to train him. Some of the staff were beginning to kid Eddy, and he didn't take kindly to ribbing. He said they'd see him riding Rocky when they came to work the next day."

"Go on."

"The night watchman found Eddy's body on his morning rounds."

"The newspapers said the cause of death was drowning."

"The autopsy showed Eddy had been drinking, so he may have fallen."

"Was he a heavy drinker?"

"Eddy was probably an alcoholic, although he would have been the first to deny that."

"Why did you keep him on?"

"Looking back at this whole mess, now, sometimes I wonder. But Eddy was one of the best trainers in the business. And he kept his drinking and work separate."

"Except for the night he was killed."

"I didn't see him that afternoon because I wasn't here, but people who talked to him said he was pretty well sloshed."

"Nobody thought it was a lousy idea for him to be drunk while he was working around a killer whale?"

"Probably lots of people did, but most of the staff was afraid of Eddy. He had a pretty violent temper. Besides, everybody figured he could pretty much take care of himself around the animals, drunk or sober."

"If Eddy was drunk, he could have slipped and knocked himself out and drowned."

"That's right. At first, people thought that's what happened."

"What changed their minds?"

"When the staff left, Eddy was working Rocky from the side of the tank. There's a sunken platform where the trainers stand. It's about a half foot below water level, so the whale can actually pull itself out of the pool. It gives the audience the chance to appreciate the full size of an orca. The last people to leave Oceanus saw Eddy standing on the stage in shorts and a jersey."

"Why is what he was wearing important?"

"When Eddy was found, he had on a wet suit. That would indicate he had changed, and was probably with Rocky in the pool in violation of park policy."

"Maybe he was standing on the stage in his wet suit and he slipped into the pool."

"That's possible. Except for one thing. There were three holes in the arm of his wet suit."

"Any holes in the arm itself?"

"None."

"I've had holes in my wet suits. Why is that significant?"

"Eddy was fastidious about his gear. He wouldn't have worn a wet suit if it had so much as a pinhole."

"What are you driving at, Mr. Austin?"

"We measured the distance between the holes."

"And?"

"We keep pretty complete records on all our animals. Part of it is to satisfy federal regulations, but it's also for our own good. We have files on the mammals' health, their physical characteristics, like length, weight, coloring. We even have a dentist come in to check out their teeth. We have some very nice dental charts, not much different than the type you'd see in a dentist's office."

"What does that have to do with the holes in Byron's wet suit?"

Austin drew in a deep breath and let it out. "The space separating the holes corresponded to the distances between Rocky's teeth."

"No mistake?"

He shook his head slowly.

"Were there any other holes?"

"No. Just those in the arm."

"You said Eddy wasn't supposed to be in the pool. Something about park policy."

Austin nodded. "Rocky had bumped trainers a couple of times. Once he raked a trainer's hand with his teeth. Just enough to leave pink marks on the skin. Another time he grabbed Eddy and pinned him to the bottom of the pool. Luckily, Eddy wasn't hurt, but after that, we passed the rule prohibiting trainers from working with the whale in the water."

"Didn't that cut down on your act?"

"Somewhat, but we could still train the whale and work it from the side of the pool. It was better doing that than having all our trainers quit or end up in the hospital."

"Rocky being his lovable self again?"

Austin chuckled. "You seem good-natured. But did you ever get mad enough to want to kill somebody?"

I flashed back on a friend I almost blew away in Vietnam during a drunken rage. "Yeah," I admitted. "I've been that mad."

"It's the same with an orca. Technically, it's just a big dolphin, but most people don't realize that even a dolphin can get testy. And an orca is more independent than a dolphin.

The navy found that out when it was experimenting with killer whales a few years ago. The whales would just go AWOL or refuse to work."

"So a killer whale can get angry. A job walkout or wildcat strike is still a far cry from a fatal attack. Lots of people would like to murder the boss, but they don't."

"True, but those navy experiments were in the open sea with relatively new whales. An orca held in captivity for a few years can get bored or frustrated, even neurotic. Change its routine, or put it under too much pressure, and it gets irritated."

"Is that what the people at your front gate meant when they called this place a whale jail?"

He gave me a sharp look. "Oh, I see you've met our friends from SOS."

"We had a nice chat. What does SOS mean?"

"It stands for Sentinels of the Sea. They're a fringe ecological group, much more radical than the main stream organizations like Greenpeace. They're real extremists."

"They didn't look very dangerous."

"Those people out front with the signs are the nicey-nicies who'll join any organization that says it wants to save the whales or the seals. They're innocents. The hard-core guys who run the group stay out of the limelight." Austin frowned. "The Sentinels are the reason Oceanus closed its doors. After Eddy's death, they picketed the place and called for a boycott. When that didn't work, we got the bomb threat. I'm sure it was the Sentinels, although they deny that, too."

"You said a whale can come under stress when there's a change in routine or too much pressure. Was that true in the case of Rocky?"

"He was kept pretty much to the same routine. But as you know, Oceanus is owned by a major corporation. That corporation's goal is to get the best possible financial return to its stockholders. The more money we make, the more money they make. The more killer-whale shows we put on, the more money we make."

"You're saying that there was too much pressure to perform, and the whale may have been reacting."

He nodded. "When a whale bites a trainer or whacks him, it's telling him it isn't happy."

"If the whale was so edgy, why would Eddy have gone in the water with him, especially if it violated company rules?"

"Eddy had been around orcas a long time. He thought he knew them better than anyone, and maybe he did. It would have been just like him to slip into the pool when nobody was around to see him—or help him. Eddy may simply have gotten too cocky."

"When can I interview the suspected felon?"

"I'd show you the orca today, but the staff might get curious why the park manager is giving a new guy the VIP tour. It can wait until you're officially on board. Otis said you're a diver. That's a good cover. We've only got a skeleton crew on right now, the trainers and a few people to feed the fish and do the dirty work. I'll introduce you to Rocky tomorrow. Be here around eight A.M."

I got up to go. "Does anyone else know I'm a private cop?"

"Just me. That's the way Otis wanted it. Frankly, I can't see what you'll find. Nothing against you, understand, but Rocky's not likely to sit down for the third degree. Hell, what do I care; it's Otis's dime. He wants to get things cleared up so he can sell us to the Japanese."

We shook hands and I walked down the stairs and out by the dolphin pool, aware Austin was probably watching me from his window. Puff saw me and came over and swam back and forth in front of me. I lingered for a minute, watching the water ballet, listening to the dolphin's chuckles and creaks, thinking about what the ancients said about dolphins. They thought dolphins embodied the souls of the dead. I smiled at the implications. If the ancients were right, Eddy Byron could find himself back at Oceanus performing with the dolphins he once trained.

5

Only two picketers were at the Oceanus front gate as I drove out. The women in tie-dyed shirts leaned against the concrete whales, drinking from plastic liter bottles of Evian water. It had been a hot day and their hair was frazzled. Their faces glistened with perspiration. They perked up when they saw me and waved the truck over. I stopped and looked around for the man and the younger woman.

"Where'd your friends go?" I asked.

One of the women said, "They had to pick up their kids."

I nodded. "Guess I'll call it a day, too."

"Wait," she commanded.

I braced myself for another off-key chorus of the whale-jail blues.

She took a sheet of paper from a canvas bag and stuck it under my nose. "This will change your mind about a lot of things."

I tucked the paper in the overhead visor. "Thanks," I said. "I'll be sure to read it."

They both smiled. I put the truck in gear and waved out the window. They waved back. Nice people. Maybe a little overenthusiastic, but hardly bomb-tossing zealots.

Route 28 was a slow-moving river of bumper-to-bumper hot cars and hotter people. The tourists had basted and baked their bodies and were leaving the beaches, heading to the bars where they'd compare tans and have a frozen margarita before going back to their motel rooms to wash the sand out of their hair. Soon they would crowd the pizzerias and fried-fish joints to chow down for the energy to hit the disco scene. Vacationing is tough work.

Near a sneaker discount store, I turned off the strip onto a side road. It was like entering a time warp. The narrow, tree-shaded lane meandered through an historic district of neatly kept old Cape Cod cottages of shingle and clapboard, well-tended flower gardens, and past a miniature white spired church. Cape Cod has a split personality. In between ghastly islands of commercial development are neighborhoods that haven't changed outwardly in a hundred years. I took a series of shortcuts east, in the direction the old-timers called "down Cape." A half hour after leaving Oceanus, the pickup rattled down a bumpy quarter-mile sand road and I was home.

Kojak was at the door. He rubbed against my leg in an outpouring of undying affection that ended as soon as I spooned a can of 9-Lives tuna into his dish. I popped a Bud and took the file folder of news clips Otis had given me to the kitchen table.

Nudged by the southwest breeze, dozens of sailboats criss-crossed the blue-green waters of the bay. I sat at the kitchen table for a minute or two, clearing my mind of clutter, and watched the white triangles move almost imperceptibly against the hazy backdrop of Strong Island and the headland at Eastward Point. Then I opened the file folder.

The news stories fell into three rough categories.

The first reports were routine one-column articles saying Eddy Byron, forty-nine, head marine mammal trainer at Oceanus, apparently drowned in the whale tank. The story might have fizzled, except for an enterprising weekly newspaper reporter who dug out the stuff about the holes in Eddy's wet suit and the connection to Rocky's teeth. The big media guns picked up on the piece and Eddy's death blossomed into major news.

The tabloid *Boston Herald* cleared its front page of unimportant copy like arms conferences, African famine, and federal budget deficits in order to run a cover story devoted entirely to Eddy's death. The centerpiece was a full column width photo of a toothy killer whale who lunged out at the reader over his scrambled eggs and toast like a creature from hell. In case anyone missed the point, the story was headlined JAWS in type three inches high. The overline said: "Killer Whale Slays Trainer." The caption identified the whale as Rocky, the main suspect in a bizarre death at Oceanus marine theme park on Cape Cod.

Herald readers have a short attention span, and the newspaper normally doesn't run stories longer than six paragraphs, but this was hot copy and continued inside for a two-page spread. The layout included a photo of Eddy Byron that had been enlarged too many times. The picture was so grainy Eddy looked as if he had the measles, but you could make out a square-jawed man with dark hair going to white. There was a picture of the Oceanus gate, sans picketers, and the whale pool with a white circle drawn in to mark the spot where the body was found. In another shot, probably a publicity photo from the *Herald*'s files, a less menacing Rocky leaped from the water to the delight of spectators.

The story was big on pictures and short on words, but you got the gist of it. At least a third of the report was a rehash of the fairly thorough account in the weekly newspaper, but the

story played up the Jekyll-Hyde contrasts of Rocky's character. The friendly killer whale who had thrilled kids and their
parents with his playful antics, was, *gasp,* in reality a homicidal maniac.

I turned to the *Boston Globe* clips. The *Globe* considers itself
more intellectual than the *Herald.* Its lead story is usually
about the elections in Romania or Botswana, and it looks
down its long nose at any hint of sensationalism. Eddy Byron's story made page one of the inside Metro and Region
section. The killer-whale picture could have been taken from
a textbook. The section editor was probably frustrated at having to downplay a story that got his newsman's juices running. He couldn't resist the *Jaws* cliché in the headline. The
Herald had all but convicted Rocky in the killing. The *Globe*
account was more balanced, with the predictable quotes from
Harvard faculty and noncontroversial statements from PR
people at other aquariums.

Dan Austin was quoted in several stories. He did a good
job walking the tightrope. He didn't admit to the holes in the
wet suit, but he didn't deny it. He said killer whales don't kill
people, but admitted Rocky had attacked trainers, including
Eddy. The cops said the case was still under investigation,
shorthand meaning they didn't have the slightest idea what to
do and hoped the whole would thing go away so they could
get back to filling their speed-trap quotas.

But the story was too hot to cool off. With the basic chan-
nels of information drying up or played out, the press put
together follow-up articles that focused on the burning question: could Rocky have done it? Most of the cetacean scientists interviewed echoed what Austin had told me: that it was
totally against the orca's character to kill a human being. Like
Austin, they, too, admitted they were talking about behavior
under *natural* conditions, and that a whale in captivity might
react differently than it would in the wild.

The best report was in *The New York Times.* The *Times*

talked to scientists and trainers all over the world. The face in one head shot was familiar. I looked closer. It was the pale man with the tortoiseshell glasses I saw leaving Austin's office. The caption said he was Dr. Henry Livingston. I found his name in the story. Livingston was director of the Cape Cod Center for Cetacean Studies, a nonprofit institution. Small world.

Livingston was cautious about laying the rap on Rocky, but some of his colleagues were less conservative. One researcher said the orca may be smart and playful, but it is still the ocean's major predator; under the stress of confinement the whale might have reacted in angry reflex. Austin's assessment again. Except for the press guys who had leaped to monumental conclusions to sell papers, nobody wanted to finger Rocky as the perp. But everyone seemed to agree that even a jolly old clown like the orca has its bad days, and any human who gets in the way of an eight-ton temper tantrum better have his medical insurance paid up.

Even the tentative suggestion that Rocky *might* have killed Eddy was like throwing gasoline onto a fire. Environmental groups worldwide jumped into the fray. Greenpeace, the World Wildlife Fund. Organizations big and small. They said the incident proved whales and dolphins belonged in the ocean, not in big manmade tanks.

I scanned *The New York Times* story and came across the name Sentinels of the Sea. The *Times* described the Sentinels as a small but highly active ecological group in the tradition of the Monkey Wrench Gang, the fictitious ecosaboteurs in Edward Abbey's book by the same name. They were similar to Earth First!, except their particular protectorate was the ocean. The Sentinels tended toward guerrilla warfare, more commonly called ecoterrorism. The *Times* said they had been accused, but never charged for sabotaging California tuna boats that caught dolphins in their nets, and were also suspected of sinking a whaleboat in Iceland.

I ran my finger down the news column. The story quoted a guy named Walden Schiller who was identified as the spokesman for the Sentinels. Schiller told the *Times* no self-respecting killer whale would ever intentionally harm a person in the wild. Rocky, he said, was like a frustrated convict who strikes out at a sadistic prison guard. Schiller's message was simple. Release *every* dolphin and whale in captivity. I could see why Simon Otis was nervous.

The demonstrations and boycott organized by the Sentinels backfired because they generated publicity. Ticket sales actually increased. People paid the fat admission price for a chance to see a killer whale with blood on its its flippers. The public has never been short on morbid curiosity. A crime scene immediately becomes a tourist attraction. The worse the crime, the greater the interest.

Rocky had been benched temporarily. Even without the killer-whale show, the park did a brisk business. After all, who knows when a dolphin might go berserk. I could just see Joe Six-pack and his family sitting in the stands not really *hoping* a dolphin would rip its trainer's throat out, but if it *had* to happen, be nice to have the Instamatic handy.

Oceanus stayed open even after the first bomb threat. Dan Austin vowed defiantly not to cave in to the threats. Then a phony bomb with a timer but no explosive was discovered outside his office door in a warning of what could happen, and Austin found religion. The next day he announced Oceanus would close until further notice. The Sentinels were the obvious target of suspicion, but Walden Schiller said SOS was not responsible for the bomb threats.

I put the file aside. I wanted to cut away all the extraneous stuff, to concentrate on Eddy, to see what made him tick. I wanted to give him life again, like Odysseus summoning the dead at the door to Hades. If I could get Eddy's shade walking and talking, maybe he'd tell me who killed him.

The news clips provided only a sketchy portrait of Eddy. He was born in Seattle and fished a few years in the Pacific Northwest before joining the navy. Later, he worked as a trainer in marine theme parks in California and Florida before coming to Oceanus. There was no indication of Eddy's next of kin.

I leaned back in my chair and looked out the window. The breeze had freshened and the white cotton curtains tumbled and snapped. The ranks of sailboats on the bay were thinning. So far, I had one dead trainer. A killer whale accused and tried in the press. And a few suspects. But suspected of what?

I picked up the phone and called Ed Shaughnessy.

"Been expecting you," he said. "Otis said you agreed to take the case. Congratulations."

"Thanks. I'm a soft touch when it comes to animals, the bigger the better. You were right, this is a weird one. What's your assessment?"

"I had two of my boys look into it. They went down to Oceanus and talked to Dan Austin. Have you met him?"

"Couple of hours ago. He seems to have doubts about the guilt of the, ah, prime suspect."

"Uh-huh. That's what he told my guys. They looked at the wet suit with the holes in it but weren't impressed. They're both ex-cops, so what do they know from whales? After they talked to Austin, they nosed around the park."

"What did they say in their report?"

"They said something was fishy. Chrissakes, Soc, what *else* did you expect in an aquarium?" Shaughnessy brayed like a barking seal.

I smiled as I pictured the bucktoothed grin on his wide face. "I guess it wasn't a bad dream, I really did put up with your bad jokes all those nights in the cruiser."

"Sorry, pal, I couldn't resist that. Seriously, they said

something was going on, but they couldn't figure it out. Staff was real friendly about answering questions, but nobody volunteered anything. And the stories all could have been cut out on the same template. So there it was, neatly tied up in a package. Guy dies. Finger points to the whale. Case closed. That's when I told Otis that if he really wanted to get to the bottom of this, he had better send someone in to see if it was really accidental."

"How could it *not* be an accident?"

"Dunno, pal. Hoped you'd come up with an answer to that question."

"We'll see. Otis said to ask you about some possible human perps."

"Yeah, we came up with three people who might have a hard-on against the park management. One is Phil Hanley, the former PR guy. He was fired and didn't like it. Then there's Lew Atwood, who was the trainer before Eddy Byron. He was fired, too. Hanley and Atwood have both been vocal about their cases, threatened to close the park with lawsuits. Maybe they decided to be more direct. Both of them live on Cape Cod. Lastly, we've got a fruitcake named Walden Schiller who runs a looney tunes whale-lover group called Sentinels of the Sea. We've got a trace out on him. I'll let you know."

"I came across Schiller's name in the news clips. You're right, he's got some strong views about Oceanus."

"If any of these guys is your boy, I'd guess it's Schiller."

"I'll remember that. The Shaughnessy gut instinct kept us from getting killed a couple of times back in the old days."

"Gut's a lot bigger than it used to be, Soc, and it's telling me something about this case."

"What do you mean, Ed?"

"You remember those times we'd be knocking on doors in some old three-decker in Dorchester never knowing if there was an acid head with a .357 Magnum on the other side. I've got the same feeling on this. You knock on any doors, make sure you stand off to the side."

"I'll do better than that, Ed. I won't knock."

We made small talk for a few minutes before hanging up. Then I called Sam to let him know I was home and working on a case. We have an arrangement. I try to sandwich my detecting in between fishing trips, but if I can't, then I line up a replacement. Sam said not to bother. The marine mechanic said it would take a couple of days to fix the *Millie D.* And that was only if the parts were in stock. The way things looked, Sam said glumly, we might not get back fishing until after Labor Day. I tried to cheer Sam up, but he was enjoying his melancholia, so I said good-bye.

Talking to Sam got me thinking about Uncle Constantine. He and Sam were a lot alike. True, Sam was a lean and flinty Methodist who wouldn't touch a drop of liquor if you threatened him with a gun. His idea of an emotional outburst was a muttered Jeepers Crow. Uncle Constantine was a powerful man who could laugh and cry in the same breath. Constantine saw life as a joke perpetrated on mankind by a mischievous Creator. But both men had been shaped by the sea.

Working the water is the most dangerous of occupations, more hazardous than coal mining. They had been closer to death than most men, realized life is as ephemeral as a castle built in the sand, and the experience gave them a sense of proportion about what is important and what is not. There was something else. They both had eyes of piercing blue.

I picked up the phone to call my mother in Lowell for an update on Uncle Constantine, but chickened out. Ma would give me hell for not calling her earlier. I sighed. It's a vicious circle. I don't call because I might get scolded. Then I get scolded when I call. I put the phone back and looked up the telephone number for Lew Atwood, the former trainer at

Oceanus, whose name Shaughnessy gave me. The telephone rang ten times with no answer, so I hung up.

I decided to blow off an interview with Walden Schiller for now. Judging from the comments in the news clips, I figured Schiller was smart and tough, probably not someone who could be conned, buffaloed, or threatened, my usual approaches with a potential suspect. Schiller would require a special strategy I had yet to divine. That left Phil Hanley, the fired public-relations man. It was late afternoon. He lived about twenty minutes from the boathouse. Since he was no longer gainfully employed, he might be home. I decided to drive over to see him.

The white one-and-a-half-story Cape Cod house was in a neat subdivision. I parked in front, went up the walk, and rang the doorbell. What was I going to ask this guy? Okay, Hanley, fess up, we know you killed Eddy Byron and framed Rocky. Okay, so you didn't pull the trigger, you got the whale to do it, bribed him with a box of herring, but you're just as guilty and you're going to fry if you don't turn state's evidence.

Soft footsteps were approaching. I wiped the ugly cop sneer off my face just as the door opened.

6

The lady standing in the doorway had short black hair, a peaches-and-cream complexion, and a nice smile that didn't match her sad eyes. I asked if I could speak to Phil Hanley. The smile melted from her lips.

"He's not home right now."

I gave her my business card. "I'll be in this evening if he wants to reach me."

She read the card and looked up at me with a worried expression. "A private investigator? Is Phil in some sort of trouble?"

"No," I said. "I just need some information having to do with his old job at Oceanus. It's pretty routine insurance stuff, but he might be able to help."

She held the card in two hands and shook her head. "He's living on his boat on Bass River. He calls me from a pay phone every night for messages. I'll tell him you came by."

I thanked her, and drove back to the boathouse. It was suppertime. I rummaged through the refrigerator and gingerly threw out some gooey black lumps wrapped in cellophane. The two white eggs in the door rack must be ready to hatch, but I wasn't in an omelet mood anyway. I opened a can of tuna. The can-opener noise attracted Kojak. He bolted out of the bedroom, having forgotten I just fed him.

Pushing him aside with one foot, I boiled some Kraft cheese and noodles, mixed in the orange cheeselike powder, folded in some Velveeta, added half a Vidalia onion for texture and half a wilted red pepper for color. Then I blended in the tuna and sprinkled the whole splendid creation with grated parmesan cheese and Italian bread crumbs. I took the noodles off the stove too soon and they came out undercooked and gummy. I persuaded myself they were *al dente*, pried the yellowish blob onto a willow pattern plate, and brought it over to the table to join a cold can of Bud.

Kojak was lying on the table imitating a furry place mat. I scraped some of the mess from my plate into his kitty dish. He jumped off the table, gave my offering a patrician sniff, cast a dirty look in my direction, and went into the bedroom for a snooze. I was at the sink trying to chisel the cheese off the plates and pans when the telephone rang. It was Phil Hanley and he was angry.

"What the hell is Oceanus doing sending a private detective to harass me?" he shouted.

"It's not like that at all, Mr. Hanley."

He wasn't listening. "Okay, I'll admit it, I took a ballpoint pen. I'll give it back. Just don't press charges."

"You can keep the pen, Mr. Hanley. Any paper clips you took, too. I want to talk to you about Eddy Byron."

"Eddy? What the hell for? My area was public relations."

"I know. Your PR work must have given you a good overview of the park. There are some insurance claims."

"Why should I give that frigging place the time of day? They dumped me without notice."

"Look, Mr. Hanley, I'm sorry to hear you were fired, and if you don't want to talk to me, I can't make you. But I can give you a chance to set the record straight. My report goes directly to the top brass at Oceanus."

"Simon Otis?"

"That's the man."

"Otis. MiGod! That *would* be sweet." Silence. Hanley was thinking. "Okay," he said decisively. "Otis may give me my job back after he hears what I've got to say."

The operator cut in and asked for more money. Hanley cursed. "Look, Socarides, I'm out of change. Meet me at my boat around ten-thirty tonight. It's a white sloop named the *Mariah* in Bass River. Come to the windmill park off River Street and grab a skiff from the beach. Head straight out about fifty feet and a little north. I'll have the mast, deck, and bow lights on."

"I'll be there."

He hung up. The dunning voice came on the phone again. New England Bell gets impatient when the coins don't drop.

A few minutes past 10:00 P.M. I turned off Route 28 near a motel that had a plaster old salt smoking a plaster pipe in front of a plaster lighthouse and drove past maple, oak, and catalpa trees, low-slung bow-roofed Cape Cod cottages, gambrels and two-story captain's houses, picket fences and privet hedges. The river was on my left, mostly cut off from view by the shorefront houses, but accessible from short dead-end streets.

Windmill Park overlooked a small public beach served by a dirt rectangle with room for a dozen cars. I parked near a sign with a picture of a goose inside of a barred circle. The Canada geese used to go south for the winter, but since people started feeding them, the big birds have become panhandlers who foul the waters. I took a pair of oars from the back of the pickup and followed a short path toward the river. The old Judah Baker windmill loomed like a four-armed monster from an H.P. Lovecraft tale.

At the edge of a seawall I paused and listened to the wet gurgle of the tide, the melancholy squawk of a seabird, and the insistent *chang-chang* of a halyard slapping against an aluminum mast. Fragments of laughter and music, caught momentarily on the damp breeze, came from a big waterfront house.

Bass River almost slices the Cape in half. It starts in a series of linking salt ponds north of the Mid-Cape Highway and flows six miles to Nantucket Sound. Leif Eriksson and his Viking longboat may have cruised up the river a thousand years ago. With the moon's veiled light filtering through a curtain of fast-moving clouds, I could almost see the silhouette of a dragon prow, hear the wind snapping in a big square sail and the nervous muttering of tired oarsmen straining against the strong river current.

A dark puddle marked a low grassy mud flat called Marsh Island. Moored nearby was a sailboat with all its deck and mast lights on.

Descending a short set of stairs to the beach, I walked over to a half-dozen dinghies upended against a grassy banking like sleeping turtles. Most looked as if they predated the Vikings. No wise sailor keeps a dinghy worth stealing on the beach. I dragged out a battered fiberglass pram that looked as if it might float to the water's edge, set the oars in the locks and pushed off.

I rowed into the channel, fighting a double combination of river current and outgoing tide that pushed me toward the mouth of the river. I put my back into each stroke. After a few minutes of strenuous rowing, I drew close enough to read the name on the sailboat's stern. *Mariah.*

The white-hulled fiberglass sloop was about thirty feet

long. She had pretty lines, with a tapering stem and a sharp bow to slice through the Nantucket Sound chop. Yet she was wide enough to provide room to stretch. I could think of worse places to go if my wife kicked me out of the house. If I had a wife.

A skiff was tied up to the sloop, but there was no sign of anybody on deck. Hanley must be below mixing a cocktail. That's what I would be doing. About a yard from the boat I shipped my oars, grabbed the rail, and with the other hand, took the pram's bowline and wrapped a figure eight around a deck cleat.

"Ahoy aboard the *Mariah*," I called.

There was only the soft burble of the current against the hull and the distant chang of that slack halyard.

I yelled, louder. "Hey, anybody home?"

The skiff bumped against the dinghy. I stared at it, wondering. The skiff didn't get here by itself.

Deciding not to wait for an invitation, I climbed on board and stepped into the roomy cockpit. The wooden cover was in place on the hatch leading below. I pushed it up and slid it off. The unlit cabin was a black hole. I reached around to the right and I found a switch. The cabin was bathed in light.

It was a roomy living space with cushioned seats that could be made into bunks, a kitchenette, table, and sink. There was a *Yachting* magazine on the table and rinsed but unwashed glasses and plate in the sink, but the boat was remarkably neat considering it was being used as a bachelor pad. I thought of the *Marie Celeste*, the old sailing vessel found adrift, table set for dinner, with nary a soul on board.

I descended into the cabin and went over to the louvered door leading to the head and forward bunk. It was shut.

"Hanley?" Maybe he was sleeping.

I pulled the door open and the light from the cabin fell on a wide bunk tapered into a triangle to fit the bow. Something lay on the bunk, covered by a Scotch-plaid blanket. The green wool pattern was flawed by an irregular dark stain. I reached forward and pulled back a corner. A man's face stared blindly back at me. His blond hair was matted with blood.

I felt his neck. His skin was still warm, but there was no sign of a pulse, which didn't surprise me. He had been shot in the head.

I covered the face, backed into the cabin, and shut the door. There was a marine radio near the companionway. I flicked it onto Channel 16 and barked into the microphone.

"*Mariah* to harbor patrol. Do you read me?"

No answer. The harbor cops must have quit hours ago. I called the boatyard.

"Come in, river marina. This is an emergency." No one there, either.

Next, I pressed the button on the microphone to call the Coast Guard.

An outboard motor buzzed in the distance. I cocked my head. The sound grew louder. I didn't like this. Maybe the guy who wasted Hanley was coming back.

The bulkhead walls seemed to squeeze in on me. I hung up the microphone and grabbed an aerosol horn off a shelf. It would give somebody a deaf ear, but it wouldn't stop him. I threw the horn back onto the shelf and rummaged in a drawer for a flare gun. No success.

There was a soft thud against the hull, then another, and the putt-putting of idling motors. Shit, there *were* two boats.

My eye fell on a gaff, a telescoping aluminum tube with a hook at one end. I stretched the sections out, locked them with a twist, and shut off the interior lights. The boat tilted from somebody coming aboard. A hand with a flashlight poked into the cabin. I stood to the side and whipped the gaff handle down about a foot behind the light. Someone shrieked with pain and the flashlight fell to the floor.

I flicked off the deck lights. Then I sprang up the steps, holding the gaff in front of me with both hands. A dark figure blocked my way. I jabbed the gaff into his midsection, felt it hit something soft and solid, and heard a surprised grunt. Another light flashed onto my left. I swung the gaff and the light was gone. I scrambled out of the cockpit, climbed over the cabin cover, and stumbled toward the bow. Maybe I could jump overboard, dive deep, and swim for it.

Shouts of "hey!" and "stop him!"

I slipped and banged my knee on the deck. I gritted my teeth against the pain and bunched my leg under me for a vault overboard.

But something hard bashed me behind the right ear. A nova exploded in my head and I fell into a deep, black pit.

7

Angry voices mumbling, as if from afar.

"Jeezus Christ who . . . Call the rescue . . . On their way . . . The fuck happened . . . Bastard went for me . . . Damned arm is broken . . . Holy shit . . . Dead guy in here . . ."

The slurp of waves, the buzz of a motor. Bright lights and confusion. Then nothing.

A coolness soothed the searing pain in my head. My eyelids fluttered. A white blur filled my vision, became a face with a mouth that opened, formed sentences.

"Don't try to move. Just lie there and enjoy the ride."

The face subdivided into facets and diamonds, dragonfly vision, then shattered into a hundred pieces. Black velvet curtains closed in. Time passed. Loud quarreling voices cut through the fog.

The first voice was high and strident. "Goddammit, he's *ours*. My man nailed him."

"Yeah, and your other man almost let him get away." A harsh voice, mocking in tone and measured in delivery. Half whisper, like someone with a touch of laryngitis. I knew it from somewhere, tried to remember, but my head hurt to think.

"Don't give me that. No one knew what the hell to expect. For Chrissake, we called you guys as a frigging courtesy. My department's got jurisdiction."

"Try again, pal." The gritty voice again. "You called us because you thought you might need help."

"That's crap. We got there first."

"But we had the first guy on board. He's still nursing his fucking arm."

"Still doesn't give you shit. My officer was attacked, too."

"Pin a Purple Heart on his chest and tell him he can testify in court. Here's the bottom line. The boat was moored on our side of the river. The mooring was inspected by *our* harbormaster. The permit came from *our* town. So the bastard's ours."

A couple of ticks of silence. "Okay, pal, you can have him. Beats me why I'm fighting for a crummy murder case that'd tie up my whole damned department."

" 'Cause you're seeing all the headlines. You want to go before the town meeting just like I do and scare the shit out of the old blue hairs. Tell the retired people they're going to have to vote the cops a fat budget because the town was hit by a big crime wave and we've got murderers running wild all over the place. Even on the water where they like to go putt-putt in their Boston Whalers."

The tension melted. Laughter. They were pals again. Somebody groaned. The laughter stopped. The groaner was me.

"Sounds like he's back in the world of the living."

"He may wish he was dead when we get through with him," the whisperer said. "You keep an eye on him. We'll be outside. Tell us when he can talk."

A third man, younger, said, "He's not going anywhere in a

hurry, but I'll holler if he gives me any trouble." Footsteps retreated. A door opened, then shut. A pudgy serious-faced man in a dark blue emergency medical technician uniform leaned over me, holding something to my head.

"How are you feeling?"

"Like twenty miles of bad road," I croaked.

He peeled back one of my eyelids. "You'll be all right. Head's bandaged up and the cold compress will keep the swelling down."

I looked around. I was on a gurney.

"Is this the morgue?"

"Naw. Cape Cod Hospital emergency. We ran you up here for a checkup. You got whacked hard with a nightstick. Broke the skin and you bled some. You'll have a headache for a while, and you'll have to keep ice on it to reduce the swelling, but you'll be okay. No fracture or permanent damage, just a mild concussion."

"I thought I heard people yelling. Was I dreaming?"

The EMT smiled grimly. "Cops from both sides of the river were fighting over you. The boat was pretty close to the town boundary line that runs right up the middle of the river. Cops in my town won. They want you real bad."

An image flashed through my mind. Hanley's white face under the blanket. "Oh damn, now I remember."

The EMT got serious again. "That's good, because some people are real anxious to talk to you. Here, hold this ice pack in place." He took my hand and placed it on a cold lump growing out of the side of my head. I turned. A uniformed policeman sat in a folding metal chair next to the door.

The EMT went over to the cop. I heard low murmurings, then they both left and a man wearing civilian clothes came in. He was around five-foot-eight, with a wide-shouldered blocky torso, put together in a series of rectangles. Squarely built body, a Fearless Fosdick jaw, made even more rectangular by the downward droop of his thin mustache, black hair trimmed in a sharply angled shovel cut over his wide fore-head, square pattern to his tan glen-plaid sports coat. Even the tinted wire-rim glasses framing his dead-looking eyes had four sides.

His cruel mouth curled into a grin. "Hello, Socarides. Long time no see."

"Hello, Detective Pacheco."

"Good, you remember me."

"How could I forget?" I said. "You're wearing the same clothes."

"I'm still impressed, Socarides. It's been over two years since you and that creep dope peddler were standing outside the Barnstable courthouse having a good laugh at my expense. Remember, I came over and said you'd better watch your step because someday you were going to mess up and I'd be there to cut your balls off?" He moved his fingers as if he were holding an invisible pair of scissors. "Guess what?" he said.

I struggled to sit up. The effort made me dizzy and sick to my stomach. Someone was bowling tenpins between my ears and just got a strike. The pain must have shown on my face because Pacheco smiled. He didn't help me, but he didn't push me down, either. I had to give him that.

I forced the words out, one by one, trying to keep him in focus. "The creep you're talking about would have gotten off even if he *was* guilty, big shot. The assistant DA said it was the sloppiest police work he'd ever seen. You're lucky you weren't put in jail for perjury."

Pacheco grabbed the front of my shirt and pulled me forward.

"You lying son of a bitch," he snarled. "He got off on a technicality because you brought in that shit evidence at the last minute."

If Pacheco kept shaking me, he'd get a load of vomit right

between the eyes. I must have turned green, because he let me go. He dragged the metal chair over, and moved it around to straddle it. He leaned back and let his sports jacket fall open so I could see the butt of his pistol sticking out of the belt holster and be frightened to death.

"You're in trouble, Socarides. Let's see what we've got." He tallied the charges on his fingers. "First, a clear-cut case of murder one. Then there's assault and battery on an officer. Two counts. And resisting arrest. That little rowboat you stole was worth a couple of hundred bucks. Grand larceny." He paused; he had forgotten something. "Oh yeah. Trespassing. I might drop that one on a plea bargain."

Pacheco was too busy playing judge and jury to notice the tall man who stood in the doorway. I raised an eyebrow and the newcomer put his finger to his lips.

"You forgot to charge me with creating a nuisance," I said.

The detective's hand shot forward and bunched the front of my shirt again.

"Don't tell *me* what to do, scumbag. I don't take advice from killers."

"Do you take it from other cops?" the tall man said.

Pacheco whirled and glared at the man, who had taken a couple of steps into the room.

"Because if you do," the man added, "I'd recommend that you read this guy his Miranda rights and stop mauling him."

"Parmenter, what the fuck are you doing here?"

The man came in and stood beside Pacheco, dwarfing him. "I was at the barracks on assignment with the drug unit. We picked up the call and it sounded like a dope bust."

"This has nothing to do with the state cops. You're out of your jurisdiction, Captain."

"Christ, I know that, Detective Pacheco. Don't mind me. I just wanted to see how a pro conducts an interrogation."

Pacheco turned back to me. "Okay, Socarides," he growled. "What were you doing on that boat?"

I brushed the wrinkles out of the shirt. "Phil Hanley asked me to meet him there."

"What for?"

"It had to do with a case I'm working on."

"What kind of case?"

I could hear myself saying, "You're not going to believe this detective, but I've been hired to clear a killer whale of a murder charge." Pacheco would probably shoot me, due process or not, just for general smart-assedness. Even without the zany story, I would have kept my mouth shut. I don't like to tell my client's business to anyone, cops included, but I'll cooperate if somebody talks to me the right way. Which Pacheco wasn't doing.

"I'm working for the people who own Oceanus marine theme park. If they want to tell you what I'm doing, it's up to them, but I don't talk without permission."

Pacheco was a throwback to a time cops could do anything they wanted, beat the crap out of a guy, rupture his spleen, and say he did it falling down the stairs. He was itching to work me over. He glanced at the tall man, who was chewing on a toothpick.

"Okay, statie. Any other big ideas?"

"Yeah. Stop trying to browbeat a confession out of the gentleman. Either arrest him or let him go."

Pacheco gagged on that one. "I can't let him go. He killed someone and attacked the cops who tried to arrest him."

"What about that, Mr. Suspect?" Parmenter said.

"Detective Pacheco's got a great imagination, but that's all it is. I had an appointment to meet Hanley. I found his body and was calling for help on the marine radio when I heard someone coming aboard. I thought it might be the murderers coming back, maybe to get rid of the body. I grabbed a gaff. It was dark. I couldn't see who they were. Nobody said they were cops. I started swinging."

Parmenter turned to Pacheco. "Did you find a gun?"

"Naw. Maybe he threw it overboard. We'll have divers look for it."

"What about a motive?"

"We just got into this case a couple of hours ago, Parmenter."

"Then I'd be inclined to believe the man's story unless you've got evidence to the contrary."

"No one asked for your opinion."

"That's true, but I'm giving it anyhow, because I don't like to see incompetent cop work that puts innocent people behind bars and lets guilty ones get away. You're going to lose this case before you begin if you violate this man's rights. I forgot to mention, Mr. Socarides' lawyer would like to sit in while you question his client."

A man in a suit stepped into the room. His tie was loose around his neck and the collar unbuttoned. I had never seen him before.

Pacheco was stunned. "A lawyer? Where the hell did he come from?" I was asking myself the same question. Pacheco was wavering. Parmeter saw the breach and jumped in.

"This is just a suggestion, Detective. Forget the attack on your cops. They should have announced they were coming aboard. I might have taken a swing at them myself if I had been in the same predicament, having just found a dead man, out there all by myself. So far, all you know is that he was on the boat. I'm sure the cops in his town will give him a good recommendation. I can vouch for him personally. Call it a night, give him a chance to clear his head, and get him to come in tomorrow to make a statement. In the meantime, check around to see if anybody heard him on the radio. A murderer wouldn't call for help. If things don't jive, arrest him, arraign him, and ask for a million dollars in bail."

Pacheco wasn't the smartest cop in the world, but he knew

he was getting into legal waters that were over his head. He nodded. "Okay, Parmenter. Your ass is on the line if he doesn't show." He pointed his finger at me. "Eight o'clock tomorrow morning at the police station."

I remembered Oceanus. "I have to be somewhere around eight. Can we make it around seven A.M.?"

He slowly rose from his chair, glowering.

"Seven. Be there," he grunted, and stormed toward the door.

"Detective," I called.

He stopped at the door and scowled darkly.

"Can I get my truck tonight without getting picked up again by your boys?"

"Get it in the morning. It might contain evidence." Then he was gone.

Parmenter shook hands with my lawyer without introducing him to me, then came over to the gurney. I sat up with my legs dangling over the side. Parmenter's hair was grayer than I remembered, but his ruddy face hadn't aged much. Pacheco tried to look tough. Parmenter *was* tough without even trying, but the laugh lines at the corners of his eyes and his thin lips cushioned the hardness. He had a firm jaw, a straight nose just a little too long for his round face, and intense hazel eyes. I always thought he looked like Gene Hackman. He shook my hand. His grip was warm and strong.

"Am I glad to see you, John. Where did I get a lawyer?"

Parmenter took the toothpick out of his mouth and flicked it into a corner. "I heard you were here from one of Pacheco's guys," he said, grinning. "I know how the lieutenant works." He jerked a thumb at the door. "I got Freddie out of bed. He's an old friend of mine. Handles real estate mostly. Probably couldn't get you off on a barking-dog complaint."

"Doesn't matter. He did the job. What brings you to Cape Cod?."

"Working with the DA on a drug money laundering case." He chuckled. "Hell, the last time I was here was to stake out the Mid-Cape flasher. Guy used to run bare-assed in front of cars on Route Six. Some nut exposed himself in the rest area we were watching, and when he saw us he drove ninety miles an hour and went off the road. Turned out to be the wrong pervert. Never did catch the flasher." His face grew serious. "You've got yourself in a hell of a mess, Soc."

"People keep telling me that. How have you been?"

"Just fine. It's been tough without Donna, but I'm doing okay. Thanks for your card, by the way."

"She was a fine woman, I'm really sorry. It's been a long time since I saw either one of you."

"Jennifer's funeral."

"That's right, Jennifer's funeral."

There was an uncomfortable silence, then Parmenter spoke again.

"I tried to get you a couple of times. After a while I just gave up. Seemed like you didn't want to talk to me."

"I didn't want to talk to anyone, John."

"I was different, Soc. We were almost family."

"That's just it. Jennifer was your daughter. I couldn't face you."

"It wasn't your fault, Soc."

"Dammit, she was on her way to my apartment when those kids rammed her car."

"That was fate, Soc. You can't blame yourself. When are you going to stop carrying the guilt for the whole world? Vietnam, the Boston Police Department, your family. You've done the same thing with Jennifer."

I didn't give him an answer because there wasn't any.

Parmenter saw the discussion was headed nowhere. "Why does Pacheco have such a big crush on you?" he said.

I picked up the ice pack and pressed it against my head. "Couple of years ago the state hired me to help a public defender trying to keep a kid out of jail on a drug charge. I think Pacheco planted the evidence. I proved the stuff came from a stash the cops had from another dope bust. The judge threw the case out. He would have sent Pacheco away if he could have, but the best he could do was to give him a stern lecture. The guy's been hoping to catch me on something ever since. Whenever I go through his town I drive twenty miles below the speed limit. Which reminds me, can you give me a ride home?"

Parmenter nodded and helped me off the gurney. I was still dizzy, and top-heavy from the bandage. A half hour later he dropped me off at the boathouse. A thought occurred to me as I got out of his car.

"John," I said, "how did the cops knew about Hanley?"

"Somebody called the station house with a phone tip. Said there was a dead man on the boat and they'd better be careful because the guy who did it might still be there. Those guys aren't exactly the SWAT team. You're lucky you didn't get shot. Any idea who called in?"

"Yeah, somebody who knew Hanley was dead. I'd like to talk to him."

Kojak was waiting for me. He rubbed against my leg and gave me the bad eye. I got out a some 9-Lives Prime Grill and gave him the whole can. I tried to tell Kojak what a rough day I'd had, but he was making too much noise wolfing down his food, so I went to bed. With luck, and a handful of Tylenol, I could catch a few Z's before my first day of work at Oceanus.

8

Morning arrived much too soon. I crawled out from between the sheets and sat on the edge of the bed, watching a golden eyebrow of sun peek over the Atlantic rim. After a few minutes I got up and went into the kitchen. I couldn't fully appreciate the miracle of the new day because my head hurt like hell and my vision swam. I washed more Tylenol down with a cup of black coffee. The pills helped blunt the pain and the coffee woke me up and brought my eyes back into focus. I called Sam and asked him for a ride to my truck. Then I cut the bandage off my head. The bruise was ugly and purple, but it wasn't visible under the hair. My face was another matter. It looked as if it had been soaked in fabric softener.

Sam arrived a few minutes later and sat at the kitchen table, puffing meditatively on his pipe. Normally he's too polite to ask questions about my mornings-after, but he couldn't restrain his curiosity.

"Hard night, Soc?"

"You could say that. I'll tell you on the way to my truck."

On the ride to Bass River, I laid out the details of the case, starting with the call from Shaughnessy. I was telling him about my arrest just as we pulled into the windmill parking lot.

Sam shook his head. "Always liked this spot," he said. "Too bad somebody had to spoil it by killing that poor fella." He furrowed his brow. "Be careful, Soc. This whole thing smells worse than a week-old pile of scallop ghurry."

"I'll look both ways before I cross the street," I said, getting out of the pickup. "Call you later to check on the boat, Sam. Thanks for the ride."

I walked over to my pickup. The floor was immaculate. Pacheco's boys probably dusted my empty Coke cans and Styrofoam coffee cups for prints. Hanley's boat was no longer at its mooring. I drove to a marina off River Street. The *Mariah* was tied up to the dock. A couple of cruisers and a car from the county identification office were parked nearby. I swung through the parking lot without stopping. I didn't want to be seen by some badge who still thinks the criminal always returns to the scene of the crime. At seven A.M. on the nose I walked into the police station to see Pacheco.

The front-desk cop showed me to Pacheco's office. The lieutenant sat behind his desk flanked by two uniformed cops. He gestured to a hard wooden chair placed directly in front of him.

"Okay," he said. "Spill it, from start to finish."

I sat down, crossed my legs, and walked Pacheco through the day before. I told him about talking to Mrs. Hanley, her husband's phone call to me, and the invitation to meet on his boat.

Pacheco slouched silently in his chair, chin on his chest, his arms folded, looking up at me from under dark eyebrows. Occasionally a uniform politely asked for a clarification. One cop kept notes. I described finding the body and my attempt to radio for help. "You know the rest," I said. "Questions?"

The two cops had plenty of them. Not once did they get angry or threatening, and they always called me sir. I took them through the story again from top to bottom and bottom to top, knowing they were looking for inconsistencies.

Forty-five minutes later they asked me to wait outside. I chatted with the front-desk officer about striped-bass fishing. Before long the door to Pacheco's office opened. The uniforms came out. One said Pacheco wanted to talk to me. I went inside and sat in the chair again.

"I talked to Dan Austin," Pacheco said. "He confirmed you were working for Oceanus." He glowered at me. "The radio story checks out, too. Couple of people at the fire department heard you."

"So you're through with me?"

"I didn't say that, Socarides. You figure it. You're a smart boy. I don't have enough evidence at this time to hold you. But this investigation is only beginning. I just know that you'll be back here for another visit."

"In case somebody asks me, what was my motive?"

"Could be anything. Money. Revenge. Jealousy. Hanley had a cute little wife, maybe we'll find out you were playing the stud with her. Her hubby didn't like it, so you took him out. Maybe we'll find there's a big insurance policy on him." He smiled. "Maybe there was dope involved."

My head was throbbing. I got up. "Maybe it's time for me to blow this pop joint."

"Not just yet."

I glanced at the wall clock. "Okay, but make it fast."

"I'm filing a complaint with the commissioner of public safety. I'm going for revocation of your PI license."

"On what grounds?"

"Withholding information necessary to a murder investigation."

"You can do better than that."

"I intend to. In the meantime, you're still a witness and we can call you in for further questioning."

I pushed my way out of the office, wished the front-desk guy good fishing, and stopped for coffee at a Dunkin Donuts. Talking to Pacheco left a bad taste in my mouth and I wanted to wash it away.

The drive to Oceanus took less than ten minutes, but it was enough time to see that the pace of events had gone from zero to Mach 1 in no time flat. Within hours of signing on to this crazy case, one of my suspects became a corpse, I'd been hammered with a nightstick, and my freedom and my PI license were in question.

The pickets must have been eating their breakfast granola, because no one stopped me at the Oceanus entrance. I drove around back and parked near the staff door. I rang the bell. When that didn't work, I pounded on the door about fifty times. The racket finally dislodged the gruff old security guard with the bulldog frown. He smelled sourly of booze and his cheek was laced with red sleep wrinkles. I said I was new on the staff. He rattled his key ring in my face like an angry wraith.

"Yeah, Austin told me about you. Christ, why didn't he give you a key? C'mon, follow me." Truly a man of action.

His office was behind the ticket booths in a space that could have been measured in square inches. He had shoehorned a cot, an office refrigerator, and a TV into the postage-stamp cubicle. His pillow had a head-sized dent in it. He took a key off a pegboard that held several key sets and squinted at the tag to make sure it was the right one.

"This'll open the backdoor," he said, handing the key over. "Come to me if you've got to get in anywhere else. My name is Ben. I'm here nights every other week."

He shuffled off, doing a good imitation of somebody with a

destination in mind. I headed toward the dolphin pool. Two
silver-gray backs and one paler glided through the water.
Puff had a couple of friends. Introductions would have to
wait. Austin stood in his office window waving his hands at
me like a conductor trying to get the piccolo section to pump
up the sound. I went over and climbed the stairs to the office.

"Socarides. What the hell is going on? The police called
me at home a while ago. They said Phil Hanley had been
killed."

I told Austin how I had called Hanley as a possible lead and
found him dead a couple of hours later.

"The whole thing is incredible," Austin said. "I just can't
believe it. First Eddy Byron, now Phil Hanley."

"Do you know anyone with a reason to kill Hanley?" I
asked.

"No, no one. Phil didn't have any enemies. He was just
your typical PR guy. Came out of Emerson College. Wanted
to be a writer, couldn't make it, so he went into newspapers,
but found there was more money in PR. He was full of bullshit and could talk a lot without saying anything, but that was
his job."

"Why did he get fired?"

"Hanley was responsible for some of the bad ink we got in
the press."

"Such as?"

"He screwed up on the Eddy Byron thing. He handled it
fine in the first days, put a spin on it, feeding the press, but
not really telling them the whole story. It looked like the
whole mess would die down. Then the story got out about
the holes in Eddy's suit and the link to Rocky's teeth. Phil
Hanley was under strict orders to deflect those questions. Say
he couldn't confirm them. Or bump them upstairs to Boston
so the reporters wouldn't bother me and we could put them
off."

"So he got fired for telling the truth?"

"Dammit, Socarides, he got fired for confirming damaging information. It was only a tiny slip, admitting that we were looking into the possibility of Rocky being involved in Byron's death, but it was enough to light a fuse under the story. I had strict orders from the top to keep a lid on things down here. I took over as spokesman after Hanley was fired. By then it was a matter of damage control."

"What about the news leak? Any idea who was responsible?"

Austin shook his head. "We tried to keep it quiet, even from the staff, but it was impossible. Barring lie-detector tests, there's no way to find out who shot their mouth off."

"What about the trainer who got fired a while ago?"

"Lew Atwood? He was no longer working at the park when Eddy was killed, but he could have maintained ties with some of the people here and picked up the story over a glass of beer and told the press. I just don't know."

"Why was Atwood fired?"

"Rocky got sick last year. Atwood should have told us sooner that it was happening."

Austin gave the image of being helpful, but he didn't say much.

"Okay," I said. "Maybe I can get to the bottom of this. I'm ready to go undercover."

He got up from behind his desk. "C'mon. I'll get you outfitted."

Austin led me downstairs to a storeroom where Oceanus uniforms were neatly stacked in a large metal cabinet. He gave me a blue shirt that matched his and a pair of khaki shorts. Then he led me to the men's locker room, left me there to change, and said he would meet me by the dolphin pool.

I put on my Oceanus uniform and caught up with Austin

again. He was chatting with a girl he introduced as Jill. She was just over five feet tall, bordering on the anorexic, with bright blue eyes in a bony face, cornsilk hair, and a wide Howdy Doody mouth. She was probably around twenty, but with her freckled nose and long hair getting in her eyes, she looked around twelve. Norman Rockwell would have loved her.

"Jill will show you around," Austin said. "She's one of our most knowledgeable staffers. After she gives you the grand tour, report to me and we'll discuss your duties."

Austin headed back to his office and Jill squinted up at me. The top of her head came to my Adam's apple. She chewed a wad of spearmint gum without saying anything. I guess I passed muster. She grinned like a sunny day and thrust out a skinny arm. Her handshake had more strength in it than I expected. "My name is Jill Wheeler," she said.

"My name is Socarides."

"Socrates like the philosopher?"

"Socarides like the fisherman and diver. Please call me by my nickname. It's Soc."

She cocked her head and considered the information. "You from around here, Soc?"

"I live down Cape. How about you?"

"My parents have a summer place in Cotuit. We're from New York, Westchester. They're vacationing in the south of France. Ever worked in an aquarium before?"

"Nope." I looked around. "I guess the toughest thing for me will be learning where everything is."

"It's easy. Just think of the park as a big cross with thick arms. It's really four buildings built around the main plaza." She pointed to the floor. "The dolphin theater here is the bottom of the cross. The roof is open now, but in the winter they install a portable glass ceiling along those metal beams so they can keep the park operating year-round. The top of the cross is the orca stadium directly opposite on the other side of the plaza. It's the biggest building in the compound. There are seats for two thousand spectators."

She swung to her right. "Off there is the main entrance and ticket booth, turnstiles, and the gift shop. The administration office and space for the staff is on the second floor. On the opposite side are the fish tanks. All the buildings are connected by underground passageways so people don't have to go outside to get from one exhibit to the other. Tucked in around the main buildings, you've got the penguin, sea lions and seals, and the bird pools. The food concessions are off the main plaza. Got it?"

"Got it," I said.

"Good. C'mon."

She was short, but most of her height was legs and I had to walk briskly to keep up with her. We left the dolphin area and headed along a descending corridor into a large circular space that was painted black. It was illuminated by the otherworldly glow from the fish tanks set into the curving wall or into freestanding islands that blocked off the center area in a mini-maze. If the park had been open, people and kids would have been milling about and oohing and aahing at the fish. But the room was empty, and the only sound was the bubbling of the aerators.

"This is my favorite room," Jill was saying in the hushed voice one uses in a cathedral. "The tropical fish are *so* beautiful. Look at all those neon colors. Come this way. You'll love this part."

The black walls and the distortion of reality caused by the moving patterns in the fish tanks threw my bearings off. But I realized we had passed from the fish room, through a short passageway lit with black ultraviolet light, and into another open space. There were fewer tanks along the walls and they tended to be larger than in the fish room.

"This is what the little kids like best, outside of the whales and dolphins," Jill was saying. "It's got the scary fish, predators and things that bite. Piranha. Angler fish, stingrays. Morays. Electric eels. Spiny fish with poison spines. Octopus. Most of them probably wouldn't hurt you unless you stepped on them, and even then I'm not so sure." She pointed at a circular tank in the middle of the room. "That's the centerpiece."

The cylindrical tank was about thirty feet in diameter and extended from the floor into the high ceiling. Around its circumference, like giant TV screens in a sports bar, were rectangular windows, each about four feet wide and a yard tall.

I moved closer and pressed my nose against the gentle curve of the glass. Long shapes the color of rain clouds glided by like phantoms. I identified a nurse shark, a lemon shark, some dogfish, and a small hammerhead. But what really caught my interest was the six-foot-long great white shark swimming on the opposite side of the tank. He drew near and passed the window, his wide staring eye only inches away from mine.

I smelled spearmint. Jill was right behind me. "That's Whitey," she whispered. "Isn't he *beautiful?*"

"Who designed this place?" I said. "Dr. No?"

"I don't think so," Jill answered. "Somebody from Florida. There's another level above this ceiling where you do feeding and maintenance."

The big shark was coming around again.

"Whitey's not a bad guy," she said. "You'll get to know him better. C'mon."

She grabbed my hand and pulled me along another dark hallway that led to the outside. Seconds later we were blinking our eyes in the sunlight streaming down on the plaza. We sat at the edge of a fountain. Water squirted from the mouths of a dozen metal fish and tinkled musically in a large sea-green basin in the shape of a scallop.

Jill crammed another stick of gum in her mouth and offered me one, which I accepted. "That's pretty much it except for the orca stadium." She gestured toward the large flat-roofed building with the picture of killer whales painted against the dark concrete. "Mr. Austin will have to show you that, I guess. Have you heard about Rocky?"

"I read something in the papers. Too bad about his trainer."

"Too bad for Rocky, too. He's still in jail."

Jill wasn't shy about telling me where her sympathies lay. "Did you know the trainer who was killed?"

"Mr. Byron? Not very well. I only got here a little before he did. They had some kind of purge and got rid of all the old Oceanus staff. That was the only reason I got the job. They needed to hire new people."

Sally Carlin was walking across the plaza. She came over and shook my hand. "What a pleasant surprise." She appraised my uniform. "I didn't realize when we talked yesterday that you were going to be working here. You should have told me."

"I wasn't sure myself. I still don't know what my duties are. Dan Austin is supposed to tell me."

"Come over to help me if you'd like. I'll be working with the dolphins."

I looked at Jill. She smiled knowingly. "I've got some stuff to do."

"Thanks for the tour."

"No problem," she said over her shoulder.

"Cute kid," I said to Sally as we strolled to the dolphin theater.

"Oh, Jill is a doll. She's always so pleasant, and smart, too. She's learned just about every aspect of the park's operation."

I stored that away. Someone who knew the ins and outs of Oceanus would be a good source to cultivate, even if I had to buy a few packs of spearmint gum.

"Puff will be glad to see you," Sally said. She blew the whistle and two dolphins came over. They were accompanied by a white-skinned animal about the same size as the dolphins. His bulbous head and friendly grin made him look like a pug who's been used too many times as a punching bag.

"Meet Puff's friend Huff and Froggy the beluga whale," Sally said. "He's actually a species of dolphin."

The beluga came up to the edge of the pool and went "wonk."

"Hello, Froggy." I said. "Hope you're not trying out for the Boston Opera Company." The dolphins stuck their noses out of the water and chirped at us. I couldn't tell them apart.

"Which is which?" I asked.

"Huff is the big one and Puff is the smaller."

"How can you tell them apart when they're not together?"

"After a while you know their personalities. There are other ways. Markings, scars and so on, especially on their fins or tails. Puff has a white spot on her fin. Birthmark, I guess."

"So Puff is a woman?"

"They're both ladies. Most of the dolphins performing in parks and aquariums are females," she said. "The males can be overly aggressive and cause problems, particularly when there's a female around."

"Not too different from humans."

She smiled. "Nicer," she said. "Oh, here comes Mike. Have you met him?"

"No, but it looks like I'm about to."

It was the guy I had seen talking to Sally from Austin's window. He was about the same size as I am, just over six feet, but whereas I like to think that I'm built in the classic, muscled but sculpted body of the Greco-Roman tradition, Mike was more of the Arnold Schwarzenegger mold. His sleeves were tight against his biceps. His legs were thick. And he looked mad as hell.

9

"Who the hell are *you?*" he snarled.

Sally said, "Mike, this is Soc. He's going to be working at Oceanus."

The news triggered an angry explosion. "Dammit, Austin didn't tell *me* he was hiring anybody."

I shrugged. "Maybe he forgot."

His eyes blazed. "Maybe he did, buddy, but don't get too comfortable in that uniform. Nobody gets hired around here without my say-so, and I didn't say." He spun on his heel and strode toward Austin's office.

I watched him go. "Who was that?"

"Mike Arnold. He took over as head trainer after Eddy. I'm sorry he was rude to you. He can be a sweet guy, but he's got a bad temper sometimes. He's my boss. Yours, too, if you're still here after he talks to Dan."

Ten minutes later Arnold was back and it was clear his talk with Austin didn't go well. His face was the color of a cranberry cocktail and his mouth was set in a tight line. I didn't blame Arnold for being burned up, but he was producing an excess amount of heat. Hell, bosses go over the heads of their people all the time. You get mad, then either quit or go on with your job. Mike Arnold was holding on to his anger, and I wasn't sure why.

He stalked over to me and said, "Austin says you're only on temporarily. That's ridiculous. We're operating with a skeleton staff as it is. Well, if you're going to be here, you can't hang out around the dolphin pool all day." He glanced involuntarily at Sally and I understood his hostility. Arnold didn't want an eligible male near his attractive dolphin trainer. "C'mon. I'll give you something to do."

He led the way out of the dolphin theater down a corridor that took us to the penguin pool, a concrete tank about fifty by thirty feet, built with irregular contours like a fried egg. The pool's sloping sides were made of blue-gray artificial rocks that were fashioned into caves, grottoes, and ledges. The water was around four feet deep.

The penguins were cute little guys a foot or two long. They sunned themselves or cruised around the pool underwater, more like fish than birds, propelling themselves with quick, jerky wing sweeps.

Arnold was scanning the water, looking for something, and at last he saw it.

"There," he said, "that's the one. He's got a red tab in his left flipper."

He was pointing at a little gray-and-white penguin who swam happily along without a care in the world.

"What about him?"

"It's Oscar. He's due for a shot. I want you bring him into the infirmary."

I looked around for a long-handled net. "How do I do that?"

"You get in the tank, and when he comes around, you grab him. Don't worry, it's safe. He hasn't eaten a trainer in ages."

"You're kidding. I'll get all wet."

"That's a shame," he said, pouting in mock sympathy. Then he grinned, not a nice grin. "You work around an aquarium, buddy, you've got to expect to get wet. Next time bring your bathing suit."

The penguin with the red tag was coming by again.

"What the hell," I said. "He doesn't look too tough." I stripped off my shirt and sneakers and climbed the low chain-link fence onto a ledge, careful not to slip on penguin droppings, then eased into the water. I waited for the birds to get used to me and kept an eye on my target. It wasn't easy. Oscar was one of a half-dozen penguins, all about the same size, going 'round and 'round, rocketing forward occasionally in short bursts of speed.

Each time he rounded the far end of the pool, I'd move in a yard. If I sashayed close enough, I might be able to cut him off at the pass. The water was up to my chest, and movement didn't come easy. Mike Arnold hung over the fence, still grinning. I hoped he got muscle cramps in his jaw. Jill had come by and stood beside him. She waved. My cheering section. I waved back, then stepped into Oscar's way and spread my hands underwater like a quarterback at center.

Oscar sensed my presence and swam to my left without panic. I lunged, scaring the hell out of him, but I managed to get a grip around his body. He flapped his short wings violently and popped out of my hands like a wet watermelon seed. My reflexes were off and my knee was still stiff from the drubbing I took on Hanley's boat the night before. I nose-dived into the water after him and came up empty-handed.

"Go get him, Soc!" Jill yelled. Arnold was splitting a gut laughing.

With the element of surprise gone, I flailed after Oscar, splashing through the water, scattering terrified penguins in my path like leaves before the wind. Squawking birds rocketed in all directions and I lost sight of Oscar in the feathery confusion. A second later I saw him in a corner. I advanced toward him. He swam back and forth in panic. We were both probably thinking the same thing. *Why me?*

Oscar zipped past on my right. I tried to grab him. Missed. At the far end of the pool, the water depth dropped sharply to about ten feet deep to accommodate an underwater viewing window. Oscar dove. I chased him past the window, waved to a couple of startled Oceanus staffers watching the show from the other side of the glass, and shot to the surface.

He was back in the shallow water, where he zigzagged, then headed for an island about dead center in the pool. It was the same slate color as the rest of the artificial rocks, around three yards wide and a couple tall. Frightened penguins crowded onto a ledge like the orchestra playing "Nearer My God to Thee" on the deck of the *Titanic.*

I caught my breath and moved slowly around the island. The penguins tried to keep the miniature mountain between them and me. I pulled myself onto the island and the birds bunched for safety near the summit. It was hard to pick Oscar out of the moving muddle. I saw a glimpse of red. Damn, the tab was on the right flipper; Oscar's was on the *left.*

Aha! Saw him.

I crawled up the side of the mountain, reached into a mass of wet feathers, and slipped on slimy droppings, smashing my elbow. I had the little monster. He squawked pitifully, but I had no mercy.

"Got you now, Oscar," I growled. "I just love plump little penguins for dinner."

Hugging him to my chest, I slipped off the island and made my way to the edge of the pool. Jill was jumping up and down. "You were terrific, Soc." She reached over and took Oscar gently from my arms. "I'll take him for his shot."

I climbed out of the pool. Mike Arnold was waiting for me.

"Good job," he said. "So good you'll get the chance to do it again."

"Wouldn't a net be easier?"

"Might hurt the little guys. You wouldn't want to do that, would you?"

My skinned elbow burned, but I decided I was going to live. My shorts were stained with penguin droppings. I headed toward the locker room. "I'm going to change into some dry clothes."

"You can do that later," he said with a wave of his hand. "I've got other stuff for you to do."

Arnold was right. It would have been a waste of time changing into clean clothes. The jobs he assigned me were the Oceanus equivalent of the Augean stables. I cleaned debris out of the seal tanks and shoveled sea-lion manure. Near the end of the day, I finished swabbing down the sidewalks. Arnold wasn't around. Probably tired himself out issuing all those orders. I looked at my watch. It was after five o'clock. No one had told me it was past quitting time, but I assumed the workday was over because the park was quiet and apparently deserted. Good time to snoop.

With bucket and mop in hand, I strolled around the park. I stopped to chat with Froggy, who greeted me with a foghorn blast, and with a stuck-up seal lion who kept his nose in the air while I tried to get his attention. Then I sauntered across the central plaza to the orca stadium.

An ascending ramp took me behind the auditorium to the seating-section entrance. The wide portal was barred by an eight-foot-high steel-rod gate that was more for show than security. I put the mop and bucket in a corner, climbed the gate, and dropped down on the other side. White arrows painted on the walls pointed the way through a passageway that came out into the top bleacher section of an amphitheater.

At the center of the amphitheater, with bleachers on three sides, was a large tank as big as two Olympic swimming pools. It was in the shape of a figure eight, with the larger

part of the pool facing the bleachers. At its narrowest junc-
ture was an oval island surmounted by two flagpoles. Flying
from each flagpole was a sea-green triangular pennant with a
picture of a leaping killer whale on it.

The afternoon sun had fallen behind the bleachers, casting
the pool partially in shadow. I descended to a poolside stage
around twenty by twenty feet, built about six inches under
the water level. My sneakers were soaked from mopping anyhow, so I stepped over a metal guardrail, sloshed to where
the edge of the pool dropped off, and scanned the dark green
bottle-glass surface.

Nothing stirred, so I called out: "Hey Rocky, are you
home?"

Home . . . hom . . . ho . . . my voice echoed in the
stillness.

For a few moments there was nothing.

Kawoof!

The sound came from the far side of the pool.

A dorsal fin as tall as a small child emerged and moved in
on me like a heat-seeking missile homing in on a target.
Halfway to the edge of the pool the fin disappeared and its
place was taken by a huge head that came straight out of the
water with hardly a ripple on the surface. The chin was
white, whiter than buffed porcelain. The upper snout and
cranium were black except for an elongated white patch behind the eyes. The head swiveled from left to right a couple
of times, and the jaws opened wide to show off more teeth
than I thought possible in a single mouth. The head disappeared and the dorsal fin again moved toward me.

Killer whales aren't dangerous to human beings. That's
what people had been telling me. But the pointed fin heading
my way marked the underwater movement of several tons of
muscle and teeth. Unanswered questions swirled in my head.
Okay, so I'm a coward. I like to think it was simply survival

mechanisms cutting in. I splashed through the ankle-deep water with all the grace of a crippled flamingo, and hastily climbed off the stage into the third row of bleachers.

None too soon. Within seconds the big black-and-white head burst from the water to rest its chin where I'd just been standing and Rocky opened his mouth to show off his impressive dental work.

From the safety of the bleachers, I checked him out. This was one formidable animal. He'd have no trouble biting a man in half. At the same time he projected some of the playfulness you saw in dolphins.

I climbed down the bleachers and walked along between the raised side of the tank and the lowest row of seats. The pool was enclosed by a thick plastic wall that allowed spectators, particularly those sitting in the high-risk rows designated as splash area, to see underwater. Rocky followed me with his head, then slipped backward off the stage. He swam over to the wall and hung vertically, with just his nose pointing out of the water, keeping afloat with gentle sweeps of his paddle-shaped fins. He could have been a very large inflatable pool toy, and not the top predator in the sea. But there was no mistaking the power lurking under the rubbery skin that covered an elongated body nearly five times as long as I was tall.

Rocky was looking at me. But it went beyond that. He was *studying* me. He was trying to decide who I was.

"Hello, Rocky," I said. "My name is Soc."

He hung there, eight tons of him, floating in the sea-green water as weightless as a bubble. Then he sank a few feet, pivoted gracefully, and dove into the depths until he was almost out of sight. After a moment he returned to where I could see him and poised there, horizontal this time, with his snout inches from the glass. I moved closer. The unspoken question ran through my mind

Did you kill Eddy Byron?

Maybe whales could read minds.

Well? Did you do it?

Less than a foot separated us, he in his world, me in mine.

"C'mon, Rocky," I said out loud, "give me something to go on. Just a shake of your bony head."

He just stared at me with his impenetrable black eye. I shrugged and turned away. Halfway up the bleachers, I heard a loud splash and looked back. Rocky was breaching, shooting out of the water at an angle, then arcing prettily back into the pool, his flight ending in a tall geyser. He did it once more and disappeared beneath the water. I went back and climbed the gate, picked up my mop and pail, and headed to the storeroom, thinking about Rocky's strange dance. He had, in his own way, given me a message that was very clear once I took my brain out of neutral. He was telling me he was glad to have company.

Dan Austin intercepted me on the way to the locker room. His shirt was unwrinkled, the slacks had a razor crease in them. His Nike sneakers were pristine white. I hadn't seen myself in a mirror, but I knew I wouldn't make the cover of *Gentleman's Quarterly*. My shorts were damp, my sneakers squished with every step, and my shirt must have looked as if someone had used it to dry dishes. The contrast with his outfit wasn't lost on Austin.

"I guess Mike Arnold gave you a rough time," he said. "Sorry about that. He stormed into my office, pissed off because I had hired you without consulting him. I had to toss him something, so I said he could assign your duties."

I looked down at my elbow, scraped raw from the madcap chase after Oscar. "He followed your orders."

"Look," Austin said. "After you change into some dry things, I'll take you over to the orca stadium to meet Rocky."

"Thanks, but we just introduced ourselves. I was near the

auditorium mopping up, so I climbed the fence. It wasn't very hard."

Austin's brow wrinkled in disapproval. He was a man who wanted everything according to his schedule. He couldn't have known I don't work that way, but he did now. He quickly covered his annoyance with a phony smile. "Good. I would have taken you over earlier, but I got too involved. Did you learn anything today?"

"Yes. I learned a penguin is harder to catch than a greased pig. But not much beyond that. This is only my first day."

"Of course. I guess I'm being impatient."

"That's understandable given the circumstances." I started off, then stopped. "By the way, do you have any material on killer whales? I'd like to read up on the subject. Might help if I knew what I was dealing with."

"Of course. Come up to my office."

I followed him up the stairs and a few minutes later was walking to the locker room with an armful of books. Sally Carlin came by and saw my load.

She smiled. "Doing some heavy reading?"

"Just some homework. I thought I should know more about the critters around here. The only fish I ever took care of was a guppy I had when I was seven. His name was Moby. I gave him too much food one day and he died."

"Maybe we'd better not let you feed our animals."

"Don't worry, I'll be too busy scrubbing sidewalks."

"I guess Mike gave you a hard time today. Don't take it personally. He can be rough on everyone, even me."

I let out a loud stage sigh. "The only thing I lost was my dignity, but I suppose you have to give up something to be in show biz. I think I deserve a reward for today, though. A cold beer would be just right. Would you care to join me?"

"I'd love to. I'll wait for you outside the locker room."

I changed back to my jeans and T-shirt. My water logged sneakers were a lost cause. There wasn't much I could do

about them, so I wrung the water out as best I could and put
them on. On the way to my car I saw Jill leaving in a beat-up
dark green Volvo station wagon. On the bumper was a sticker
that said, *This Car Brakes for Whales.* I waved to Jill, who
waved happily back. Sally and I left the lot together, with me
following her red Honda to a place she said the staff hung
out. Minutes later we were in a funky art deco movie bar on
Route 28. It was decorated with posters of Marilyn in *The
Misfits*, Cagney in *Public Enemy.* The mug of beer for a buck
and a half wasn't a bad deal. Sally ordered a margarita.

We made small talk for a few minutes, then I asked Sally
how she had come to Oceanus. She said she was from Hart-
ford. She majored in marine biology at UConn.

"How did you get into the marine mammal field?" I asked.

"It was a book I read in college. It was written by a
delphinist named John C. Lilly. He said dolphins were probably as bright as humans, because their brains were as big and
as complex as man's. He thought people might actually be
able to speak to dolphins someday if they got rid of their
preconceived notions about man's place in the universe and
started thinking unconventionally about dolphin research."

"What do you think?"

She pondered the question. "Lilly came in for a lot of
criticism from other scientists. They said just because a dolphin's brain is big doesn't mean it can communicate with
man. I guess they were right, but I do think that there is
something unexplainable there. I sense it when I'm working
with the animals, that sometimes we communicate on a nonverbal level."

"Arion's dolphin?"

"What do you mean?"

"It's an old Greek legend. Arion was the best harp player
in Greece. The crew of the boat he was on grabbed him and
said they were going to kill him and take his money. They
said he could throw himself into the sea if he wanted to,

which he did, but first he played a beautiful song on his harp. And when he jumped into the water, a dolphin who'd been attracted by the music came and carried him safely to land. Nonverbal communication. You still haven't told me how you got to Oceanus."

"After college I worked for the Connecticut marine fisheries division. I did shellfish pollution surveys and things like that. It was interesting, but Lilly's work was always in the back of my mind. When a position opened up, I joined the educational department at the Mystic Seaquarium in Connecticut. Later I moved into the training program. I heard Oceanus had an opening for a trainer and came to Cape Cod." She regarded me with interest. "First a quote from Euripides, then an ancient dolphin legend. You seem to be familiar with the classics."

"I should be, I studied them for a couple of years in college. It was my mother's idea. She was afraid I might grow up to be like my grandfather Nikos, who knocked off half the occupying Turkish army on Crete. But the siren call of my Cretan genes was too strong. I quit college, joined the marines to save democracy in Vietnam, escaped with my body in one piece and my mind a wreck, got a job as a Boston cop, got burned out, and moved to Cape Cod to fish." I didn't mention my private-detective work.

"How did you hear there was an opening at Oceanus?" she asked.

"The fishing boat I work on was laid up with engine problems. I was looking around for something to do while the boat was being fixed. I've about had it with the unreliability of fishing, anyhow. A friend who knows Austin called me and said there was some part-time dirty work available, but it might evolve into a real job if and when the park ever reopens. Any news on that?"

Sally licked the salt off the edge of her glass with her tongue. "Dan keeps saying he's going to reopen soon, but

your guess is as good as mine, and mine isn't very good. It's
all this business with Rocky. First Eddy's death, then the
boycott, the picketing, and particularly the bomb threat."

"What do you think? Did the whale kill Eddy?"

"I don't know. There's some evidence it was possible,
but . . ."

"But you don't believe that's what happened."

She pushed her drink aside. "Look, Soc. I've worked
around marine mammals for five years. Mostly dolphins, I
admit, but I spent some time helping with Rocky. And in my
opinion he's one of the most gentle creatures I have ever
met."

"That doesn't cut it," I said. "Just about every murderer
you read about in the papers has got a neighbor who'll say
how nice he was and helped take out the rubbish. I knew a
guy in Vietnam who was like Father Christmas to the local
kids. He'd pick them up, hug them, give them candy. He had
a couple back home he missed a lot. Then one day after some
of his guys got hit in an enemy ambush, he went into a village
and wiped out half a dozen families, kids, mothers, grandfa-
thers. Machine-gunned them first then threw in a couple of
grenades. Funny part was, I think he really liked kids."

Sally looked up from her drink. Anger flared in her eyes.
"Dolphins and orcas are a lot different from humans," she
said firmly. "They only kill for food."

A raw nerve. "I'm new at this," I said, backing off. "Maybe
I'll learn."

I never found out if my tepid apology was accepted because
Mike Arnold walked into the bar and came over to the table.

"I saw your car outside," he said to Sally, ignoring me. He
didn't expect to find his attractive dolphin trainer drinking
with his newest and lowest slave.

"Won't you join us?" Sally asked.

"Thanks," he mumbled. "I'm meeting some people." He
glanced pointedly at me. "Bring your scuba gear when you

come in tomorrow." Then he went to the other side of the rectangular bar and sat directly across from us. I took a sip from my beer mug and glanced over the rim. Mike was staring at me with unfriendly eyes.

"Am I doing something wrong having a drink with you?" I asked. "He looks as if he's sorry the penguins didn't eat me."

"Mike and I have been out a few times, that's all."

I looked at the clock and drained my beer. The air was getting too tense to be productive. "I have to be on my way, but maybe we can get together again."

"I'd like that," she said, and I think she meant it. We stood and shook hands. Sally took her drink and said she was going to stay to chat with Mike. I said I'd see her tomorrow at work. Minutes later I was on Route 28, driving over the old concrete bridge that spans Bass River. People were fishing for flounder off the bridge. I let my eyes range downriver where the *Mariah* had been moored.

Two dead men, Eddy Byron and Phil Hanley, equaled one inescapable conclusion I'd do well to keep in mind. Working for Oceanus can be hazardous to your health.

10

"Hey, Kojak, old buddy, listen to this," I was saying. "Did you know the killer whale can swim thirty miles an hour? That's faster than my pickup truck goes."

Kojak finished inhaling the food from his plate, let forth with a fishy burp, then walked a few steps before the exhaustion of eating caught up with him. He collapsed in a ragged black pile of fur, rolled half over onto his side, and licked the rest of his dinner from his whiskers.

I was sitting at the kitchen table with the books I had borrowed from Dan Austin in front of me and my hand curled around a cold can of Bud.

"Okay, so you're not impressed. How about this? Orcas travel in packs of six to fifty. They hunt as an organized team, the way wolf packs do, circle their prey and attack on signal. This should interest you. They play with their victims like cats."

Kojak lifted his head. His owlish yellow-green eyes blinked. He had no idea what I was talking about because he is a pacifist when it comes to the rodents who claim squatters' rights in the boathouse. Countless generations of mice have been born, grown up, and died of old age under Kojak's nose. He probably attends christenings.

Despite Kojak's cavalier attitude, I found Austin's books informative. I knew now that the male orca could grow to thirty-two feet and weigh nine to ten tons, and the female who doesn't watch her waist may reach a dainty twenty-eight feet and five to six tons. It can dive a mile and hold its breath thirty minutes.

Technically a dolphin, orkie is the largest and swiftest marine mammal that eats warm-blooded prey. The Romans named it *orca*, which means "sea devil," and it isn't hard to see why they did. It has forty-six to fifty teeth in powerful jaws with a large gape that close in an interlocking trap for gripping and tearing. One orca was seen to leap clear of the water holding a five-hundred-pound sea lion in its teeth. As Austin and Sally said, though, when it's not hunting, the orca is a gentle animal with a highly developed social responsibility toward members of its group.

The first orca captured was named Moby Doll. She was harpooned in 1965 by a sculptor who wanted a model for a statue. He couldn't kill her, so he took her captive, gained her confidence, and showed that killer whales are not the bloodthirsty villains people have said they were. They even like humans. And they learn quickly. Before long killer whales were taught to wear fake sunglasses and to have their teeth brushed by a trainer who stuck his head in the whale's mouth for a fake dental exam. Orcas became popular performers with the public, and every marine amusement park with a mind for making a buck wanted at least one.

I read on. An orca has a lousy sense of smell and its eyesight isn't all that great, but it's got a sonar system that could put the best nuclear submarine to shame. By bouncing low-frequency clicks focused into a narrow beam off objects in its path and reading the echoes, the orca gets an accurate sound picture in its brain. It can tell the size and position of underwater objects, especially when it's looking for food. It uses high-frequency clicks run together in a scream to communicate over long distances.

I closed the book I was reading and pushed it away. Everything I read verified what Austin told me and Sally had implied. Except for that crazy incident in British Columbia, there was no record whatsoever of a killer whale ever having killed a human being. I got up and went out onto my deck.

The bay was a huge ebony disk of emptiness. Kerosene lanterns glimmered in the camps along the narrow barrier beach. The Big Dipper wheeled above, its stars blinking coldly in the black sky. I waited for inspiration, but none came. No light bulb went off over my head the way it does in the comics. All I had gotten from two hours of reading was a cranium full of information and a headache from drinking too much beer on an empty stomach.

I went back in the house and opened the refrigerator. It was the cook's day off, so I would have to throw something together. I found the leftovers of a Greek salad: an onion, tomato, olives, cuke, and a scrap of feta cheese. On the door rack were the same two eggs that hadn't been near a hen in months. The secret in cooking old eggs is to overwhelm their staleness with stronger ingredients. I mixed the eggs in a bowl and poured them in a buttered cast-iron frying pan. I sprinkled on the feta and vegetables, and while the omelet cooked I toasted a frozen bagel and popped another beer. I was about to sit down to enjoy a feast fit for the gods when the telephone rang. I picked it up and said hello.

"Hello, Aristotle," my mother said. "Good, your telephone is not broken."

My mother did not really think my telephone was broken.

It was her way of telling me she was angry because I hadn't called her. I stood in the kitchen with the phone clenched in one hand, a can of beer in the other, trying to think of a plausible excuse that would get me off the hook. With a few words she had reduced me to the age of twelve. And I am not twelve. I am approaching middle age. Furthermore, I am six-foot-one, a combat veteran of Vietnam, and an ex-cop. I have spent some time in the amateur boxing ring and have scar tissue on my face to prove it.

To understand why a woman who is barely five feet tall can make a big tough guy like me squirm requires some explanation. And the best place to start is at the beginning. It was my mother who named me after the Greek philosophers. With Hellenic logic, she reasoned that if I bore the names of great men famed for their intellect, I might follow in their footsteps. As I grew older she became convinced she had made the right decision. For she saw something in me as a child that reminded her uncomfortably of her grandfather Nikos, whose looks I have inherited, and whose temperament she fears I bear.

Her memories of Nikos persuaded her to push me into college to study the classics, a course I abandoned to fight with the marines in Vietnam. Later, when I had the chance to resume my studies, I became a city cop instead. Even worse, I dropped out of the tightly knit Greek community in Lowell. After the woman I thought I might marry was killed in a car crash, I moved to Cape Cod and left my younger brother, George, to run the family business while I indulged my fondness for alcohol and self-pity. Through the years I have accumulated a substantial and pathologically addictive burden of guilt. Even my cat takes advantage it.

Ma was ready to lay a scolding on me. I was too tired to respond with the usual litany of lame excuses she has heard a hundred times. I said simply, "I'm sorry I haven't called."

The admission of filial malfeasance caught my mother by surprise. There was no outburst of the usual motherly martyrdom. Only a silence on the other end. After a moment she said pleasantly, "That's all right, Aristotle. I know you are busy."

Encouraged by the success of this newly discovered strategy of candor, I said, "Actually, I was planning to get in touch with you. I talked to Cousin Nick in Boston the other day. He said something about Uncle Constantine coming to Massachusetts. Is that true?"

"*Neh*, Aristotle. Yes. Your uncle will be here soon. And it is why I talk to you. I want you to do something for me."

"Sure, Ma, what is it?"

There was another pause. My mother is no fool. She can be as sweet as the honey in a piece of baklava, but she didn't make Parthenon Pizza into the premier frozen-pizza company in New England by being a dummy. It is no accident that the characteristic the ancient Greeks admired most about Odysseus was his craftiness. The brain under my mother's pepper-and-salt hair is much too guileful to be fooled by any deviousness on my part. She knew I always tried to wriggle out of family obligations, but if she wondered why I was being the dutiful son, she didn't show it.

"You know Constantine is very sad since your aunt Thalia dies from cancer. His children live far away and they are no good anyhow and never come to see him. He is very lonely. He wants to be busy again. He wants to come see me and the family here. So he finds a job to do on Cape Cod. Work is the best way to forget, he says."

"What kind of work, Ma?"

"He wants to go under the water again."

"Uncle Constantine wants to dive? He hasn't done anything like that since his sponging days. He's as tough as nails, but he's too old to go diving."

"You are right, Aristotle. I tell him that when he calls me. But he gets angry. He is *not* too old, he says. He is stronger than ever. He says he will come in his boat and show me."

"I thought he sold the boat when he retired."

"He did. But he buys it back. Aristotle, I'm very worried."

"I'm sure everything is okay. It's not a bad trip if he sticks to the inland waterway, and Uncle Constantine knows the sea better than anyone I know."

"No, I don't worry about the trip, but later, when he dives. The boat is old, too, like Constantine. I am afraid he will hurt himself."

My mother worries so much about everything and everybody that it's easy to toss off her anxieties, but I had my own misgivings about Uncle Constantine's plans.

"What do you want me to do, Ma?"

"When he comes to Cape Cod, maybe you talk to him. Stay with him. Make sure he doesn't hurt himself."

I wondered how I was going to baby-sit a man in his seventies while I was undercover at Oceanus, but I'd figure a way. "Sure, Ma. No problem. Do you know how to get in touch with him?"

"He has your address and telephone. I tell him to make sure he calls you. He says he will. You should hear by now."

"He could have been delayed by anything—weather, engine trouble. But I'll call around to some of the big marinas and leave a message for him to call me pronto when he gets in. I'll talk to him."

"You are a good boy, Aristotle."

"Don't worry. How's the rest of the family?"

"Good. Father and George are working hard. Your sister Chloë is helping out in the office. It is very busy. We are selling many diet pizzas."

The idea of a diet pizza struck me as being something of an oxymoron, but my mother and father have had steady success since they left their mom-and-pop pizza joint and got into wholesale production.

"I'll have to try one the next time I come up," I said.

"Yes, Aristotle. Make it soon."

We said good-bye and hung up. I took a sip of my beer. It was warm and flat. Then I tried my omelet. It was cold, but I was hungry and ate it anyway.

II

Sam and I met at Elsie's Restaurant for breakfast the next morning. Eating at Elsie's is like playing Russian roulette with all the chambers loaded. The blackboard special was cranberry Belgian waffles. The waffles tasted like balsa wood. The cranberries were hard as bullets. Sam spit a mouthful into his paper napkin and made a face, lowering his voice so Elsie wouldn't hear. "Soc, I've tried every dish under the sun in my life, but this is the most god-awful thing I've *ever* eaten."

I tried a pulpy nugget liberally lubricated with Vermont Maid maple syrup, decided it was a lost cause, and used my napkin, too. Then I rinsed my mouth with the caffeine-flavored dishwater that passes for coffee at the restaurant. Elsie came by to ask how the waffles were. Sam and I swore up and down it was the best breakfast we could remember. It doesn't pay to lie, I guess. She gave us more waffles, on the house.

Sam was looking kelpy around the gills as we left Elsie's. My stomach was full of blast-furnace clinkers.

"Good to get some air," Sam said. "I'm going down to the boat. The mechanic's coming early to work on the engine. Says it could take a few days, so we won't be fishing for a while." He looked up and sniffed the air. A lemon sun hung in the unclouded blue sky. "Darned shame. Weather's perfect."

I promised to call Sam that afternoon and headed off to Oceanus. I had time to spare and made a detour off Route 28 to Bass River. Windmill Park was deserted. I got out of the truck, walked over to sit on a green wooden bench, and watched a fishing boat head toward Nantucket Sound. A harpoon was lashed to the pulpit. It was a tuna boat going out to hunt for bluefin that could pay ten thousand dollars or more per fish on the Japanese market. I watched the boat wistfully, wishing for a day at sea and the purity of fishing. I sat awhile, thinking, then looked at my watch. Time to go. Reluctant to leave the bucolic spot, I got back in the truck and drove to Oceanus.

Again I got there before the pickets. I let myself in the staff door, changed into a clean pair of shorts and jersey, and wandered out onto the central plaza. Sun-sparkled droplets of water played pitty-pat in the fish fountain. I found my mop and bucket and strolled over to the dolphin theater, stopping first at a big observation window on the lower level to watch Huff and Puff and Froggy the beluga perform a graceful underwater ballet. Then I climbed the stairs to the dolphin pool. Huff and Puff saw me and swam over, chirping like crickets.

"Sorry, guys," I said. "Don't have a sardine to my name." The beluga came up and let out a basso grunt. It was either a hello or tongue-lashing. Hard to tell with a beluga.

If I wanted to poke around without interference, I had to move fast. With my mop over my shoulder and my bucket in hand I walked quickly across the plaza to the orca stadium.

The iron gate was ajar. I set the mop and bucket down, went through the gate, and followed the passageway that opened onto the spectator section. Pausing at the top row of bleachers, I swept my eyes around the stadium. A man stood in the ten-foot-wide space designated as the splash area between the lowest row of bleacher seats and the pool's plastic wall. His back was to me.

I walked down to the poolside. The man faced the pool and was unaware of me. I said hello. He didn't answer. A second later I saw why. He was wearing earphones. The headset was attached to a rubber cord that was plugged into a tape recorder. Another cord reached from the recorder over the transparent plastic wall and ended in a foot-long black rod suspended in the water.

The man wore dark blue slacks and a yellow shirt instead of the regulation blue and tan, so I guessed he wasn't on the Oceanus staff. He had black hair going to gray at the sides, worn longish over his collar. He was tall, over six feet, but almost fragile looking, as if a good northeast wind would knock him down. His shoulders were bent into a slight stoop, like someone who spent a lot of time hunched over a desk. He was jotting notes into a clipboard with a Bic ballpoint pen. Finally sensing I was there, he turned his head. I recognized him as the man I had seen leaving Austin's office the day of my interview. He was the same guy whose picture was in *The New York Times*. He examined me with alert eyes that were almost black, magnified by thick-lensed glasses perched on a large nose that protruded from a gaunt face. I expected him to be annoyed at having his work interrupted, but his mouth widened in a friendly smile. He took the earphones off and handed them to me.

"Put them on," he said. "Rocky is being very talkative this morning."

I slid the earphones onto my head and heard a hiss of

background static. Rocky was about twenty feet back from the glass, hanging vertically just below the surface in the Christmas-ornament pose he favored. Slowly, he lifted his tail into a more horizontal position to face me head-on and opened his mouth in a toothy grin. A couple of clicks came over the earphones. The clicks grew more frequent and rapid, running together.

Yeeeeeoooooooeeeeeeee.

The piercing, primeval banshee shriek filled my ears. A chill went up my spine. It was like listening to an alien creature calling across empty space from another world. I ripped the earphones off my head.

"Wow," I said.

"Tell me what you heard on the hydrophone."

"It sounded like Dizzy Gillespie blowing a high E riff in my ear."

A sparkle of amusement glinted in his dark eyes. "Absolutely wonderful, isn't it? They make that sound when they're communicating."

"What was Rocky saying?"

He took the earphones back and draped them around his neck. "You would have to compare it to other orca sounds to be absolutely sure, but given Rocky's situation, I'd guess he's saying he's lonely, probably bored, and wants to know where everybody is." He glanced at my Oceanus jersey. "You're new here, aren't you? I thought I knew everybody on the staff. I don't think I've seen you around."

"I started yesterday. My name is Socarides, but just call me Soc. Normally, I'm a fisherman, but the work hasn't been there. Austin says there's a chance of something full-time when the park reopens. He's got me doing scut work. I guess he figured his regular people would quit if he asked them."

"Well, that doesn't surprise me. I've run into a few prima donnas around here." He extended his hand. "My name is

Henry Livingston. Call me Hank. It's *Doctor* Livingston, actually, which earns me a lot of kidding, as in 'Dr. Livingston, I presume.' But don't get sick around me, because my specialty is marine mammals, not humans. I run a little research outfit called Cetacean Explorations out of my house in the town of Sandwich. We do consulting work for Oceanus and other marine parks and aquariums on a contract basis." He pointed to the black rod hanging in the pool and tapped the clipboard with his pen. "That's a transmitter as well as a microphone. I'm seeing how killer whales respond to human sounds, feeding him words and sentences to see how he answers. Have you met Rocky?"

"We introduced ourselves yesterday. He seemed glad to see me."

Rocky wasn't wasting an interested audience. He plunged to the bottom of the pool like a dive-bomber, then turned and shot halfway out of the water, giving us a nice view of the shiny whiteness of his belly before he hit the surface in a foamy echoing explosion.

"He's even happier today having two of us around," Livingston said. "Orcas are very social animals. He's been quite lonely without his daily routine to keep him busy. I've advised the park to get someone in here every day to play with him, run him through his tricks, anything to keep that magnificent body and that large brain active. You don't have any experience working with killer whales, by chance?"

I glanced out at the sixteen-thousand-pound projectile throwing itself halfway to Mars and didn't have to fake a look of horror. "This is the first job I've had in an aquarium, Hank. Maybe I should start off with something smaller. A goldfish would be about right."

A bemused smile played across Livingston's lips. "Oh, yes, I suppose you've heard about that business with Eddy Byron."

"Yeah, I read some stories in the newspaper."

"If it makes you feel any better, the newspaper stories are so much hot air. Killer whales are the gentlest creatures alive when it comes to human beings."

"This is all very confusing," I said. "The papers said people had been hurt by Rocky."

"Oh sure, people have been injured, but that's a big difference from being killed." He handed me his clipboard. "Here, hold this, if you would while I retrieve the microphone." He reeled in the black rod, coiled the cord, and put the electronic equipment next to an L. L. Bean travel bag on the lowest tier of bleachers. He dug a pipe out of the bag and lit up.

"Killer whales have been getting bad press for centuries, but most of the stories are apocryphal," he said. "There's the one about the Canadian loggers working on a hillside overlooking the water. A pod of killer whales passed below and one of the loggers deliberately rolled a log down on top of a whale and injured it. The loggers were rowing back to camp that night when whales attacked the boat and tipped it over. The man who rolled the log disappeared, but the whales never bothered the other logger. I would love to talk to the survivor, but he vanished, too, after telling the tale."

We walked slowly around the perimeter of the pool. Rocky paced us, swimming lazily along the edge of the tank as if he were listening to us talk. Even at minimum speed, his huge body created a low tidal wave that splashed over the top of the transparent wall.

Livingston stopped and contemplated Rocky. The killer whale did a somersault and came back to the surface to hang there with his head partially out of water.

"That's typical orca behavior around human beings, by the way," Livingston said. "These whales are intensely curious creatures. They seem as fascinated by us as we are by them."

He puffed on his pipe. "The most often heard scare story came from Herbert Ponting, a photographer with the Scott expedition in Antarctica. He was on drift ice and orcas started crashing all around him. It scared the pants off him and his story has been told and retold for decades as proof positive the whales are dangerous. But the animals left Ponting alone as soon as they realized he was a human. I think they saw his shadow on the ice from below, thought it was a seal, and just followed their natural predator behavior."

"Was that the last reported attack?"

"Oh no, there have been dozens. Back in the seventies a schooner was rammed and sank off the Galapagos. A couple of the survivors said three orcas had punched the holes in the boat. In 1976 something damaged a yacht off the Cape Verde Islands. Again there were killer whales in the area and again, of course, they were named as the attackers."

"What do you think?"

"It is possible the culprits were killer whales in both cases, but I'd say proof was sadly lacking. There was one notable case. A surfer off California was lying on his board when something grabbed him. He made it to the beach and needed a hundred stitches to close up the three gashes in his thigh. Witnesses sighted a dorsal fin and a black-and-white body. The distance between the gashes was the same as that between a killer whale's teeth, and they were clean incisions, not like the tearing wounds that would have been made by a shark."

Eddy Byron had three holes in his wet suit.

"That sounds like a pretty strong case for an orca attack."

"I don't deny that. The orca doesn't have great eyesight, but its echolocation can pick out the stripes on a bass, so its natural sonar should have been able to distinguish between a seal, which is fair game, and a man on a surfboard."

"Why didn't it, then?"

"I think the whale simply made an error. For all its sophisticated electronics, I'll bet there are times a nuclear submarine mistakes a whale for another sub. Why shouldn't a whale get confused? God knows what it thought the surfboard was. But again, the attack was not fatal, the man made it to shore without being bitten again, and the whale went away."

"That's it?"

"Pretty much. Even as recently as the 1960s, navy diving manuals were warning divers that orcas will attack humans. But every diver who has been in the water with an orca is evidence just to the contrary."

"Austin told me about a trainer being killed in British Columbia."

He frowned. "I'm not sure what to make of that. My feeling is that it is dangerous to work with more than one whale in a confined space. It's been pretty well established that marine mammals can become neurotic in captivity."

"Then a captive whale can be dangerous?"

"I said *neurotic*, not psychotic. But to answer your question, incidents of orca attacks are not unusual in captivity. Even dolphins can become touchy. It must be much harder for an orca, because of its size and its freewheeling predatory instincts, to put up with captivity. It could get frustrated, and that frustration would show up in anger. I think in British Columbia a pack mentality set in. The whales' natural instincts overrode their learned behavior. The same thing could happen with trained circus bears."

"The other day I ran into some pickets who called this place a 'whale jail.' Does what you just said about captivity back them up?"

Livingston looked at me with more than casual interest, his dark eyes probing. Then he shrugged. "They have their right to express their opinion. But I think the situation is much more complex than they would have people believe."

"In what way?"

"There's an international debate raging over creatures like Rocky. On one side are some conservationists who think no marine mammals should be held captive. They would prefer that the public be exposed to marine mammals in the wild, and suggest places be set up where dolphins, for instance, can interact voluntarily with humans. On the other hand, you have people like Dan Austin and the owners of parks like this who say the problems whales and dolphins have in captivity are no different from the ones zoos have with big animals. Just look at the dolphins living much longer in captivity than they would in the wild, they say, or at the number of dolphins being born in these parks." He grinned. "Their position isn't surprising, given the kind of money a place like this generates."

"Who's right?"

"Whoever has the most political power. When the pros and cons clashed in Australia, the government banned the capture of cetaceans for export. Nothing like that ever happened before, and it stirred up people on both sides of the issue around the world."

"Do you think anything like that would happen in this country?"

"One never knows. There are some groups working toward that end. Most of the time they run into a combination of big-money lobbying by the marine-park industry and the tendency of government toward inertia. But when something like Eddy Byron's death happens, all bets are off. What you see out at the front gate is only a small manifestation of the global debate."

"If you don't mind my asking, Dr. Livingston, where do you stand on this?"

"Before I answer that question, I should mention a third group. They say there isn't enough evidence to prove captivity is harmful, but even so, it is a small price to pay for greater public appreciation of the world around them, more support for conservation, and adds to the sum of our human understanding of the world around us."

"Is that what you think?"

"I think cetaceans, more than any other wild creatures, are the closest to feeling emotions the way humans do. As a human being I can't help but empathize with Rocky and other marine mammals who show such fascinating anthropomorphic characteristics. I know they are not here of their own free will and that bothers me. Personally, I would like to see every whale and dolphin released in those cases where they wouldn't suffer from the shock of being returned to the wild. At the same time, as a scientist, I realize that I can best study these remarkable animals in a controlled situation like this. And I know that if people come in here, especially children, and see marvelous creatures like Rocky, yes, even doing their silly tricks, they will a develop an appreciation for these animals. That means greater public support when government wants to pass conservation and protection laws and appropriate more money for research. We would never know as much about them as we do if they were all still in the wild." He shook his head and laughed. "So where does that leave me? I suppose it leaves me sitting on the fence."

It was my turn to shrug.

He gathered up his electronic equipment and said, "Well, sorry I have to go. Nice meeting you."

"Thanks for answering my dumb questions."

"Not dumb. No, not dumb at all," he mused. He took a business card out of his wallet and gave it to me. "Come by my office sometime, we'll talk some more. I'm sure I'll see you around the park. I'm here several times a month." He gathered his electronic equipment into the canvas bag and climbed to the top of the stadium, giving me a wave before he disappeared around a corner.

I turned back to Rocky. He was swimming back and forth behind the glass. I wondered again what unimaginable stories lay behind that big round eye.

"You'd make my job a hell of a lot easier if you could talk," I said. I chuckled inwardly at my human chauvinism. Rocky *could* talk, to other killer whales. It wasn't his fault if I couldn't understand him. "Sorry, buddy," I apologized. "You know what I mean. You can talk fine, it's just that we dumb humans aren't very good at understanding stuff that doesn't come easy to us."

I collected my mop and pail and walked back to the plaza. It was good, or bad timing, depending how you looked at it. Mike Arnold was coming toward me. He had a grin on his face that made Rocky's look positively benign.

I laid the mop handle on my shoulder like a rifle and stood at attention. "Well, what is it today, skipper? Do I chase penguins, clean up after the sea lions, or slop the seals?"

Arnold's grin widened, but it still didn't make him look any friendlier.

"Naw, that stuff can wait," he said. "I got something better for you to do. I'm going to introduce you to Whitey."

12

Whitey glided past the window, his tapered head weaving rhythmically from side to side, syncopated with the fluid movements of his tail. He passed so close his pectoral fin grazed the window glass. I remembered looking at pictures of the sixty-foot-long monsters who roamed the ancient seas when herds of mastodons grazed on land. The shark's streamlined form is so near perfection it hasn't evolved in a hundred million years. The same pointed snout, dorsal fin, and knife-cut tail mark the hungry little dogfish Sam and I see stealing the bait off our hooks.

Whitey wasn't big as white sharks go—maybe six feet in a species that can go over twenty, but the heavy body and wide mouth had an air of menace you couldn't hide behind a cute nickname. The other fish swimming around in the tank ranged in size from a poodle-sized sandshark to a harmless nurse shark about eight feet long.

I turned to Mike Arnold. "Let me get this straight. You want *me* to get in the tank with *him?*"

"You got it right, except for one thing. Whitey's a *her*."

"Gee, that makes me feel one hell of a lot better. Now tell me why anybody would want to get in there with that?"

"To begin with, it's part of your job if you want to work as a diver at Oceanus."

"Austin never said being shark bait went with the salary."

"He musta forgot, so I'll lay it out for you. It costs big bucks to run this park, that's why the tickets are on the high side. The customers like the whale and dolphin shows, but we want them to get their money's worth. So two times a day a diver goes in the shark tank and swims around. No big deal. It gives the customer a thrill, they take pictures and buy film in the gift shop. We sell posters, too. Maybe we can get you in one."

"Thanks. I've always wanted to get into show biz, but Whitey isn't my idea of a leading lady and I forgot my scuba gear."

"No problem. We've got a suit and tank you can use." He shrugged his bodybuilder's shoulders. "Look, pal, it's no skin off my ass if you're too scared to do this. Austin wants to open the park soon and the staff has to be ready. We won't have time for training then. If you don't want this job, we'll just hire somebody else."

The ghostly forms scudded past the window. I watched them for a few seconds and recalled that sharks have been called the ultimate eating machines. I was in a quandary. Nothing in my job description said I had to go into the tank, but I couldn't back out unless I made a fuss, and that would call unwanted attention to me and hinder my ability to snoop.

I looked at the window again. "Okay," I said, "but you go in first and show me how it's done."

Arnold sneered. "C'mon, tough guy."

He led the way across the dimly lit fish room and opened a

door that was part of the wall. We climbed a stairway to a space about eight feet high between the false ceiling over the fish room and the roof. Electrical conduits and pipes snaked across the floor to the open tops of the fish tanks, which were serviced by metal walkways.

The shark tank was built of thick concrete, elevated several feet above the rest of the ceiling. We climbed a short set of stairs to the rim, which was encircled by a narrow walkway. On the walkway next to the pool were two sets of scuba gear and two wet suits. But the big metal bird cage hanging over the pool was what really caught my eye.

The cylindrical cage hung by a cable from a boom and power winch in the ceiling. It was about six feet high and had a trapdoor at the bottom. Metal semicircles arched across the top. I put my hand on an aluminum bar.

"You're going to tell me this thing is for a two-hundred-pound canary, right?"

Arnold chuckled. "Naw, it's an antishark cage."

I pushed the cage gently and it swung back and forth over the pool.

"I'm just full of dumb questions today, Arnold. If the boys and girls below are as harmless as you say, why do you need an antishark cage?"

"It's for dramatic effect. You lower the diver into the pool. The crowd oohs and aahs. They think, hey, this is dangerous. They really get excited when the diver gets out. They think he's going to be eaten alive and they'll get it on film. Cage makes a good elevator besides, but we won't use it today."

Arnold started stripping down to his underwear and I did the same, reluctantly. In a few minutes we were in our neoprene wet suits safety checking the dive gear. The equipment was fairly new and appeared in good working condition. Arnold reached into his gear bag and pulled out a wooden stick around three feet long and a couple of inches thick. He slid the ski-pole loop at one end over his wrist and slapped the stick into the palm of his hand like a beat cop getting ready to bust a few heads.

"This is a shark billy," Arnold said. "Jacques Cousteau and his crew came up with the idea. It's got these little nails at one end so it won't slip against the shark's skin. If a shark gets too close, you push him away real gentle. He'll keep coming back, but the stick tells him to keep his distance. Oh yeah, there's one small thing; important, though."

"What's that?"

"Be gentle with it, especially around Whitey. You whack the shark or hurt it, she'll get pissed off and go for you." Arnold pulled the face mask over his nose. "Watch me," he said. "I'll go in real slow so I don't scare the fish."

He bit down on his regulator and put one leg over the lip of the tank, followed with the other, and sat on the edge next to a set of rungs on the inside wall. He gave his body a half turn and slipped into the tank. Holding on with one hand, he adjusted his mask and tested his regulator underwater, then released air from his buoyancy compensator. Descending hand over hand, he sank slowly toward the gray shadows below.

I went down the stairway into the fish room and peered into the shark tank. Arnold's fins were coming into view, followed by the rest of him. He sank toward the sandy bottom and moved into the open circle of boulders arranged like the megaliths at Stonehenge in England.

Startled by his appearance, the fish darted out of his way. Whitey shot toward the top of the tank, then cautiously made her way down again, doing her best to avoid the bubbles streaming upward upward from Arnold's regulator. Resting on his knees, Arnold kept his movements as languid as a jellyfish. After a minute the sharks adjusted to him and resumed their mindless circling. He saw me looking through the window and gave a kid's wave, all fingers. The movement attracted a small shark who got the courage to move in on Arnold, but he pushed it away with his billy. After a few minutes Arnold began climbing the side of the tank. I went upstairs. Maybe it wouldn't be as bad as I imagined.

Arnold's head broke the surface. I helped him climb out and he gave me a hand pulling on my scuba gear. I hooked a leg over the rim of the tank.

Arnold handed me the shark billy. "Remember," he said. "Don't poke too hard with this or you'll trigger their defensive instincts and you could get bitten."

I nodded, took the billy, then eased into the water, not the least bit confident I would come out again in one piece. I started down the ladder, moving rung by rung as I had seen Arnold do it. As I descended I tried to remember what I had read about sharks.

The first rule for divers in shark-infested waters is never attach a speared kill to your belt. Blood from the fish will attract sharks who have a better sense of smell than a kid in a cookie kitchen. They'll go for the fish and take part of you with it. The sight of a wet suit makes a shark wary, but a hungry fish will attack a diver. I looked down, hoping these guys had eaten their breakfast. Another rule: don't thrash around; sharks are attracted to water vibrations. Above all, don't get scared. A shark might attack if it senses your fear. Most important, once you've committed all this stuff to memory, discard it, because no one can ever predict *what* a shark will do.

The sharks were all around me, but they veered off rather than come near, which was fine. My fins touched the sandy bottom. A few kicks propelled me toward Stonehenge. I pulled myself into the center circle and looked up. Even if you never get closer to a shark than mako steak in a fish restaurant, you have to admire the beauty of the creatures.

With their metallic gunmetal skin they look more like machines than living things.

I shook my head. Something was going on. After Arnold's initial arrival, the sharks had settled down. They were acting differently with me. They seemed hyper, wired, disturbed. Some of the smaller fish darted across the tank in short nervous sprints and swam against traffic, confusing the other fish, bumping into them.

Within seconds a new pattern evolved. The fish circled just above my head, forming a regular merry-go-round, with me in the middle. I pivoted on my knees and waited for a chance to kick my way to the top of the tank, but there was no break in the silver-finned canopy. Besides, I had other things to worry about.

A shark around three feet long broke ranks. It raced in and bumped my shoulder with its snout, then shot off and quickly circled the tank. Sharks will graze a target before taking a bite. This guy was gearing up for an attack.

I tightened my grip on the billy and had it ready when he lunged again. A shark attacking head-on presents an impossible target, but I was lucky. I jabbed with the stick and it caught it behind the gills, deflecting the attack. The shark didn't like being poked and moved off to regain its courage. I tried to keep it in sight, but it was becoming tougher, because every shark in the tank was moving in a deadly carousel. The small shark angled in for another attack. It was a fatal miscalculation.

Whitey hadn't shown the same signs of agitation as the smaller sharks. That lethargy ended when the smaller shark cut in front of Whitey, who reacted like a punchdrunk pug moving on instinct. She clamped her jaws into shark flesh and shook her head violently. The smaller shark came apart in an explosion of blood and guts. Instantly, two other sharks raced in to get the crumbs, setting off a chain reaction.

The shark tank went crazy.

Gray bodies hurled themselves in every direction, jostling, bumping, biting in a mad frenzy. They whirled above me like a flock of frenzied birds. Each slashing attack brought new jets of blood to drive the sharks to even greater levels of fury. This was no place for me, but it was impossible to surface through the cloud of whirling bodies and snapping teeth.

I moved as close as I could to a Stonehenge megalith and hunched over, turtle fashion, my elbows and knees in the sand.

Sharks dipped and wheeled. One bumped into my shoulder and ricocheted off.

Blood pounded in my temples. I wanted to scream.

Something hard slammed into the top of my head.

Whitey. I braced myself. The rubber wet suit would be a frail armor against the shark's razor-sharp teeth. I pulled my elbows and knees close together and curled into a fetal position. I was trying to present as small a target as possible, hoping Whitey would take a bite out of my fin and be happy with it. I closed my eyes and clamped my teeth down on the regulator almost hard enough to chew through the plastic mouthpiece. The metallic clink of the air valve and the rapid exhalation of bubbles were loud in my ears.

Something bumped my head again.

This was it.

13

Nothing happened.

I opened my eyes and glanced up, fearfully expecting to see the razor-sharp teeth in Whitey's half-moon mouth about to clamp onto my head. But I saw only the bottom bars of the shark cage about three feet above me. The door hung open and must have been what bumped me. Uncoiling my legs, I pushed off against the floor of the shark tank and shot through the narrow opening like an arrow. Once inside the cage, I quickly reached down, closed the door and latched it.

The cage began to rise. None too soon. Bodies bounced off the bars like a stampede of drunks making last call at the 'Hole on a Saturday night. My problems weren't over. The cage was made to protect a diver from big sharks, not smaller fish like the yard-long one who was trying desperately to get at me. Caught up in the frenzy, he was squeezing between bars, his eyes wild, his mouth snapping wildly.

Even a minor shark bite has the potential to kill you. The only variable is the degree of shock.

My back was to the bars. The shark was halfway into the cage, going for my midsection. I brought the shark billy up, fast, and rammed it down Junior's throat like a plumber unclogging a toilet. The shark sank his teeth into the wood and jerked his body. He would have wrenched the billy from my hand if the loop hadn't been secured around my wrist.

Okay, hotshot, you want the stick, you can have it.

I shoved the billy so far down his throat the nails on the end must have tickled his tail, and slid the strap off my wrist. Junior backed off and disappeared into the whirling maelstrom, taking the billy with him.

The cage neared the surface.

I looked down in amazement. Every fish in the tank had gone insane. The water was clouded with fish blood and bits of flesh. Another few seconds and the cage was clear, swinging off to the side on its boom. As soon as there was solid floor under me I opened the door, dropped onto the walkway, and ripped my face mask off.

Mike Arnold had the winch control box in his hands. I was shaking, half with terror, half with rage. My legs felt like inner tubes, but I went for him anyhow. I managed a round-house right that would have dislocated his jaw if it had landed solidly. It's never a good idea to lead with your right hand, and even worse form to try to hit someone while you're wearing fins and an air tank with hoses dangling from it. I tripped over my fins and fell forward. The blow glanced off Arnold's cheek. I would have fallen onto my face if Arnold hadn't grabbed my wrist and steadied me.

"Hey!" he shouted. "Take it easy!"

With my left hand I tried to claw out a piece of his throat. It was a clumsy move, and Arnold held that wrist, too. I struggled for a second, but didn't get anywhere. Arnold was one strong dude. I stopped pulling away and stood there glaring at him until my panting slowed and my breathing became more normal.

"You can let me go," I grunted. "I won't take a swing at you."

Arnold had more faith in human nature than I would have in his place. Doubt lingered in his eyes, but he released my wrists.

"Are you okay?" he said.

"Sure. I'm just fine. I've always wanted to go swimming in the middle of a shark feeding frenzy."

I went over to the pool and looked down. Sharks were still swarming. It was hard to see what was happening because the water was so dirty. I couldn't believe I had escaped with my skin in one piece.

I turned to Arnold. "What the hell happened?"

"Jeezus, I don't know. I *swear* it. You saw me go in. There was no problem. I admit I wanted to bust your ass, but I never would have sent you down if I knew they'd go crazy."

He had a point. The sharks hadn't bothered him.

"What did I do that was different from you?"

He shook his head. "Nothing. One second it was okay, the next all hell broke loose. I got the cage down to you as fast as I could." Arnold was stricken. If he were acting, he was doing a good job of it.

He came over and stared down at the bloody bedlam. His eyes widened in astonishment.

"Holy shit," he said. "It's a goddamn crazy house down there. I've never seen anything like this before. Austin will go out of his frigging mind."

I peeled off my wet-suit jacket. "I'd love to stick around while you explain it to him, but I'm going to get some dry underwear and take a few hours off. I think I wrenched my shoulder. Any objection?"

He opened his mouth. Nothing came out.

"Thanks," I said. I got out of my wet-suit bottoms and pulled my shorts and jersey onto my soggy skin. Leaving Arnold to mop up, I went outside and walked over to the main plaza, where I sat on the edge of the fountain. I was still trembling. I put my head between my knees and took several deep breaths. I was sitting this way when Sally Carlin came by.

"Soc, are you all right?" she said.

I sat up and gave my best imitation of a grin.

"Yeah, thanks. I just went for a swim with Whitey and his friends and the party got a little rough."

She looked puzzled. "I don't understand."

Sally was a sweetheart, but I wasn't in the mood to explain. I jerked my thumb back at the aquarium building. "Ask Mike Arnold. He'll tell you all about it."

I got up and started for the locker room. Realizing I was being a rude jerk, I turned and said, "I'll tell you about it later if you're still interested." She nodded, her face wreathed in concern.

The locker room was deserted. I sat on a bench and reviewed the last twenty minutes. Was this another accident like Eddy Byron's? Suppose it *wasn't* an accident? On the other hand, how could it *not* be an accident? The sharks ignored Mike Arnold. I'm down a few seconds and every shark in the tank starts tying a bib around its neck. I couldn't figure it. But one thing was deadly certain, it didn't pay to get careless near some of the full-time inhabitants at Oceanus.

I wanted to talk to Austin about the attack, but that could wait until Mike gave him the bad news about his sharks. I changed into jeans and T-shirt and went out to my truck. My shoulder felt fine. I just needed an excuse to get away and took advantage of Arnold's guilt, real or not, for some time off.

A lone picket was at the gate. It was the goateed man. I stopped the truck and said, "Good morning. Not much business for you today."

I guess staffers from Oceanus usually didn't stop to chat because he smiled and said, "Good morning. A few people still don't know the park is closed, so we want to be here to show the flag and to make our point. We're not angry at the staff. We know you're just doing a job. It's the management and owners we want to reach."

"I'm glad you're not mad at us," I said. "By the way, where's the main office of the Sentinels?"

He laughed. "You're not talking about Greenpeace. SOS has no formal organization. There are no dues, no big fundraising campaigns or mailing lists." He tapped his chest. "We like to think that each one of us in SOS carries his own membership card right here, in his heart."

"No executive director or president?"

"Oh no, the nearest thing to a leader is Walden Schiller. I guess you could call him our spokesman. Are you interested in joining? You'd be doing yourself and the planet a favor." He glanced toward the park entrance. "This is not a healthy place to be, my friend."

I nodded, put the truck into gear, and headed out toward Route 28. It was nice of the picketer to warn me about Oceanus, but he wasn't saying anything I didn't know.

14

The headline on the SOS flier got right to the point.

It said: WE ARE AT WAR.

The copy was equally direct.

In this war, two sides are fighting, the industrial world and the natural world. The stakes are Mother Earth and the Great Sea that nurtures Her. Casualties mount every day. Japanese whale fleets still murder whales. Hundreds of sea lions are netted or shot. Thousands of dolphins die in tuna nets. But nowhere is the combination of the greed and cynicism that allows this needless destruction more readily apparent than in this country's aquariums and marine amusement parks, where intelligent and beautiful creatures will die, far from their families, after leading unhappy and unhealthy lives.

If you agree that no morality in the world can sanction the kidnapping and imprisonment of orcas or dolphins for entertainment and profit, take these three simple steps:

First, do not patronize marine amusement parks that imprison dolphins or whales or buy any products made by their owners, often large corporations. Second, write or call your representative in Congress to support any law which prohibits the capture, transport, and imprisonment of marine mammals. Third, support the Sentinels of the Sea as it fights against the unholy governmental and corporate coalition that sanctions marine murder. You too can join the battle to save the planet.

The flier given me by the woman picketer in the tie-dyed shirt had no address. Nor did it ask for contributions the way most environmental organizations did. I took a bite of toasted tuna on an onion roll with melted Muenster cheese and sliced olives. I was back at the boathouse enjoying the comfort of dry underwear. The flier told me very little beyond what I already knew, which wasn't very much. I picked up the phone and called Shaughnessy to see what he had on SOS.

"That was an easy one," Shaughnessy said, "at least up to a point."

"Up to what point?"

"The Sentinels like ink in the papers and coverage on the boob tube when it comes to their protests and such, but they're a little shy about their personal business. They have no national officers and no official enrollment."

"I'm starting from zero, Ed. All I've got is a blurb from *The New York Times* and a promotional flier. Anything you've dug up is money in my pocket."

"Then here's a few coins for you to jingle. Have you ever heard of Earth First!?"

"Yeah, I saw a piece on '60 Minutes.' They're a radical

environmental group that raises hell with the logging industry. They go around spiking trees and putting sand in bull-
dozer gas tanks."

"That's right. They've been getting the most press of the
environmental groups that got fed up with the process back
in the seventies and eighties."

"What do they have to do with the Sentinels?"

"They have a lot in common. Both groups don't believe in
compromise. They say the politicians have been corrupted by
the big-money interests, so they take direct action, even if it's
against the law. They call it 'monkey-wrenching,' as in
throwing a monkey wrench into the works. Some people call
them ecological terrorists, and I think they promote the image."

"What do the mainstream environmentalist groups like
Greenpeace and the Sierra Club think about monkey-
wrenching?"

"Thumbs down, Soc. They say the stuff the militants do is
counterproductive and turns people off who might ordinarily
back a cause. The mainstream guys really tear their hair out
over SOS. The Sentinels make the other radical groups look
like Cub Scout packs."

"In what way?"

"The goals are pretty much the same, but their methods
are different. The fringe groups say they're not terrorists because they only act against inanimate objects. They don't
hurt people. Earth First! may spike a redwood, something
that could injure a lumberjack who hits the nail with a power
saw, but they do their best to warn them. It's not the
same with the Sentinels. They say flat out some things they
do may hurt somebody, but that's better than hurting the
planet."

"Depends on your point of view, I suppose. Have they
killed anyone?"

"Not yet. They may have promoted this creepy image just to scare people."

"They're doing a good job with me. What have they done to make the headlines?"

"Can't say for sure, Soc. They're out in the open with the tame stuff, like picketing. But they pull a 'who, me?' about the covert action. The Mexican government wants to speak to them about the tuna-fishing boat that went to the bottom shortly after SOS picketed it for catching dolphins in its tuna nets. Iceland would like to ask them questions about a couple of whaleboats that were put out of commission."

"That must do wonders for our international relations."

"Oh, they've been busy in this country, too. Somebody poured powdered abrasive into the canning machinery bearings at a California tuna-packing plant. Thousands of dollars' worth of damage there. It was an inside job."

"Was SOS involved?"

"The Sentinels denied it in public, but their people owned up off the record. Here's a cute one. They picketed an aquarium in Florida because it took lousy care of its animals. The aquarium got nasty, brought in the law to make some arrests. A few weeks later, more than a hundred thousand dollars in tropical fish died mysteriously. Seems someone put copper sulfate in their tanks. Another inside job. They're better at infiltrating their targets than the FBI."

"Sounds like they're prejudiced against fish. What kind of membership do they have?"

"Even SOS can't answer that question. There are no membership lists. Probably a couple of thousand by best estimates."

"Where does Walden Schiller fit into this?"

"Schiller is usually referred to as a spokesman for the SOS, almost the way the Sinn Fein speaks for the Irish Republican Army. Supposedly he's detached himself from administration, but those in the know say he sets the long-range policy goals and reviews all covert operations before they go down. The Sentinels have no national officers because the FBI would jump on the leaders if they could prove SOS has been naughty."

"Mr. Schiller's mother didn't raise a dummy for a son. What's his background?"

"He's forty-one years old, comes from Massachusetts. Old Yankee family. He broke out of the mold, though, skipped Yale to go to California for his education as a marine biologist. He became radicalized out there and joined another environmental group on the Coast. He left them in 1988."

"Why did he leave?"

"He claimed they were going mainstream, so he founded SOS. He's divorced, one kid. His wife was a Massachusetts woman, and when she moved back home, he decided to spend some time here so he could visit his son and bring his gospel to us unenlightened easterners. He left the West Coast operation in the hands of a lieutenant. He shows up all over the place. He's picketed as far south as Sea World in Florida, outside the Boston Aquarium, and down in Mystic. His most passionate target these days is Oceanus."

"Where does he have his headquarters?"

"SOS has a main office in California, and Schiller goes back there a few times a year. He operates out of his apartment in Cambridge. No salary. SOS is a shoestring operation. Apparently it survives on contributions and speaking fees. You'll like this, though. He stays down your way during the summer. Wellfleet."

I told Ed to hold and reached for the Cape Cod telephone book. Only one Schiller was listed in Wellfleet. It was a woman's name, Ursula Schiller.

"I've got a possibility," I said. "I'll go see if it's my man."

"Good luck, but for Chrissakes, be careful. Sounds like Schiller's elevator doesn't go to the top floor."

"Thanks, Ed, I'll keep your advice in mind. One more question. Do you think the Sentinels are capable of making a bomb?"

"Let me put it this way, Soc. If I got the Sentinels pissed off at me, I'd start checking under my car before I turned the ignition key."

Shaughnessy's blunt appraisal was still on my mind as I turned off Route 6 into Wellfleet, a twenty-minute drive from my boathouse. Wellfleet is a picture-postcard town sandwiched between the Atlantic Ocean and Cape Cod Bay. Its big harbor shelters a busy fishing fleet, and seafood gourmets still consider the Wellfleet oyster the best in the world. The coffee shop on Main Street is called the Lighthouse and the bell in the robin's-egg-blue steeple of the Congregational church rings ship's time. But today the town has more writers and artists than fishermen.

I drove through the village and turned onto Chequesset Neck Road, a narrow macadam strip that runs along the buff-colored cliffs overlooking the harbor. The Schiller mailbox marked the entrance to a crumbling blacktop driveway that wound up a hill through scrub pine and locust trees. The drive ended after a quarter mile at a slate-colored Victorian house with a mansard-roof turret. It looked like one of the houses Charles Addams used to draw in the *New Yorker*.

An old Chevy van was parked in the drive. I pulled up next to it and walked around to the side of the house. A man stood on a ladder slapping dark blue paint on the first-floor window trim. He was getting more paint on his full ginger-colored beard and his clothes than on the trim, but his sloppy brush technique didn't surprise me. Cape Cod is full of homegrown painters, carpenters, and builders who learned their trade out of a book.

I cleared my throat. "Excuse me. I'm looking for Ursula Schiller."

The man wiped a glob of paint off his nose and looked at me curiously. "Ursula isn't around. In fact, she rarely uses the place."

"How about Walden Schiller? Is he ever around?"

"Sometimes. Who wants to see him?"

"My name is Socarides."

He daubed the trim with a wet brushful. "Got a message for him?"

"Yes, please tell him I want to talk to him."

I handed up my business card. The painter studied it thoughtfully and climbed down the wobbly ladder.

"I'm Walden Schiller," he said.

Reality didn't jibe with my mind image. I had pictured Schiller as a lean and ascetic glassy-eyed fanatic. This guy looked more like a young Santa Claus. His eyes were Kris Kringle blue and they twinkled with good humor behind square steel-rim glasses. He was about five-foot-eight, slightly overweight, with the wide shoulders of somebody who chopped a lot of wood. His torn jeans and green-and-white Boston Celtics cap were splattered with dark paint stains.

He removed the cap to wipe the sweat off his forehead and got a new paint smear on his receding hairline. His hair was pulled back in a short ponytail tied with a rubber band.

"Sorry not to be more friendly. I've been trying to touch up that trim for days. It really takes a beating from the sun and salt air. Every time I get up on the ladder, somebody or something gets me down. You got my interest with your card, I must say. Why does a private detective want to see me?"

"I want to talk to you about Oceanus."

He gave me an engaging grin. "Now you've *really* got my attention." He rinsed his brush in a pailful of turpentine and covered the paint can. "Let's go out back."

We walked behind the house and sat in a couple of wood-slatted Adirondack lawn chairs. I looked at the two-story turret. "Interesting place you've got here."

"Thanks, but it's not mine. It belongs to my aunt Ursula. I pay rent just like anybody else, although I get a discount for doing work around the house. The Schillers are an old Yankee family that has never been known for largess, even, or should I say *especially*, to other Schillers, whom they regard as bloodsucking leeches. So tell me, what's happening with my favorite whale jail?"

"The owners hired me to prepare a complete report on the Eddy Byron affair." I didn't tell him I was working undercover at Oceanus, and there was no reason for him to find out unless he showed up on the picket line. From Shaughnessy's description of Schiller as a behind-the-scenes guy, that didn't seem a possibility. My candor was also partially pragmatic. Schiller didn't impress me as somebody I could blindside.

"That still doesn't explain why you came to see me." There was no hostility in his voice, and his mouth was set in a bemused smile, but his eyes were steady and inquisitive.

"Eddy died, and that might have been the end of it," I said, "but SOS made sure it wasn't. You called for a boycott after Eddy's death. You still have pickets out there. You wanted the park closed, and it was. A bomb threat shut it down. I wondered if you had something to say. And besides, it was a nice day for a drive to Wellfleet."

Schiller picked some paint out of his beard. "Mr. Socarides, do you know anything about the Sentinels?"

"You can call me Soc. In answer to your question, I know you're not the national Audubon Society."

He laughed. "I sincerely hope not. We're more of a grassroots organization. No mailing list, no salaries, no big administrative budget. The mainstream groups think we're a bunch of environmental rednecks who go around raising hell. It's an image we don't discourage, although it's more complicated than that. We think Mother Earth is in big environmental trouble, and since the planet is mostly ocean, we've chosen to make our stand with our feet in the sea."

"Why did the son of an old Yankee family decide to get his toes wet?"

"Precisely *because* of that family, Soc. The Schillers hail from Fairhaven originally, right next to New Bedford. My ancestors made a fortune financing the ships that murdered whales for lamp oil and corset stays."

"Hard to believe that you're carrying the cross for something your ancestors did a hundred years ago."

"You're right. I could have been like all the other Yankees who shrugged off the fact their families made their fortunes from whaling or slavery or child labor in the textile mills."

"Why didn't you?"

"My grandfather's fault. He was a rara avis, a Schiller with a conscience. His father was the cold-blooded old bandit who made big bucks slaughtering whales. But Grandpa was an environmentalist before there was such a thing. Butterfly collector, bird-watcher. He even persuaded the family to contribute land for a park. A very little park. He idolized Thoreau. It was his idea to name me Walden after the pond where Thoreau had his cabin. He was a gentle guy, and he did some good, but after I moved to California, I saw that somebody had to take direct action."

"What changed you?"

Schiller's eyes grew icy, and he set his mouth in a tight line.

"You must have read about the dolphins being killed by the tuna industry. Yellowfin tuna will school beneath pods of dolphin. The boats set their nets around the dolphins and herd them in with the tuna. Some dolphins escape, but most die in the tuna nets."

"I've heard most of the tuna companies brag now that their product is dolphin safe."

"That's a major development. For years there was lots of talk and no action. The Marine Mammal Protection Law was passed in 1972 to protect the dolphins. When it came up for renewal in 1988, some of us wanted to show it wasn't working, that dolphins were still being slaughtered."

"Did you?"

He nodded. "I got a job as a crewman out on a tuna boat and brought my camera. The boat used helicopters to spot the dolphins. Then they'd be herded toward the mother ship with chase boats or bombs in the water. The mother ship would set the net. They'd catch a thousand dolphins in a set, and almost all of them died. Even when you try to release them, the mortality is high. They get crushed, they drown, their beaks get broken and their flippers get ripped off. The deck would be awash in dolphin blood. The animals would get mangled and torn apart in the machinery. There'd be more blood in the water. Then the sharks would come in." His voice became tight with emotion, dropping almost to a low growl. "Dolphins don't die quietly the way fish do. They squeal and shriek with terror and pain. They flail around trying to get out of the net. It was like a scene from Dante."

"You had a lot of guts to do that. The crew probably would have tossed you overboard if they knew what you were doing."

He shrugged. "They thought I was shooting pictures for my family. The toughest part was keeping my mouth shut, even participating in this slaughter. The pictures went national and the politicians got into the act. Congress didn't have the courage to buck the tuna industry by banning the practice of setting on dolphins. They passed new regulations that limited the killing, but didn't stop it. A lot of the tuna boats are foreign vessels, so they're not directly subject to U.S. regulations. Maybe sixty-to-eighty thousand dolphins are still killed each year. It made me see the futility of going through the process. I decided direct action was the only option."

"What sort of direct action?"

"Here's one example. The tuna boat I shipped out on sank at the dock one day."

"Did the Sentinels have anything to do with that?"

"We like to think it was Divine Providence."

"Was Eddy Byron's death Divine Providence, too?"

"In a way," he said, wrinkling his brow. "We think Oceanus bears the responsibility for the trainer's death. They confined the whale to that tank. A killer whale normally cruises fifty to one hundred miles in a day. No pool in existence can duplicate the animal's environment in the sea. It's bad enough keeping a dolphin captive, but it's even tougher for an orca because of its size. Both animals are sonic creatures; they use sound to locate themselves and the food they eat. The echoes must bounce off the tank walls and drive them crazy. It would be like a human living in a room with mirrored walls. We humans take them away from their family members, put them in this crummy tank, then add stress by making them perform those dumb tricks. They can get ulcers, just like humans."

"What's that got to do with Eddy Byron?"

"I doubt the whale killed Byron on purpose. I think he was like a convict who's had a rough day and takes a swing at the first prison guard who makes him blow his stack. The whale might have been in a bad mood. Maybe it didn't mean to kill the trainer, but it's a powerful animal. We're saying that this was an unnatural act for an orca, and it proves what a lot of people have been saying right along. Whales and dolphins do not like captivity. No orca has ever killed a human in the wild. But there isn't a pool in the world large enough to house an orca without risking aggressive behavior."

"What do you hope to accomplish at Oceanus?"

"Oceanus was planning to expand. That means it will need more dolphins and whales."

"Where does it plan to get them?"

"I'll tell you where, it plans to get them at sea, somehow, to yank them away from their pods, and we're not going to let that happen. We've got a toehold there. We're delaying that expansion. We're going to keep that park closed and use the trainer incident as a springboard to shut down whale jails across the country. We won't rest until every marine mammal held prisoner goes free."

"That's a tall order for a small organization like SOS."

"We know our impact is limited, but we think we've got a chance."

"What do the mainstream environmental groups think of this?"

He leaned forward in his chair and curled his lip in contempt. "Look, Soc, Greenpeace has a budget of ten million, but only a fraction of that goes into direct action. They'll harass a Russian or Japanese whaler for the TV cameras, but they're more interested in selling bumper stickers and T-shirts. You don't see them out there picketing unless there's a network cameraman around. The mainstream environmental groups liked us at first. They said we inspired them. That we brought passion to the cause that they couldn't match. Now they think we're a bunch of crazies, ecoterrorists. But they know we can galvanize public opinion and force the issue politically by raising hell."

"What about those who say places like Oceanus are educational?"

"Let me tell you how educational they are," he said, his eyes narrowing. "The marine amusement parks are a twenty-five-billion-dollar business in this country. Kids could be educated just as well looking at mock-ups. They don't have to watch a trainer ride on a killer whale's back or see a dolphin play toss ball."

"What will you do if Oceanus decides to reopen?"

"They would be very unwise to do that."

"Why, will they get another bomb threat?"

"Making a bomb threat would be against the law, Soc."

"Sinking a tuna boat is against the law, too."

Walden Schiller spread his hands apart. "It's against the laws of man, my friend. The rules we impose on ourselves can change from day to day or they can be repealed, depending on who has power at a given time. The laws of nature are absolutes. And we think it is absolutely morally wrong to keep dolphins and killer whales in captivity. These are intelligent creatures. They can manage their own lives, and if they had the choice, they would greatly prefer the open seas to a concrete or metal tank and a life of being a circus clown. So if a tuna boat is killing dolphins, or if an aquarium keeps animals in captivity, they are breaking laws of nature, and that should be remedied, even if doing so breaks the artificial laws of man."

"Hypothetically speaking, if the choice came between a dolphin or orca or a human, would you choose the animal?"

"I regard these creatures as remarkable, maybe superior beings, who deserve to be free. And I will do anything I have the power to do to make that freedom come to pass. *Anything.*"

"Even if it hurts innocent people?"

"Our philosophy is called Deep Ecology. In other words, we think a mouse has the same rights as a man, equal title to the earth. That the human species may be a cancer on the planet. So when you measure a human being against the fate of the world, he comes out a second best. We don't want to injure anyone, we just say leave things alone and you won't have to worry about being harmed."

Neither one of us spoke for a minute. The air was charged. Schiller had revealed more of himself than he intended. He squinted at the house. The grin came back on his face.

"Damn, I've run off at the mouth. I'd love to talk all day, Soc, but I've got to get back to my painting before I succumb to inertia."

I got out of the chair. "That's all right, I appreciate your time."

"No problem. Maybe after you get through working for Oceanus, you'll be primed to join the Sentinels. No dues. No monthly meetings. You just have to have a general anarchist inclination. I'd guess you've got already got an antiauthority streak or you wouldn't be working outside the system as a private investigator. Give us a try."

"I'll think about it."

Schiller nodded and got up to walk me to my truck. We were shaking hands when a battered blue Jeep bumped into the drive and two people got out. They looked as if they'd been at a 1960s peace rally. The blond guy had a shoulder-length hair and a beard like shredded wheat. He was dressed in army camouflage and wore airman's sunglasses. His companion was a thin woman in faded jeans with heavy-lidded eyes and long face set in a sullen expression. Her raven hair was parted in the middle and worn straight down. I bet myself she smelled of patchouli. The man glanced right by me as if I weren't there, but the woman stared like someone eyeing an insect that should be squashed. Walden went over to greet his friends. He didn't introduce us, so I got in the truck.

As the pickup bumped out the long driveway I reviewed my impressions of Schiller while they were still fresh in my mind. One thing was very clear. Under his elfin exterior there was a steely resolve and sharp intellect. His observation about my attitude problem when it came to authority was pretty accurate, and it told me something else. While I was sizing up him, trying to get a handle on where he was coming from, Schiller was doing the same with me.

15

Dan Austin sprang up from behind his desk. "Migod, man, are you all right? Mike Arnold told me what happened in the shark tank. Christ, that's absolutely incredible."

Seeing Austin was the first thing I did after returning to Oceanus from my talk with Walden Schiller. "I'm fine, but I can't say the same for your fishies," I said, sliding into a chair. "The shark tank looked like a bowl of Manhattan clam chowder. Were there any survivors?"

Austin sat down and rubbed his eyes like a man with a migraine headache. "Damn few," he grunted. "Whitey's got a few scars, but she'll pull through if they don't get infected. Some of the smaller fish are okay. The nurse shark got torn to shreds. She was a big target and couldn't defend herself. We'll have to restock. It's going to take months to round up some new fish and it will cost us money I'd rather not spend. Christ, it couldn't have happened at a worse possible time."

"I'm sorry about that."

"Hell, it's not *your* fault. I'm just glad you didn't end up like the nurse shark." He shook his head. "God knows what set them off. Do you have *any* idea what happened?"

"Sure. Mike went down and the sharks ignored him. I was underwater ten seconds and every shark in the tank started acting as if it were dinnertime and I was the early-bird special."

"Dammit." He slammed his hand down on his desk. "What the hell is going on around here? First Eddy is attacked, then you."

"Maybe the whales and fish have had it with us, like the birds in Hitchcock's movie."

Austin scotched that theory with a doubtful frown.

"I don't believe it either," I said. "Speaking of Eddy, I'd like to see the wet suit he was wearing when his body was found."

Austin went over to a closet and unlocked the door with a key from his pocket. He pulled a wet suit off a wooden hanger, brought it over, and spread it across his desk. It was like the one I wore in the shark tank, orange red with black three-inch stripes running vertically along the arms, sides, and legs.

"The police had this for a while, but they didn't know what to do with it. I persuaded them to give it back to me so the media wouldn't get hold of it and do another hatchet job." He laughed. "Frankly, I don't know what to do with it either. Here's what you're looking for."

Austin pointed to the black neoprene just above the elbow. I pushed my hand into the sleeve and stuck a finger through one of three rents in the quarter-inch rubber fabric. The cuts were around two inches long, separated by about an inch of space.

"These holes look as if they were made by a pair of shears," I said.

"That clean slash is characteristic of a killer-whale bite," Austin said. "A shark bites into its victim and jerks its body and head back and forth. The sharp edge of its teeth rips out a piece of flesh and leaves a ragged hole. The whale's teeth point backward and inward. They close in an interlocking grip that would leave gashes like an ax."

"You told me before that Eddy had no wounds on his arm."

"Right. He did have some scratches and welts whose location corresponded to these holes, but the skin wasn't broken."

I pulled my hand out of the sleeve. "Something isn't right. Rocky could have ripped Eddy's arm off in a second, yet he didn't." I opened my mouth and tapped my front teeth together, top and bottom, then bit the loose skin on the back of my hand hard enough to leave tooth marks. "He grabbed Eddy like this, very deliberately, like a puppy holding on to your pants cuff. His teeth went through the rubber, but Rocky was careful not to chomp down on Eddy's arm, although he couldn't help leaving a few scratches on the skin."

"Maybe he just missed."

"I can't buy that. You said it yourself. Orcas can jump out of the water and take a fish from a kid's hand without even grazing the fingertips."

"What you're saying is perfectly true. But Rocky could have become angry, grabbed Eddy, and pinned him to the bottom of the tank. That occurred before with Eddy. This time he wasn't as lucky."

"It doesn't sound like luck. Rocky gets mad and reacts; any wild animal would do that. But between the top and the bottom of the tank the whale made a conscious decision *not* to rip Eddy apart. He thought about what he was doing. And cared, too."

"You're forgetting time has no meaning to an animal.

Rocky couldn't have known Eddy was drowning. Animals don't know their own power."

"You've been in this business longer than I have, Mr. Austin, but I respectfully disagree. I think these animals *do* know their own power or Eddy's death wouldn't be such a big deal."

Austin stared out the window. "You may be right. I wish I knew." He glanced at his watch. "Unlike killer whales, though, humans do have a sense of time. I'll be late for an appointment if I don't get moving. Tell me, what are your plans?"

"I'd better get back to work so my fellow staffers won't think I've got an in with the boss."

"Fine. Sally is out by the dolphin pool. Why don't you give her a hand? If Mike Arnold asks, say I thought you needed a break from diving after your close call in the shark tank."

"I appreciate that," I said, getting up. "By the way, Mike sent me down in the tank in anticipation of the park reopening soon. Is that a possibility?"

"Yes, it is. I'd like to start getting the park ready next week and to actually reopen by August."

"What about the possibility that the park may have new Japanese owners? They might have something to say about the opening."

"Personally, I think the Japanese will pull out of the deal. They won't buy Oceanus as long as there is controversy, and I don't see that ending. The smart thing would be to use that controversy to make a few dollars. I don't know for sure if Rocky killed Eddy Byron, but I do know he's made headlines around the world. That translates into big box-office receipts. And every time one of our friends in SOS screams about this place being a whale jail, it will give Oceanus even more publicity. I think I can persuade Bay State to see my point. They are, after all, interested in the bottom line."

"What about the bomb threats?"

He frowned, probably remembering the phony bomb somebody laid at his office door. "I could do without those. But if Oceanus doesn't open, it will go under financially. I think I'll take the bombs over the banks. Besides," he added with a skeptical grin, "you will have wrapped up your investigation by then and the whole mess will be settled."

"In that case we'll both need some luck."

Sally Carlin stood by the dolphin pool watching Huff and Puff, who were taking turns jumping out of the water to touch their noses to a black-and-white rubber ball suspended about ten feet above them. After each contact the dolphins swam to Sally, who rewarded them with a piece of fish. Sally saw me and blew a short blast on her whistle. It must have been a signal to take five because the dolphins stopped leaping and circled the pool, noisily blowing steamy exhalations from their blowholes.

Sally came over, threw her arms around my shoulders, and gave me a friendly squeeze. Her hands smelled from handling fish, but I don't think I would have minded if she used codfish oil for cologne.

She let go after a second, but clasped my hand in hers and held it tightly. There was an expression of concern in her eyes. "I was afraid you had quit. It's a miracle you weren't hurt in the shark tank."

"I'd swim with Whitey any day if I were sure I'd be greeted like this."

Sally squeezed my hand self-consciously and let go.

"I get carried away at times. Blame it on my mother. She's Italian. I got the color of my eyes and my emotional temperament from her. Are you okay?"

"I'm fine. I'm still trying to figure out what happened."

"I just don't understand," she said, cocking her head. "I've seen Mike dive in the shark tank dozens of times without a problem."

"I've heard sharks can sense when a person is nervous and will attack."

"Do you really believe that's what happened?"

A picture flashed through my mind. Long gray bodies streaking through the water. "No," I said. "I wasn't in the tank long enough for the sharks to get a fix on my frame of mind."

"Even so, Mike shouldn't have sent you down on your second day." Her eyes flashed with anger. "He's been an absolute jerk about you. I told him to grow up."

"I'm not sure if I want him any bigger. He may have done me a favor, though. Dan Austin felt sorry for me and suggested I work with you. So I'm at your service."

"I'm delighted. I've just been doing routine tricks with the girls. They get bored if they're not challenged."

She knelt and slapped the water. At the signal the dolphins swam over and stuck their heads out. Sally stood and swung her arm like Clemens winding up on the mound at Fenway Park. The dolphins came all the way out of the water, beating their tails furiously. Defying gravity, they walked backward side by side across the surface. Reaching the far side of the pool, they dove under and darted toward us, two rippling shadows. Sally was ready when they popped up at her feet. She reached into her bucket and tossed a chunk of fish into each open mouth. Huff and Puff chattered their appreciation.

Sally pointed and made a wide circular motion with her arm. The dolphins dove and came up in the middle of the pool in a graceful rainbow leap. Seconds later they were back for more fish.

"I get it," I said. "They do the trick and you reward them. It's something like training a dog."

"A dolphin is a lot more intelligent than a dog, but you are right, the basic principle is the same. A hungry dolphin is trainable; a full dolphin isn't. You have to keep them hungry when you work with them."

"Isn't that a little rough on the dolphins?"

"We keep them *hungry*, not famished. But it goes beyond trick equals reward." She bent over and rubbed the dolphins' heads. "They are very tactile creatures and like to be stroked, so it's important to praise them when they perform. A dolphin may do a trick just for a pat on the head, but you can't depend on it and the customers who normally fill these seats pay to see a show."

"Are you the only one they'll work with?"

She shook her head. "Normally, we'd have assistant trainers running the performances. Most of them are young people who look good in a wet suit. So while it is important to build up a good relationship with an animal, we don't want them to work for just one trainer. Let me show you."

Sally repeated the jump command. The dolphins leaped out of the water again and came back like a couple of kids trick-or-treating on Halloween. She handed the bucket to me. "Here, you feed them this time."

I popped a piece of fish into their mouths and they chattered their thank-yous. Sally picked up two soccer-size rubber balls and told me to throw them into the center of the pool.

"Now, stick your arm out straight as if you were telling somebody to go *that*away."

I did as I was told. Huff and Puff dashed toward the balls. After a second of confusion, while they figured out who was going to grab what, each grasped a ball in his flippers, zoomed back, and jumped from the water in front of us. Sally reached out to take one ball and I got the other. I handed out chunks of fish again.

Sally bent and rubbed the dolphins' heads.

"They're a lot like a child in some ways," she said. "They like to play. They love treats. Most of the time they're happy, but occasionally they're cranky. And sometimes they get into mischief."

"You mentioned reward. What about punishment?"

"I don't know what you mean."

"You talked about rewarding good behavior. Do you ever punish them for bad behavior? Like a child?"

"Oh, I see. Oh no, if the animal doesn't want to work, we don't push it."

"Does he still get fed?"

"Maybe not right away. But if you want to train a dolphin, hunger is the only pressure that works. There's another way I can get a message across. If I want to let them know I'm not pleased with their behavior, I just leave the side of the pool. Dolphins are social animals. In the wild, they would be swimming with their pod. They crave companionship and touch and don't like to be left alone."

"Some people might say keeping a dolphin hungry or in solitary confinement are forms of punishment."

"Some people do. I agree there's a thin line, but no park would allow a trainer to harm a dolphin. Not because of any moral reasons, I'm sorry to say, but because marine mammals are just too expensive and difficult to acquire under the current laws. A good trainer senses the animal's mood. You've got to get inside the animal's skin. If it's having an off day, there's not much you can do about it."

"Those are the good trainers. What do the bad ones do?"

"The majority of trainers I've known love the animals they work with. Perhaps too much, because it's easy to get attached to them."

"What about the minority of trainers?"

"I don't even like to think about that. I've heard of cases where trainers have beaten the animals or even worse. That sort of cruelty sickens me."

"What sort of a trainer was Eddy Byron?"

She hesitated. Not a long pause, but long enough to tell me she was thinking about my question. I'd stopped playing Micky the Dunce and she sensed the change.

"I think he knew what he was doing. You know something, you ask an awful lot of questions."

I'd been moving too fast. Irritation showed in her eyes. I did some backpedaling.

"I'm sorry. It's self-interest. Some of the critters around here bite."

She relaxed. "I don't bite."

"I'm glad to hear that, Sally. This may sound stupid, but I was wondering. Does a dolphin ever get angry the way a person gets mad?"

"Normally they aren't aggressive, but they can show fits of temper. Say another dolphin tries to take its food. Or a dominant male might nip or whack a young male who tries to mate with a female in the pod."

"No, I mean, do they ever get angry with divers? Self-interest again."

"Oh sure. People have this vision of dolphins always being happy. It's their smile, I guess. But they have moods just like people do. If you were in the water and didn't feed them after they did a trick, they might swat you with their tail. Dolphins have snapped at trainers to show their displeasure. They'll push you around. Or an animal will simply get burned out. Too much pressure on it to do tricks that don't come naturally. Even a dolphin can become dangerous to work with. They could knock you unconscious with their tail if they wanted to."

There it was again. *If they wanted to.* Dolphins were animals

who could make a choice. They weren't just all nerve endings, teeth, and bottomless appetites like sharks. And Rocky
was the biggest member of the dolphin family. Rocky could
tell you he was annoyed by pushing you around. *If he wanted
to.* Or he could just as easily kill you. Again, *if he wanted to.*

I wanted to ask Sally more questions, but decided to post-
pone it. Mike Arnold was striding toward us.

He came over and stuck his face in mine. "Are you
through here?" he said. I guess he wasn't feeling sorry about
the shark tank anymore.

"Dan Austin told me to give Sally a hand."

"I know that. I've talked to him. I just want to know if
you're through."

Arnold had toned down his Simon Legree act, but he still
managed to look as if he wanted to horsewhip somebody.
Sally caught the hostile vibrations. "Thanks for your help,
Soc. I'm about done."

"Good," Arnold said to me. "Jill needs a hand in the fish
house."

He spun on his heel and marched off toward the administration building. The tension evaporated. Sally and I looked
at each other. We both shrugged at the same time and
laughed.

I made believe I was wiping sweat off my forehead. "Mike
seems more angry about me than he should be. Is there
something here that I'm missing?"

Sally frowned. "Mike doesn't like to see me talking to any
male under the age of a hundred. He thinks that because we
dated and because he hired me that he has a proprietary interest in me."

"Is he wrong?"

She leveled her eyes at me so there would be no mistake.
"Yes. He is. Very much so."

It wasn't exactly an invitation, but I've never been subtle.

"In that case, would you like to get together some night for food and fascinating conversation?"

"You may be sorry. I inherited my appetite from my mother."

"Your eyes, your temperament, and your appetite. That's three reasons I have for liking your mother. How about tonight?"

"Fine with me. Seven okay?"

"It's a date."

The fish house was behind the dolphin theater. I opened the door and stepped into a ten-by-ten room with Formica counters, a large cutting board, and a couple of sinks. Jill was coming out of a walk-in freezer. She gave me her Miss Sunbeam smile.

"Hi! You arrived just in time. I need a strong back."

She held the steel door open and I went from summer to dead of winter. The freezer was lined with metal shelves stocked with cardboard boxes, most marked either "herring" or "mackerel." Jill put her hand on one box and slid it off the shelf a few inches. I got on the opposite side and together we carried the box out to the other room and set it on a counter. Jill pulled a dozen frozen fish from the carton, grabbed a cleaver from a wall rack, lopped the tails and heads off, and started to chop the fish into bite-size pieces.

"Thanks for the hand," she said. "There's a dolly in there, but I always have a hard time getting the box off the shelf. There's an extra cleaver if you want to help. Watch out for your fingers."

I grabbed a fish and started chopping. The cleavers made a *chuck-chuck* sound as we worked. The mountain of chopped fish grew higher. Jill pulled more herring out of the box and divvied them up.

I said, "Is this for the dolphins?"

Chuck-chuck.

"Yep. For the beluga, too. Isn't Froggy something?"

"Yeah. Friendly guy."

"He's a she. Like the dolphins."

"Is Rocky a she, too?"

"Nope. He's a he."

Chuck-chuck.

The pile was getting bigger. Eyeing it, I said, "How much do those guys eat?"

"Huff and Puff eat about fifteen pounds of fish each a day. The beluga eats the same. We'll chop a few more, then we can set some whole fish aside for Rocky. We won't have to worry about the shark tank. They've already been fed," she said with a sidelong glance. "Mike Arnold wasn't too happy about cleaning up the mess."

"It couldn't have happened to a nicer guy."

She gave me a sly grin. "How do you like your job so far?"

"It's not like anything I've ever done before. How long have you worked for Oceanus?"

"Since March. I was part of the new crew."

"I didn't know there was an old one."

"Oh sure. There used to be a totally different staff here."

"What happened to them?"

"The park was closed a few weeks last winter and everyone was laid off. When they reopened, Mr. Austin hired almost all new people. Something about starting with a clean slate."

"I didn't realize the park was closed."

"Mr. Austin wanted to do some renovations, and Rocky got sick."

"Sick? He looks pretty healthy to me."

"He's fine now, but I guess back then he couldn't do his tricks. Mr. Austin blamed the trainer."

"Eddy Byron."

"Oh no, Mr. Byron came to work here after Mr. Austin fired the old trainer. I don't know the man's name, but Mr. Austin said he was responsible for Rocky getting sick. At least that's what Ben told me. I guess things were pretty crazy for a while."

"So you came in as part of the new staff?"

"Uh-huh. I was friends with a girl who had this job. Sort of a glorified gofer. She expected to come back and was really upset when she heard they weren't hiring old staff. She got a job at a ski mountain and moved to Colorado. I was looking for work. I came in one day and Mr. Byron hired me right on the spot. How'd you know about this place?"

"I heard through the grapevine that they needed somebody, preferably with diving experience. The fishing boat I work on is out of commission and I took this job to pay the rent. You live on the Cape year-round?"

"I do now, but I'm basically a summer kid. My family built a house on the Cape years ago when I was little. I dropped out of college and I'm staying at the family house while I find myself."

"Good luck." There are probably hundreds of college-educated young people like Jill on the Cape who move into the family summer house to find themselves; most never do. "How was Eddy to work for, compared say to Mike Arnold?"

"Oh, he was okay, I guess. He could get down on you, but it wasn't personal the way it is with Mike. And he wasn't so arbitrary. I think Mike's insecure, so he takes it out on people."

"How do they compare as trainers?"

"Mike's competent, but Mr. Byron really knew his stuff. I don't know if he really liked the animals, you know, like Sally. God, I think she'd go out on a date with a dolphin if it asked her."

I stifled a snort. "I heard Eddy had a weakness for the grape."

"Huh? You mean he drank. Oh sure, usually at the end of the day. That's when he got really mean. The staff stayed out of the way. We couldn't figure out why Mr. Austin put up with it, but he's the boss. Well, I guess that's all the fish we need. Thanks for helping."

We scooped the fish into plastic buckets and washed up. She said good-bye and gave me a grin. "You remind me of my brother. He wears an earring, too. My father can't stand it."

I touched the gold ring in my ear. "My father can't stand it either."

Traffic on Route 28 was frozen solid like flies in amber. You can't fight the Cape's summer glut. You just have to expect delay. I was listening to Jimmy Buffet on the tape deck singing about sailing and hopping a plane and flying to Paris. A couple of minutes passed.

A break was coming in the oncoming traffic. I flicked my headlights, leaned on my horn, hooked a hard left on the steering wheel, and shot through the breach to a two-story brick building on the other side of the road. I parked next to a sign that said STATE POLICE and went inside the building. The cop behind the front desk took my name and picked up his phone. A minute later Parmenter came out and shook my hand. He was wearing his state-police uniform, the blue tunic and dark blue riding pants with the knee-high boots.

"Soc, what a hell of a nice surprise. Come on out to my office."

He put his arm around my shoulder and guided me to a cubicle just big enough to hold a Parmenter, a desk, a phone, and a couple of chairs. I sat down in one of them and Parmenter went to get us some coffee. He returned with two paper cups, settled behind his desk, and looked at me. "How come you're not in jail?"

"Beats me. Maybe it's because I haven't done anything wrong."

He grinned. "How are you feeling?"

Parmenter's sharp cop eyes must have noticed my face still looked pale and puffy. I tenderly touched the scalp above my right ear. "I'm a little sore, but my head is still attached to my shoulders, so I can't complain."

"You're damned lucky the town cops didn't drill you full of holes." He raised an eyebrow. "This social or business?"

"A little of both. First the business. Has anything broken on the Hanley case?"

"Lieutenant Pacheco doesn't confide in me, but I've got a couple of friends inside his department who say the investigation is dead in the water. No murder weapon yet. They've had divers in the river. No apparent motive. No enemies anyone knows of. He was probably killed less than an hour before you found him. Shot with a twenty-two which wouldn't have made much noise."

"So where's he go next?"

"Pacheco would love to pin the thing on you, but the DA won't go for it on the basis of the evidence so far. Just don't get too cocky."

"I won't. Would you keep an eye on the case for me, John? I don't want any surprises."

"I'll do my best, Soc."

I stood up to go.

"Thanks, John. That's all for the business part. I just wanted to tell you it was good to see you the other night. And not just because you saved my ass, although I'm grateful for that, too."

"The feeling is mutual, Soc."

We looked into each other's eyes in the way men can do without embarrassment when they've both loved the same woman. We shook hands then I went out to my pickup and rejoined the folks who were spending half their vacation stuck in traffic.

16

The *Millie D* was moored in a jog next to the fish pier. Sam saw me drive up and waved from the deck.

"How's it going?" I said, climbing aboard. Sam opened his mouth and shut it as a pipe-factory clanging came from the engine compartment. A hoarse voice yelled, "Christ in the raging foothills!"

He jerked a thumb toward the bow and shook his head. "*That's* how it's going, Soc."

A large greasy lizard emerged from the engine compartment. The lizard grinned. "Almost got it, Sam. Have to go back to the shop for another tool."

Sam nodded glumly and introduced me to the marine mechanic. His name was Fred and he took our handshake as an invitation to bare his whole life in a stream-of-consciousness narrative. Where he was born, where he'd gone to school, how many times he'd been married (twice), how many kids he had (three), where they lived, and what they did. He rattled on for twenty minutes about everything except the state of the engine repairs. He paused to take a breath and that's when I jumped in. "Fred, how's the work on the engine going?"

"Oh *that*," he said absentmindedly. "Looks like the electrical system."

"When do you think you'll get it fixed?"

"Damn soon." He looked at his watch. "Hell. Didn't know it was so late. Got to be back at the shop for quitting time. Sam, I'll be here first thing in the morning. Bet you'll be able to take her out fishing tomorrow. Nice to meet you, Soc." He climbed off the trawler and walked jauntily to his truck, first stopping to tell his life story to a couple of unlucky fish packers.

Sam watched him go. "I'll be able to retire on all the fish that man has promised I'd catch," he grumbled.

"Is there anything I can do?"

"Yep. Go down to the Catholic church and light a few candles. I'll head over to see Charlie Jones the Methodist minister and promise to sing in the choir if he asks the Lord to fix the engine. That's the only thing that'll help us now."

"Sam, your optimism is too much to bear. I'll talk to you in the morning."

Kojak heard the truck drive in and was waiting for me just inside the front door. I gave him a can of 9-Lives tuna and egg and took the cordless phone out onto the deck.

As I punched the numbers I thought about Sally Carlin and wondered why she hadn't like my questions about Eddy Byron.

Jill's revelations puzzled me, too. Closing the park for renovations made sense, but firing the staff didn't. Rocky looked the picture of health. It was hard to imagine him sick. Do whales come down with the flu? Austin hadn't mentioned the park's closing or Rocky's sickness. But he made it clear from the start he didn't want me at Oceanus, so I couldn't expect him to be forthcoming.

A woman said hello on the phone. I asked for Lew Atwood, who was the trainer Austin fired before hiring Byron. The woman said Atwood would be home later that night. I gave her my name and number and left a message asking him to call when he got in. I hung up and went into the boathouse to change for my date with Sally. I was laying out a clean navy shirt and a pair of pleated tan slacks I'd picked up for free at the Episcopal church clothes swap, when the phone rang.

It was my younger brother, George.

"Soc," he said breathlessly. "Ma asked me to call. Can't talk long. I gotta drive Maria to her girlfriend's house. Have you seen Uncle Constantine?"

"Constantine? Last I knew he was coming up the inland waterway."

"Yeah, I know. He called today from the Cape. Ma wasn't around, and she wants to make sure he's okay. She's still ticked off because I didn't ask where he was. The guy's in his seventies for godsakes and tough as nails, but she's worried he won't get three meals a day. I can't figure it, but you know how she is. Anyhow I gave him your number. He said he was going to celebrate the end of his trip. Has he called you?"

"Not that I know of. I've been home about an hour, but I was gone most of the day."

"Great, damn, just great. Ma's really getting on my case. Okay, Maria, I'm coming! Keep your pants on." George was carrying on a conversation with his wife at the same time.

"George, you've got three cars. How come Maria doesn't drive herself?"

"She says the Caddies are too big and the Cherokee's too stiff to drive. C'mon Maria, you call that vulgar? I'll show you vulgar. Okay, get the kids in the car, I'm coming." Back to me. "Hey Soc, what do I know? I just go along. Married life, it's great. You ought to try it sometime."

"Thanks, George, maybe I'll get lucky someday. What does Ma want me to do?"

"Check around. You know lots of people down there. Maybe they've seen Constantine's boat."

"The Cape is bigger than people think, and there are a hell of a lot of boats here this time of year, but I'll see what I can do. If I get any news on Uncle Constantine, I'll give you a call. You do the same."

"Will do, Soc. All right, okay, Maria. Sorry, got to go. Bye."

I stared at the phone and shook my head. Then I got dressed for my date.

Sally Carlin lived on the second floor of an old carriage house that had white clapboards and black shutters. It was a spacious sunny apartment with a wood stove, wide oak-board floors polished to a high gloss, and a view of the Sandy Neck dunes through the big picture window. Sally was wearing a sleeveless bluish purple summer dress that picked up the color of her eyes. She had let her hair tumble around her shoulders.

Kissing me lightly on the cheek, she took my arm and guided me to a comfortable leather living-room chair. She asked if I liked Campari and soda. I said yes and she went into the kitchen to make us drinks. The living room was done in an eclectic combination of contemporary chrome and glass and old wood. Most of the photographs and prints on the walls had to do with the sea. Dunes, waves, boats. An Edward Hopper reproduction. A Cape Light poster by Joel Meyerwitz. Dolphins and whales under and over the water.

Sally came back carrying two glasses of ruby liquor that tinkled pleasantly. She sat on the hassock in front of my chair.

I tasted the cold bittersweet Campari. "How did you guess I was taking you to an Italian restaurant?"

"Intuition. It comes from working around marine mammals. You have to use a lot of nonverbal communication."

"You find that helps you deal with humans?"

"Why not? We're a lot alike in many ways. We're both intelligent, emotional, childish."

I nodded.

She sipped her Campari, looking at me over the rim of her glass, then set it down on a coffee table. "I have a confession to make. I wasn't exactly candid with you at the park today when you asked me what kind of a trainer Eddy Byron was."

"I didn't mean to put you on the spot. I was just curious."

"Oh, I understand. The question just caught me by surprise." She pondered for a moment. "You have to know there are all kinds of trainers. Most of them empathize with the animals. They know captivity can be a hardship and do their best to ease it. I like to think I'm one of them. Then there are others who think of the animals as performing machines. If they don't work when you push the button, you tighten a nut here or rewire a new circuit there."

She was trying to tell me something. "And Eddy was one of those?"

She smiled sadly.

"How do you rewire a dolphin or an orca?"

"You use operant conditioning. It's a system of behavior manipulation, a combination of punishment and reward, but the punishment can be harsher than just walking away from an animal or denying it food. I'm talking about actual physical abuse."

"Why would anyone do that? I thought dolphins are relatively easy to train because they're smart and friendly."

"That's true, Soc. It's not hard to take something the dolphin does naturally, like making those magnificent leaps out of the water, and connect the reward of fish to it. But the animals will balk at something they wouldn't ordinarily do in the wild."

"What kind of things?"

"Things like putting a bomb on a ship. Things like attacking divers and killing them."

"Wow," I said. "I guess you're not talking about Oceanus."

"No," she said, her voice gaining an edge. "I'm talking about our own fine country's navy. They've been training marine mammals for warfare."

"How successful have they been?"

"Successful enough to pour millions into research. I'm sure the navy has kind trainers who treat the animals well, but I've read about the animals being held in small pens, beaten and kicked, and punished with electrical shock."

"What does that have to do with Eddy Byron?"

"Eddy was part a navy unit that trained marine mammals in Vietnam."

Sally's accusation rubbed off. "Sometimes people use a broad brush on ex-Vietnam types like Eddy and me. Just because some marines killed women and children doesn't mean we all did. Being part of the unit doesn't mean he used the methods you're talking about. Or that he brought his training ideas to Oceanus."

She shook her head at my defense of Eddy. "But he *did*, Soc. He did."

"How do you know?"

"I *saw* him."

There was no mistaking the cold fury in her eyes. "Okay, I believe you. Tell me about it."

She took a deep breath. "It was one night this spring. Eddy sometimes worked with the animals after the staff left. I stayed late in my office to catch up on paperwork. On the way out I went by to check the dolphins. Eddy was there. He didn't see me at first. He was standing by the side of the pool. He was holding a rod in his hand. I went over and asked him what it was. He tried to evade the question, but I kept on. He admitted that it was something like a cattle prod, and he was going to punish the dolphins. He said they had been giving him a hard time, being too aggressive, pushing him around when he was in the pool. I was appalled. I told him I wouldn't allow that kind of treatment. He'd been drinking. We argued. I threatened to report him if I ever saw that thing again."

"Why didn't you report him then?"

"I should have. But I was confused, angry for not being aware of what was going on. The dolphins had been more skittish than usual; I should have sensed something was wrong. But the real reason I didn't report him was that Eddy and I had been involved. Not a long time, a few months maybe. Later, I raged at myself for being so blind. I could have killed him. The next day I told him we were through."

"What was his reaction?"

"Oh, he laughed. He said I had a lot to learn, not just about dolphins, but about men. I guess he was right about that."

"Do you think he would have used the prod on Rocky?"

"Rocky is a different proposition. He's bigger than the dolphins. And orcas are more independent. They may be more intelligent than dolphins. I don't know. It would have been dangerous."

"Maybe that's the reason Eddy's dead. It *was* dangerous. Maybe he tried punishing Rocky and the whale killed him."

"It's occurred to me, but I haven't wanted to believe it."

"Well," I said, "is it possible?"

She got up, walked over to the picture window, and stared out at the bay. After a moment she turned and smiled. "I'm getting hungry. Do you think we could get something to eat?"

I looked at my watch and suggested it was time to dive into a bowl of linguini. We took the pickup to a restaurant in Hyannis that knew how to make pasta *al dente*. Neither one of us went for the linguini. I tried the manicotti and she had saltimbocca—veal with prosciutto and Marsala wine. We washed dinner down with a bottle of Chianti Classico and lingered over cups of cappuccino, talking about food the way people do when they're eating.

The evening went fast and around ten o'clock we found ourselves sitting in the pickup outside the carriage house, dealing with the awkward moment that comes at the end of a first date, when an invitation into a lady's house can be a prelude to romance. She was probably tallying up the evidence of the evening, trying to decide if she should ask me in. She solved the social exercise with an adroit maneuver that deflected my attention without discouraging it all together.

"I had a great time tonight," she said. "I'd love to ask you in for a drink, but I have to get up early tomorrow. Would you like to come over later this week for dinner? How about the day after tomorrow?"

"I'll be there. Unless Mike Arnold puts me back in the shark tank."

She got serious. "I'm still wondering about that."

I shrugged. "Maybe they didn't like my new after-shave lotion."

It was a lame joke, but Sally was polite enough to laugh. We kissed each other good night, on the lips this time, warmly, and I drove off intending to head straight home. But something made me change my mind. I had been chewing over my parting comment about the after-shave lotion. The weak attempt at wit may have contained a germ of wisdom. Maybe I had it all wrong. Maybe the sharks *did* like my smell. It was a crazy idea, but this whole case was crazy. At the end of Sally's driveway I pointed the pickup toward the other side of the Cape. Toward Oceanus.

· · ·

The four flat-roofed buildings that made up the park complex loomed darkly like a cyclopean fortress against the charcoal backdrop of the star-speckled night sky. I drove across the deserted parking lot and left the truck in the shadows near the administration building, not far from the employees' entrance. As I made my way to the door with flashlight in hand, the breeze picked up, bearing with it the rank exhalations of the salt creek and marsh. The summer chorus of night insects drowned out my softened footfall.

I slipped inside and shut the door quietly behind me. I didn't need my flash. Lights had been left on at strategic locations so Ben wouldn't fall into a pool by accident as he made his rounds, but the park lay mostly in darkness. I followed a passageway to Ben's office and listened. Tinny voices and canned laughter filtered through the door. There was another sound, like a distant buzz saw. I turned the doorknob, pushed the door open, and stuck my head into the office.

A smooth-faced man on the TV was selling a formula for hair remover to a studio audience. Ben lay stomach up on the cot, snoring. Spittle from his mouth dripped down his chin. On the floor next to the cot was a glass half-filled with amber liquid. Poor Ben had passed out before he finished his drink. I stepped inside, careful not to wake him. The Mormon Tabernacle Choir could have sung "Glory, Glory Hallelujah" in Ben's ear and he wouldn't have heard it. You can never tell what a drunk will do, so I was as quiet as possible as I reached across his supine body to the pegboard and carefully lifted off a couple of labeled key sets. I stepped out, closed the door softly, and walked to the storeroom.

Hanging from hooks along one wall of the windowless space were a dozen red-and-black wet suits. The first one I picked out was small, made for a woman. I looked at the others and found three that would fit me. I wasn't certain which suit I wore in the shark tank, so I set them all aside. One by one, I examined, then smelled them. All I got were rubbery lungfuls of neoprene.

I set the last of the suits aside and looked around the room. Some dive gear was stacked in a corner. Air tanks, fins and masks, belts, and a couple of buoyancy compensators. Called a BC for short, the buoyancy compensator is an inflatable vest with straps to hold the air tank.

I picked up a BC and examined it minutely, giving it the same sniff test I used on the wet suits, but found nothing unusual. I looked in all the pockets. Nothing. I put the vest aside and followed the same routine with the other compensator. Again, nothing.

Waitaminute.

I tried again. There was a faint fishy smell. That should not be unusual. After all, this *is* an aquarium. I stuck my nose into each pocket. Yes. The fish odor was stronger. I held the BC under the light and spread the pocket open. Caught in the crease at the bottom of the pocket was a whitish powder. I tore off part of an equipment checkout schedule on a clipboard, and used my Swiss army knife to scrape the white powder into the paper, which I folded and tucked in my shirt pocket. After one last look around, I switched off the light and left the storeroom.

I walked across to the other side of the park, avoiding the plaza, following the shadows around the open space until I came to the orca stadium. I didn't know what I was doing there, or what I hoped to find. I was just drawn to the place. I pulled out the other key ring from Ben's office and went to unlock the gate.

It swung open at my touch.

Moving cautiously, I went through the gate and followed a

passageway to the bleacher section. At the top of the bleachers I looked down. The auditorium was in darkness. Wishing
I had Rocky's skill at echolocation, I crept down an aisle to
the splash area between the lowest bleacher row and the
plastic wall of the pool. I paused to listen. There wasn't a
sound. Not even Rocky was stirring. I took a few steps and
stopped, sweeping my eyes around the stadium. Blinked and
looked again.

An aisle went along the outside of the bleachers from the
lowest row to the top of the stadium. Bordering the aisle
was a low wall. Visible beyond the wall was the gray,
star-speckled sky. And cast in relief against the stars was the
figure of a man. He stood there like a statue carved from
basalt.

Keeping my left hand on the curved pool wall as a guide, I
soft-shoed along the splash area until I came to the outside
aisle and started to climb the steps. I planned to move closer
and turn on the flashlight.

I glanced down for a second to be sure of my footing.
When I looked again, the man was gone.

Flicking on the flashlight, I pointed it up the aisle. Nothing. I moved the beam higher. A big man, dressed in ninja
black, was moving fast toward the top of the stadium.

I sprinted up the aisle, trying to keep him in the bobbing
bull's-eye of light. A quick movement, half shadow, half human, and he disappeared around a corner. I was at the top of
the aisle, pounding down the passageway toward the gate. As
I rounded the back side of the bleachers there was a metallic
clang. I ran up to the gate. Smart guy. Cool, too. He had
locked the gate behind him. I dug the key from my pocket,
slid the bolt, and dashed out into the central plaza. But the
moment's delay gave my quarry the time he needed. He had
vanished.

I slammed my fist into my palm, then went back into the

stadium, where I stood in the aisle looking down at the darkened stadium and pool.

Why anyone would sneak in to see Rocky?

From the pool came a splash and a *weeooof!*

The sound echoed throughout the quiet amphitheater. I
pictured eight tons of black-and-white predator moving
through the inky water, and a chill passed along my spine. It
was a nonintellectual, primordial reaction passed down by
primitive ancestors who knew that when the sun went down,
sharp-toothed creatures ruled the night. But the fear was
real, nevertheless.

Ben was still zonked out, snarking and
snorting in his alcoholic sleep. I hooked the keys onto the
pegboard. Minutes later I was on my way home.

Back in the mildewed luxury of the boathouse, I slipped off
my dating clothes and pulled on a pair of shorts and a T-shirt
and fed Kojak. Then I sank into an overstuffed chair and
thought about the powder in the BC pocket. I was too wired
to sleep and needed some mental chewing gum, so I flicked
on the TV and was mindlessly watching a Three Stooges
flick when the telephone rang. I glanced at the wall clock. It
was after 1:00 A.M. Who the hell would be calling me at this
hour? I picked the phone up and said hello.

"Mr. Socarides?" I didn't recognize the voice.

"Speaking."

"This is Sergeant Winslow at the Barnstable police station
in Hyannis. There's a gentleman here who says he's related
to you. He'll only say his name is Constantine. Do you know
him?"

"Constantine? Of course I do! That's my uncle. Is he
okay?"

The cop laughed sardonically. "Hell, yes, he's fine. But
he's been involved in a little trouble."

"What sort of trouble?"

"It's too complicated to explain over the phone. Could you drop by so we can get this thing straightened out?"

I threw on a sweatshirt and flip-flops as I talked. "I'm on my way," I said.

17

Less than thirty minutes later I walked into the two-story brick police station on the outskirts of Hyannis and gave the dispatcher my name. She mumbled into an intercom and a tall red-haired cop came out to meet me.

"I'm Sergeant Winslow," he said gravely. He shook my hand and crooked his finger for me to follow. We went down a hallway and into a small room with a couple of plastic chairs and a table in it. He motioned for me to take a seat and sat in the other one, then folded his arms across his chest and screwed up his mouth in puckish thought.

"How old is your uncle, anyway?" he said after a moment.

"I'm not sure, Sergeant. He lives in Florida. I haven't seen him in years. Early seventies, maybe."

Winslow shook his head as if I'd just told him fish fly and birds swim.

"Unbelievable. I hope I have as much energy when *I'm* seventy. No, scrub that. When I'm *sixty*. Well, we've got your seventy-year-old uncle in protective custody. He had a little too much to drink."

I winced. I never saw Uncle Constantine drunk, but I used to hear the family tut-tut talk. I tried to put the best face on it.

"His wife died not too long ago, Sergeant. He's been pretty broken up about her death. Maybe he was feeling bad and had a few pops."

"No, I don't think he was feeling bad." Sergeant Winslow chuckled. "From what I understand he was feeling pretty good, but he'd better get remarried if he wants to live to be eighty."

Winslow was being too damned elliptical. It was starting to annoy me.

"I don't get you, Sergeant."

"We got a call earlier tonight from a watering hole down near the harbor. The bartender was screaming at the dispatcher. Said some customers were tearing the joint apart. We get called there a couple of times of month in the summer. Mostly college kids who can't hold their liquor. This sounded more serious. The dispatcher could hear crashing and yelling. So we sent over a couple of cruisers in a hurry. The cops come in the front door and there's a brawl in progress. No, let me rephrase that. It was more of a riot. And your uncle was right in the middle of it."

"*My* uncle?"

He nodded.

"Migod, was he hurt?"

The cop did his annoying chuckle again. "Naw. He had a few bumps and scrapes, but the other guys got the worst of it. They ended up at Cape Cod Hospital. Nothing serious. The main damage was to their egos."

"What happened?"

"We're still trying to piece this thing together, but I got

the impression it started with an argument involving some women."

It was my turn to chuckle. "Women? C'mon, Sergeant. That's my seventy-year-old uncle you're talking about."

"Yeah, I know, but the bartender saw the whole thing. A couple of girls were having a drink. These two goons from Billerica came over to their table and gave them a hard time. Your uncle decides to butt in. The guys have one too many, and it's made them mean. So instead of laughing it off and minding their own business like they should have, they decide they're not going to take any grief from this old geezer. They try to shove him around. He took a few knocks, but before they know it, both of them are looking up at the ceiling."

Oh Jeez. My heart sank. My mother practically ordered me to keep an eye on Uncle Constantine. I could see myself saying, Sure, Ma, everything's okay, Uncle Constantine just got himself plastered, brawled with a couple of lardheads over some women in a bar, got busted by the cops and thrown in the slammer. I sat back in my chair and groaned. "What's going to happen?"

"I know what I *hope* is going to happen. You're going to take your uncle home and make sure he behaves himself. We didn't arrest him. We've got him here so he won't hurt himself." He paused, thoughtfully. "Or anybody else."

"What about the guys in the bar? Do they want to press charges?"

"Uh-uh. They're a little embarrassed. They go to court and the story will get back to their hometown. How they were whupped by this old man. They've agreed to pay all damages. They wouldn't have a case anyhow. The bartender will vouch for your uncle, and the girls whose honor he defended think he's the most wonderful man in the world."

"I appreciate your telling me this, Sergeant. You can

release him in my custody. I'll see he stays out of trouble."

"You may not want to make any rash promises you can't keep. Remember, I've *met* your uncle. Just tell him to do his fighting in the next town."

Winslow rounded up a uniformed cop, who led the way to the cell block. The policeman stopped in front of a cell and opened the door so Winslow and I could go in. Uncle Constantine was asleep on a cot, his back to me. He looked like a heap of soiled laundry.

Sergeant Winslow said, "Hey, Constantine, you've got company."

Uncle Constantine stirred, grunted in reply, then rolled onto his other side so that he faced us. He blinked the sleep out of his eyes. Slowly, he sat up on the cot and blinked again. He didn't seem to know where he was, then the light of recognition dawned in his face. His broad mouth widened in a grin. He yelled joyfully.

"*Ar*istotle!"

He came off the cot like a stone from a catapult, threw his arms around me in a bear hug, squeezing so hard I could hardly breathe. He smelled of sweat and the liquorishy fragrance of ouzo. He released me just long enough to plant a wet kiss on my cheek, then locked me in his vise grip again.

"*Ar*istotle," he repeated. One big hand clamped my shoulder in an iron grip and the other grabbed the back of my hair and tugged on it affectionately.

"See," he said to Sergeant Winslow. "I tell you my nephew will come. This is my sister's boy." He pushed me away and held me at arm's length. "Aristotle. You have grown tall. I remember when you are only this big." He held his hand at waist level. "It's your mother's cooking."

Uncle Constantine always seemed ten feet high when I was a kid. Age and the death of his wife had taken a toll. He was more round-shouldered than I recalled, and the magnificent white-thatched head drooped slightly more than it did in his younger days. But his deep voice was robust, his muscular body was as hard as it was when he carried me around my house, and his blue eyes glittered with electrical vitality.

Sergeant Winslow said, "You can go, Constantine. We're releasing you in your nephew's custody."

Uncle Constantine unleashed me and flung himself at Sergeant Winslow. He wrapped his arms around the cop and gave him a mushy kiss on the cheek. Winslow's face turned the color of his hair.

"Thank you very much, my friend. You are a fine policeman, and a gentleman, too." Uncle Constantine released the stunned cop and led the way out of the cell.

Sergeant Winslow hurried to catch up. "Wait. You've got to fill out some forms."

Fifteen minutes later we were in the parking lot. Constantine drew a deep breath of the cool night air and flexed his biceps. "*Eleftheros,*" he said. "Freedom. *Efharisto,* Aristotle. I thank you for coming to save me. Sergeant Winslow is a very good man. But, fooh. His jail stinks like a pigpen."

"Glad to do it, Uncle Constantine. I'm really happy to see you. What happened at that bar?"

He dismissed the question with a shrug. "Today I come to Hyannis in my boat. I call your brother George and say trip is over, I want to celebrate. So I find this place near the dock. I have an ouzo. Very good. So I have another one. Maybe another. I am very happy to be on land. Then something makes me not happy. Some pretty girls are at a table. Two big boys bother them. I go over and say, please, let girls alone. The big boys don't like what the old man says. They try to frighten me. Then they push me away. I push back." He clenched his hands into fists. "Pretty soon, *poom!* I bump one on the nose. *Poom!* I bump another one on the chin. Then

the police come. Nice Sergeant Winslow gives me a hotel
room. I tell him to call you. You come, and I am free. Good
boy, Aristotle."

"Ma called me a few days ago. She was worried about you,
Uncle Constantine."

He pretended he was angry. "She *always* worries for me,
my little sister," he said, "She doesn't want me to come here
in the boat. I tell her it's okay, but she is still angry, she wants
me to stay home. The trouble with your mother is she's too
stubborn." He glanced around as if my mother were in earshot. "This thing with the police," he whispered. "Don't tell
your mama, okay?"

"That's the *last* thing you have to worry about, Uncle. You
can stay with me tonight if you want to and call her in the
morning from my house."

"*Ohi*, Aristotle. Take me to my boat. I sleep there. The
Artemis is my home now."

"Okay, Uncle Constantine. I'll give you a ride."

Constantine's boat was tied up to one of the floating piers
at the Lewis Bay Marina. He had lucked out on the mooring.
The fishing boat that normally occupied the spot was off
several days on a trip. We walked out onto the pier past
sailboats and cabin cruisers quietly nestled in their slips and
stopped next to the *Artemis*, where we stood in the moon-
light.

"Did you have any trouble coming up from Florida?" I
asked.

"A few leaks. Sometimes the engine gets lazy. But I take
care of it. No problem. The *Artemis* can go through a hurricane."

Even at night with most of the boat in shadow, the *Artemis*
didn't look seaworthy enough to withstand a good sneeze. It
smelled heavily of diesel fuel and old wood, but who was I to
argue? She had safely borne Uncle Constantine all the way

from Florida. It occurred to me that I still didn't know what he was doing up north.

"It's great to see you, Uncle, but what brings you to Cape Cod?"

"Two reasons. I come to New England to see my family. You, your mother and father, brother and sister, and all the cousins. And I come for work."

"What kind of work, Uncle?"

He put his hand on my shoulder and his finger on his lips. "Big secret." Then he yawned. "I tell you tomorrow. Too much ouzo. Your uncle is very tired. You come by and we talk. Maybe you help. Now I go to sleep. *Kalinihta*, Aristotle."

I squeezed his arm, glad to see him. "*Kalinihta*, Uncle Constantine."

18

Humphrey Bogart had just iced the slimy Nazi commander Conrad Veidt and Claude Raines was ordering his men to round up the usual suspects. Rick and Captain Renault walked off into the fog at the start of a beautiful friendship and *Casablanca* rolled to an end.

After springing Uncle Constantine from jail, I couldn't sleep and stayed up to watch the very late show. I flicked the TV off during a commercial for a Zamphier panflute album, went out on the deck, and breathed in the damp night air off the ocean.

Round up the usual suspects.

Good idea, but who *were* they?

So far, I had only one solid suspect in Eddy Byron's death. Rocky. All the evidence pointed to him. The holes in Byron's wet suit. The previous attack. The electric prod.

The stuff was circumstantial, but murderers are rarely caught with a smoking gun, bending over a warm corpse. Rocky had motive; Eddy was leaning on him, driving him nuts, maybe to the point of being homicidal. Rocky had opportunity; Eddy was alone with him. And he had method. Forty-six sharp teeth and more muscles in one flipper than ten weight lifters had in their whole body. If Rocky were human, I'd tell Simon Otis to cut a deal on voluntary manslaughter.

Still.

I scanned the black dome of the sky and picked out the constellations.

This case should be a wrap, but it wasn't. Too many loose ends. Like Hanley's death. It wasn't random. There was an undeniable connection between Oceanus and Hanley. My phone call. Hanley told me he was going to lay out the skinny on Oceanus. A few hours later he was dead.

Walden Schiller was another enigma.

Jolly little elf, the whale hugger, bubbling over with goodwill toward all creatures great and small. As long as they aren't human beings. Schiller was a ten-car pileup waiting to happen. He wanted Oceanus closed. He wanted Rocky and every marine mammal in captivity sent back to the wild. He would stop at nothing to do it. He said so himself. He engineered the boycott and the picketing, and I'd bet he was behind the bomb threats.

Then there was the prowler I chased at Oceanus. Who was he? And what was he doing there?

The usual suspects.

Sally *seemed* to be baring her soul about Eddy Byron, but was she telling me all she knew? Doc Livingston *seemed* to be a caring, inquisitive scientist. Austin *seemed* to be helpful, but he was selective, leaving out the parts about Rocky's sickness and the park closing and the staff firing. Jill *seemed* to be an innocent cutie . . . C'mon, Socarides, next you'll suspect Huff and Puff are sharks in dolphin costumes and the beluga is really a barracuda.

A shooting star streaked across the black sky and burned out like an ember caught by the wind.

I went back into the boathouse and tucked the folded paper holding the white powder I'd collected from the buoyancy compensator into a zip-lock bag. I put the bag and a note into a five-by-seven manila envelope. I propped the envelope up on the kitchen table so I wouldn't forget it. From a kitchen cupboard, I took a fifth of Old Grand-Dad a client had given me and set the bottle next to the envelope. I dug my dive gear out of a closet and put the equipment near the front door. Then I kicked Kojak off my pillow and went to bed.

As I slipped into a restless sleep, my mind went back to Eddy Byron. Suppose he *had* tormented Rocky into a murderous reaction? What happened to the electric prod?

Dawn, the daughter of morning, arrived much too soon. Kojak had snuck back during the night, curled up behind my knees, and forced me to the edge of the bed. Talk about mysteries! How does a cat on a bed expand far beyond its normal size?

Sam would have been up an hour ago. I called him and we agreed to meet at Elsie's place. The special that morning was cranberry pancakes. Sam and I figured the cranberries were left over from the Pilgrims' first Thanksgiving. We dined on overdone eggs and carbonized bacon instead. For all its faults, Elsie's cooking did stick to your ribs. After breakfast Sam went off to deal with Freddie the marine mechanic and I drove to Oceanus.

I set my dive gear in a corner of the locker room and went to see Ben. He was drinking coffee at his desk. He looked at me with small rheumy eyes and wiped his nose with the back of his index finger.

"What can I do for you, bub?" he said hoarsely, leaving no doubt from the tone of his voice that he didn't much care for an answer.

I pulled the fifth of whiskey from behind my back and held it up. His eyes darted toward the bottle and he licked his lips involuntarily.

"Got this as a birthday present. I don't drink the stuff—strictly a beer man—so I was wondering if you knew someplace where it wouldn't be wasted."

He reached over, took the bottle, and examined the label. "Yeah, I know just the place." He peeled the aluminum foil from the top, unscrewed the cap, and poured two fat fingers' worth into his coffee mug. "Want some?"

I shook my head. He said, "Suit yourself," and indicated the unmade cot. I sat down. He took a gulp of his spiked coffee. "You're the new guy. What's your name?"

"Socarides. Most people call me by my nickname. It's Soc."

He pondered that. "Sock, like you put on your foot?"

Funny guy, Ben. I made a fist and brandished it. "No, *Soc!* —like somebody gives you in the jaw."

That satisfied him. He drank more coffee and poured another couple of fingers of whiskey. One bottle might not be enough.

"What do you do here?" he asked.

"I'm a diver, primarily. But Mike Arnold's got me doing every dirty job that comes along."

Ben muttered something about Arnold I couldn't make out. "Don't worry. Place is going to hell in a hand basket. We'll all be collecting unemployment before long."

"You mean that business with the trainer. What was his name? Eddy something?"

He wiped his nose again and took another gulp. "Eddy Byron. He was some crazy bastard, going swimming with that goddamn fish. I told him he'd get his ass bit someday. He used to laugh. Well, he ain't laughing now."

I leaned forward. "Say, Ben. I might be helping train the animals here. I'm wondering if they're going to ask me to work with that whale, and to tell the truth, I'm not sure they can pay me enough money to do that. I've seen Rocky. He's one big mean-looking mother. You think he really did it to Eddy Byron, like some people say?"

"Sure he did."

"Was it pretty bad?"

"Naw. No blood or nothing like that. The other security guard found him. He told me about it. We trade shifts every other week. I was the early man and went home at one A.M. He was making the rounds the next morning, checking out the orca stadium. There was Eddy's body, floating right next to that wall you can look through. He called the rescue squad, but they couldn't do anything." Ben shuddered. "Hell of a way to go, being bit by a big fish, if you ask me."

"That's quite a story. I heard Eddy was a good trainer. Someone said he was like a bandleader. They said he had this big stick that he used sometimes, that he'd point it and the animals would do just what he wanted."

"Shit," Ben said. "Whoever's telling you that is blowing smoke up your flue. If Eddy could make that damn fish do what he wanted, how come the damned thing ate him?"

"You've got a point there. Then there was no stick?"

"Didn't say that." He took another swig and belched. "Sure, I seen him with it that night."

"What was he doing?"

"Walking over to the orca stadium."

"Did you talk to him?"

"Hell, no, we never had anything to say to each other. He minded his business, I minded mine." Ben grinned evilly. "He drank his hootch, I drank mine. Sure you don't want a slug? It'll get your motor started."

I got off the cot. "No thanks. I've got to get moving before Mike Arnold finds me."

"I'm not afraid of Arnold," he said. "Austin neither.

They're not going to find anyone else who wants to sit around a big fish house like this for what they want to pay me." He screwed the cap onto the whiskey bottle and tucked it in a desk drawer. "Thanks for the booze. You need a slug, it's in here."

"I'll remember that," I said.

Mike Arnold was working in the orca stadium. He stood on the stage at the poolside, wearing a red-and-black Oceanus wet suit, and didn't see me take a seat in the bleachers a few rows behind him. He raised his arms like the hood ornament on a Rolls-Royce. Rocky's big black fin came straight at Arnold, who didn't move.

Rocky slithered entirely out of the water and lay on the stage next to Arnold, dwarfing the man. Arnold didn't seem alarmed. He gave Rocky a fish and stroked his back. Then blew on a whistle. Rocky slid off the stage and back into the pool. He went through his whole repertoire of tricks. He jumped straight out of the water. He swam along the side of the pool and waved his fin at the empty bleachers. He did several arcing jumps. And with each trick I grew more respectful of his grace and power and of Arnold's control of him.

I walked down to the splash area and applauded. Arnold turned and saw me. His smile melted.

"What the hell are you doing here?"

"Reporting for duty. What is it today? Piranha? Crocodile? Plesiosaurus?"

He shook his head. "This is Saturday. You don't have to come in weekends. Somebody should have told you."

"No problem. It gave me a chance to see the show. Pretty impressive."

His eyes narrowed. He was combing my voice for sarcasm. "Rocky does all the work," he said.

"I saw him come up on the stage. Aren't you worried? I mean, after the accident."

"Don't believe everything you read in the newspapers." He glanced out at Rocky's dorsal fin slicing through the water. "Rocky won't hurt me. We get along just fine. He likes to do tricks. You treat Rocky right, and he'll do anything you want him to. You just can't take him for granted. He's sixteen thousand pounds of predator. Forget that and you've got trouble."

"Is that why you're not going in the water with him?"

"Yeah, partly. House rules. The park owners say no one in the water until we figure out where Rocky's head is. We can do most of the tricks from the stage except the one where he jumps out of the water with someone on his nose or the trainer rides him. We had to scrub that trick anyhow. Rocky doesn't like people on his back. Orcas are like that. They've got their individual personalities. Some you can bat around like a kid's teddy bear. Some are touchier'n hell. You walk on tiptoe around them. It's like that old joke. What do you call an eight-hundred-pound gorilla?"

"You call it 'sir.' "

Arnold laughed. "That's right. Same with Rocky."

I walked over and leaned against the plastic wall. "Guess you're right. If he really wanted to make trouble, he could snatch you right off the stage."

"Yeah, he could bite me in half, but he won't."

"Rocky's not like a shark, you mean." I hadn't meant to stick it to Arnold. The comment just slipped out.

I thought Arnold would do his usual pit-bull imitation, but he looked embarrassed. "Hey, I never expected what happened. Remember, I was the guy who got you out in one piece. Hell, it was Austin's idea to put you in the tank in the first place."

Austin? That was a new one. Arnold could be lying, shifting the blame elsewhere, but I couldn't deny he came to the rescue in jig time. "I remember, and I appreciate it." I looked out over the pool, wondering if Eddy Byron's electric prod lay under the green water. "Guess I'll enjoy my day off. See you Monday," I said.

"Yeah," Mike replied.

Arnold was a skilled trainer. He could make Rocky jump through hoops. Could he make him kill someone? The idea was too ridiculous. But he did have motive. He was next in line for the top job, and maybe more important, he and Eddy were rivals for Sally's attention. Come to think of it, I was, too, and that didn't make me feel very secure.

Leaving Oceanus, I drove into Hyannis and stopped at a public telephone in a CVS drugstore. I dialed the Boston police lab, gave the operator my name, and asked for Charlie Reed. A minute later Charlie came on the phone. He had a boyish voice that always sounded as if he had just run in from wherever he was, which was often the case.

"Soc," he said. "What a great surprise. How are you?"

"I'm fine. I'd be even better if you could do a favor for me. I'm going to send a package up to Boston on the next P-and-B bus leaving the Cape. There's a powder sample inside. Could you run a quickie analysis?"

"Is it dope?"

"No, I don't think it's anything like that, but I don't know. That's why I'm calling the best lab tech in the business."

"Thanks for the endorsement. Tomorrow's Sunday. First of the week okay?"

"This could be important, but I guess I'll have to wait, unless you've got a good lab assistant who doesn't mind working tomorrow."

"You know better than that, Soc. It will be a great sacrifice, but I'll just tell my wife that I can't go shopping with her in New Hampshire like I was dying to do."

I knew he'd say that. "I'll call you tomorrow night."

Moments later I dialed another number.

"Parthenon Pizza," a woman's voice said.

"Hi, Athena," I said. "Can you put me through to my mother?"

"Sure, Soc. Hold on, I'll connect you with the bakery."

My father picked up the phone. "Allo, who's there?"

"It's me, Pop. How are you?"

"Ah, Aristotle. I'm fine. I'm very glad you call. Mama is very worried about Uncle Constantine."

"That's what I called about. He arrived last night. I've talked to him and everything's fine."

"Good, Aristotle," he said with relief. "I try to tell her everything is okay, but you know how she is, very stubborn."

"How's the frozen-pizza business, Pop?"

"Everything is good. You come to Lowell sometime and your brother George shows you the new oven. Hold on." He stopped to talk to somebody else in Greek then came back on the phone. "Come up soon. Bye."

My mother's voice came onto the phone. "Hello, Aristotle. Papa says your uncle Constantine is here. He's good?" There was anxiety in her voice.

"That's right. I saw him last night. He's in Hyannis and he's fine."

"*Doxta Theos*, thank God," she said. "He stays with you?"

"No, Ma. I offered to put him up, but he wanted to sleep on his boat."

She laughed and said, "That's your uncle. Stubborn as an old donkey. He does what he pleases. Did he say what he is going to do?"

"Only that he has some kind of work on the Cape. He didn't tell me what kind."

"Ah, he is such a little boy," she said tenderly. "Aristotle, it is very important that you keep your eye on Uncle Constantine. See he takes care of himself. He forgets how old he is sometimes." There was concern in her voice.

"I'll do my best, Ma," I said.

"I know you will. You're a good boy, Aristotle."

Lew Atwood wasn't at his house, but the teenage girl who answered the door said her father was working at a boatyard in Barnstable on the north shore of the Cape. I dropped Charlie's package off at the bus station, then put my seersucker jacket and tie on in a shopping-plaza parking lot and drove cross-Cape to the bay side. The old gent in the marina office pointed out his window to a guy pumping gas into a white cabin cruiser at the fuel dock. I waited until he hung up the nozzle. Then I walked over to the dock and introduced myself.

Atwood was about fifty-five with a ruddy wind-burned complexion and gray hair cropped close to his head. He smiled. "You called me the other night. Sorry I didn't get back to you. Got home late. Are you sail or motor?"

"Neither. I'm working for Oceanus and I'd like to talk to you."

The smile flipped upside down and became a frown.

"Let's go over to the shed," Atwood said. "I can't smoke on the fuel dock."

He clipped a walkie-talkie to his belt and asked the old man in the office to keep an eye on the gas pump, then he led the way to a barn-size gray-shingled boat storage shed. He lit a cigarette out of a pack of Winstons and gazed at me with hooded eyes. "What does someone from Oceanus want from me?"

I gave him the usual half-truth. "I've been hired as a consultant by Bay State Investments. They want me to prepare a complete report on the Eddy Byron incident. Something to do with insurance."

"You wasted your time coming to see me. I was long gone when Eddy came on the job."

"Yes, I know Mr. Byron was hired after you. But if you could shed some light on the situation at the park before the accident, it might put Mr. Byron's death in perspective."

Atwood took an angry puff on his butt and ground it out under his shoe. "Why the hell should I help Oceanus?"

"You wouldn't be helping them necessarily. I'm simply pulling together information on the Oceanus operation so people who are smarter than I am can figure out what went wrong. If you've got criticisms, I'm not going to whitewash the facts; what you say will go in my report. Maybe knowing more about Mr. Byron's death can prevent another trainer from being killed or injured at Oceanus or anyplace else."

He blew smoke through his nostrils like a dragon. His features hardened.

"You knew I got the ax," he said.

"I heard you were let go after the whale got sick."

Atwood rose from his chair and paced back and forth a couple of times before he came over and stuck his finger in my face.

"Okay, Mr. Consultant," he growled, "I'll tell you what *really* happened. Sure, Rocky was sick. Hell, I saw it first. I was working with him one day and noticed the sound he made through his blowhole. He was having a tough time breathing. He was swimming in tight little circles and had trouble keeping his balance. I caught it right away. I'd been working closely with Rocky for months. We got Doc Livingston to take a look at him. Turned out to be respiratory problems."

"Is that serious?"

"It *can* be." Atwood settled into his chair again and sat back, crossing his arms. "We don't know a lot about orcas. There just hasn't been enough research. But a killer whale is basically a big dolphin, and pneumonia kills more dolphins in captivity than anything else. It's more complicated, though."

"Complicated in what way?"

"Say a dolphin dies in an aquarium. They perform a necropsy and the cause of death is put down as pneumonia. They don't say if the animal probably died from something else."

"Why not, Mr. Atwood?"

"Nobody wants to admit they're only telling part of the truth. Sure the animal got pneumonia, but that was only a secondary infection resulting from an ulcer or some other stomach ailment that was produced by the real cause of death, plain old stress. It's pretty much an open secret in the marine-park industry."

"Why would anyone be afraid to admit a dolphin died of stress?"

"Because they don't want to get the federal regulators or the animal-rights people down on their neck. Saying an animal died from stress is like admitting you've been leaning too hard on it."

"How's that, Mr. Atwood?"

"You've got to start at the beginning. First the animal is yanked away from its family and companions. Then he's stuck in an artificial environment that limits his movements and he's fed dead fish instead of the live ones he's used to. Just when he starts getting acclimated to swimming around in a tank that bounces his signal back every time he tries to echolocate, we humans come along and start demanding that he jump through hoops to get his supper. It puts a lot of pressure on him, like your bosses calling you up and saying you've got to get your report here done this afternoon or you won't get paid."

"Was Rocky under stress?"

"Every marine mammal in captivity is under *some* kind of

stress. Depends on the management of the park. How tough they are with the training, or how much pressure they put on the animals to perform."

"What about the management at Oceanus?"

"Oceanus is no different from anyone else. They all say they're out to educate the public, but that's crap. They're after the bucks. Oceanus was planning a major expansion program built around the killer-whale show. They wanted Rocky to perform as often as he could. I was always being pushed to teach him new tricks."

"What happened after you told Austin that Rocky was sick?"

"Livingston pumped antibiotics into him."

"How did he respond?"

"I never got a chance to find out. Austin told me to take a few days off. I guess the treatment worked. Rocky is still alive. But that wasn't the end of it. Austin blamed me for Rocky getting sick. He said I could have prevented it, or that I should have told him sooner. That's a bunch of bullshit. Austin was just covering his ass. So he fired me."

"Do you think Rocky's sickness had any bearing on Eddy Byron's death?"

"Directly, no. Rocky is a real gentle animal. Even now, even with Eddy dead, I find it hard to believe he'd ever hurt anyone. The most he'd do is nudge me once in a while or sulk if I was working him too hard, and I'd lay off."

"Are you saying he couldn't have done it?"

"That's what I'd like to say, but I can't. I read about the rips in Eddy's wet suit and I'll be damned if I can explain those away. Then there's the whole lousy setup. All at once I'm gone. Rocky's got to deal with a new trainer using different training methods. You know how it is when you're feeling awful and someone starts to bug you. You want to strangle them. Maybe Rocky was just confused from being sick and the changes at the park and he went over the edge."

"What did you mean about different training methods? I thought they were all pretty much the same."

"They are to a point. First you have to build trust between you and the whale. The whale has nothing to base that trust on, so the most positive thing you can do is feed it. The whale gets used to having a human around. It learns a human is interesting and nonthreatening. It sees that play is fun. Then you try to maintain that bond. It's amazing the things they will allow you to do, whether performing or not."

"It must take a lot of time and patience."

"You have to know how to react to the whale's behavior. It takes a sixth sense. But that's only half of it. The whale must be ready to accept you in or out of the water."

"Does that mean Eddy would have had to go through the bonding thing all over again with Rocky?"

"Absolutely. You can't take anything for granted. It's no sure thing Eddy and the whale would have hit it off. A whale might not like the person he is working with. Or if a stranger tries to feed the whale a fish, he might not take it. A whale loves tactile things like being scratched or having its dorsal fin rubbed, but only with people he's accepted."

"Theoretically, then, once you've established this bond, you could pretty much get the whale to do anything, within its physical bounds and those of its own intelligence."

"That's right. Of course, every animal has a different personality. If the animal hates what you're trying to get it to do, drop it. You have to stay on your toes."

"Are you suggesting that Eddy didn't stay on his?"

"Not exactly. I just think the training method he was using was just plain dangerous."

"In what way?"

"Eddy preferred a technique the guys in the industry called

the 'macho' method. Some of the parks began using it a few years ago. That's when the problems started with the whales, in my opinion."

"What was so macho about it?"

"You spent a lot of time in the water with the whales. The idea was to get real close to the animal, give it lots of spontaneous play, petting and scratching, more variety in its routine so the whale will perform because it *wants* to please, not because it's hungry."

"No more fish for a trick?"

"That's right. You fed the animal more regularly with less of its food coming as a reward for tricks. The rewards were the petting and the giving it action. You punished it with boredom. If the animal did something you didn't like, you stopped working with it and didn't talk for a minute or two. Your silence tells the whale you're not pleased."

"Sounds pretty civilized to me. What was so dangerous about it?"

"The trainer becomes the focus of the whale's attention rather than the food. There is less control, and the whale could become unpredictable. Look, Mr. Socarides, those animals weren't designed to react to that kind of training. They operate by their own set of rules. Like one guy said, it's not like training dogs, it's more like working with grizzly bears. Top predators, in other words. At the same time, pressure was on to get the animals to perform newer and more complicated stunts. Some trainers in the industry were worried about safety. No one listened to them until trainers started getting attacked at a few parks around the country. Eddy still wasn't convinced."

"I take it you didn't approve of the macho technique."

"I thought it was a recipe for disaster. I used the old methods. Later, I found out that Byron had made a change in the training. I called Austin and warned him he was asking for trouble."

"What was his response?"

"He told me to shove it. Said I wasn't working at Oceanus and to mind my own business. Not long after that, a couple of trainers were injured at Oceanus. I heard the park went back to the old methods and ordered the trainers out of the water. That would have confused Rocky even more. Austin never gave a damn about the animal. He's just interested in the bottom line."

"But they found Eddy *in* the water."

"I'm not surprised. Eddy had a reputation. Nobody ordered *him* around. He would have done exactly what he wanted to do. Then again, Rocky could have snatched him from the side of the pool."

The walkie-talkie on Atwood's belt crackled. Somebody at the dock needed gas. He got up and we walked back toward the marina.

"Sorry I have to go," he said. "It felt pretty good getting this stuff off my chest."

"I appreciate the time. I'll make sure your comments get into my report. Do you plan to get back into marine-mammal training?"

"Hell yes. This job is just to get me through the summer while I look around. My wife's got a pretty good spot with an insurance company and my daughter was planning to waitress at a restaurant, so it would be tough on them to just pull up stakes. We'll probably end up in Florida, or the West Coast."

"Well, good luck in whatever you do."

"Thanks. I hope this whole mess gets cleared up soon. I don't like seeing all this crap about Rocky in the papers, like he was some kind of man-eating monster. We were real buddies. I really miss him."

"You sound like somebody who likes his work."

"I've trained whales and dolphins for years. I love them. I'd put them higher on the evolutionary scale than a lot of human beings. It kills me to see them locked up in these tanks, and if I had my way, I'd let them all go. But as long as they're in captivity, I'll try to make their lives as comfortable as I can."

We shook hands. I went back to my truck and sat. What next? I could try to dig up more suspects, but I had the nagging feeling that it was Rocky, not Eddy Byron, who held the key to this case. I thought of Dr. Livingston. He was the scientific expert on killer whales. Maybe he knew something that could make all the pieces fall into place. I took his card out of my wallet and looked at the address. He lived in the town of Sandwich, about fifteen minutes away. What the hell, I reasoned. It was worth a try.

Livingston lived off the Old Kings Highway at the end of a long driveway in a contemporary house shaped like a typewriter case. A silver Toyota four-by-four was parked in the drive. I went up the flagstone walk and rang the bell.

A moment later he came to the door. He had a straight stem pipe clenched between his teeth. His annoyed expression changed to one of mild astonishment when he saw me. He took the pipe out of his mouth.

"Well," he said. "This is a surprise."

"I happened to be in the neighborhood and I remembered your invitation to drop by to talk. If it's not convenient—"

"Oh no . . ." he interrupted. "Come in. I was just thinking of taking a break. I've been running some statistics through my computer. It's incredibly dry work and I'd love the excuse to stop for a bit."

He led the way to his living room, settled me in a long sofa with wooden ends, and asked if I wanted some iced coffee.

"Sure, Dr. Livingston."

"Call me Hank," he said. "Let's see. And your name was . . ."

"Socarides. Most people call me Soc."

He nodded and went out to the kitchen. I enjoyed the view of the marsh from the window that ran the length of the room. A few minutes later he came back with two glasses and settled into an Eames chair.

"I had an ulterior motive in dropping by," I said.

He raised his eyebrows.

"I've heard rumors that the park might open soon, which means I could be working with Rocky." I laughed nervously. "I'm not sure if that might be good for my health because of, well, you know, that business with that trainer. We talked about killer whales in general the other day, but not about Rocky in particular."

Livingston chuckled. "Well, I don't blame you for being jittery. Rocky is a pretty formidable-looking character. But how can I help?"

"I'd just like to know a little more before I decide if I want to get in the same tank with him."

Livingston tapped his pipe tobacco into an ashtray.

"I could tell you that Rocky is nothing but a big oceangoing panda bear, but that would be unfair as well as inaccurate."

"Does that mean I should look for another job? Something less hazardous, like working in a bomb factory?"

"No, not necessarily. But you should realize killer whales behave differently in captivity than they do in the wild. It's been a problem, not just at Oceanus, but at other parks. And it hasn't always involved humans. At one park a female orca broke its jaw attacking another killer whale, and bled to death. The park people should have known better than to put two female whales, one with a newborn, in the same tank, where they'd play out a female-dominance ritual."

"That's whale on whale. How about whale versus human?"

"Attacks are far more common than most people realize. Dozens of trainers have been injured by killer whales. One whale pinned a trainer against a wall. Another took a trainer in his mouth. At one park, after a guy ended up with broken ribs, pelvis, and femur, the park owners banned divers from the water and fired the top management. This all happened before the business with Eddy Byron and the fatal attack on a trainer in British Columbia."

"Couldn't they work the whales from the side of the pool?"

"I hope you won't be shocked if I tell you decisions in the marine-park business are often made on the basis of what's healthy for the cash register, not what is good for the trainer or the animal. Sure, you can put a whale through its paces from the edge of the pool. But it's far more dramatic when the trainer rides on the whale's back, or jets out of the water on the whale's nose. That's what people buy tickets to see."

"What happened at Oceanus?"

"Once, during a performance, Rocky jumped out of the water and landed on the trainer. I didn't see it happen, but maybe the whale just miscued. Rocky bit another trainer on the hand. Nothing serious, which tells me the whale was only warning him. Then some of the trainers were knocked around a couple of times, pushed up against the side of the pool, but they could have been working Rocky too hard on bad days. Rocky was sending signals that shouldn't have been ignored."

"What about the thing with the head trainer? Byron, I guess his name was."

He tamped some tobacco into his pipe and lit up. "It was during a training session. Eddy was trying to ride on Rocky's back. It wasn't a big deal. They used to do it all the time, but Rocky rolled over and knocked Eddy off a couple of times. I happened to be at the stadium. I told Eddy to give it a break. Rocky obviously wasn't going to play piggyback. Eddy was one of the best in the business, but he was stubborn. He got on Rocky's back again and held on to his dorsal. Rocky rolled him off. This time he actually grabbed him in his mouth and dove with him to the bottom of the pool. The whole thing only took a few seconds. After Rocky showed Eddy who was boss, he let him go and swam away."

"What did Eddy do?"

Livingston laughed. "You should have seen him. He popped back to the surface sputtering and gasping. It would have been damned funny if it hadn't been so near tragic."

"How badly hurt was he?"

"That was the incredible thing, Soc. Eddy didn't have a mark on him, not even where the teeth had grabbed him. It was as if Rocky knew he had to be firm but gentle with a squishy thing like a human being. It scared the hell out of Eddy, as you might imagine. When he got some color back into his face, he got angry. Eddy Byron considered himself the best marine-mammal trainer in the universe. He'd been trying to build a relationship with Rocky, being a pal to him. He thought the whale would do anything he wanted. So when Rocky attacked him, it was a betrayal. Eddy took it personally. From that time on I think he began to hate Rocky."

"You make it sound a little like Ahab and Moby Dick."

"You know, I had the same thought and I wondered if I were stretching the analogy. Moby was just reacting naturally when he bit off Ahab's leg in self-defense. Yet it was Ahab, the human being who supposedly had the benefit of reason and intelligence, who was acting like an enraged animal to get his revenge. Hell, you would have thought Rocky had chewed off Eddy's leg instead of just singeing his dignity. After I helped him out of the pool, Eddy glared at Rocky a few minutes, swearing under his breath. Then he stalked off."

"How did Austin find out about it?"

"I told him and he talked to Eddy. To his credit, Dan moved quickly. He banned trainers from the whale tank until further notice. And he ordered Eddy to discontinue the training method he was using and go back to the old way."

"How did Eddy like that?"

"Not well. He argued with Austin, but the orders stuck. Anybody else would have shrugged his shoulders and gone back to work, but not Eddy. He felt humiliated and blamed Rocky. He went along with the change but he didn't really go along. I think Eddy actually hated Rocky, and his attitude spilled over with the other animals at the park."

Livingston finished his coffee. "Well, I'd like to chat about whales all day, but I've got to get back those onerous statistics whether I like to or not."

I got up. "No problem. I appreciate your taking the time to talk to me."

"I don't know if I've helped you in any way in making a career choice."

"I think what you told me was that whales have gone after trainers, but they probably had good reasons."

He nodded. "That's it in a nutshell."

Livingston walked me to the door. Before he let me out, I said, "You've worked with these animals a long time. What do you think about John Lilly? I'm just curious."

"Lilly? I see you've been doing some reading. My reaction is the same as most legitimate scientists. Lilly had some interesting ideas, but he went off the deep end. I thought it was ironic that as part of his research he hammered electrodes into the brains of animals he thought might be equal, and possibly superior in intelligence to man."

"He did that?" The bruise on my head twinged. "Doesn't seem quite friendly, does it?"

"You'll find a lot of ambiguities in this business. You hear a lot of holier-than-thous," he said, smiling bleakly, "but none of us is quite as clean as we would like people to think. Thanks for stopping by."

We shook hands and a few minutes later I was driving along Route 6A. Livingston's closing comment wouldn't go away. With a couple of exceptions, maybe, none of the people I had met in the course of this investigation could say with a straight face that they were squeaky clean. And to tell the truth, I was beginning to feel a little grimy myself.

19

Uncle Constantine had company. Two attractive young women were stretched out in aluminum lounge chairs on the deck of the *Artemis*. The lotion on their aerobically trim bodies glistened under the dazzling rays of the summer sun.

I walked along the finger pier and leaned against the boat. "Excuse me," I said, sounding like a lost kid, "I'm looking for my uncle."

One of the women, a blonde, lifted her head an inch off the plastic webbing of the chair and peered at me through burgundy sunglasses. "You must be Aristotle." She gave me a lazy smile. "Your uncle's below." She rose and went over to the hatchway.

"Constantine," she called down sweetly, "your nephew is here to see you."

I climbed on board as my uncle's snowy thatch of hair emerged into daylight, followed by his muscular nose, his generous mustache, and his crooked grin. "*Hopa!* Aristotle!"

he roared like an old sea lion. "You don't forget your uncle."
He threw his arms wide and gave me a rib-crushing hug and
a battery of back thumps. His face had lost the grayness I had
seen in the Hyannis jail. He wore a clean white shirt and
baggy black pants. His hair was combed and slicked into
place, his mustache looked waxed, and he smelled as if he had
taken a shower in cologne.

"Come meet my new friends." He grabbed my arm and
introduced me to the women. The blonde was named Kara.
Her brunette companion was Maureen. They were in their
midtwenties. Both were from Boston. Uncle Constantine had
excellent taste. The ladies were leggy and tanned, but these
were no airheads. Kara was a psychologist for Mass. General
Hospital. Maureen was a lawyer for a law firm that had more
names in it than a telephone book.

"They come to visit me," Uncle Constantine said happily.
"I show them *Artemis* and we have lemonades. Wait." He
scuttled below.

"How do you know Uncle Constantine?" I asked.

Kara removed her sunglasses. She had pretty green eyes.
"We met the other night. He defended our honor against a
couple of drunken idiots who were bothering us." She
laughed. "It was like a scene out of *Indiana Jones*. I've never
seen anything like it."

Maureen said, "We'd just gotten off the Nantucket boat
and were having a couple of drinks when those two goons
started drooling down our necks. Your uncle was incredible.
He came over to help us. He was very courtly, very polite,
but they went after him. We told the police it wasn't his
fault."

Kara added, "Maureen and I were just saying how hard it
is to find someone like your uncle. Most of the men we know
are so full of themselves. He's been telling us about his wife
and fishing for sponges in Florida. It's been fascinating."

Uncle Constantine emerged with a tray bearing a pitcher and a thick tumbler. He splashed some lemonade into my glass, replenished everybody's drink, and sat on the deck between the two women. He drank half his down in a single gulp and wiped his mouth with the back of his hand. "No more ouzo, Aristotle. Only lemonades and coffee." He squeezed his forehead. "Too much headache. Too much stomachache. Too much trouble with police."

Life's funny. My mother had practically ordered me to take care of Uncle Constantine. From where I sat, it looked as though he were taking care of himself damned well. We talked for a while until Kara looked at her watch and said they had to go. She and her friend shook hands with me, then hugged my uncle.

"Don't forget," Maureen said. "You promised to take us out for a cruise."

"Tomorrow I work, but you come back next week and we go out. We bring food and ouzo and—" He glanced at me, aware he was about to break the pledge he made minutes before. "No ouzo," he said manfully. "We drink lemonades."

"Bye, Connie," Maureen said, kissing my uncle's cheek. "You have our number, so be sure to give us a call."

The women folded up their chairs, climbed off the boat onto the pier, and walked across the parking lot, their progress scrutinized by every male in the marina. They waved and got into their car. Uncle Constantine waved back, then roared with laughter and gave me a slap between the shoulder blades that knocked the wind out of me.

"Put your eyes back in your head, Aristotle," he said.

I shrugged. "Nice girls."

He put his arm around me and drew me close in a conspiratorial huddle. "For fifty years I am married to your aunt Thalia. All this time I never touch another woman, not even the pretty tourist girls who come to Tarpon Springs with makeup on their faces. But excuse me, I'm a man." He tapped his brow. "So I look. But I don't touch. Never. Now my friends say, 'Constantine, don't be lonely, find yourself another wife to keep you warm at night.' But I think, what if what the priest says is true, and we all come together in heaven again? The angels will shake their heads and say, 'There goes Constantine and his two wives. Poor man, he can't say a word.' So even now, with Thalia in heaven, I still don't touch. Come inside. We talk business."

I followed him into the pilothouse. He moved fast despite his limp. He pawed through a pile of charts, grunting triumphantly when he found a chart of Nantucket Sound. He rolled it flat and put his finger on a smudged X that was penciled in to mark a position about ten miles south of where we stood.

"*This* is our business," he said. "We make a big salvage job here."

"Salvage? For what?"

He lit a thin cigar and took a few puffs. His eyes twinkled. He was deliberately drawing out the suspense. He used the same gimmick when I was a kid listening to sea adventure stories at his knee. He threw out the hook, and once he was sure he had my attention, he reeled me in.

"One hundred years ago, a big storm comes off Cape Cod. Lightning and thunder, and a wind that makes waves as big as a house. A boat sails from New York. English, with iron hull, no motor, three masts. She carries too much weight. Down she goes. Some of crew is rescued, some die. But nobody knows where boat is. Until now, Roger finds."

"Who is Roger?"

"My good friend I drink with in Tarpon Springs. I know him from many years. Roger makes much money on antiques. Buys them cheap, sells to rich people. One day Roger buys a big load of books. Inside one book he finds a map and other papers. Map shows this place." He pointed to an *X* on the chart. "Roger and me, we play dominoes. His legs are bad now and he is in a wheelchair. One day he says, 'Constantine, I have a map that shows wreck of boat off Cape Cod. Big, rich cargo. Close to shore.' I say, 'Roger, I bet you this wreck is empty.' But Roger says, 'No, Constantine. Only a few people know where the wreck is, and the cargo is not like silver and gold that drives everybody crazy and makes them look for ships. The boat has tin.'"

"Tin?"

"Sure, Aristotle. Fifty thousand pounds from Singapore. Worth thousands of dollars. Maybe more. So Roger says, 'You have the *Artemis*. You have family in Massachusetts. I lend you money to go up north and find the boat. We split fifty-fifty."

"Uncle Constantine, I hate to disappoint you, but it's real tough to find a wreck, even one this close to shore."

He chuckled and pinched my cheek so that it hurt. "You are very smart, Aristotle, but your uncle Constantine is smart, too. I work for years looking for sponge beds. I know the sea is very big. I tell Roger the same thing. So he buys me sharp eyes to see with. Look!"

Uncle Constantine pulled a plastic dropcloth off a home-made stand of plywood built next to the helm. Clean-lined boxes of electronic gear gleamed in the sunlight streaming through the windows. Dumbfounded, I ran my hand over the side-scan sonar, the magnetometer, and sophisticated depth sounder. State-of-the-art treasure-hunting tools.

"This is top-of-the-line stuff, Uncle Constantine. Do you know how to operate it?"

He covered the equipment and smiled mysteriously. "I come to Cape Cod from Florida last week. For four days before I bring boat to Hyannis I go back and forth with the

machines. Back and forth, up and down, until I find something. Then I come here."

That's why my mother didn't hear from Uncle Constantine. He had arrived off the Cape, but lay low while he did his
treasure hunting.

"Did you find the ship?"

He slid the chart under my nose and put his finger on the
penciled *X*. "Here, Aristotle. Easy job. Forty feet of water.
Now I dive down for closer look."

Alarm bells went off in my head.

"Uncle Constantine, when was the last time you did any
diving?"

He waved me off. "Aristotle, I dive since I am sixteen years
old. It makes no difference when I stop. You are a diver, too;
it runs in the blood. You help me?"

"Of course I'll help you." My mind was churning. Maybe I
could delay him until his boat broke down or he lost interest
in the project.

"Good," he said, clapping my shoulder. "We go out tomorrow."

Tomorrow? Damn. I nodded. I'd have to think up something else. "This is costing a lot of money, with the equipment and running a boat up here from Florida. How do you
and your friend Roger expect to make any money?"

Frowning as if he had a stomach pain, Uncle Constantine
said, "Ah, Aristotle, now you sound like your mother. She
thinks life is to make money so I can die a rich old man in my
bed. *Phooey*. Hard work, yes. Good woman and children, yes.
I do all that. But life is to *live*. Life is to dream, Aristotle.
That is why we do it, not for money. When you are old like
me, or cripple like Roger, you will know. Don't ever stop
dreaming, Aristotle."

I wrapped my arms around him and gave him a hug, feeling the bones under his muscle. He seemed almost fragile,

and I realized that what I had mistaken for his strength was his unquenchable spark of vitality.

"I won't stop dreaming, Uncle Constantine. I promise."

I left the marina and headed back to Oceanus to pick up my scuba gear for the next day's dive with Uncle Constantine. On the way I tried to pull together what I had so far.

Outside of Eddy's dead body, his perforated wet suit, and a lot of talk about what a fine lad Rocky was, I didn't have one tangible piece of evidence. Unless I could find Eddy's electrical prod. It was hard to believe Eddy would be dumb enough to use shock treatment on an eight-ton killer whale, but if he were angry enough and drunk enough . . .

Ben said he saw Eddy with a "stick." The prod had not been found near the whale tank. Did that mean it was in the pool? I might just have to go take a look. Hold on, pal, better chew that one over. I had seen the holes in Eddy Byron's wet suit. More important, I had seen the teeth that might have made them.

Before retrieving my scuba gear from the locker room, I walked over to the orca stadium. The gate was unlocked and partly open. For a suspected murderer, Rocky was a popular guy. I went through the passageway, emerged into the bleacher section, and saw a slim, blond-haired figure in a blue jersey standing on the stage next to the pool. It was Jill.

I hailed her, my voice echoing in the empty stadium. Jill whipped around like a startled doe, then waved. I walked down to the splash area. Jill stood in a half foot of pool water. Her socks and sneakers were neatly placed next to a towel on a bleacher seat. She had a Canon 35mm camera and zoom lens hanging from a strap around her neck.

I sat down next to the sneakers. "Taking pictures for Rocky's family album?"

"I just like to have photographs of the animals I work with."

Whooof!

Rocky's tall dorsal fin and glossy black back surfaced about twenty feet away. He cruised by, his huge body creating tidal waves that sloshed onto the stage. Jill quickly brought the camera to her eye. She fired off a round of shots, the camera's motor drive going *kerchunk, kerchunk.*

"He's not being very cooperative," I said. "Has he smiled for the camera?"

"A couple of times," she said. "I made him say cheese."

She sloshed across the stage and came over to sit beside me.

"What brings you to Oceanus on your day off?" she said.

"I could say I like this place so much I can't stay away, but I wouldn't be telling the truth. I came by this morning because nobody told me I get Saturday and Sunday off. Now I'm here to pick up the scuba gear I left on my first trip. As you can see, I'm very organized."

Jill toweled her feet dry and put her socks and sneakers on. "That's okay, I often come in on my day off to see Rocky and the dolphins. I could spend hours watching them, they are so graceful."

Rocky swam underwater where we could see him behind the transparent pool panels. He was looking out at us.

"You're right about that. For a big hunk of blubber, Rocky moves like Pavlova."

Mesmerized, we sat without speaking, watching the whale's underwater ballet. Jill spoke finally. She turned, her child's face as serious as it could be. "Soc," she said, "what do you think about Rocky and the dolphins being here?"

"I don't get you, Jill."

"You know. Do you think it's right for them to be prisoners against their free wills?"

"I haven't thought about it, Jill."

"Well, *please* think about it, for me."

Jill's cornflower-blue eyes were pleading. Her lips were compressed as if she were trying to will me to answer. The playful gamin had vanished. In its place was an intensely serious young woman.

What had Uncle Constantine said when he left the jailhouse? *Eleftheros!* Freedom! Constantine was a free spirit who hated bonds of any kind. I felt the same way. I chafed at restraints. I was looking for freedom when I quit a paying job and moved to this sliver of sand where the only barriers were the ones I erected around myself. My Cretan genes again. The Greek air is holy; surely freedom was born here, said Nikos Kazanzakis. But was freedom just for people?

"I guess I don't like seeing any living thing locked up against its will," I said. "Maybe that's why I've always been uncomfortable in zoos, even as a kid."

The grim look evaporated from Jill's face. She was beaming. "I *knew* you'd say that, Soc. How far would you go to set them free?"

"Hold on, Jill. I said it bothered me to see them in captivity. I didn't say anything about turning them loose."

The serious look again. "I'm sorry. I spoke too soon. We just wanted to know where you stood."

"I don't understand, Jill. Who is this 'we' you're talking about?"

She sighed deeply. "Soc, do you really know who I am?"

"Sure, you're a college dropout lucky enough to have parents who own a house on Cape Cod, and you're trying to find yourself. That's what you told me."

"That's not the whole story. I'm like you, Soc. I'm not what I seem to be."

"Jill, I don't want to seem impatient," I said gently, "but

we could spend the entire afternoon playing metaphysical word games, so why don't you get to the point."

Her mouth curled in an impish grin. "Okay, since you asked for it, I will, Mr. Private Detective."

My chin dropped down to my belt buckle. Jill knew I was a private cop! Good undercover job, Socarides. Less than seventy-two hours on the job and this kid blows your cover!

There was no use denying it; she had me cold. "How did you know?" I growled. I was irritated at myself.

"Walden told me."

"Walden Schiller? How do you know him?" Even as I asked the question I knew the answer. It lurked in Schiller's passionate story about the tuna boats, how he had shipped out as a crew member to take the controversial pictures of the dolphin massacre, and in Ed Shaughnessy's story about the inside-job sabotage at the tuna factory and aquarium. Shaughnessy had said they were better at infiltrating targets than the FBI. "Let me guess," I said. "You're spying on Oceanus for the Sentinels of the Sea."

Jill nodded. "Walden said he had been visited by a private investigator. We compared notes. It didn't seem likely there would be two detectives with a name like yours and a gold earring. We figured it must be you. Right?"

"Very careless on my part. I just assumed there would be no connection between the people at Oceanus and Walden. But why are you telling me this? You could have watched me bumble along and gotten a big laugh at me doing my cloak-and-dagger imitation."

She studied my face for a moment. "Walden said he picked up some sympathetic vibes from you. That's just the way he is. He acts on intuition. He thought we might be able to work together. He said it was worth taking a chance even if we had to let you know we had somebody in here."

"Wait a minute, Jill. As you know, I've already got an employer. The corporation that owns this park you want to see closed. They want me to find out if Rocky really killed Eddy Byron."

"So that's *really* why you're here? We thought they put you in because they suspected SOS had somebody on the inside."

I shook my head. "That's *my* story. What's yours?"

"SOS wants to find out what's going on at Oceanus, too. It goes beyond Eddy's death, though."

"What do you mean?"

"We're not sure what it is yet, but I think I'm on the verge of something big, *really* big."

"Tell me about it."

"I can't," she said, frowning. "Not yet, anyway."

"Okay, Jill. You're dealing this hand. Walden obviously has something in mind. What is it?"

"We're amateurs at what we do," she said. "Sometimes it helps, but sometimes it doesn't. Walden thinks it would be better to have an extra set of eyes and ears in here. He just wants to share information, that's all."

"And if I don't go along?"

"Nothing, Soc. Things will stay the same. We won't say anything about you, and we hope you'll say nothing about us. We took a chance with you. There's nothing to prevent you from telling Oceanus about me. They'd fire me and pat you on the back, if that's what you want."

"No," I said. "It's not what I want." I pondered the proposition carefully. SOS and I had different agendas, but we both wanted to learn what was going on at Oceanus. And Jill was right, she could have blown my cover without hurting hers. It took a certain amount of trust and naïveté to come straight out with an offer.

"Okay," I said. "It's a deal." I grabbed her hand and pumped it.

"I just *knew* you'd do it." Jill pecked me on the cheek and picked up her camera. "I've got to go. Talk to you later."

She sprinted up the stairs and disappeared around a corner, leaving me alone with Rocky. He swam to the side of the pool and stuck his massive head out of the water. I walked over and pressed my nose up against the glass.

"Okay, big guy," I said. "You gonna tell me that you knew all along that I was a gumshoe, aren't you?" Rocky opened his mouth and grinned with his big white teeth. "Yeah," I muttered, "I thought so."

20

Sam cast a glance at the sunbaked tourists filling the bar without seeing them. "Maybe I should quit fishing," he said morosely.

We were sitting in a corner booth at the 'Hole. It was late afternoon, and except for Sam and me, there wasn't a local in the place. The pickup trucks had been vanquished from the parking lot by Volvo station wagons and mini-vans from Connecticut and New York. The bearded guys in work clothes who usually hung out at the 'Hole had been scared away by hordes of tanned kids with braces on their teeth. I was drinking from a cold mug of beer, thinking how the summer invaders seemed to get younger every year. Sam was having his usual ginger ale on the rocks. He leaned on the table, his long jaw cradled in his hands.

I slurped the foam off my beer. "C'mon, Sam, you're too young to retire."

"Didn't say I was retiring. I could do lotsa things shore-side. I could fix outboard motors. Maybe build dinghies. Or I could sell the *Millie D*, get something smaller, and take out fishing parties for charter."

"True, you could do all those things, Sam. But do you really want to bait hooks and open beers for some city guys so they can tell their buddies about the one that got away?"

"Dunno, Soc." He sighed. "It just gets real discouraging. Millie told me I shouldn't have bought the boat 'cause of the big mortgage payments. Said it was dumb to get into debt at my age, but I was stubborn and went ahead with the loan. We've been doing pretty good lately with the price of fish holding. Just when you think you're ahead, something happens like the engine going kerflooey."

"You've had engine trouble before, Sam. It goes with the territory."

"That's my point. Even if I get it fixed this time, something else'll go wrong on another trip." He sighed heavily. "Maybe it's just that mechanic, Fred. I can't get a straight answer from him. Every day he fools around we lose money. Heck, you know I never get mad at anybody, Soc. Live and let live is my motto. But if I have to listen to that fella's life story once more, I'll grab him by the scruff of the neck and toss him into the harbor."

I raised an eyebrow. Sam was the quintessential laconic Yankee. He rarely got riled about anything. I only saw him worked up once. The Coast Guard had radioed us to say the rescue squad was rushing Millie to the hospital for an emergency appendix operation. I thought he was going to jump off the boat and run home over the wave tops.

I took another sip of beer. "Is Fred working on the engine today?"

"He's down at the fish pier, I'd wager. Fella spends a lot of time there, but is he working on the boat? Lord only knows."

I didn't take Sam seriously about quitting, but I shared his frustration.

"Don't worry about it, Sam. I'll swing by the pier and see if I can get Fred moving. You go home and rest up while you've got the chance."

Sam brightened. "I'd really appreciate that, Soc. Do me good to say hello to Millie. Haven't seen her much in the last couple days."

He headed out. I had another beer then drove to the fish pier. Fred was leaning against a piling, chatting with a couple of young guys on the loading dock. They were busy stacking fish boxes. Fred followed them around, his jaw flapping like a jib sail in a stiff breeze.

I went over and said, "Hi, Fred, how's the work coming on Sam's boat?"

Fred detached himself from the fish packers, who rolled their eyes and escaped into the walk-in freezer. "Coming along fine, Soc. Real fine." He grinned cheerfully. "Just taking a break. Been working on her all day."

"Glad to hear that. So she must be about ready?"

Fred chuckled like someone who's just heard a kid utter something cute but dumb. "Didn't say that, Soc. Tomorrow's my day off. I think I can start putting her together again Monday, though, and we'll just have to see how things are going."

I could see how things were going. I gave him a grin that was as white and wide as his and equally as insincere. "Okay, Fred, I know you'll do your best."

"Sure thing. Say, did I ever tell you about—"

"I think you did, Fred. Got to go now. Catch you Monday."

I got in my pickup truck and drove back to the boathouse. I told Kojak he'd have to wait a couple of minutes for munchie-munch. Then I picked up the phone, called the boatyard Fred worked for, and asked for the boss. A guy who talked as if he had a cigar in his mouth came on and said his name was Dom. I told him who I was. I said we had to get back fishing and wondered if he could light a fire under his mechanic.

"Christ!" he exploded. "Give me a break, pal, I'm up to my eyeballs with customers who want work done yesterday. I sent you a mechanic, what the hell more do you want?"

"I'd like a mechanic who we don't have to pay for on-the-job training."

He must have heard the same complaint before because he was ready with a smart-ass answer. "Look, pal, this is the way it is. It's tough to get a mechanic who knows what he's doing and wants to do it, so we got drunks and assholes working for us. You want another mechanic, fine, I'll take Fred back and send you a drunk."

"I'm not getting through to you. Fred has decided to make our engine his life's work. He's stiffing us for overtime, and that's just plain thievery in my opinion."

"Hey, wait—"

"No, you wait. You won't have any more problems with help because you're not going to have any work when I get through telling the fishermen's association how you do business. And when they get through calling their buddies in every one of the fifteen towns on Cape Cod." The fishermen's association had fallen apart years ago, but Dom didn't know that. "Now you can tell me to go to hell, and hang up, but first ask yourself one question. Is Fred worth ruining the reputation of your boatyard?"

There was mumbling on the line. "Okay, okay. I'll come by and check it out myself. Monday early enough?"

"How about tomorrow?"

"Jesus! Tomorrow's Sunday."

"You'll just have to skip church."

"Shit. Aw, all right. I'll be there."

"We'll be looking for you."

I hung up and called Sam.

"Looks like you won't have an excuse to quit fishing," I said. "I talked to Fred's boss. He's going to come by tomorrow morning to look at the engine."

"Hmmph," Sam said. "How'd you do that?"

"I used a little sweet talk. I'll be busy tomorrow. Can you be at the fish pier to make sure he doesn't leave without getting the job done?"

"No problem, Soc, and thanks. Hope you don't think I was serious about quitting. I've got a long way to go before I retire, but I tell you, it's times like this, especially when my back is acting up, that I think maybe it's getting nearer."

"Hang in there, Sam. I'll talk to you tomorrow."

I didn't mean to be abrupt, but Kojak was rubbing into my leg, purring like an outboard motor, putting his whole weight into the calf. I did a waltz step trying to evade him and trotted over to the kitchen cupboard. All that was left was a can of 9-Lives Tender Veal and Cheese dinner. It wasn't his favorite flavor, but it would have to do. I made a mental note to pick up some cat food.

I was spooning the last of the stuff into Kojak's dish when the phone rang. I rinsed my fingers off, picked up the phone, and said hello. It was Parmenter.

"Glad to find you at home," he said. "I tried to get you earlier today."

"I was out taking care of business."

"Yeah, I know all about your business. I called the 'Hole and the bartender said you left a little while ago."

"Damn snoopy cops. I should know better than to fake it with an old flatfoot. How are you, John?"

"I'm fine. You asked me to keep you posted on the Hanley thing, so I thought I'd bring you up to date. I talked to a couple of insiders on the investigation. They say Pacheco has hit a stone wall. No murder weapon yet. They checked out your gun registration. Hell, Soc, you still got your thirty-eight Police Special."

"It makes a nice paperweight, John. Hanley was shot with a twenty-two, so that rules me out."

"Not entirely. Pacheco says you could have an illegal pistol that's not licensed. He's talking search warrant."

I glanced around at the chaos in the boathouse. Magazines and papers and old clothes thrown over the secondhand furniture, cat fur everywhere, Kojak wolfing down his dinner. Pacheco wouldn't be able to find a howitzer in this mess.

"It's a little late for a search warrant, isn't it?" I said. "I could have mailed the twenty-two to the moon by now. Pacheco could plant a throw-down while he was nosing around, but the bullet wouldn't match the one that killed Hanley unless he finds the real thing. Is he still plugging for a malfeasance hearing to take my PI license away?"

"He's just going through the motions. I wouldn't worry about it. I've got a few buddies in the Department of Public Safety and I've filled them in on Pacheco's wild ways."

"You didn't have to do that, John. He could make it difficult for you."

"Hell, Soc, he can't touch me. I'm near retirement anyhow. But that's not the reason I called. I've got a tip. A couple of Pacheco's guys interviewed Hanley's wife. One is a young cop whose father I know from the staties. Pretty sharp kid. Mrs. Hanley has an alibi, but you never know in a case like this. Maybe she had somebody else knock her husband off, so this cop asked about their marital problems."

"Did she say what caused them?"

"Yeah. Hanley was a drunk. He had gotten off the booze, gone to AA, and was doing pretty good, I guess. Even a chance the marriage would mend, his wife says. My cop friend said she was pretty open about her marriage troubles, but whenever he asked her about Oceanus, she clammed up, said she didn't know much about her husband's business."

"That doesn't sound likely."

"Uh-huh. Especially with people whose marriage is on the rocks. They don't talk to each other about the important things, like why their marriage is going down the tubes, but they've got to fill in the silence, so they gab about what a bitch of a day they've had at work or home, because it's easier. I know the drill, I've been there myself."

"Hanley was going to spill something he hoped would get him his job back. Maybe that's what she knows. If it got him killed, she might be in danger, too."

"I was thinking the same thing, Soc. Maybe you should talk to her."

"I'll get on it as soon as I can, John. Thanks for the tip. I owe you on this, too."

"You don't owe me a thing. Remember, I was almost your father-in-law. Scary, when you think about it."

"I couldn't think of anyone I'd rather have." I was looking at the picture on the fireplace mantel of a sable-haired woman. Jennie Parmenter. I had my arm around her in the photo and we were both smiling happily at the camera.

"Thanks for that, Soc, I appreciate it. Okay, back to business. This works both ways. If you learn anything, let me know. I'll be on the Cape another week until this drug case is wrapped up, so give me a call anytime at the barracks."

"I'll keep in touch."

I put the phone down and went out onto the deck. I looked out over the bay and whispered Jennie's name, savoring the sound. I had often pondered what life would have been like if Jennie hadn't been killed in a car crash. Marriage definitely. Kids probably. I would have stayed on the Boston PD and retired fat and cynical to bore my grandchildren with cop stories. Jennie would have just become more beautiful as she got older; I was sure of that. I took a deep breath of the cool air, feeling its fullness in my lungs, as if the thought of death made it necessary for me to reaffirm my own existence. Waste not fresh tears over old griefs, Euripides had said. He was right, of course, but I knew the sadness and the great emptiness would always be there.

The last of the sailboats in the bay were heading home and the barrier beach was a strip of gold satin in the rays of the setting sun. Beyond the beach was the Atlantic Ocean, the great mysterious ocean, but surely no more mysterious than the ways of the gods.

I put my thoughts of the past aside and went back in the house. Stretching out on the green flowered sofa, I began to list what I knew about this case since square one, when Shaughnessy called, but dozed off after a few minutes. I might have slept through the night if I hadn't been awakened by a suffocating weight and the cheesy fragrance of cat breath. I shoved Kojak off my chest and sat up. It was dark outside. The wall clock said ten o'clock.

I decided to get ready for my dive the next day with Uncle Constantine. Damn. Jill's revelations had distracted me. I forgot to take my scuba gear with me when I left Oceanus. I could always pick it up in the morning, but Uncle Constantine wanted me on his boat at dawn. If I left now, I could be home and in bed by eleven. I went into the bathroom, splashed cold water in my face, and wearily headed out the door to Oceanus.

An old Buick station wagon I assumed belonged to Ben was the only car in the parking lot. I went in the backdoor and walked by his office. The television set was on. I could hear the laugh track for a TV sitcom. I knocked gently. There was no response. I opened the door. Ben was sacked out on his cot. I left him undisturbed and walked to the storage area.

My gear was in a blue plastic duffel bag with my name stenciled on the outside. I found the bag where I had left it under the rack of wet suits. Acting on impulse, I left the storage room and headed toward the orca stadium. The gate was unlocked. Rocky had company again. Instead of going down the passageway nearest the gate, I walked around behind the bleachers to the other entryway. Moving quietly, taking my time, trailing my left hand along the wall so I wouldn't lose my way in the gloom, I stopped every few seconds to listen. All was quiet.

I slipped into a passageway. My eyes were becoming accustomed to the darkness. I stopped once more where the passageway opened onto the bleacher section and looked down at the orca pool. The underwater lights were on and the pool glowed a creamy chartreuse. I stood hidden in the darkness at the top of the bleachers and let my eye travel down along the outside aisle until it came to the dark figure of a man.

Taking a deep breath, I moved down the aisle to introduce myself.

21

My sneaker found a Styrofoam cup the maintenance crew must have missed. The crackle of plastic underfoot had the impact of a shotgun blast in the hushed stadium.

The prowler whirled at the sound, put his head down, and charged.

Umph! It was a lousy match. He was taller and heavier and I bounced off him like a pop fly hitting the wall they call the green monster at Fenway Park. I flew backward, twisting my body in midflight. My right shoulder crunched against the rubber mat covering the aisle. The impact knocked the wind out of me and loosened every filling in my head. I lay on my side like the Dying Gaul and gasped for air.

The guy's leg brushed my chest. I reached out and grabbed a thick calf. His forward momentum dragged me a couple of feet. I held on, grimly, with both hands. He went down like a falling redwood tree, crashing onto the mat with a loud grunt of pain.

I rolled over, got my legs under me, and sprang after him, ready to get an arm around his neck and sink a knee into his spine. But he twisted onto his back and kicked out. The full force of his leg power would have slammed into my rib cage and launched me down the aisle like a bowling ball, but he reacted too soon. His feet caught me lightly on the chest. I sidestepped and went for him again, trying to grab his head to smash it against the floor.

Fingers came out of the darkness and clamped onto my cheek, searching for my eyes. I jerked my head back and smashed the hand away with a karate chop. The motion threw me off balance. A fist battered into my shoulder and I tumbled backward.

He could have finished the job and enrolled me in dance class at the Elysian fields, but he disengaged. He was up and running. I tried to do the same, but my foot slipped on something in the aisle and I fell. I reached down and felt the cold metal of a flashlight. It wasn't mine, so it must be his. I scrambled to my feet and dashed after him, trying to ignore the pain stabbing at my shoulder.

At the top of the aisle leading into the passageway I paused and clicked on the flash. The cone of light caught an elbow and a heel disappearing around a corner. He was moving behind the bleacher section. If he got to the gate before me, it could be a repeat of the other night. He could lock me in again and get away. I sprinted through the passageway, rounded the same corner, and played the flashlight beam toward the gate.

Captured in the yellow bull's-eye was a man wearing a black shirt and slacks and a black baseball cap. He was big, over six feet, with a top-heavy torso, football-pad shoulders, and short legs. The flame of recognition flickered in my brain.

"Flagg!" I shouted reflexively.

The man stopped and turned to look directly at me, his dusky face frozen in astonishment. Then his mouth widened in a wide and white-toothed grin.

"Shit," his deep voice said. "That you, Soc?"

"Naw, Flagg, it's your grandmother."

He let out a whooping laugh. We approached each other and shook hands.

I was stunned. "For Chrissake, Flagg, what the hell are *you* doing here?"

"I was wondering the same thing about you. Douse that light. I don't want the world to know we're having a reunion."

I snapped the flash off and we stood in the darkness, both still panting from the chase. "I should have known it was you in that ninja suit from the way you took me out. You okay?"

"Knees got scraped and hurt like hell. But I'll live. How about you?"

"Every bone in my shoulder is broken and it's only sheer luck you didn't pop my eyes out."

"Naw, Soc. It wasn't luck. You knew what you were doing. Except you shouldn't sneak up on a guy in the dark like that. Can't tell what he's packing."

"Knowing you, Flagg, you're probably carrying an arsenal. I work here, what's your excuse?"

"I guess you could say I'm working here, too, ex officia." He chuckled. "Hell, man. Fishing and detecting businesses must have gone to hell for you to have a real job."

"I can explain the whole thing. Let's get out of here. I know a bar in Hyannis where we can talk."

We went through the gate and I secured the padlock.

"By the way," I said as we headed for the exit, "how'd you get in?"

"I got passkeys, you've got a night watchman who likes to drink. It wasn't hard."

"I didn't see a car."

"You weren't supposed to. It's parked up the road. I walked here. You can give me a ride back."

Remembering why I had come by the park, I said, "Okay, I've got to pick up my scuba gear first. Meet you out by my pickup."

He kept on going while I went to Ben's office and listened at the door. The TV set was still on, but there was a new sound, like the noise of a tractor trailer climbing a mountain road. Ben's snoring. I went to the storeroom, got my diving gear, and hauled it out the employee door to the truck. Flagg was leaning against a fender. He got in the pickup and I dropped him off a couple of hundred yards from Oceanus where he had pulled his car onto a side street. Then I drove to a country-and-western bar in Hyannis with Flagg following.

John Flagg and I met a million years and miles ago, or so it seemed. I was in the marines and Flagg was an ex-paratrooper in Operation Phoenix, a hard-assed unit whose job was to destroy the Viet Cong infrastructure. Flagg was a Wampanoag Indian from Gay Head, a tiny town on the island of Martha's Vineyard off Cape Cod. He had become a hired gun for the same white man's government that had stripped the dignity and identity from Native Americans, and the fact troubled him. I was the eldest son of successful Greek-Americans with a strong sense of their ancient culture. I had every chance in life, but I blew it off, leaving the tightly knit community and deserting the family business to save the world. Despite our different backgrounds, Flagg and I shared a common rootlessness and a vague guilt neither one of us was happy with.

We first met at the NCO club in Quang Tri province. I saved his butt from a drunken marine who wanted to carve him up with a switchblade, and Flagg and I became good friends. Our dreams of fishing for striped bass back in the real world ended when my unit turned some captured VC over to Phoenix. Flagg's guys threw the POWs out of a helicopter when they wouldn't talk. I blamed Flagg and didn't learn until years later, after I cast my hatred aside, that I had tagged him with a bum rap. The last I knew, Flagg was working for a troubleshooting CIA subsidiary that had more letters in its name than a can of alphabet soup.

Flagg and I found a table away from the bar crowd. I ordered a Bud. Flagg, who doesn't drink booze, asked for a Perrier. The waitress looked at him. "We don't have that foreign stuff. You get Poland Spring." She whisked off, a champion for Made in the USA.

He warned me with a flat-eyed glare against wisecracks about his upscale taste.

"Was that you I chased out of the orca stadium the other night?" I said.

"Yep. I saw you by the whale tank and beat-feet when you started up the aisle. Looks like you got smart this time. Came around from behind. Too bad you made all that noise, you might have surprised me."

"I stepped on a plastic cup. What the hell were you doing there?"

"Just listening to the wind."

"Flagg, it's great that you've gone back to your Wampanoag roots, and it wouldn't bother me at all if you went around wearing a headdress full of eagle feathers, but I wish you'd stop with your noble redman metaphors."

"Guess we all look alike to a white man. Feather headdress is for Plains Indians, not Wampanoag," he said with mock seriousness. "It's like I told you before, Soc, you can crash through the woods and scare everything, or you can sniff the wind, listen and watch, and maybe something will come to you."

Speaking of which, the waitress came with our drinks. I chugalugged half my beer and ordered another before she left the table. Flagg sipped at his mineral water.

"Forgive my Caucasian obtuseness," I said. "But you must admit it's odd when someone who works for a spook agency so obscure most people in the Company don't even know about it spends his nights baby-sitting for a killer whale. What did you expect to hear on the wind at Oceanus?"

He seemed to drift off into a trance, his broad face went stony, and his voice came as if from a distance. "That whale, he talks if you listen to him."

It was funny to hear Flagg say that. I had done the same thing, watched Rocky and listened. Deep down, I guess, I yearned to know what went on in his brain, not just about Eddy Byron.

Rocky was born in the ocean, knew its rhythms and moods because he was part of them. Migod, what sights those great round eyes must have seen before he was captured! He knew his blue world, not like I did, skimming the surface in a boat or timidly making ridiculously shallow dives, but to its depths. He could tell us about his wonderful stories of the deep, if only we knew how to hear him.

"I think I know what you mean about the whale, Flagg. But why would you be interested in anything he had to say?"

The distant look faded and he refocused his gaze on me. "Navy business. Now it's my turn to ask questions. You putting in overtime at Oceanus?"

"I'm working for the park's owners. They hired me to go undercover, to look into the death of Eddy Byron, the whale trainer. Seems his demise is stirring up a hell of a mess that could hurt a big real-estate deal, and they want the whole thing settled. Your turn again."

"Huh," Flagg said. "Well, now." A glint of amusement flickered in his onyx eyes. "Remember back in 'Nam we used to say we should have gone navy, stayed on a ship with showers and dry bunks just lobbing shells at shore installations that couldn't shoot back."

I chuckled ruefully. "Sure, Flagg. It beat slogging through rice paddies any day. What's that got to do with Oceanus?"

"The navy was even smarter than we thought. Wasn't just us ignorant grunts doing all the dirty work. The navy figured out how to use dolphins and whales for military missions."

The military connection again. Sally Carlin said Eddy Byron had been in Vietnam.

"Go on," I said. "This is real interesting."

Flagg nodded. "Back in the 1960s, the Department of Defense started looking at dolphins and whales. It began with low-key stuff, like training them to pick tools up or torpedoes off the seabed. Then they got them got them to push divers along so they wouldn't have to use up so much energy. Training system they used was called 'operant conditioning.' I'll explain it to you if you want me to."

"You don't have to, Flagg. It's a system of reward and punishment. Give the animals a fish when they do a trick, punish them when they don't."

Flagg reacted as if he had just seen a goldfish swimming in his Poland Spring water. He put his glass on the table and squinted at me. "If you want, I'll let you tell *me* what *I'm* doing."

"Don't be touchy, Flagg. You know me, I'll scavenge a fact here and there, but I don't know the big picture. It's still your deal."

He stared at me with hooded eyes, then nodded. "Okay, I'll lay it out for you. The military said, hell, if we can train a dolphin to carry a lost tool, maybe we could get them to put a magnetic mine on an enemy ship. So they trained the animals to attach a limpet bomb under an enemy ship and swim away. Friendly ship had a metal plate welded to the hull so the fish could ID it. That got the navy thinking about defending their own ships. They figured a dolphin would make a good underwater guard. Vietnam came along and they had the chance to field-test their theories. They used dolphins as guards in Cam Rahn Bay."

"Dolphins are pretty friendly guys. How did the navy manage to turn them into underwater Dobermans?"

"Simple. The animal would push the enemy frogman to the surface where a patrol picked him up. Worked okay, I guess, because they used dolphins in 1987 in the Persian Gulf to guard a command barge during the Iran-Iraq War. Then the navy decided it wasn't enough to herd an enemy frogman. They started to arm their dolphin guards and gave them instructions to shoot to kill."

"That's ridiculous, Flagg. I can see how the dolphin might push a diver around. It's part of their natural instinct. But how they hell are you going to teach them to kill somebody? They like people, although it beats me why when we do stuff like this to them."

"Dolphin didn't *know* it was killing anybody, Soc. Navy stuck a cone with a forty-five in it on the dolphin's nose and taught it to ram enemy frogmen. Thing had a trigger attachment. Dolphin bumps a frogman and *bang*, guy's been perforated. Navy wanted them to guard a Trident nuclear-sub base up in Bangor, Washington. They were going to use sea lions for the same thing. Project was called the 'swimmer nullification program.'"

I shook my head. The military must have whole battalions of guys thinking up these euphemisms to sugarcoat its functions, which were mainly killing people and blowing things up.

Something occurred to me. A killer whale was essentially a big dolphin. Could an orca be programmed to kill?

Intrigued, I said, "Was the program a success?"

"Naw. Those crazy dolphins were lousy guards. Like you said, they like people. The navy tried to train them to ram a target trainer, but they'd just swim away or put their snout on the guy's shoulder. Then up at the Trident base some of the dolphins died. They were from the Gulf of Mexico and couldn't take the cold water. Guess nobody figured that. Some of the animal-rights groups raised hell. A judge said the navy had to do a study to see if the dolphins would be harmed by bringing them to the base, and the project went down the drain."

"So was that the end of the dolphin draft?"

"Nope. The navy's still serious about it. The Naval Ocean Systems Center in San Diego spends fifteen to twenty million bucks a year, which is small change, but still not bad. They had over a hundred dolphins in San Diego and Key West. Dolphins get shipped to San Diego for boot camp, then go to other bases for specialized training."

I shook my head. "You have to admit it's a cute trick, getting someone who'll work for a few fish."

"Shit, Soc, it gets even cuter. Remember what I said about the gun-toting dolphins? Some genius came up with another idea. The dolphin carries a long hollow hypodermic needle on its snout to inject CO_2 into the enemy frogman."

"That's not nice," I said. "You stick a diver with pressurized gas and his guts will get forced out of every hole in his body."

Flagg stared at me and smiled.

"Okay, Flagg, where do you fit in?"

"Some people don't like what the navy's been doing. Aside from the moral part, using dolphins for war, they say trainers have kicked and beaten animals, that a lot escape every year wearing muzzles on their snouts. Animals can't eat and they starve to death."

"Is any of that true?"

"Navy says the animals get mistreated sometimes, and about a fifth of them escape with muzzles on them. Everything else they deny, or won't comment on. San Diego's pretty tight-lipped about what it does, probably because the whole subject is so controversial. Back a while ago in Boston there was a big flap when the aquarium wanted to trade an ornery dolphin to the navy for one that'd be easier to train. The aquarium backed down after protesters picketed the place and threatened a lawsuit."

"You still haven't told me where you fit in."

"Getting to that, Soc. Like you said, Byron's death stirred up a hell of a mess. That Boston deal, even the flap in Puget Sound, was just a little thing compared to this."

"What's Eddy Byron's death got to do with the navy?"

"It's got the whale huggers all raising hell. You know what the goody-goodies say when some punk kid wastes a cop who just wanted to talk to him. Wasn't the kid's fault. He's just a product of his environment. That's what they're saying about that whale. Keeping him in that tank just made him mean. I don't blame him. They make me do tricks for the kiddies all day, I'd get some pissed, too. Anyhow, the whale people have been beating up on Congress. They want laws that'll free every marine mammal in captivity, even the ones the navy's using."

Walden Schiller had told me the same thing. "Do you really think there's any chance of that?"

"I don't, but the navy's nervous. They might have to let on what they're doing. The taxpayers might get mad if they find out their dough's been spent to tie a bomb onto Flipper's head and send him off on a kamikaze mission. Navy gets nervous, my bosses get nervous, so they say, you're from around Cape Cod, go on down to Oceanus, poke into it, and see what's happening. The park is closed, and I don't want to make a big fuss by showing my badge. Park's security perimeter looks pretty weak, so I do a little reconnaissance and get caught at it. Two times. I must be slipping. Glad it was you, Soc. Learn anything yet?"

"Not much. I'll tell you what I know. I may need your help later on."

"You got it whether you talk now or not, but I guess you know that."

"Yeah, Flagg, I know. And thanks. Here's what I got."

I started from the beginning, telling Flagg how I was hired by Bay State to look into Eddy Byron's death because the furor was jeopardizing the sale to the Japanese. I told him about Hanley's death, my interview with Austin, what Sally Carlin had said about Byron's Vietnam background and his training methods, and filled him in on my talks with Jill, Arnold, and Doc Livingston.

Flagg let me ramble on without interrupting. When I was through, he sat there silently, thinking. Finally he spoke.

"So the way you see it, Byron did something to the whale that got him killed."

"It's looking that way, but I'm not sure. Something about Oceanus smells worse than an old sneaker."

"I think so, too. But I've done all the creeping around in the night that I can get away with. Only thing I can do now is check out the background of everybody involved."

"I talked to someone else you might be interested in. His name is Walden Schiller."

Flagg cocked an eyebrow. "Head guy for the Sentinels. You're a jump ahead of me, Soc. That was the other part of this job, check him out. What did you think of him?"

"Intelligent. Uncompromising. Fanatical."

"You think he'd ever do anything violent?"

"He said he would do anything in his power to accomplish his aims."

"That makes me feel real good, Soc. Knowing that guy's got a few pounds of Semtex."

I stared at him for a second. "Semtex? What the hell are you talking about?" Semtex was a plastic explosive loved by terrorists because it's tough to detect and can be molded into any shape. A couple of pounds of Semtex brought down Pan Am flight 103 and killed two hundred and seventy people.

"The Czechs exported tons of the stuff," Flagg replied. "SOS got its hands on some. Don't ask me how, 'cause it's too embarrassing to the feds. Now Uncle Sam is afraid SOS will use it."

I remembered the way Walden Schiller's eyes turned to ice when he talked about his cause. "That's not good, Flagg, not good at all."

"I agree. We're doing the best we can on it, working with the FBI. Got any suggestions?"

"I'll just keep digging around. I'll let you know if anything turns up."

"You do that." He wrote something on a slip of paper. "Here's my number if you want to reach me."

We shook hands and he left. I watched him shoulder his way easily through the crowd and thought how strange and nice it was to run into Flagg. Sometimes his born-again Native Americanism annoyed me, but I knew he was trying to carve a cultural identity out of the shambles that years of white man's indifference and misguided paternalism had left of the Wampanoags' heritage. It was that same ancestry, I suspected, that gave Flagg his uncanny intuition, a sensitivity that picked up vibes far above or below the normal range of human understanding. If he hadn't exercised those talents the last time we worked together, on a hunt for a missing undersea robot, I might not be sitting in the bar enjoying the pleasures of country-and-western music.

The jukebox was playing a Johnny Paycheck song, "Take

This Job and Shove It." I ordered another beer. Flagg was right about Rocky. If I listened real well, he'd have something to tell me. The question was, would I understand him when he did?

I drank my beer and headed out the door. It would have been tempting to lose myself in a quiet little binge, but I had promised Uncle Constantine I'd dive with him the next morning. From what I had seen of my uncle so far, I had the feeling I would need all the strength I could muster.

22

A sea gull eyed me sleepily from a piling at the Lewis Bay Marina. The bird's shiny yellow beak was pointed into the light southwest breeze that fluffed in off the water. I got out of the pickup and walked over to Uncle Constantine's dock. Without a couple of well-oiled beauties like Kara and Maureen on board to distract my eye, the *Artemis* looked in rough shape.

She was a graceful vessel about forty feet long, with an upswept bow and a square stern, and in her day she must have been the pride of the Tarpon Springs sponge-fishing fleet. Her newly painted white hull and red-and-blue trim gleamed in the morning sunlight. The paint gave her a colorful jauntiness, and it covered the dings and knicks in the wood, but it couldn't hide them. The nails holding the hull planking together were already bleeding rust streaks.

On the plus side, she was the perfect work boat, broad in the beam, with a wide deck forward of a small pilothouse. I hoisted the duffel bag holding my dive gear onto the deck and climbed on board. From below came the strains of bouzouki music. I yelled out my uncle's name.

"Aristotle," he shouted, "come, come."

I went down into the galley. Uncle Constantine sat at a dinette table digging into chunks of hard-crusted bread soaked in a bowl of hot chocolate. He turned down the volume on a portable tape player and brandished a dripping tablespoon mounded with soggy bread.

"Aristotle, you want to eat? Good stuff."

"Thanks, Uncle, it's too early for breakfast. Coffee's okay." Cocoa and bread isn't a bad meal if you're in a hurry, but Uncle Constantine has an incredible sweet tooth and I knew he'd lard the mixture with sugar. He shrugged as if I'd just passed up an invitation to dine at the Ritz and took a long-handled brass coffeepot with an hourglass shape from the stove. He poured the thick coffee into a demitasse cup and set it before me. I took a sip. The strong syrupy concoction was a nice change from Stop & Shop economy instant.

Uncle Constantine spooned the last of his breakfast from the bowl, wiped his mustache neatly with a paper towel, and patted his stomach.

"So, Aristotle," he said grandly, "you ready to make a million dollars?" He was smiling like a kid with a pass to the circus.

"Anytime you say the word, uncle."

He thumped his fist lightly on the table and his eyes lit up like lanterns. "Good. We go *now*, Aristotle."

Uncle Constantine scrambled up the companionway to the deck and went into the pilothouse, with me following. He deluged the old diesel engine with a stream of curses and pleas in Greek and English and it started in a cloud of purple exhaust fumes and noisy exhortations that sent a score of gulls into the sky. Uncle Constantine made last-minute checks while the engine warmed up. Then we cast off the dock lines and he pointed the boat's high-curved bow into Lewis Bay like an ancient trireme leaving an Aegean port.

The *Artemis* passed a miniature white-and-black light-house, plowing ahead as steadily as a good-natured draft horse, the chug-chug of the engine echoing off the shorefront houses. Within minutes she broke out of Lewis Bay into Hyannis Harbor. The long stone breakwater that extends into the harbor from Hyannisport was off to star-board. Behind the stone jetty, the golden light of morning glistened off the white-painted houses of the Kennedy com-pound, known as Camelot North before that awful day in Dallas. We passed Point Gammond on our portside and headed southeast into Nantucket Sound.

Fair Athene of the flashing eyes was keeping watch, be-cause Nantucket Sound was as calm as a bathtub and the water that hissed past our hull was Bahama green. Mistaking the *Artemis* for a fishing boat, gray-winged gulls hovered and dipped in our foamy wake. The air was a wonderful combina-tion of salt, fish, and kelp. I drank it in like an addict, filling my lungs with each intoxicating breath until I got dizzy.

Pushing aside an adjustable wrench and a box of greasy engine parts, Uncle Constantine unrolled the NOAA marine chart of Nantucket Sound. He brushed away the ashes falling off the tip of the cigarette in his mouth and traced our course with a gnarled forefinger. Our heading would take the *Arte-mis* southerly, then east into Nantucket Sound after we passed the Bishops and Clerks gong buoy. Maybe ten miles in all. Our destination was between Cape Cod's flexed arm and Nantucket. The sound is comparatively shallow. There are shoal areas less than a dozen feet deep right in the middle of it. We'd be diving in water between forty-five and fifty feet.

Uncle Constantine asked me to take the helm. He went below and returned a few minutes later with a tray holding two coffee cups and a plate of baklava. I bit into a diamond-shaped pastry, savoring the taste of honey and walnuts sandwiched between paper-thin layers of filo dough, and chased it down with coffee. It was a match made in heaven. I offered the plate to my uncle. He nibbled at the pastry and grinned.

"Not good to eat too much before a dive. You get the bends."

Uncle Constantine was repeating the warning he'd probably heard when he was a young sponge diver back in Greece. He knew from personal experience eating had nothing to do with the bends. The body-twisting cramps hit a diver who surfaces too quickly because the nitrogen trapped in the blood from breathing air under pressure is suddenly released. Bubbles froth around the joints like champagne, and the agonizing pain can transform a diver's body into a human pretzel. Sometimes it kills. Uncle Constantine had been lucky. The bends only left him with a limp.

"How's the Tarpon Springs sponge fleet doing?" I asked.

Uncle Constantine lit up another Lucky and took a puff. "Very good, Aristotle. Thirty boats go out. We get many sponges, best in years. Market is good, too. Sponges go all over the world. We sell most in Europe now."

"How badly do the synthetic sponges hurt your market?"

Uncle Constantine pretended he was spitting. Then he made believe he was scrubbing his back. "Plastic sponges okay to clean dishes, but not for skin."

"Have you been sponging with the *Artemis?*"

My uncle knew I was fishing for information. "Aristotle, you want to know if your uncle Constantine can still dive. You think I am oldest diver in Tarpon Springs? George Stampas is three months older than me."

I let it drop, but I was still worried.

I walked out onto the deck to inspect my uncle's diving suit. It was lying neatly folded with the bulbous helmet on top of it. I squatted and felt the soft canvas fabric. There wasn't a patch on it.

I went back in the pilothouse. "That's a nice suit," I said. "Looks new."

"Only the best, Aristotle. Two-layer nylon canvas, gum rubber in between. They make them in Japan." He tapped his head. "But we still make the helmet in Tarpon Springs."

Absentmindedly playing with his blue worry beads, Uncle Constantine squinted against the sun, his eyes reflecting the sparkle from the water, his leathery face wreathed in a smile as if he were looking into the face of an angel. I thought how very fond I was of him. And how sad it was that he was getting old and would die. I had distanced myself physically and psychologically from the warm and sometimes suffocating embrace of my family, choosing the life of a loner, always ready to pull up the drawbridge. It was a decision they lived with, but could never understand. I didn't understand it myself, but I regretted it more than they would ever know.

My father is a kindhearted, hardworking guy, but as a kid, I never saw him because he always labored incredibly long hours. A shrink would say I fixated on Uncle Constantine as sort of a substitute father figure, and it might be true. He was so different from all my family. He had a wildness about him and a love of the sea that struck a chord in my own psyche. Without too much trouble, I could picture him standing in the prow of an ancient black ship as it coursed through the misty isles, ready to dare the gods of Olympus. I laughed inwardly, and despite my misgivings about this salvage project, I was glad to be there beside him, flying on the wings of *Artemis*, goddess of the hunt, in search of grand adventure.

"Uncle Constantine," I said, "do you remember the story you told me years ago, about the giant octopus that attacked you?"

"Sure I remember, Aristotle."

"I've always wondered, was he really as big as a house?"

He thought about it, then held his hands about a foot apart. "Maybe as big as a *bird*house. But don't worry. I catch him long time ago and your aunt Thalia cook him for dinner."

I put my arm around his shoulders and gave him a hug, then got my own dive gear ready. I laid out the neoprene wet suit, hood, booties, fins, mask, sheath knife, and weight belt. Next to them I set my buoyancy compensator. I had brought along a spare tank as well. I checked the air pressure and the regulator action. Everything seemed in good shape.

Uncle Constantine rapped on the pilothouse window to get my attention. I went inside and he asked me to take the helm. He put on a pair of reading glasses and consulted the numbers scrawled in a battered brown notebook. Then he began to give me directions. Right, left, ahead, back, over there, stop, go again. While I maneuvered the boat around Nantucket Sound like a drunken sailor, he read his notes, checked his watch and compass, grimaced at the sea, peered at his chart, and kept his eye on the loran receiver. Loran is shorthand for long-range navigation, a system that collects and displays the signals sent out by land stations. You check the readings against the coordinates on the chart and can know your position within a few hundred feet.

My uncle made a circle on his chart to mark our location. It was next to the *X* he had penciled in earlier. He took the wheel and handed me a pair of scarred binoculars, pointing off our starboard bow.

"I run the boat, Aristotle. My eyes not so good now. Look to southeast maybe quarter mile for the orange marker."

I scanned the water as Uncle Constantine moved the boat on a long shallow arc. At first there was nothing to see except the low blue-green waves. Then I caught a glimpse of Day-Glo orange.

I pointed in the buoy's direction.

"Over there, Uncle." He gunned the engine and we moved closer. Within minutes we came up on an inflated plastic sphere the size of a basketball. Uncle Constantine put the engine on idle and I took the wheel. He tossed over two anchors to hold us, then killed the engine. According to the fathometer, depth was forty-seven feet. Without wasting a second, Uncle Constantine went below to start the air compressor, then came out on the deck to unfold his dive suit. I offered to make a quick reconnaissance dive to make sure we had the right target, but he would have none of it.

"This is *my* wreck, I go first, you dive later." He slapped my back. "I teach you how to be good tender."

Keeping his clothes on, Uncle Constantine sat down on the dressing bench and stretched his legs out. He shoved his stockinged feet into the diving suit and stood erect. I grabbed the suit by the shoulders and pulled it up. He sat again, and from a bucket of soapy water, lubricated his wrists and worked his hands through the tight rubber sleeve cuffs. I fastened the back of the suit. Next came the breastplate, a copper collar eased past his ears and nose and attached by wing nuts to the suit. Then I helped him on with his lead-soled shoes, lacing them around the ankles with leather thongs.

"My God, Uncle, how much weight are you going to be carrying?"

"Not too much. Twelve pounds in shoes, eighteen pounds in suit, collar is twenty-two pounds, helmet thirty-eight pounds, and seventy-pound weights on feet." He figured using his fingers. "Maybe one hundred seventy-two pounds. Not bad for an old grandpa, eh, Aristotle."

"Not bad for *anyone*, Uncle. Do any divers in Tarpon Springs use scuba? It's a lot lighter."

He laughed and lit up a cigarette. "Only crazy man. Hard-hat sponger can work two or three hours in the water. How long you stay under, Aristotle?"

"Twenty-five minutes. I see what you mean. Still, does anyone else in Tarpon Springs use a rig like yours?"

"Sure, maybe one or two. Most use mask and wet suit, like you have, with hose and compressor. I don't like. Too dangerous."

"More dangerous than the hard-hat rig?"

"Sure, Aristotle. What happens when your tank is empty? You going to run to store to buy more air? I stay down as long as compressor works. Compressor feeds into a tank, so if it stops, I still have reserve. I have trouble, suit gives me buoyancy. I fall asleep, can't use exhaust valve, suit fills with air and up I come." He mussed my hair. "Too much talk, Aristotle. Help me finish."

He wrapped a short piece of line tightly around his waist as a belt, then hung a small weight off his chest from a loop of rope just below the collar of the breastplate. The weight would help him walk with a forward pitch. He tied a nylon line from a long coil around his chest, explaining that it was a safety line and his means of signaling me on the surface. He would jerk the line three times if he wanted to take in slack. Four times to stand by for him to come up, five if he found the tin ship. Any more jerks meant he was having problems. The biggest danger was getting the airline tangled. He warned me sternly to keep an eye on it.

He stood for a few seconds and wriggled to make sure the suit was neither too tight nor too loose. He took a final puff on his cigarette, flicked it over the side, then sat down and gestured toward the helmet. I set it on his head and gave it a clockwise turn. Air poured through the hose in his helmet and into the suit, blowing it up until he looked like the Michelin man. With the height added by the diving shoes and the wide shoulders of the suit, he cut an imposing figure, more like a many-eyed monster from the deep than a seventy-plus-year-old man who refused to recognize his own mortality.

He tested the chin valve to make sure it was working, curled his finger and thumb in an okay sign, and pointed to a small steel staging hanging over the side. I would have collapsed under all the cumbersome weight he carried, but Uncle Constantine put one leaded foot in front of the other. With me holding an arm, he scuffled slowly to the ladder, got his legs onto the staging, and clutched the rail to steady himself. I played out some slack in the hose. He winked at me through a circular porthole. A second later he stepped down to the water level, leaned forward, and jumped in feetfirst.

His suit had filled with air and he only sank an instant before he bobbed up again to float at armpit level in the low waves. I towed him by the lifeline as close to the Day-Glo buoy as I could. He hit the exhaust valve to release air from his suit and sank into the sea. He waved from just below the surface, then faded into the ocean in a circle of bubbles.

For the next few minutes I tended the safety line and watched coil after coil of air hose slither into the water like a reddish-brown python. Then it stopped. He was on the bottom, probably getting his bearings. The line tugged again. He was walking. He went another twenty feet, stopped, then headed off to the right, his progress marked by widening circles of bubbles.

Holding the line between my thumb and forefinger, as if I were jigging for flounder, I pulled at it lightly so as to take in slack without dragging him back.

Time passed. I listened to the low throb of the compressor, the cry of seabirds, the slurp of waves against the hull. The sun's warmth made me sleepy.

A sharp tug on the safety line jerked me out of my lethargy. Uncle Constantine knew about tenders; he was just making sure I was still awake. Minutes passed. Three more tugs. A quick pause, then two more. He repeated five in a row so there would be no mistaking his message. He had found the tin wreck! I got up and paced the deck, frustrated because I wasn't with him. I stripped down to my bathing suit and pulled on my wet suit. I wanted to be ready to go when he surfaced.

The safety line jerked violently. One, two. Then one. Then a half-dozen times. For several terrible minutes I felt nothing. I pulled gently on the line. It wouldn't give. Tugged again. The line didn't move. It was as if Uncle Constantine had tied the line to a solid object and walked off. The rising bubbles surfaced in one place, indicating that he wasn't moving.

I had my air tank on in one minute. I jumped feetfirst over the side and followed the hose down. The water was murky, maybe a dozen feet of visibility. A large dark object loomed against the lighter sand on the bottom. It was the hulk of a ship, lying at a slight angle with its hull sunk nearly three-quarters into the sand. It was covered with vegetation, but still largely intact.

Uncle Constantine was near the wreck, kneeling on the bottom as if in prayer, his arms curled in front of him in a fetal position. I swam over and stuck my face a few inches from his helmet and looked in the front porthole. His features were contorted in a mask of pain, his eyes scrunched tight. I rapped with my knuckles on the helmet and his eyes snapped open. He raised his arm and pointed above his head. I looked up, saw nothing but the hose and safety line snaking toward the surface, so I rose a few yards and discovered the problem.

The lifeline was tangled in the jagged bow of the old wreck. Uncle Constantine could blow his suit up until he looked like a float from the Macy's parade, but he was going nowhere with the line tightly snagged. I wondered why he hadn't cut it. His knife was still in its sheath. I whipped out my blade, severed the line and dove down to where my uncle was. The rest should have been easy, but I was having problems of my own.

First came a light-headed feeling, as if my skull were a helium balloon. Then a headache that made me dizzy. Waves of nausea swept through me. I could taste the bile in my mouth that presaged a fit of vomiting. It is not a good idea to throw up underwater, because you can choke. I fought down the lump rising into my throat, grabbed Uncle Constantine by the sleeve, and pointed toward the surface.

He was still clutching his chest, but he understood what I wanted, and let his suit inflate. He began to rise, rapidly, and I held on for the ride. We popped up thirty feet from the *Artemis*. Still fighting the stomach-churning nausea, I swam to the boat with Uncle Constantine in tow. I grabbed the edge of the staging, pulled myself up, and unbuckled my tank harness and weight belt. Then with me pulling on his suit, Uncle Constantine ponderously climbed into the boat and sank to the deck. Quickly, I unscrewed the helmet. He was as white as a haddock's belly. After a few gulps of fresh air, his cheeks regained color, but his face was still crumpled in agony.

"The pills, Aristotle," he whispered hoarsely. "The pills, below, in the first-aid kit."

Yanking the fins off my feet, I practically fell down the companionway into the galley and ripped the first-aid kit off the bulkhead. Buried in with the Band-Aids and antiseptic salve was a plastic prescription vial. I dashed back onto the deck and spilled the pills into my hand. Uncle Constantine reached out and took two of them, chewing the tablets down without any water. He closed his eyes. For a moment I thought he was gone, but soon he began to breathe more regularly.

He reached out for my hand and gripped it tightly. *"Epharisto*, Aristotle," he said hoarsely, *"epharisto.* Thank you, nephew."

I squeezed back. Then I let go and staggered to the rail, leaned over, and spilled my guts into the sea.

23

I gave a final dry heave over the side, wiped the spittle from my chin, and came back to check on Uncle Constantine. His face had an unhealthy pallor, but the pills had done their work. He was grumbling like a nascent volcano. I helped him out of his suit, then peeled off mine. Hooking our arms together for support, we went below and collapsed, exhausted, into the bunks.

After several minutes Uncle Constantine groaned. I tensed, thinking he was going to have another seizure.

Instead, he rolled out of his bunk, came over, and put his face six inches from mine. His brow was crinkled in worry. "You okay, Aristotle?"

I said, "I'm fine, Uncle."

He sighed with obvious relief. "Good. Anything happens to you, your mother kill me."

Something was wrong. I was supposed to be worried about him. I sat up. "How about you, Uncle? How do you feel?"

He thumped his chest with his knuckles. "Tough as a barnacle, Aristotle."

"Naw, Uncle, you're tougher. What happened down there?"

He sat on his bunk and snorted. "Everything fine. I go down, walk around, find the ship. You get my signal?"

I nodded.

"So, I want to see tin. I climb up onto ship. Still everything okay. Then pains come. I can't breathe. I try to get off ship, fall. Lifeline gets tangled."

"Why didn't you cut the line?"

"I can't move. Too much pain, here." He touched his chest.

"What were those pills you took?"

"Nothing, Aristotle." He dismissed my question with a wave of his hand. "Just something makes me feel better."

I worked as a street cop long enough to know a heart attack when I see one. The pills were probably nitroglycerin. My uncle's heart problems were news to me. I was out of the family loop and usually learned a relative was ill when I went to his funeral. My mother runs a better intelligence service than the CIA. If a cousin sneezes in Athens, Ma is on the phone within five minutes with a prescription. She would have known about my uncle. That's why she sounded so worried.

I leveled my eyes at him. "I don't believe you, Uncle Constantine. That wasn't nothing down there."

He flashed his teeth in a devilish smile and slapped my knee. "We feel better after some medicine." He opened a cabinet, pulled out a bottle of ouzo, and poured the colorless liquid to the tops of two mugs. A licorice smell filled the cabin.

Uncle Constantine picked his cup up in a toast. "*Yasou,*" he said.

I shook my head, and clinked my mug against his. "*Yasou*, Uncle."

The ouzo *was* damn good medicine. The sweet liquid fire trickled down my throat, washed away the brassy taste in my mouth, and helped clear my head. I couldn't figure it. I felt fine in the moments before I dived. The nausea came on after I went to my air tank. Now, except for some residual dizziness, I felt pretty good again.

We finished our ouzo therapy and went on deck. Uncle Constantine took care of his dive suit and I tried an experiment. Taking the regulator from my tank, I stuck it in my mouth and breathed. Nothing happened at first, but after a few minutes I felt light-headed and a slight pressure began to press on my brain. I yanked the regulator from my mouth and gulped in fresh air. Soon I felt fine again. The problem was in my air tank. If I had gone down for a normal, prolonged dive, I could have been in trouble. To test my theory, I switched tanks and tried the same procedure. There was no problem with the spare tank. It didn't make sense. Both tanks had been filled at the dive shop at the same time. If one were fouled by a faulty air compressor, then the other one would be contaminated, too.

Uncle Constantine came over and saw me fiddling with the tanks.

"Everything okay?"

"No, Uncle. Something was wrong with my air supply."

He rapped a tank with his knuckles. "I told you. Too dangerous. You want to know about tin?"

I had forgotten about the old wreck. "Of course! Did you find it?"

"You bet," he said, beaming. "Wooden deck all rotted out, so I see many ingots in the hold. They just lie there, Aristotle. We get a basket down and a winch. Pull them up in no time, tomorrow."

I hesitated. "I don't know about tomorrow. We'll have to talk about it."

He looked disappointed, but only for a second. "Okay, we talk about it, then we go dive." He squeezed my shoulder and went back to tend to his gear.

The *Artemis* came into Lewis Bay around midafternoon. After we secured her, I told Uncle Constantine I was going to be busy the next day or two, but I promised to dive with him again as soon as I possibly could. He wasn't happy at the delay, but he understood.

I put my gear in the pickup and drove to Larry's Dive Shop. Larry was out with a dive club, but the kid in the shop said he was due back any minute. I leaned against my truck and before long a van piled into the parking lot and squeaked to a stop. The doors flew open and a half-dozen excited young men and women piled out. The compact ginger-haired man who was driving the van saw me and turned the group over to an assistant, then came over and shook my hand.

"Socko, my man. Just got back from a club dive off Monomoy. Let's go inside and have a brew." We went into the shop and he led the way to a cubbyhole at the back. The space was cluttered with tanks, spears, fins, and other dive paraphernalia. Larry liberated a six-pack of Rolling Rock from a tiny refrigerator and popped a couple of cans.

He took a noisy slurp of foam. "Glad to see you, dude."

"You might not be so glad when you hear what happened today." I told him about my aborted dive with Uncle Constantine. "I had the tanks filled here. Any chance your compressor's on the blink?"

"Shit no," he said with a shake of his head. "Impossible. I filled my tanks the same time I did yours and I didn't have any problems today. 'Sides, didn't you say only one was bad?"

"That's right, the other tank was fine. So what gives?"

He pondered a moment. "There was something in the tank besides air, I'd guess. It didn't smell. It didn't kill you. Just made you sick. Could have been pure oxygen. But taking a guess, I'd say you were breathing in carbon dioxide."

"Carbon dioxide? How the hell would CO_2 get into one of my tanks?"

"That's the hard part. I don't know."

The bad tank was out of my sight a couple of hours yesterday in the locker room at Oceanus. My buoyancy compensator was clearly stenciled with my last name. Someone could have taken the tank, let some air out, and substituted carbon dioxide. I wouldn't have been the wiser until I dived.

My thoughts must have shown on my face, because Larry was looking at me expectantly.

"Got any ideas?" he said.

"Maybe. Is there any way you can test what's in this tank so I can know for sure?"

"I can give it a try, Soc. Meantime, you can take a fresh tank from the storage shed in case you plan on making a dive."

"Thanks, Larry," I said. "I might just do that."

From Larry's I drove to the boathouse. I gave Kojak a handful of Whisker Lickin's to curb his appetite, then popped a Bud and went out on the sun deck. I flopped in a deck chair and stared out at the blue waters of the bay. Twice since joining the Oceanus staff I had run into trouble, first in the shark tank, then on the wreck dive. One time could have been an accident, but not two. I went back into the boathouse and called the number of the Boston police lab. A minute later I was talking to Charlie Reed.

"Hey, Soc," he said, "I tried you earlier today, but you were out. I got a reading on the stuff you sent up."

"That's what I'm calling about. Anything exciting?"

Charlie chuckled. "Was that some kind of test to see if I had lost my touch?"

"I don't get you, Charlie."

"That powder you sent me." He chuckled again. "It was fish blood."

"*Fish* blood?"

"That's right. Dried fish blood, crystallized and very highly concentrated, I'd say."

I was back in the shark tank, dead eyes and sharp white teeth whirling around me, Whitey and his friends nudging me with their noses. Sharks can smell the blood of a speared fish for miles. In the close confines of the shark tank, they would have picked up the dried fish blood in my pocket in no time.

"You still there?" Charlie was saying.

"Yeah, just thinking. Anything else?"

"Nope. If you give me a couple of weeks, I might be able to track down the species."

"Thanks, Charlie, but don't bother. I think I know the species."

I hung up and stared into space. My air tank could have been contaminated by accident, but the dried fish blood did not get in my pockets by itself. Somebody put it there. A weight nudged my ankle and I looked down. Kojak had finished his appetizer and wanted the main course.

After feeding Kojak, I called Sam. His depression had vanished. The head mechanic showed up as promised. He labored all day on the engine and promised to have it ready the next morning. I asked Sam to put the Nickerson kid on standby in case I was too busy to go fishing, and said I'd get back to him later that week. Then I called my mother.

"Hi, Ma. It's me," I said. "I've seen Uncle Constantine twice. He's fine."

If she was surprised at my call, she didn't show it. My mother definitely had class.

"Ah," she said, obviously relieved.

"I was wondering, though." I didn't want to alarm her by describing my uncle's heart attack, so I slid into it through the backdoor. "Is there something you didn't tell me about Uncle Constantine's health? I saw him taking some pills and I wondered what they were for."

"Yes, Aristotle, I don't want you to worry, but Constantine has a heart attack after your aunt Thalia dies. He becomes very sick, but he gets well again. He is very strong, not not as strong as he thinks. Does he still want to go under the water?"

"Yes. But not for a few days."

"He is much too stubborn. Always the same, when he is a young man he leaves Crete and goes off to Kalymnos to find sponges." She sighed impatiently. "Before you go out on the boat, you have your uncle call me. I want to talk to him."

"I'll do my best, Ma."

"I know you will, Aristotle. Now I have to go now and cook some food for Papa. Remember to call me. Bye."

With my family duty temporarily out of the way and Sam put on hold, I could get back to detecting. Tonight's assignment was dinner with Sally Carlin. A tough job, but somebody had to do it. I dug a clean pair of tan chinos out of the closet and found an aqua short-sleeved shirt I'd only worn once or twice. Then I stood under the shower and let the hot water wash the salt accumulation off my skin.

I lounged around in in my cutoffs and read the *Boston Globe*. The Red Sox were still in first place, but I knew it wouldn't last. The Sox always start the season like a shooting star, but the blaze of glory fizzles by the end of August. I

looked at the clock. Time to go. I got dressed, slipped a pair
of Top-Siders over bare feet, told Kojak not to wait up for
me, and went outside where my chariot awaited. On the way
to Sally's I stopped off at a liquor store and picked up a good
Riesling.

It was nearly sunset when I parked outside the carriage
house. Sally greeted me at the door with a kiss. She was
wearing a white cotton short-sleeved jersey with a scoop
neck, a pair of loose-fitting cinnamon slacks, and leather san-
dals. Her hair was tied about halfway down its length. She
seemed to flow rather than walk across the room, trailing a
light flower scent I liked but couldn't identify. She wore gold
earrings. Somehow it didn't surprise me to see they were
made in the shape of dolphins.

The table was next to the French-door screens. A bayberry
candle in a crystal holder had been placed in front of each
setting. I asked if she needed help.

"You can open the wine if you'd like," she said, handing
me a corkscrew. "Dinner's about done. I hope you like
chicken Florentine." She opened the stove door and a
mouth-watering fragrance filled the kitchen.

"I hated spinach as a kid, but the second they started calling it Florentine my whole attitude changed."

She closed the oven. "Good. I'm the same way. I would
hide the spinach under my mashed potatoes, but my mother
always caught me. Did you ever wonder why it was okay with
your mother to leave the vegetables you liked, but you had to
eat the ones you hated?"

"I gave up trying to figure out my mother a long time
ago."

I popped the cork from the wine and poured it into two
slender goblets on the table, then lit the bayberry candles.
Sally turned the lights down, put some Mozart on the stereo,
and brought out a wooden bowl with a salad made from red

lettuce, fresh garden tomatoes, cucumbers, black olives, and a honey-mustard dressing. The Riesling was sweet and not too dry. Halfway through the salads, she got up and came back with a platter of boned chicken breasts and a covered bowl of wild rice.

Private investigators are probably below a used-car salesman and just above a pimp on the socioeconomic scale, but the job has its advantages. I was having a candlelight dinner with a beautiful woman. And when I got tired of looking at her, which was highly unlikely, I could let my gaze drift through the French doors and out to Cape Cod Bay. It was low tide and the chocolaty mud flats extended nearly a mile into the water, broken into purple ribbons by elongated tidal pools. The orange sun sank into the bay, leaving behind a pearly light.

We made small talk about the weather and traffic, as comfortable with each other as a couple of old friends. I discovered Sally was not only beautiful, she was a good cook. "That was delicious," I said, resisting the urge to lick my plate.

"Good, I'm glad you enjoyed it." She cleared the table and returned with two snifters of brandy. We sipped from the snifters, enjoying the slightly full feeling that comes with a good dinner.

After a minute she set her glass down. "I've been thinking." My antennae perked up. When a woman says she's been thinking, she really means it. "About our talk the other night. You asked about Rocky, if he would have attacked someone who punished him."

"I remember. You didn't answer my question."

She brushed a stray hair back from her forehead. "I guess it's no secret how I feel about this whole thing," she said. "It devastates me that some people think Rocky is a murderer. Rocky and the dolphins at Oceanus are more than just clever animals who can do tricks. They're intelligent, but they are *feeling* creatures. They're very much aware of their environment. They're very much aware of us. They *know* they could hurt us if they want to, but they don't. I've felt right along Rocky didn't kill Eddy, but after our talk the other night, I'm not so sure."

"I didn't mean to distress you."

"No, Soc. You did me a favor. It's really made me think about this. In answer to your question, yes, I think Rocky could have been goaded into an attack. I'm still convinced that Rocky is innocent. I know him. He's far too gentle to have hurt anyone. But what I don't know is how he'd react under high stress, if a human had been hurting him, whether his natural reflexes would just take over."

"It was only a supposition," I said.

"Yes, but it could have happened. Don't you see, Soc, if we can prove Eddy was torturing Rocky, it might make a difference. Then at least people would understand that Rocky's not a ferocious killer."

"In other words, Rocky could have killed Byron, but he had good reason. How do you prove that?"

"By locating the electrical prod. It wasn't anywhere near the pool when they found his body. But it could have fallen into the water. No one else knew Eddy had the prod, so they wouldn't have looked for it. I've wanted to search for it, but it's been difficult because everybody's been banned from the water. And even if I got into the pool, it would take me forever to search the bottom. You've seen how big and deep it is, like a small lake."

I could see where this was heading and I wasn't sure I liked it.

"What are you suggesting?"

"Soc, you're a diver. Could you go down in the tank and look? It would mean so much to me."

Sally and I had been on the same track. We both felt the

electric prod might tell us something. In time, I might have made the dive myself, but I hadn't summoned up the courage to go swimming with Rocky. I would have procrastinated forever, hoping something else would develop.

"When do you want to do this?"

She was ready for the question. "How about tonight?" she said.

A breeze came in off the bay, and the candle flames flickered, casting moving shadows across her face. There was no mistaking the determination in those lovely eyes. Sally had me with my back to the wall.

I took a deep breath and let it out. "Okay," I said, "let's do it."

I couldn't slip out of this one without looking like a coward. I wouldn't do that, even if it killed me. But if I had known a dive with a possibly homicidal killer whale was on Sally's dinner menu, I might have taken a chance with my own cooking.

24

Forty minutes later Sally and I stood on the platform at the side of the orca pool watching Rocky's wobbly dorsal fin knife through the water.

"It's normal predator behavior for Rocky to be curious about something new introduced into his environment," Sally was saying. "So don't worry if he approaches you."

I looked out over the orca pool. "Do you mind if we don't call Rocky a predator until I come out of the water?"

"Of course, but it won't change a thing. Rocky *is* a predator, the biggest. He doesn't have any natural enemies, so he isn't scared of anything. He'll be very bold about inspecting you, but that doesn't mean he's going to *eat* you."

"Thanks, I'm glad to hear that."

"It's the same as walking through a cow pasture. The cows will clomp after you. You know they won't hurt you, but it's still unnerving, because they're so big."

The glistening black back roiling the surface only hinted at the powerful body that lay beneath. I tallied Rocky's vital statistics like the master of ceremonies at a boxing match.

In this cor-nah, at twenty-fi-yuv feet and sixteen thousand pounds, Rocky the killer whale!

I shook my head. "Sorry to disagree with you," I said, "but Rocky is no guernsey."

Sally put her arm around me as if she were comforting a bashful kid on his first day of school. It was a natural gesture and didn't embarrass me.

"He's as gentle as one," she said. "Whales and cows share the same bovine ancestors, and both are very curious. Orcas are as fascinated by human beings as we are of them. Just expect Rocky to pay a great deal of attention to you. You're the most interesting thing he's seen in weeks. And don't forget, I'll be in the water with you."

Sally was wearing a form-fitting red-and-black Oceanus regulation wet suit that looked as if it had been brushed onto her supple body. She did have a point. If Rocky devoured anyone, it would be a tasty morsel like Sally and not a chewy old shamus.

Her afterdinner suggestion to look for the electrical prod caught me by surprise, but I wasn't totally unhappy. I had been toying with the same idea. The prod might be the only tangible piece of evidence in this whole weird case. Ben said Eddy was brandishing a "stick" the night he died. It wasn't around in the morning when Byron's body was found. Ben may have been seeing things, but if the prod were in the pool, I would conclude that Eddy had unwisely zapped Rocky, and the killer whale zapped back.

Case closed, Mr. Otis. Rocky did it.

Being nudged into action by a beautiful young woman who cooked like a dream wasn't the worst thing that could happen. I was pleased she trusted me and guilty for parading under false flags. As far as I knew, she didn't suspect I was a private cop.

We cleaned up from dinner, then Sally and I got in the pickup and drove to Oceanus. I parked in the shadows of the administration building and we went through the employees' entrance. There was no sign of Ben. I guessed he had made his one swing around the complex and was back in his office taking a snooze. He seemed unable to maintain consciousness past the "Johnny Carson Show," but then I can't get through it either.

Sally stopped at the locker room to pick up her wet suit. At her suggestion I grabbed a bucket of herring from the fish house. We met at the fountain and proceeded to the orca stadium. As one of the mammal trainers, Sally had her own key to the gate. We locked it behind us and carried the gear into the darkened bleacher section.

From a central switch box Sally turned the underwater lights on in the whale pool. The water glowed like a great puddle of distilled moonbeams. We set the gear down next to the plastic wall. Before leaving her apartment Sally had changed into a teal exercise outfit. She slithered out of it, revealing a two-piece bathing suit in matching color. Her long chestnut hair was untied and fell free over her tanned shoulders. She looked like a Nereid, one of the lovely water nymphs whose parents were Nereus, the Old Man of the Sea, and Doris, the daughter of the god called Ocean.

She put on her wet suit and I stripped down to my boxer shorts and got into mine. I strapped on my buoyancy compensator, wondering if the air in my tank was clean, but quickly dismissed the worrisome thought; I had picked the tank at random from the shed at Larry's dive shop.

Sally hung a whistle around her neck, walked to the edge of the pool, knelt down, and slapped the water several times. Sound travels four and a half times faster in water than it does in air. The noise would have sounded like gunshots to Rocky, who was about fifty feet away. His head popped out of the water and he moved it back and forth, showing us his white chin.

"That wig-wag motion is typical orca behavior," Sally said. "He's seeing who's here."

She blew lightly on the whistle and gestured hands-up in a come-along signal. Rocky disappeared in a circle of bubbles. Sally quickly stepped aside and suggested I do the same. Seconds later, I saw why. Rocky exploded from the water and slid his immense body onto the stage between us. I was ready to scramble for the highest row of bleachers, but Sally went over to Rocky, knelt down, and rubbed the whale's blunt nose.

"Hello, Rocky." She crooned like a mother talking to a baby, not to an eight-ton hunk of blubber with a mouthful of sharp teeth and a tail that could crush a man. This close, where I could measure Rocky's bulk against my own body, he was enormous.

She gave him a herring. He chomped it down like a bonbon.

"Rocky, I'd like you to meet a friend of mine. His name is Soc and he's an okay guy." Sally gestured at me. I went over and knelt beside her. She took my hand and put it on the top of Rocky's nose. His skin was smooth and surprisingly soft. My presence was not unnoticed. Rocky was watching me with his great liquid eye.

Sally patted his head and made a signal with her hands again. Huffing through his blowhole, Rocky wriggled backward and slid into the water, so all but his head was submerged.

"Okay," Sally said. "Let's go in. Me first." She dove off the platform, disappeared for a few seconds, then emerged several yards from Rocky. She pushed her hair away from her face and waved. "Come on in, the water's fine."

I checked on Rocky, who seemed to be doing the same to me, shrugged my shoulders, and jumped in. Buoyed by my inflatable vest, I breaststroked over to Sally. She waited until I was by her side, then we struck out together. We swam around twenty feet and stopped. I turned onto my back and looked for Rocky. He was gone. Where the hell was he?

Wooo-oof!

It sounded like an exploding steam valve. I spun around in the water. Barely fifteen feet away was Rocky's head. It was only visible for a second before Rocky rolled partially onto his side, fixed me with his big black eye, and slid under the water. I thought about my dangling legs and hoped they didn't look like pork chops to Rocky.

He began to circle. The four-foot-high dorsal fin sliced through the water, keeping a respectful distance away, which was fine with me. 'Round and 'round. I pivoted to keep pace with him, but soon got dizzy. Sally swam over and hung on to me to gain a moment's rest from treading water. I put my arm around her waist to help. The warmth of her body penetrated the double thickness of our wet suits.

"You can start your search anytime," she said. "I'll try to keep Rocky busy up here so he won't get in your way, but don't be surprised if he checks you out again. One more thing. You may feel a slight tingling at the base of the spine when Rocky uses his sonar on you."

"Okay," I said. "I'll swim around the inside rim of the pool and kind of spiral into the center. Then I'll retrace my path back to the sides again. If I don't find anything, I'll slip into the smaller pool and do the same thing. It's an inexact way to cover ground, but the water is pretty clear, and I'm sure I'll see anything on the bottom."

She nodded and let go. I paddled back to the pool's edge near the stage and let air out of my BC. I swam straight down to the blue-painted concrete bottom of the pool, inflated the vest to a slight positive buoyancy so I could hover, and set off around the perimeter, swimming with the transparent wall off to my right.

Moving my fins in unhurried but steady scissors kicks, I swam about a yard above the bottom, covering ground rapidly. But less than a minute into the search I stopped.

A huge shadow was passing over my head.

I looked up and saw Rocky's white underside. He was just below the surface, rounded flippers angled down. Swimming with a lazy side-to-side motion of his tail, he moved across my line of vision like a miniature dirigible.

I gritted my teeth and pushed ahead. The pool was his turf, after all, and he could do anything he wanted.

Tap-taptappity-taptap.

It sounded like somebody hitting the distant keys of an old Underwood typewriter. I rolled over and looked above and behind me. Rocky had dived almost to the bottom, and was following me. He must be echolocating, because my spine prickled as Sally said it would. This continued until I was halfway around the pool, then Rocky broke off and disappeared.

I kept on, moving my head to take in as wide a radius as possible with my search, and completed the entire circuit of the pool without finding a thing.

Back where I started, I angled in and started a smaller circuit, moving toward the center of the pool in ever-decreasing concentric circles. Rocky returned to keep me company. He passed overhead, but stayed a respectful distance away. I caught a reassuring glimpse of Sally's red wet suit from time to time.

At the pool's center I paused a few seconds to get my bearings, then started on a reverse spiral that ended at the island. I surfaced and yanked the regulator out of my mouth. Sally was standing on the elongated island that divided the larger section of the pool from the smaller one.

"Did you find anything?" she asked.

"Nothing. I'll try the smaller pool."

She nodded. "Is Rocky behaving?"

"He's following me around like a lost puppy, but he's being a good boy. See you in a couple of minutes. This shouldn't take long."

I swam around the island to the smaller pool, dived to the bottom, and did a repeat of my search pattern. Within minutes I had surfaced again. Sally was still on the island, sitting with her long legs in the water. I shook my head. "If there was a prod in there, Rocky must have eaten it."

Sally tried to hide her disappointment, but it showed in her eyes. "Well," she said, "at least we know. Let's go back."

She slid into the water beside me and struck out across the pool. She swam in slow easy strokes so I could keep up with her. Scuba gear isn't made for surface movement, and even with the added push from my fins, I fell several paces behind her.

I was getting used to Rocky's antics and thought nothing of it when he disappeared at the far side of the pool in a frothy bull's-eye of ripples. Ten seconds later he exploded from the water in a great graceful arc that took him completely out of the water and he splashed down in a huge geyser. Sally and I bobbed in the seas he created. It was a beautiful maneuver, and I marveled at his agility.

It just didn't seem possible for all that bulk to move as if gravity didn't exist. I watched to see if he was going to jump out of the water again. He swam around the edge of the pool, as if he were going to repeat his circling pattern, then cut in suddenly toward the center. He began to pick up speed, moving on a straight-line trajectory, his black dorsal fin cutting the water like the conning tower on a nuclear submarine.

Sally swam in a slow, measured Australian crawl, oblivious of Rocky, who was rapidly moving in on her blind side.

I watched Rocky, expecting him to turn or submerge as he had before. Instead, his head came out of the water and he opened his beartrap mouth wide. The significance of the movement penetrated my thick skull. Fingers of fear clutched my heart.

Jeezus, he was going for Sally!

I shouted, "Sally, get out of the pool!" My mouth was half-full of water and the words were garbled. Sally caught their urgency even if she didn't understand them. She stopped swimming and turned to face me.

"Behind you!" I screamed again.

She swiveled around to face Rocky, her back to me, but she didn't move. Poor kid must have been petrified with fear.

Adrenaline surged through my body. I put all the strength of my legs into frantic kicks. My arms windmilled, although I didn't have the faintest idea what I could do against an animal the size of a locomotive.

The whale had cut the distance to Sally in half, trailing a white wake behind him.

I flailed away in panic, got closer by a few yards. Too late. Rocky was less than two dozen feet away.

His pink mouth looked big enough to swallow a car. I had never seen so many teeth in one place in my whole life. It was the same awful sight that must have filled Eddy Byron's vision in the last seconds of his life.

I swam even harder. Sally was turning to face me now. I expected her features to be twisted in fear.

But she was laughing.

Rocky had come to a stop. Grabbing the whale by the nose, Sally pulled herself up and stood on his flippers. She wrapped her arms around his huge head, rubbed him on the side of his snout, then kissed it. I swam closer, gulping for air.

"Are you all right?" I yelled.

"Of course. Watch."

Rocky began to pivot as if he rested on underwater ball bearings. Faster and faster in a leviathan ballet. Sally held on to his nose with one hand for balance, leaned back, and waved at me with the other. After a few dizzying seconds of playing ring-around-the-rosy, they stopped.

Rocky turned kittenishly onto his back and swam around the pool with Sally riding on the whale's belly. After a few seconds Sally slid off. Rocky turned right side up. I swam over to them.

"Rocky just wanted to play," Sally said. She giggled like a teenager, hanging on to his pectoral fin and stroking his back. "Rub his skin. He likes it."

I moved in and gingerly touched the whale's back near the dorsal fin. That's when I noticed the fin had two V-shaped nicks in the trailing edge. Rocky didn't exactly purr, but he must have liked the body massage because he floated there while we hung on. After several minutes Sally said, "That's enough. We don't want to spoil him." She gave him a couple of affectionate pats, pushed off, and swam to the side of the pool with me following.

Rocky angled off fighter plane style. I brought my knees up to my chest instinctively and stuck my head underwater to see what he was up to. Rocky was below me near the bottom of the pool, swimming belly up like a big dog looking for a tummy scratch.

Sally had climbed onto the stage. She took my air tank and weight belt, then helped me out of the pool. Rocky had followed me. His head was out of the water near the stage.

"See if he'll take a fish from you, Soc."

I reached into the bucket and held the fish over the pool. Rocky moved in closer until he was under the herring. He eyed me for a second, then opened his mouth. I dropped the fish and it disappeared down his gullet.

"I guess you passed the test," Sally said. She gave him

another fish and patted him on the nose. He moved out into
the water and turned on his side to wave a flipper at us. Then
he dove deep and disappeared.

Sally shook her head sadly. "He's pretty happy to have
company. People have been avoiding him because they think
he's dangerous. Next time I'll show you his grand finale trick.
He'll jump out of the water with me standing on his nose."

"Is there anything he won't do for you?"

"Yes, he won't let me ride on his back. Some whales are
like that. It must be sensitive there. He'll knock off any
trainer who tries it, even me. Almost all the incidents you
heard about with trainers happened when they tried to ride
him."

Sally had been smart enough to bring along some towels.
The night was warm and humid, but a cool breeze was coming in the open sides of the orca stadium and we both shivered. We took turns toweling each other's back. I found myself lingering, gently buffing her smooth skin long after it
needed drying. I could have done it all night and I don't
think she would have minded. I know I wouldn't have. She
slid back into her exercise suit. I pulled on my slacks over my
squishy underwear. We collected our stuff, slipped out of
Oceanus as unobtrusively as we had come in, got into the
pickup, and headed back to her apartment.

We didn't talk. She was alone with her thoughts. My mind
kept doing instant replays of the same terrifying picture.
Rocky advancing on Sally, his mouth wide open as if to de-
vour her. Me frantically struggling to get to her before Rocky
did. Sally playing games with the whale. I felt like a fool for
trying to rescue her.

Back at the carriage house, I took her up on the offer of a
shower and she loaned me a bathrobe of brushed terrycloth.
It was snug around the shoulders, but Sally liked extra large,
so it covered the important parts. She told me to throw my
underwear in the dryer. While I was doing that, she went

into the bedroom to get rid of her wet bathing suit. She quickly showered, and came out a minute later wrapped in another terrycloth robe. She turned the lights down and relit the candles. Then she went to the kitchen and poured two snifters of Grand Marnier. She brought them over to the sofa, where I sat trying to piece together the mindless mosaic of this bizarre case.

She took a sip of brandy and stared at nothing.

"Well," she said, "we didn't find the prod."

"Sorry," I said.

She smiled and put her hand on my arm. "Don't be. It wasn't a waste. I'm glad you had the chance to see Rocky isn't the deranged beast the press paints him as. Do you still think he killed Eddy Byron?"

"Yes," I said. It wasn't the answer she was looking for.

A crimson flush appeared on her cheeks. Her smile vanished. I didn't give her the chance to reply.

"And that's why I worry when you get in that close to him," I said. "You still think he's a big panda who wouldn't harm a fly. Maybe you're right, but maybe you're wrong, and maybe there's something bent about him."

"You don't know that."

"As far as I'm concerned, Rocky is a prime suspect until proven otherwise. If he were human, he'd be posting bail."

Anger flashed in the gentian eyes.

"Who *are* you, really?"

For an instant I thought Sally had fingered my real identity in another example of blown cover.

"What do you mean?"

"I mean who do you think you are in the scheme of things? Don't answer, because I'll tell you. You've got the same egotistical disease that afflicts all of our species. You think human beings are the center of the universe. That we are superior in every way. The whole cosmos revolves around what we do. You're conditioned to hate or fear anything you

don't understand. You couldn't *conceive* that there are creatures on earth who may be as intelligent as we are, maybe
even superior to us. Creatures who control their environment
without destroying it, who don't wage war or assault their
mates, who only kill for food."

Tears welled up in her eyes. I had touched a nerve again. I
was good at that.

"Look, Sally."

"No, *you* look. I thought you were different. When you
put aside your foolish fears and agreed to go in that tank
tonight, I said to myself, here is someone who is not afraid of
the truth. I can see I was wrong. You're just like the rest."

I extricated my foot from my mouth and tried again.

"I'm sorry I upset you, Sally. You're right about one thing.
It is very hard to get rid of notions you've had all your life.
When I saw Rocky coming at you with his mouth open, all I
could think of was *Jaws.* I didn't know it was organized play-
time, but I did know about Eddy Byron. I knew he was dead,
that he was found in the pool, and that Rocky may have killed
him."

"I was *never* in any danger," she snapped.

"That's easy for you to say. You've worked around these
animals before, so you can sit there and get angry and say I'm
just being silly. But no matter how rational I try to be, I've
still got the shivers because for a second back at Oceanus I
thought Rocky was going to hurt you, and that scared the
hell out of me." I got up to go. "My stuff must be dry by
now."

Sally put her hand out and held on to my sleeve, tugging
me back onto the sofa.

"No," she said softly, "let's talk."

But we didn't talk, at least not verbally.

We communicated on a more primal level, locking eyes,
then moving closer. She smelled of soap and water. I touched

her arm and ran my hand inside and up her sleeve, past her shoulder, tracing her shoulder blade with my fingers, then under her hair, massaging the smooth warm skin at the back of her neck. She quivered and closed her eyes, and I kissed her under her ear, tasting her deliciousness, feeling the warmth of her skin. She arched her neck, tilted her chin up, and parted her lips. I grazed her cheek and kissed her on the mouth, moved to her pulsating throat, then back to her mouth again.

She sighed with pleasure and slid her hand under my robe, ran her fingertips across my chest then moved them lower, leaving a trail of fire where they touched. I pulled my hand out of her sleeve and slipped it inside the robe. She was naked underneath.

With my fingertips I explored the graceful curve of her shoulder and the firmness of her pointed breasts, pausing to explore her flat stomach before moving to the warmth inside her thighs. Then I helped her off with her robe and followed the same trail with my lips. Her body shivered, and with urgent, searching hands she caressed my face, my neck, and my chest. I peeled out of my robe, and using it as a blanket, we stretched out on the sofa. We kissed, gently at first, then harder, probing with our tongues, breath coming quickly, inhibitions dropping even faster, until our bodies merged in the flickering yellow glow of the candlelight.

25

The long rosy fingers of a Homeric dawn reached through the window and gently pried my eyes open. Sally and I lay like two spoons in her bed, having moved there from the sofa during the night. Her back was against my chest; her skin was fever warm and her hair tickled my nose. I inhaled the flower scent of shampoo and listened to her low, even breathing, thinking what a lovely sound it was.

Reluctantly, I unglued myself from her body and slipped out from under the sheets. Sally stirred, but didn't awaken. I watched her for a moment, thinking that the peaceful sleep of a lovely woman might convert even an old agnostic like me to religion. Nothing so exquisite could be a cosmological accident.

I dug my shorts out of the dryer and got dressed. On a kitchen memo pad I jotted a note telling Sally I went home to change and would see her at Oceanus. Half an hour later I pulled up to the boathouse. I ripped a piece of paper scrawled with Sam's handwriting from a nail on the front door and stepped inside, almost tripping over Kojak, who lay in ambush on the threshold. He didn't like being left alone all night and his whiskers were curled in a furious frown. But when he saw me pouring him a bowl of milk, he rubbed against my legs, purring and generally making a nuisance of himself. Kojak's a cheap date. I guess we were pals again.

Sam's message said if the *Millie D* were fixed, he'd go fishing the next day, but not to worry because the Nickerson kid could fill in if I couldn't make it. I changed into a clean shirt and slacks and went out to my truck, stopping briefly at Elsie's for a coffee to go.

I got to Oceanus ahead of everybody else and went to punch in. A note was clipped to the back of my time card. It said: *Meet me 10:00 A.M. in the fish house. Jill.*

I tore the note up and went to the locker room to change, then walked over to the dolphin pool looking for Sally. She wasn't there, but Mike Arnold was. His eyes lit up at my arrival. Before long, I was helping unload boxes of fish from a truck, moving them on a hand dolly from the delivery door to the fish house.

Ten o'clock came, but no Jill. I dillydallied until ten-thirty, then checked Jill's time card. She had punched out the night before. I didn't worry about it. She might have changed her mind. Or she might have been up partying all night and slept in. She was still only a kid, after all.

Sally and I ran into each other later that morning. We said good morning, but before we'd exchanged more than a couple of words, she mumbled an apology about being busy and started to hurry away. As she walked off I asked her out for lunch, but she said she had made plans. I watched her go, scratching me head, wondering if I would ever know enough about human nature. I went back to work and around noon I got in my truck and drove over to the Lewis Bay Marina.

A cabin cruiser longer than a blue whale occupied the slip

next to the *Artemis*. The name painted on the boat said it was the *Berger King* from Naples, Florida. A young deckhand saw me poking around on Uncle Constantine's boat and called over. "You looking for the old guy?"

"Yeah," I said. "Seen him around?"

He nodded and pointed to the restaurant overlooking the marina. "He and my boss are having a drink."

The place was crowded with hungry tourists, and I didn't see Uncle Constantine until he waved from a corner table. I walked over and he pulled out a chair. "Aristotle, come sit down and meet my friend Mr. Berger."

I shook hands with a big-shouldered guy about sixty with a year-round tan and a jaw you could balance a champagne glass on. He had longish hair and little-boy bangs that probably cost him a lot of money at the Hair Club for Men, but the Prince Valiant look didn't go with the prizefighter's ruins of a nose, the deep-set wrinkles, and the shoe-sole skin. He was dressed in a "Miami Vice" outfit, white slacks and a pale violet T-shirt. He was drinking Beck's beer dark. My uncle held a clouded glass that probably contained his favorite medicine.

Berger pumped my hand with enthusiasm and grinned crookedly. He had the opportunistic eyes of a traveling salesman.

"Good to meet you, pal. Your uncle here has been telling me all about you."

"Yes, Aristotle, I tell Mr. Berger about our wreck diving."

"Damn interesting stuff, too," Berger said.

So much for our top-secret project. "Oh," I said. "How much has my uncle told you about our work?"

"Enough so that I want in on it. Damn, I want to see that silver Madonna for myself."

I glanced sharply at Uncle Constantine. He shrugged and looked out the window.

I came back to Berger. "Silver Madonna, you say?"

"Yeah, the statue your uncle saw in the hold of the ship. That right, Constantine?"

My uncle leaned forward. "I tell Mr. Berger *maybe* I see a Madonna. But not for sure."

Berger guffawed. "Hell, Constantine, don't go cozy on me. You were saying a few minutes ago you could see the lapis lazuli in her pretty blue eyes."

Time for damage control. "Mr. Berger," I said. "I should warn you about wreck divers. They can get real excited underwater, and their imagination goes into hyperdrive. It's quite possible my uncle saw nothing like the things he described. You never know for sure until you get the stuff out of the water." I stared hard at my uncle. "Something you think is silver might only be tin, for instance."

Uncle Constantine avoided my eyes. He puckered his mouth and patted his shirt pocket as if he were searching for the pack of Luckies in plain sight on the table in front of him.

Berger punched me lightly on the shoulder. "Tin. Hah. Dammit boy, you don't have to play games with me. I know there's a risk involved, but I'm not afraid to put my money where my mouth is. No pain, no gain, I always say, and I've done real well by that."

"Mr. Berger has three hamburger stores in Florida," Uncle Constantine interjected. "They are very busy."

"Biggest-grossing fast-food franchises in the state, and most of the money I've made squeezing herds of cows between buns has gone into real estate, good stuff, not under two feet of swamp water. So if it's money bothering you, don't worry, lad."

"No, Mr. Berger, it's not money. I wonder if you could excuse us. I'd like to talk to my uncle. I'm on my lunch hour, so I don't have much time."

"Sure thing," he said, grabbing my hand and pumping it

again. "Talk all you want. Constantine, we're going to be neighbors for a while. I'm gonna to stick around here and look for a horny widow. If I don't hear from you, I'll invite myself over. I'd like to get going on this real soon. Right, *pard*ner?"

I grabbed Uncle Constantine's arm and guided him out of the restaurant to a picnic table next to the marina.

"Okay, Uncle Constantine, what's going on?"

"Don't get mad, Aristotle. I explain. Mr. Berger, he comes in his big yacht yesterday. I see he is from Florida, so we talk. He has been to Tarpon Springs, and he says, why am I on Cape Cod, no sponges here? I say, there is better than sponges. We have some drinks, then talk some more."

"Is that when you told him about the silver Madonna?"

A shrewd look replaced the innocent expression in his eyes. "Mr. Berger is no fool, Aristotle, but even a smart man is a little greedy. I just make sure he has something to be greedy about. You hear me tell him. I *never* say I see a Madonna. I say *may*be I see one. I don't tell him maybe I see a tin ingot that looks like a Madonna."

I shook my head. "Damn, Uncle. That's fraud."

"No, Aristotle. He makes the story in his head. It's nothing."

"Like those pills, and your heart attack the other day. I suppose *that* was nothing."

"No heart attack," he said, rubbing his midsection. "Bad cooking."

"Don't give me that, Uncle," I said firmly. "I know all about it. I talked to Ma."

"Paff. Your mother worries too much. Okay, so it's heart attack, but no big deal, I have pills. I take them, makes everything okay. Don't worry, Aristotle."

Uncle Constantine's cavalier attitude didn't calm my fears. I *was* worrying. He was the most vital, alive man I had ever met. I didn't want to see that spark of life extinguished because of an old tin ship.

I couldn't hide my exasperation. "Uncle Constantine, why do you want to kill yourself over this wreck? You know damn well that by the time you get through with the legal work that has to be done for a state permit, and the actual salvage work, you'll be lucky to break even. You might *lose* money, even if you pull in a whole boatload of suckers like Mr. Berger."

Uncle Constantine pointed to a chubby-legged girl about two who was walking along hand in hand with her mother.

"Cute, no?" He was stalling. Seeing it would do no good, he shrugged and said, "Aristotle, you remember when you are a little boy what I tell you about the cross in the water?"

"Sure, I do, Uncle." In January, the Tarpon Springs Greeks celebrate the Epiphany with the blessing of the waters. The archbishop throws a gold cross into a bayou and young Greek guys from the town dive from a circle of rowboats. The kid who brings up the cross is blessed by the archbishop and supposedly has good luck for the rest of the year.

Uncle Constantine said, "Then you don't forget what happens when I am seventeen."

I smiled. "The girl who held the white dove with blue ribbons on its feet."

"Ah, good, you remember. She lets the dove go. It is the signal to dive. She is so beautiful, I can't see anything else. So I am still standing on my boat when *splash!* All the boys dive. My friends George and Mike get to the bottom first, but I want that cross more than anybody, so I swim hard, grab it, come up, and hold it high. They pull me out of the water. The archbishop touches my head and says, 'Blessing, blessing on these waters,' and everyone cheers, even George and Mike. Then we walk through the streets, all the winners from other times, singing and taking money for the poor. I am the hero."

I put my hand on his shoulder. "You used to tell me the archbishop must have used his strongest blessing, because your good luck started right away."

His eyes lit up. "*Neh*, Aristotle. Yes, yes. After the dive there is a big *glendi* on the sponge docks. Much food and music. I talk to the girl with the dove. Then at the Epiphany ball, I dance with her all night long. A few years later I marry her, your aunt Thalia. My luck stays good. I have two children. I buy the *Artemis* and pick many sponges. I get the bends, but I don't die."

"You've had a good life, Uncle."

"Sure, Aristotle, I know that. Maybe *too* good. One day God looks down and says, 'This miserable man Constantine, he laughs all the time, he gets all the good luck, there isn't enough for other people, so we'll take some away and see how much he believes.' So God moves my kids far away and I never see them. He gives me a bad ticker and makes me get old so I can't work and nobody wants to hire me. Still I laugh. So God says, 'We'll give this fellow a big test,' and he takes Thalia away from me."

Thalia. She was a vivacious and lovely woman, named after one of the three Graces, Good Cheer, and the name fit her well. I knew my aunt's death had been tough on the old man, but he masked his grief under his natural exuberance. It was easy to forget his sorrow was probably tearing him apart.

"I'm so sorry, Uncle Constantine. She was always my favorite aunt."

The words seemed inadequate, but I must have said the right thing because he snapped out of it. He put his hand on my knee and said, "Don't feel bad, Aristotle, you and me, we go out, we get the cross and good luck will come back again."

"I don't understand, Uncle. What cross?"

"Aristotle," he said softly. "You're uncle's not crazy in the head. I can't dive with the kids in the bayou. But I can go bring up the tin wreck. *That*'s my cross." He grinned. "Then maybe God will say, 'This man is an old fool, give him back some luck before he kills himself and comes knocking at our door.' So, you help me?"

I saw a golden opportunity to carry out my mother's orders. "Okay, Uncle, I'll help you. But you have to promise something."

"Sure, Aristotle, anything."

"I want you to stay out of the water."

"Now who's crazy. Then how do I get my cross?"

"You don't," I said. "I'll get it for you."

Uncle Constantine was stubborn, but he was no fool. He grabbed my hand and shook it and put his other arm around my shoulder.

"Okay, you drive hard bargain, but we do it your way."

Oscar the penguin saw me coming and gave me the bad eye as only a penguin can.

I leaned over the fence and he moved to the edge of his perch, his beak pointed at the sky, his stubby wings slightly raised, as if poised for flight.

"Look, pal," I said. "It wasn't my idea to chase you all over hell and give you that shot." I tossed him a fish. He gobbled it down, but he didn't turn his back on me.

"You know, Oscar, you've got a lot of hostility in you for a penguin." That did it. He dove into the water and shot across the pool to the other side. I threw a handful of fish goodies over the fence and walked away with the squawks of a full-blown food fight ringing in my ears. A few minutes later I was at the dolphin pool. Froggy the white beluga came over to greet me. He stuck his funny clown's head out of the water. I knelt down to pat his head and gave him a fish.

"Hey, Froggy, you're one of the locals. What's really been going on at this crazy place?"

He moved his head back and forth and said *wonk.*

"Yeah," I said. "I thought so."

I heard voices. Sally and Mike Arnold were approaching. I stood up and went over to meet them.

"Mike," I said. "Am I glad to see you. Look, I threw my back out unloading fish this morning, so I've got to leave a little early to see a chiropractor."

The smile on his face faded and his mouth curled in a skeptical frown. He must have been thinking three is a crowd because he told me to buzz off. Sally said she hoped my back would get better soon, but she avoided eye contact. I punched out and jotted down Jill's address from her time card. Minutes later I headed out of the parking lot. My back had fully recovered. Like the old song says. Miracles do happen.

I drove along Route 28 until I found a pay phone. I tried calling Jill. The phone rang a dozen times. No answer.

Twenty minutes later I pulled up outside the neat Cape Cod house Phil Hanley used to live in before he died. I reviewed what I knew about Hanley. He was dead. Somebody had killed him. He might have been killed to shut him up. And his wife might know what it was that he knew. Which could put her in a dangerous position.

I left the truck, went up the walk, and rang the bell. The door was answered by a dark-haired boy about six years old. His nose was runny and his large eyes were red-rimmed, as if he had been crying. There was a fresh Band-Aid on his knee. He was nibbling soggy bites out of a chocolate-chip cookie that was bigger than his head.

He looked at me curiously. "Hi," he said.

"Hi," I answered. "Is your mommy home?"

The kid opened his mouth to answer, but he was whisked

back into the house and Mrs. Hanley stepped into the doorway to take his place. She looked as if she had just seen her
kid talking to Bruno Hauptmann. There was fear in her face,
fear of me. She stood there like a mother lion defending her
cub.

"Do you remember me, Mrs. Hanley? My name is Socarides."

"Yes, you're the private detective," she said guardedly.
"What do you want?"

"May I talk to you a few minutes?"

"What about?"

"Your husband."

She bit her lip. "I'm not interested in talking to you. Now
go, please, before I call the police."

The boy pulled on my shirt. "I fell off my trike and hurt
my knee, want to see it?"

"Sure, tiger." I squatted and looked at the ugly bruise
around the edge of the Band-Aid. "You're a brave boy not to
cry."

"My daddy said it was all right for boys to cry if they got
hurt."

"Your daddy was right. Even big boys like me can cry when
they get hurt."

He nodded gravely. "Did you know my daddy?"

I stood up. Mrs. Hanley's eyes pleaded for me to go.

"A little," I said. "He was very nice."

The boy's mother said, "Go in the kitchen and get another
cookie while I talk to the man."

He shot into the house and we were alone. I knew I was
putting her through an ordeal just by being there. The last
time I showed up on her doorstep, her husband was dead
within hours. But I kept pushing because I didn't want her to
end up the same way.

"Look, Mrs. Hanley," I said, "I'm very sorry about what

happened to your husband. But I just need to ask a few questions. It could be very important. All I'm asking is five minutes. So do us both a favor before you slam the door in my face. Please call the state-police barracks and ask for Captain Parmenter. He'll vouch for me. I don't know the number. It's in the phone book under Commonwealth of Massachusetts."

She thought about that for a moment, then said, "Go around back and sit on the deck. I'll meet you there."

She closed the door and I walked out to the deck and sat in a lounge chair. The deck overlooked a small backyard and a split-rail fence that divided the property from the backyard of another house. On the other side of the fence an old man and woman crawled along on their hands and knees, working a vegetable garden.

Before long the deck sliders swished open and Mrs. Hanley came out. She was carrying a plastic pitcher and two glasses.

She sat down in the other chair and studied me. "Captain Parmenter said you were harmless. That you only got irritable when you couldn't get a beer. I don't have any beer. Will iced tea do?"

"It's fine. Did he tell you anything else about me?"

She poured a glass of dark liquid and offered it to me. "Yes, that you almost married his daughter. I'm very sorry about what happened."

"So am I."

We were on more or less an even plane now. We had both lost somebody we loved.

"I've sent Bobby in for a short nap. We can talk now."

"He's a neat kid."

"Thank you. He really misses his father; they were pals. So he's attracted to any grown-up male."

The tea had fresh mint the way I like it. Mrs. Hanley had aged since I last saw her. Sooty semicircles underlined her eyes. Her face was puffy from lack of sleep. It was the look of a woman in mourning.

"I'm not here to cause you any more pain, Mrs. Hanley. I'm trying to find out who murdered your husband."

She shook her head. "I just can't fathom who would want to hurt Phil. He had no enemies. He liked everybody, and they liked him. That was why he was so good at his job."

"He seemed bitter at being fired."

She bristled, visibly. "Of *course* he was bitter. He was fired for telling the truth."

"Tell me about it."

"Phil was responsible for dealing with the press. He was honest with them, answering all the reporters' questions. So Austin fired him."

"I've heard the same story, Mrs. Hanley. It doesn't strike me as the kind of knowledge that would get a man killed. Is there more?"

"Yes, I think so."

I waited.

She arranged her thoughts, then said, "You have to understand something. My husband was an alcoholic. His drinking was the reason our marriage fell apart. It got even worse after he was fired from Oceanus. He went totally off the edge. Hitting bottom is the best thing that can happen to an alcoholic, Mr. Socarides. We were able to get him into intervention with a counselor, and into a detox program. He'd been pulling himself together. He went into AA. He hadn't had a drink in months. There was a good chance he and I would get back together."

"Breaking up must have been very difficult."

"Yes, it was, but pushing for a separation was for his sake as well as mine. You see, I was always picking up after Phil, making his alcoholism easy. But the person most responsible for saving Phil was Steve. Phil met him in AA. He became

Phil's sponsor, the one he called when the urge to drink came back. They became quite close. Phil told me he and Steve had talked about Oceanus, but he never told me what they discussed."

"What was Steve's name?"

She smiled. "It's Alcoholics *Anonymous*, Mr. Socarides."

"Of course. Where did Phil attend AA meetings, Mrs. Hanley?"

"It's the one in Orleans, at the Episcopal church. Phil was embarrassed at first, he didn't want anyone he knew seeing him at an AA meeting, so he didn't go to the one in our town."

"That's a good lead, Mrs. Hanley." I got up to leave. "I won't bother you any longer. Thanks for the time and the tea."

"He really loved it, you know."

"Loved what, Mrs. Hanley?"

"His boat, the *Mariah*. He told me that living close to the water, smelling the sea, and hearing the cry of the terns helped clear his head, made him see how he was destroying himself."

"I know exactly what he meant, Mrs. Hanley."

The sliders opened and the boy came out. He went over to his mother and gave her a hug. "I couldn't nap," he said.

"That's all right. Go over and see Mr. and Mrs. Johnson. Maybe they'll let you help in their garden." Without another word, the boy ran across the lawn to the split-rail fence. The faces on the old couple lit up. They helped him through the fence and handed him a rake. Mrs. Hanley was watching her son. "It's all so maddening," she said. "Phil was coming back, we were going to pick up where we had left off. We could have rebuilt our lives."

"You can still have a life, Mrs. Hanley. Your boy needs you."

"Yes," she said. She turned to me, her eyes blazing and tearful at the same time, and I thought she was angry at me for being too quick with a platitude.

"Get him," she whispered. "Please, Mr. Socarides."

"Pardon me?"

"Get whoever took my son's father away from him."

She extended her hand to grip mine tightly, and we held on to each other in a silent pact.

26

Jill lived ten miles west of Hyannis in a two-story square-built captain's house surrounded by a privet hedge that looked as if it had been cut with a nail clipper. I drove onto a semicircular gravel driveway edged with blue-blossomed explosions of hydrangea and looked out over West Bay. Dusk had fallen, and the hues of sea and sky flowed into each other like errant strokes from the brush of a careless watercolorist. I watched the rays of the setting sun go from pink to purple until a pulpy blackness oozed in and covered everything like a slow-moving tidal wave of blackstrap molasses. Then I got out of the truck.

With a flashlight in hand, I went up the walk and punched the front doorbell. The Big Ben chimes echoed in the silent caverns of the old house. I pressed my ear against the door to shut out the night chorus of insects, hoping to hear the sound of footsteps. Inside there was only silence.

I walked over to the garage and peeked through the window. The Mercedes inside must have belonged to Jill's parents, who were in the south of France, but there was no sign of her battered Volvo. Playing the flashlight beam ahead of me, I followed a flagstone path around to the back of the house. A narrow border of impatiens and dusty miller ran alongside the foundation. I stopped at one point where some of the pink and white flowers were crushed by a waffled imprint in the soft earth.

Boot prints led to a window and another set pointed away. Some tracks were scuffed as if a hurried attempt had been made to cover them. I put my sneaker into a footprint. It was about the same size as mine, a ten, definitely not that of the petite Jill. I flicked the light up at the window. Crumbs of dirt lay on the sill and dark paint showed where the white paint had been chipped off by a jimmy. I tried the window. It was unlocked.

The window slid open easily. I slithered inside and seconds later stood in a large living room listening to the monotonous tick-tack of a grandfather's clock. Hooding my flashlight beam with my fingers, I moved though a dining room into the kitchen and explored the rest of the first floor, then climbed the stairs to the second story. There were three bedrooms, but only one showed signs of having been recently occupied. The four-poster bed was unmade and the dresser had a brush with long strands of blond hair in the bristles. I found some postcards from France addressed to Jill, but nothing that might tell me where she was.

I sat on her bed, gathering my thoughts, hoping some object in the room might tell me a story. Nothing came to me. After a few minutes I went back downstairs and slipped out through the window I used to get in. I figured the person or persons who'd broken in before me had gone. I snapped the light off and moved quietly around to the side of the house on the way back to my pickup.

A shadow detached itself from the shelter of a rosebush

and stood in front of me, blocking the way. From behind came a rustle not much louder than a snake sliding through the grass. A muscular arm wrapped itself around my face and yanked my head back. The cold, hard sharpness of a knife blade pressed against my exposed Adam's apple.

A classic commando move, done as nicely as I'd ever seen. With this maneuver, you could take a sentry out and the only noise he'd make would be a bloody gurgle. I froze like a kid in a game of statues. My heart rate tripled. I didn't dare breathe. A couple of eternities went by. The knife stayed where it was. I was still alive, but the chances of dying in my sleep had taken on long odds. Even worse, a mosquito was trying to drill a hole through my nose.

The shadow in front of me had a voice.

"I'd advise you not to move, Soc. Ned has a steady hand, but he'll get nervous if you struggle."

I said, "Ig nargh movag."

Another figure came in from the left. Hands lightly patted up and down my body.

"He's clean," a woman said.

"Thank you, Sara. All right, Ned, you can let him go. Please don't try anything foolish, Soc. We don't want to hurt you, but we will if we have to."

The arm released me. I had no intention of doing anything foolish because Ned's big knife had moved from my throat to the small of my back, where the point pricked the skin covering my kidneys.

I said: "I thought the Sentinels were nonviolent, Walden."

The shadow took a few steps forward.

"We are. As I told you, we're basically opposed to violence. But it's all relative, you know, if you think of us as surgeons removing cancers. To the body, a mugger's knife or a doctor's scalpel are both violent intrusions, but one cut is meant to harm and the other to help."

I wasn't in the mood for hairsplitting. "Tell Ned that if he doesn't take the shiv out of my back, I'll revoke his license to practice medicine and stuff it down his throat."

Schiller laughed. "I don't think so. Ned used to be a Green Beret. You can relax, Ned, our friend here isn't going anywhere."

The knife was removed from my back. I could still feel the dimple from the sharp point. I swatted the mosquito and brushed him off my nose.

"Thanks," I said. "Excuse me for being unfriendly, Walden. I have an attitude about guys who sneak up and stick a knife under my chin."

"Ned is just using the skills he was taught by the Establishment. So tell me, what were you doing skulking around Jill's house?"

"What were you doing breaking into it?"

"Hear that, gang? I told you we did a lousy job covering our tracks. I asked you first, Soc, but since you've been so gracious about the confusion a few minutes ago, I'll answer your question. We were looking for Jill."

"What a coincidence, Walden, I was doing the same thing. Jill and I were supposed to meet this morning. She had something important to show me. When she didn't come into work, I began to worry. I found out where she lived and tried to call her. There was no answer, so I came out here. I was hoping I'd find something."

"Did you?"

"Yeah, Walden, I found you."

"Do you know what Jill wanted to show you?"

"No," I said. "Wouldn't she have told you?"

"We were supposed to meet here last night. Jill was going to tell us what she had. She was pretty excited. But she never arrived, and she hasn't called. We've been watching the house. You were right to worry. We think something happened to her."

"Like what?"

"She said she was on the verge of something big, but she wanted to get the proof together and present it as a package."

"What are your plans now?"

"We'll sift through the information we have. Maybe there's something there to point the way."

"I know this is a radical idea, but did you ever think of reporting her disappearance to the police?"

"We don't work with the Establishment," he snarled. It was the same transformation from elf to troll that I had seen the first time I talked to him. "Besides, we think Jill could be hurt if the police go blundering into something they know nothing about."

"Okay, Walden if that's the way you want to play it, I'll keep poking around. Maybe I'll turn up something."

"Good, but you'd better be a little more careful than you were tonight. The next people who jump out of the bushes at you might not be so friendly."

He stepped back. It was a signal for the others to leave. They melted into the darkness, following Schiller around the front of the house, their boots crunching into the gravel driveway. A few minutes later came the distant sound of a motor winding through the gears.

I stood there listening to the buzz of insects, and for the first time I noticed that my T-shirt was soaked with sweat.

I stopped at the boathouse to change clothes and gave Kojak a quick tummy scratch on the way out. Fifteen minutes later I was looking for a parking space outside the Episcopal church.

The young guy tending the coffeepot by the door leading into the church basement gave me a wide grin and stuck out his mitt.

"Hi," he said. "I'm the official greeter tonight. My name is Ed."

I shook his hand. "Call me Soc. It's a nickname."

"You got it, Soc. Want some coffee?"

"Thanks. Just black is fine."

"No problem." Ed filled a Styrofoam cup and handed it over. I took a sip and looked around the room. The conversational hum grew louder as people filtered in and filled the rows of wooden chairs facing a table. The crowd was a mix: young and old, men and women, rough-hewn blue-collar workers still in their work clothes and clean-cut professionals. You could probably find teachers, cops, firemen, secretaries, businessmen. Even a few tourists who had stopped by to meet the locals. It was a good-feeling place. Most of the people were smiling or laughing. New arrivals were greeted like old buddies, with friendly handshakes and encouraging pats on the back.

"I'm new at this meeting, Ed. You don't have a guy named Steve who comes here, do you?"

"Sure," he said. "I think we've got three of them."

"The one I'm looking for is a lawyer."

"Jeez, Soc, I don't know what these guys do. I just moved into town myself. Whoops, looks like the meeting's about to start."

The seats were nearly full. I took an empty one near the back corner. A middle-aged woman with blondish hair and a nice face sat at the table. There were a couple of plaques in front of her. One of them said, *Easy Does It.* The other one said, *One Day at a Time.*

The woman smiled. "Hello. For those who don't know me, my name is Jean. We'll start with the serenity prayer."

Following her lead, the group joined in, "God grant me the serenity to accept the things I cannot change, courage to change the things I can, and wisdom to know the difference."

The prayer was followed by a moment of silence for the sick and suffering, then the reading of the AA preamble, with a call for people to share their experience, strength, and hope. The treasurer gave a brief report. Jean launched into her "drunkalogue," a touching and personal story about her kids and husband before she went sober. More strength and hope. Then she asked for a topic.

Somebody in the group suggested they talk about honesty. A tall man in a tan summer suit with no tie stood up and said he first got honest with himself when he admitted he was powerless over alcohol and his life had become unmanageable. Others followed, telling in their individual ways how they had confronted the demon rum and how they were managing to struggle with it. I began to think that an AA meeting must be the most civilized place in the world.

There are a lot of drunks on the Cape. The economy tends to be seasonal, the winters quiet and damp. Sometimes the folks who retire here discover it isn't paradise, so they try to drown the loneliness and pain of old age with a good snort. On any given night, it seems, half the Cape's population is at an AA meeting, and the other half probably should be.

People continued to talk about the ones they had hurt, wives, husbands, sons and daughters, mothers and fathers, and about the jobs or friends they had lost or the the dumb things they had done. The tales were told sometimes sadly, sometimes joyfully, but always optimistically. The feeling of strength in the air was palpable. The meeting lasted about an hour. At the end we held hands, said the Lord's Prayer, and told each other to "keep on coming."

The group broke up into knots of chatting people. I went over to the table and said hello to Jean, who was gathering up her papers, explained I was new, and asked if she could point Steve out to me.

She smiled. "Which Steve?"

"He's a lawyer."

"Oh sure. Over there."

She pointed to the man in the tan suit who had been the first to talk about honesty. He was heading for the door with a young couple. I caught up with him and asked if we could talk for a moment. His mouth widened in an easy grin, he took me by the arm and guided me off to one side so others could pass.

He was a thick-boned man with graying reddish-brown hair, probably in his midfifties. If it is true that a face is a map of a man's life, Steve had seen some hard miles. His face was creviced by too many losing bouts with the bottle. But the deepest furrows were the smile lines around his mouth. Laugh crinkles framed deep-set green eyes that had the focused intensity of a priest's.

"What can I do for you, friend?"

I handed him my business card. He shook his head. "I don't understand."

"I'd like to talk to you about Phil Hanley. I understand you were his sponsor."

Steve looked around. "We can't talk here. The janitor has to close up. Tell you what, there's a Wendy's out on the edge of town. I'll meet you there in ten minutes."

I said it was fine with me. He broke off and went on saying his good nights in the parking lot. I got in my truck and drove to the fast-food joint. I was sitting at a small Formica table when Steve arrived.

He settled into his seat with a cup of coffee and got right to the point. "How did you know about me?" he said.

"I talked to Phil Hanley's wife today. She told me you were Phil's sponsor and that he met you at AA. I took a chance you might be there."

He shook his head. "Lynn is a nice girl. She's taking Phil's death hard. She feels it was her fault, that if she hadn't thrown him out of the house he'd still be alive. Her boy's a real fine lad. How are they doing?"

"Not great, but she'll tough it out."

"I've told her she can call on me if she needs help. Well, Mr. Private Detective, what can I do for you?"

"Hanley's old bosses at Oceanus hired me to do some snooping for them. The job had nothing to do with him directly, but I thought he might be able to help. Hanley told me he had information that could get him his job back. I never found out what it was because he was dead a couple of hours later. Mrs. Hanley seemed to think you might know what Phil had on his mind."

"What's your interest in this?"

"It's become personal with me. Phil may have been murdered because he was going to talk to me that night, and I was the one who found his body. There's a town cop who's drooling at the chance to nail me on the charge. He doesn't have enough evidence to stick, but he might decide to manufacture some. Then there's my case. It's become a logjam. If I can pry something loose, maybe the river will start flowing. Finally, there's Mrs. Hanley. You're right, she's a nice lady and shouldn't have to bring up a little kid by herself. I can't get her husband back, but maybe I can see justice gets done."

Steve shook his head. "The shame of it all is that Phil was doing so well. He was sober. He was looking for work. He and Lynn were putting their lives back together. It's damn tough to stop drinking."

"I know," I said.

He puckered his lips in a quizzical expression. "You in the program?"

"No, but some people think I should be."

"If you ever need a sponsor . . ."

"Thanks, Steve. Remember what you said back at the church. First you've got to be honest enough with yourself to admit you've got a problem. When I get to that point, you'll be the first one I call. Meanwhile, I'd appreciate it if you could tell me more about Phil."

Wrinkling his brow thoughtfully, Steve said, "Phil and I were pretty close. It gets that way with someone you sponsor. We used to talk about a lot of things. He was still pretty bitter about being fired from Oceanus. I guess that's how we got on the subject of his old boss."

"You mean Dan Austin?"

"One and the same."

"How did his name come up?"

"Hold on, I need more coffee." He got up and when he came back he said, "I'm a pretty good lawyer. Before I hit the sauce, I worked for an old respected law firm in Boston. The pressure finally got to me. I moved down here hoping to clear my head, but it only got worse. I bottomed out, and with the help of my friends and family, I got dry and I've been that way ever since. I started a law practice on the Cape and occasionally my old firm will refer a client to me. Last year Austin came by. He was the original guy behind Oceanus, did you know that?"

"No, I didn't."

"He told me all about it. He'd managed a few parks, then finally got enough seed money to start construction on Oceanus. The park was his dream. It cost him more than he thought it would. His original funding evaporated, and that's when he went to Bay State Investments. They agreed to pick up financing in return for an interest in the park and a hand in running it. They bought a pile of his shares. He became a minority stockholder, essentially nothing more than an employee of Bay State."

"Why did he come to see you?"

"It was during the park's construction. There were major delays because he wanted to dig out a marsh in violation of the state wetlands act. The town conservation commission turned it down. The town was fighting it tooth and nail. They were worried the project would alter the whole ecosystem around the marsh. And Bay State's participation was contingent on a permit going through. I started shuffling the papers for an appeal, but then Austin called one day and said he didn't need me anymore."

"What happened?"

"I really don't know. He got his permit somehow, managed to leapfrog over the town objections. I'm not surprised. Massachusetts is probably the most politically corrupt state in the country. A little money in the right pocket goes a long way on Beacon Hill. Anyhow, he thanked me, and that was the end of our professional relationship. He went on to bring in Bay State money, build the park, and apparently it was very successful. Tell me, though, what are you doing for Bay State? I'm curious."

"They want to sell the park to a Japanese outfit. Some complications have arisen, and they asked me to look into them."

His eyebrows arched. "Sell to the Japanese? That's odd."

"What is, counselor?"

"Dan Austin had first refusal on any sales deal. If he could come up with the down payment, he could buy his park back. The park was doing quite well, and Dan had a percentage of the take."

"I guess it wasn't doing well enough. Did you and Hanley discuss anything else about Oceanus?"

"I told him about my work for Austin on the wetlands appeal. That was about it. He said he was going to do some digging on his own. He might find something."

"Did he say where he was going to dig?"

"Yeah, as a matter of fact. He did PR with the Department of Environmental Management before he came to Oceanus. He said he was going to talk to some friends up in Boston."

"Something to do with the marsh project?"

"I'd say that's a fair guess. That's really all I know. More coffee?"

"No thanks." I started to rise. "Thanks for your time."

"I was glad to do it. Before you go, though, remember, if you want to get into the program or even talk, just give me a call. The only ticket to the program is admitting that you're powerless over alcohol."

"I'm powerless over a lot of things, Steve, but I'll remember your offer."

We shook hands and left Wendy's together. I headed back toward the boathouse, intending to call Sally and find out why she acted as if I no longer existed. But on the way home I made a detour to the 'Hole and stayed there longer than I should have.

27

No one answered at Jill's house the next morning. I let the phone ring a couple more times then put it down and took a tentative sip of coffee, trying to drown the sand crabs clawing at my stomach. Too many beers had chased too many tequila shots the night before, and my body was lodging a grievance. There was another reason for the lead feeling in my gut; I was worried about Jill. The currents swirling around Oceanus had swallowed Eddy Byron and Hanley like tatters of seaweed on the tide. Now Jill may have been pulled under, too.

I dialed the state-police barracks. Parmenter came on a minute later. He was in a good mood. His narcotics case was ending with a whimper. The lawyer charged with laundering drug money was going for a plea bargain. In return for a lighter sentence, he would blow the whistle on the big boys. While Parmenter talked I rubbed my head where someone had driven nails into my temples and wondered why the Socarides family had withheld its supply of temperance and wisdom when I was born.

"By the way," he was saying, "I talked to the DA. Pacheco's been on his ass about you. The DA knows the guy's reputation, so he's been putting him off, but nothing is moving on the Hanley case. Pacheco is stupid enough to try to hang that thing on you. I'll keep an eye on him."

"Thanks, John. Could you do me another favor? There's a girl missing and she could be in trouble. I don't want to make a big fuss yet, but maybe your guys could watch out for her while they cruise around the Cape." I gave him Jill's name and address and a description of her old green Volvo, and told him to call me at Oceanus if he heard anything. Parmenter promised to keep in touch. I hung up, fed Kojak, then showered, dressed, and headed off to work.

The locker room was empty when I got there. I stripped off my jeans and T-shirt and hung them on hooks in the lower compartment of my locker. The day before I had thrown my dirty jersey and shorts into the top section. I pulled the soiled clothes out to toss them in the hamper, and a letter-sized envelope that must have been on the shelf fluttered to the floor. I picked the envelope up and looked at it. It was blank. I tore it open. Inside was a film-processing claim ticket and a sheet of lined paper ripped from a notebook. There was a Hyannis address on it. This was definitely not a U.S. Postal Service delivery. I tucked the ticket and paper into my wallet and finished dressing.

Mike Arnold wasn't around, so I busied myself feeding fish for a couple of hours. Just before noon I decided to feed myself. I strolled over to the dolphin theater to see what Sally was doing for lunch. On the way I said hello to Huff and Puff, who did a double tail dance for me. Froggy gave me his usual croupy greeting, but no Sally. I went to her office and passed Mike Arnold, who was on his way out. When he saw

me, he turned to Sally and said, "I'll meet you in five minutes." It was his way of putting a verbal brand on Sally in case
there were any rustlers in the hills.

Sally sat at her desk. She had a pencil in her hand and a
smile on her face.

"Hi, Soc," she said. "I was wondering where you've been
keeping yourself."

"I'm glad to hear that. I thought you were avoiding me."

The smile faded. "No, Soc, it's not like that at all."

I sat in a chair next to her desk. "Then what *is* it like,
Sally?"

"I don't know what you mean."

"It's really not very complicated. We seemed to hit it off
the other night, but since then I've had to make an appointment just to say hello to you. I'm wondering what's going
on."

She placed the pencil down on the desk and stared at it.
Then she turned to me with sad eyes.

"The other night was a mistake."

"How so, Sally? I thought we got along pretty well."

"We *did*, Soc. It's just that . . . look, I'm sorry, I understand why you're angry. It has nothing to do with you. It's
me. I seem to make mistakes with men. First Eddy, then
Mike. I didn't want to make another."

"You and Mike still seem to be an item."

Sally's cheeks flushed with anger. "Looks can be deceiving,
Soc. Mike and I have an understanding. We're just friends."

"Platonic friends?"

She shook her head in frustration, like somebody trying to
explain Mozart to a deaf child. "I like you, and that's the
problem. I've already had two relationships go sour. I can't
trust myself. And I have a hard time trusting others."

"Whom *do* you trust, Sally? Huff and Puff?"

"Yes," she countered, sticking her jaw out at a stubborn

angle. "If you must know, I trust them more than I trust anyone. I would trust them with my life. That's more than I can say about any human being I've ever met."

Human beings are a pretty wretched lot, but I was getting sick of hearing about noble sea creatures untainted by original sin, as if every dolphin or whale in the sea qualified for sainthood. "For godsakes, Sally, you're talking about them as if they had souls. Sure, they're smart and beautiful, but they're just animals. Even your guru Dr. Lilly admitted that when he hammered electrodes into their brains."

She reacted as if I had slapped her face. "They are *not* just animals. They are more than that. They are the purest and gentlest creatures on earth."

"Even Rocky?"

"Yes," she said flatly. "Even Rocky. I thought you understood. I knew you were nervous about going into the pool with him the other night, yet you did it, because you were interested in the truth. I admired that."

"Is that why we made love? You were rewarding me for my bravery."

"No! Of *course* not. That's vile, that is positively vile." Her eyes welled with tears.

I don't handle rejection very well, maybe that's why I picked a fight with Sally. I got out of the chair and prepared to blast out of her office and leave her standing there looking at my back, but Sally was ahead of me. She stood and grabbed the clipboard off her desk, then stormed past me.

I stood there, seething, more angry at myself than at Sally. Great going, pal, you just made a nice lady cry. Then I abandoned the office and slammed the door behind me, but it wasn't the same because there was nobody to see my big exit.

The photo-store clerk handed me an eight-by-ten manila envelope in return for the claim check and some cash. Jill's name was on the order slip taped to the envelope. I sat in the pickup and opened the package. Inside were three 35mm contact sheets of color film, each with thirty-six exposures.

Jill must have been compiling a family album for Rocky. She had taken shots of him from every conceivable angle. Right and left profiles, head-on, pictures of him breaching, or peering through the Plexiglas pool wall. One contact sheet was filled with close-ups of Rocky's dorsal and pectoral fins, and his tail. I remembered the day I saw Jill banging away at poolside with her camera. Could she have put the envelope in my locker? I shook my head. Rocky's mom would have loved all the photos of her baby boy, but I couldn't figure why Jill had gone out of her way to make Eastman Kodak a little richer.

I drove to the marina to check on Uncle Constantine. He was sitting on the deck of the *Berger King* with its owner. He saw me and shouted.

"*Hopa*, Aristotle, come aboard."

I climbed onto the yacht. Uncle Constantine and Berger were seated on the wide deck in turquoise deck chairs. They were sipping cool drinks from tall glasses and smoking cigars as thick as my arm. A backgammon table was set on a table between them.

Berger sprang up and grabbed my hand. "Boy, am I glad to see you. Your uncle has been beating the holy hell out of me. We're using loaded dice, too. I should know, they're mine." He slapped Uncle Constantine on the back, so that some cigar ash fell on the board. "Hell, he's going to own my damn boat before long."

"Maybe in ten years," Uncle Constantine said, smiling. "Come, Aristotle, sit and have a drink."

"I'm on my lunch hour, Uncle. I was wondering if I could talk to you for a minute."

"Go right ahead," Berger said. "I'll make some more drinks. Don't be long, Constantine, I want a chance to get my money back."

"Don't worry, Harry. I want to win this yacht." Berger guffawed happily and headed into his cabin.

We climbed off the *Berger King* and onto the *Artemis.*

"You and Mr. Berger seem to be having a good time."

"Sure, Aristotle, Harry is nice fellow. I tell him treasure hunting maybe not a good idea. He says he doesn't care. He is just bored. Another lonely widow man like me, no good without our wives. He's glad to have company. Me too. Come, I make some *mezes.*"

He disappeared into the galley and came out a few minutes later with a platter laden with appetizers. Cubes of feta cheese, dark olives, stuffed grape leaves, sliced tomatoes, some pita bread, and a bowl of *tzatziki,* yogurt with grated cucumbers and garlic. He fetched a pitcher of lemonade and we sat on the deck eating like Dorian kings. After we finished lunch and cleaned up, I brought out Jill's contact sheets and showed them to him.

He squinted at the sheets, first holding them close, then at arm's length. "Ah," he said. "*Delphis.* We see them all the time in Florida." He made a leaping gesture with his hand. "They jump ahead of the boat. You see dolphins, you have good luck." He put on his glasses and squinted at the contact sheet again. "Ah. These no dolphins. Whales, like they show on TV for Sea World in Orlando. Smart cookies, these whales."

"That's right, Uncle. Very smart cookies."

Uncle Constantine used the Greek word for dolphins. *Delphis,* he had called them. In the old legends, Apollo disguised himself as a dolphin and led settlers to the site of the most famous oracle. A place called Delphi. An oracle would come in handy about now. Maybe she could tell me what was going on at Oceanus. As I remembered, the oracle's answers were usually ambiguous. Their value was in what you made of them. Like the contact sheets.

Lunch hour was nearly over. I waved good-bye to Mr. Berger and told Uncle Constantine I'd come by the next day to talk to him about the tin wreck.

"Take your time, Aristotle. We play some more backgammon."

Back at Oceanus, a note clipped to my time card said a Mr. Parmenter had called. I went to a pay phone and dialed the state-police barracks. Parmenter came on. "Well, we didn't find your missing girl," he said, "but we have her car."

"Where was it?"

"On one of those dirt roads next to the Cape Cod Canal. A jogger running along the canal service road noticed it and called the town cops. They ran the plate through the stolen-car list. They got a negative report and figured the car broke down and the owners could come back for it."

"Any sign of the owner?"

"No blood on the seats, if that's what you had in mind."

"Yeah, I'm afraid that's exactly what I had in mind."

"Nothing like that. We're running a search of the surrounding woods, but I don't think we'll find anything. If I wanted to get rid of somebody's body, I'd toss it in the canal and hope the tide would take her out to sea."

Parmenter was right. Jill's slender body would have been like a piece of flotsam caught in the savage currents of the canal.

"Thanks, John," I said. "If you need to get me later, try me at home."

"Will do."

The afternoon seemed to drag on. Neither Mike nor Sally was around. It must have been a long lunch. I was spinning my wheels at the park, so I punched out early and took the film back to the photo store in Hyannis. The store had one of those do-it-yourself color enlargement machines. You stick your negative in and the machine projects the picture onto a screen. You can enlarge and crop to order and have a copy within a few minutes. I ran the negatives through the machine, pausing for an instant to check each exposure.

Jill had used a zoom lens for distant shots, then focused in on specific body parts. The pictures looked pretty routine first time around. I studied them again and began to see differences. Some of the pictures of the dorsal fin and the tail were grainy, as if they were copies of other photos.

A line was starting to form behind me. I quickly ran off a couple of five-by-sevens of the dorsal fin, since that was the physical feature Jill seemed most interested in. I choose one of the high-grain pictures and a sharper one for comparison. The prints came out in less than ten minutes. I took them over to the counter and borrowed a magnifying glass, studied them a few minutes, then I borrowed a loupe that gave greater magnification.

Something was very odd.

I went back to the machine to stand impatiently in line and blew the prints up to eight-by-ten size just to be sure. I wasn't mistaken. In one picture Rocky's dorsal fin was as I remembered it from my swim in the pool with him. Two notches on the trailing edge. On the grainy print, there was *one* notch. I bought a magnifying glass and went across the street to a bar. Over a beer I examined the prints again. It was puzzling. Maybe he picked up another notch at Oceanus. Or maybe not.

I took another look at the Hyannis address Jill had written on the slip of paper that was with the film ticket. Jill must have thought it was important. I decided to learn why.

The houses by the sea on the east side of Hyannis were probably quite elegant back in the thirties and forties, when families came to the Cape from Boston to drink in the salt air. But cottages had been shoehorned into lots that were too small for them, and now the neighborhood looked as if it had been squeezed together.

The address I was looking for was a two-story gray-shingled house overlooking the harbor and hidden from the street by a stockade fence. About a hundred yards beyond the house I turned down a drive and parked at a town landing. The high fence extended almost to the beach. A fishing boat maybe fifty feet long was moored next to a short, wide pier. The upper story of the house was visible, as was the roof of a smaller building behind the main one.

My daypack with the stuff from the Dougie's Clam Shack job was still in the truck. I slipped the contact sheets into it and pulled out my binoculars. I watched the house and pier for fifteen minutes, then drove back onto the road and parked on a side street where I could see the front door without being seen.

After a half hour of nothing, I began to think about the bar I had passed on the way in and how nice a cold beer would taste. I had my hand on the ignition key, ready to turn it, when Livingston's four-by-four drove up. A gorilla of a man who looked as if he belonged in the World Wrestling Federation got out on the passenger side and opened the gate in the stockade fence, then shut it behind him after the Toyota.

Lines were beginning to intersect. Jill was missing and her car was found in Sandwich, the same town Livingston lived in. Jill writes down an address, and Livingston shows up there. Coincidences possibly, but not very likely. There was nothing I could do now. I studied the house and its surroundings for a few minutes, imprinting them in my memory. Then I started my truck and put it into gear, thinking that it was odd but true, but often you can see more clearly in the dark than in the daylight.

28

Flagg's answering service said he was busy. I growled that it was urgent. The androgynous voice on the phone insisted he was in an important meeting in Boston and could not be interrupted.

"Please tell Mr. Flagg when he's done with his meeting that I need his help this evening." I gave the operator the address of Livingston's Hyannis house and hung up. I was in a bind. The same voices of intuition telling me this was too big to handle alone urged me make haste. I got in the pickup and headed for Hyannis.

Wisps of fog were rolling in off the harbor and the air smelled like the underside of an old wharf as I drove past Livingston's house and parked at the deserted town landing. Hooding the beam of my flashlight, I walked along the wet sand a few yards above the gurgling edge of the tide. Minutes later I stood next to the pier behind the house and listened. The mist-muffled summer-night sounds of music and laughter came from a couple of bars across the harbor.

Climbing a slight incline to the backyard, I made my way around a couple of skiffs and a pile of metal lobster traps to the smaller house. It was a one-story cottage of weathered shingle and white trim about the same vintage as the main building. The cottage was dark except for a dim yellow glimmer. I peeked in the window. The curtains were drawn. I went around to the front door. It had a new Yale padlock on it.

The second-floor lights were on in the main house. I walked across a short expanse of lawn, climbed a stairway onto the porch, and listened at the front door. All was quiet. I tried the knob. The door was locked.

Two vehicles were parked in the drive, Livingston's Toyota and a white Camero I hadn't seen before. I left the porch and went around the side of the house to an old flower bed I had passed. The flowers were long gone, but the bed was bordered by a row of white-painted rocks. I picked out a boulder the size and shape of an eggplant then walked back to the cottage and examined the lock. The wood was old and soft around the latch screws.

I raised the boulder and brought it down hard against the lock. The noise sounded like a cannon. The cottage faced away from the house onto the harbor. I hoped the sound wouldn't carry to the second floor.

The lock held. I cursed, and smashed it again, skinning my knuckles. This time the screws pulled out of the wood. I waited a minute and listened, heard nothing that worried me, then pushed the door open.

The cottage exhaled a damp musty smell of long disuse. I poked the flashlight inside and followed it with my nose. The door opened onto a short hallway. I made my way quietly down the hall and turned into a small kitchen that had a 1930-ish white-enameled GE stove and a Kelvinator refrigerator. Light came from a doorway off the kitchen. I walked that way and stepped into the small living room.

The source of the illumination was a Mickey-Mouse–face night-light plugged directly into an outlet. It didn't throw much illumination, but its soft glow was enough so I could see the blanket-covered form on the couch.

The last time I looked under a blanket I found Hanley's corpse. Preparing for the worst, I peeled back the blanket and switched the flash on at the same time. The circle of light fell on Jill's face. Her mouth was gagged with a red neckerchief. She was lying on her side, her wrists and feet tied with nylon cord to the wooden arms of the couch. I knelt beside her.

"Jill," I whispered, "it's me, Soc. Are you all right?"

She nodded vigorously.

"Good. I'm going to untie you and get you out of here, okay?"

I put the flashlight down and reached behind her neck to undo the gag. Her eyes widened, and she jiggled her head like someone with the palsy. I thought she was excited to see me. I was wrong. The floorboards creaked behind me. I turned. It was too late. Somebody dropped a ten-ton vault on my skull.

I blinked my eyes open and almost immediately wished I hadn't. My head felt as if somebody had jabbed a dinner fork into it above the left ear. Now the scalp was tender on both sides. I tried to rub away the pain, but my arms were tied above my head. My feet were equally immobile. And I was not alone.

A table lamp had been turned on. Two men were in the room. Livingston was bending over me. Standing near the kitchen door was the dark-haired gorilla.

Livingston opened his mouth. "Soc, are you all right?"

It was the same question I asked Jill, which was pretty funny, because I was lying on the couch in her place. I nodded slightly.

Livingston straightened and dragged a chair over. He sat

down and leaned forward. "Well, I guess we can dispense with games. I know you're a private detective."

I almost laughed. Was there anyone who didn't know I was a private cop? I needed to stall while my head cleared. "How about some water?" I said.

He nodded and motioned with his hand. The tap ran in the kitchen and seconds later the gorilla handed Livingston a glass. Livingston held it to my mouth and I took a couple of sips. The water was lukewarm and tasted like old copper pipes, but it relieved the dryness in my mouth. I took another sip.

"How'd you know I was here?" I said.

Livingston laughed softly. "We discovered we had run out of beer upstairs, and my friend Gordie remembered we had a couple of six-packs in the cottage refrigerator." Gordie must be the gorilla. Preppy name for a guy built like King Kong. "He heard you breaking in, and while you were talking to Jill he crept up behind you and hit you over the head with the large gun he always carries."

"Where is Jill now?" I said.

"She's fine, Soc." Livingston motioned to Gordie, who handed him my daypack. He took Jill's contact sheets out of the bag and held them under my nose. "We found these in your truck. Do you know what they are?"

I shook my head.

"You still haven't told me where she is."

"She's going with us, Soc. I think she knows more than she's telling and I want to talk to her at length. Besides, I want to show her what she got herself into." He put his arm on my shoulder. "We'll be leaving you for a time, but we'll try to make you a little more comfortable."

He motioned to the gorilla, who produced a switchblade and slit my bindings. I sat up and rubbed my wrists and ankles, watched him tuck the knife away, and wondered if I could make a break. I quickly decided against it when I saw the Smith & Wesson .357 Magnum Gordie pulled out of his belt. He came over, grabbed my arm, and sat me on a worn braided rug next to an old-fashioned radiator. Then he took a pair of handcuffs from his pocket, snapped one bracelet around my left wrist and the other around the radiator. Livingston took some cushions off the couch and tossed them and the blanket at me.

"You can stretch out and take a nap if you get tired," he said. "Sorry we can't make you more comfortable, but we didn't expect you, and we're in something of a hurry. We'll be back tomorrow night. Gordie, get something for Mr. Socarides to drink."

It was clear Livingston was in charge. The gorilla brought me a six-pack of Heineken's and a wine bottle full of water.

He knelt down next to me and said, "If you have to take a piss, just go in your pants."

"I can think of better targets, Gordon. Your face, for instance."

He grabbed me by the shirt, but was cut short by Livingston's annoyed voice. "C'mon, Gordie, we've got work to do. I want to make sure we catch the ebb tide."

Gordie released my shirt and stood up. "Talk to you later," he said. He was grinning as if he looked forward to our reunion. He switched off the table lamp and hurried to catch Livingston. The door shut and I was alone. About ten minutes later the sound of an idling motor came from the direction of the pier where the fishing boat was tied up. Great rescue attempt, Socarides. Jill is going on a boat ride, and you've become a permanent cottage fixture.

I jerked at the handcuffs. It was a futile gesture. I wasn't going anywhere unless I dragged the whole cottage along with me. My head still hurt where Gordie had sapped me. I popped a beer with one hand and sat with my back against the wall, brooding over my situation, staring sullenly at the vapid grin on the plastic Mickey Mouse face. I was thinking about Laurel and Hardy, Oliver saying another fine mess you've gotten us into. I paused in my ruminations.

I was no longer alone.

A shadow loomed in the kitchen. I thought Livingston had changed his mind and ordered Gordie to take care of me. I had only a couple of weapons. My feet and the beer can. Maybe I could trip him if he got close enough and throw beer in his face.

The shadow moved closer, but not close enough to reach with my feet. A flashlight beam blinded me, then moved down to where my wrist was handcuffed to the radiator. There was a derisive chuckle.

"Looks like you got yourself into something of a pickle," a deep voice said.

I had been holding my breath. I let it out and said, "I got tired and decided to take a nap, Flagg. What the hell took you so long?"

"I came down as soon as I got out of my meeting and heard about your call. Made it from Boston in fifty-five minutes, Soc. That's almost as fast as the plane does it. Spent another ten minutes snooping around. Long enough for you to get into deep shit."

"Stop gloating. If you'd been here as a lookout, I wouldn't be in this predicament." I paused. The pitch of the boat engine had changed. It was revving up.

I pulled at the handcuffs. "Dammit, Flagg, they're getting away."

"You know where the key to the cuffs is?"

The boat was moving from the dock; I could tell by the sound of the exhaust.

"Yeah, it's on the goddamn boat that's halfway across the harbor by now."

"Huh," Flagg said. He reached inside his windbreaker, pulled out a Glock 9mm, and pointed the muzzle inches from the chain between the cuffs. "Turn your head the other way," he said. I did as I was told, covering my left ear with a cushion that only cut off half the explosion that followed. Fragments of flying steel from the shattered chain bit into my hand, and my ears were ringing. I didn't care. I was free. Flagg helped me up.

"I can call the cops or the Coast Guard on my car radio."

I shook my head. "They've got a girl on board. Someone starts shooting, she could get dead real fast."

"You got any better ideas?"

"No," I said. I thought about it a second. "Yeah, I've got an idea." I grabbed his arm. "C'mon, I'll fill you in on the way."

29

Flagg's blue Ford Fairlane was parked about a hundred yards from the house. He had the car in low gear and moving fast while I was still closing the passenger door.

"Where to, skipper?" he said, as if in afterthought.

"You know where the Lewis Bay Marina is?"

"You got it," He spun the steering wheel like a telephone dial and the Ford squealed around a corner. Coming out of the turn, Flagg stomped the gas and the car leaped forward in a tire-squealing, neck-wrenching surge of power.

Moments later he pulled onto Main Street, cut off an Isuzu Scout and ran a slalom course between the summer slow-pokes. He hooked a left and less than a quarter mile from Main Street the Ford shot into the marina parking lot and screamed to a stop in a banshee screech of brakes.

Grabbing my pack, I hit the pavement running and yelled at Flagg to follow. I pounded along the dock and climbed onto the *Artemis*.

"Uncle Constantine!" I shouted down the hatch. "Wake up. I need you."

There was a stirring below and a sound between a sigh and a groan. A light went on, and Uncle Constantine's gnomelike face peered up at me.

"Holy Mother of God, Aristotle," he croaked, "what—"

I cut him off. "No time to talk, Uncle. I've got to borrow your boat. I'll explain after we get under way."

"Okay, nephew, okay. Lemme get dressed." He pulled on his clothes, muttering under his breath in Greek.

"I'll get the engine going." I dashed into the pilothouse just as Flagg climbed aboard. Flagg is built more like a pro football defenseman than a sprinter, and he was puffing with exertion. But I had my own problems. The *Artemis* refused to start. I coaxed, wheedled, whined, threatened, and implored. Uncle Constantine came in, still muttering, tucking his white shirt into his black work pants. He squinted curiously at Flagg.

I said, "This is a friend of mine, Uncle. I'll make a formal introduction once we get moving."

Uncle Constantine nodded and stepped up to the helm. "You're too rough," he said, gently patting the wheel. "The *Artemis* is a woman, Aristotle. You've got to handle her easy, but you have to show her who is the boss."

He ran his fingers over the controls. After a couple of false starts the engine coughed into life and the hull vibrated as power took hold. We gave the engine a few minutes to warm up, then cast off the mooring lines and headed into Lewis Bay. Livingston's boat was probably fifteen minutes ahead of us. His broad-beamed vessel was no wave-busting cigarette boat, but neither was the *Artemis*, despite her goddess-of-the-hunt namesake.

Uncle Constantine extracted a bent cigarette from a crushed pack of Luckies and stuck it in his mouth.

"Now maybe you tell me where you want to go."

I pointed ahead. "There's a boat I want to follow. She just pulled into Hyannis harbor."

He lit up. "Okay, Aristotle. We go like the wind."

He leaned forward against the wheel and increased power on the throttle. The *Artemis* shuddered and jerked slushily forward, gaining a knot or two as we rounded the point with the miniature lighthouse on it. I grabbed a pair of binoculars and scanned the bay. The bright half-moon cast the harbor in a leaden sheen, but a mist hanging over the water cut down visibility.

Almost dead ahead, maybe a quarter mile separating them, were two sets of moving lights. I watched them for a few minutes, shifting my view from one to the other.

One boat was moving southeasterly to the left, toward Monomoy Island off Chatham. The other was veering to the right on a southwesterly course that would take it near Martha's Vineyard. I lowered the binoculars. My brain was in turmoil. If we followed the wrong boat, Jill could be lost forever.

Something came to me. Back at the house, when his goon was handcuffing me to the radiator, Livingston said he wanted to catch the *ebb* current. He was very specific. Not high tide or low, but the ebb.

"Uncle," I said, "do you have an Eldridge tide and pilot book?"

"Sure, Aristotle." He opened a drawer and pulled out a yellow paperbound book covered with grease smudges. Eldridge's has been the Bible for sailors around the Cape and islands for more than a hundred years. I pawed through the pages and found the reference to a "curious phenomenon" off the Cape that vessels can use to get a little shove under their hull from Mother Nature. In Nantucket and Vineyard sounds, the ebb current flows *west*.

The charts in the book indicated the tide was on the ebb in the sound. We were coming abreast of the Hyannisport breakwater. I had to make a decision. I pointed off to the right. "I think that's the one we want, Uncle."

He nodded, moved the throttle up another notch, and aimed the bow on a westerly heading. Flagg, who'd been hanging back, leaned over my shoulder.

"Are you sure?"

"No," I admitted, "but there's a good chance I might be right." I explained my tide theory.

"Huh," he said, in Flagg's version of a compliment. "You're not so dumb as you look."

I turned to my uncle. "This is a friend of mine. His name is John Flagg and he works for the government. We're trying to catch up with some bad people on that boat. I think they have a girl on board. We're afraid to call the police in because she might get hurt."

A grave expression came into my uncle's blue eyes. He shook Flagg's hand and offered him a Lucky, which Flagg declined.

Fifteen minutes passed. The *Artemis* slogged through the rolling seas. The fog had thinned out and we seemed to be staying right on Livingston's tail, but I wondered how long the *Artemis* could stay cranked at top speed before every rusty nail was shaken loose from its hull.

Flagg borrowed the binoculars and stepped out on the deck. A few minutes later he came back into the pilot-house.

"Don't know if this is a coincidence or not, but I think someone's on our tail." He handed the glasses to me. "Take a looksee."

I went out on the deck and pointed the binoculars stern-ward. It was tough to keep the focus in one place, because the deck pitched and yawned. I braced my back against the pilothouse and propped my elbows against my chest. Flagg was right. There was a craft behind us, maybe a half mile back, moving like a caboose in the boat train formed by Livingston's boat and the *Artemis*.

I stepped back inside. "Doesn't mean anything," I said. "Lots of traffic in the sound this time of year. Look, there are a few other lights around us. It could be a big cabin cruiser or a fishing boat."

"Could be," Flagg said without enthusiasm. I caught the doubt in his tone. Remembering his fine-tuned intuition, I decided not to ignore it.

"Okay," I said. "You're probably right, we're being followed."

He showed me his teeth in a lazy smile. "Now you going to tell me what this all about?"

As the *Artemis* plunged into Nantucket Sound with the lights of Cape Cod's southerly shore sparkling off to our right, I gave Flagg a guided tour through the twists and turns that had been added to this crazy maze since I last talked to him. I told him about Hanley's wife, Jill's disappearance, my finding her again, the contact sheets that didn't make sense, and Livingston's mysterious hint that Jill and I had stumbled into something major.

Flagg asked a question now and then. Mostly he listened impassively during the monologue. When I was through, he grunted. "I've felt in my bones there was something else going on here, but I couldn't put my finger on it."

"While you try I'm going below to make some coffee. We could be in for a long night."

It was a cloudless evening, and in spite of the competition from the bright light of the moon, the stars seemed ready to pop out of the black sky. The breeze on the deck was cool and damp. I glanced behind us, past the white frothy wake to the yellow pinpoint off our stern, and wondered whose eyes were looking at me. I had the feeling we would know before long. I went below to make a pot of coffee. When it was ready, I poured three mugs full and took them to the pilothouse. Flagg and Uncle Constantine were chatting like old buddies.

"Aristotle," my uncle said. "Your friend here says he knows you from long ago in the war."

"That's right, Uncle. Flagg was in the paratroops and I was in the marines." I passed the steaming mugs around. "Now that we're on the subject of Vietnam, Flagg, tell me about Eddy Byron. Unless there's a problem with security."

"I just gave you a security clearance," he said. He sipped on his coffee. "Eddy was in 'Nam about the same time we were. He was in the navy, started off as a SEAL, but he flunked basic training. SEALs that wash out get a chance to go into demolition or the navy marine-mammal program. Eddy decided dolphins were a lot safer than demo, so he ended up at the research center in San Diego. When the war got hot, he shipped out and trained the animals to do stuff like guarding bases and taking out enemy frogmen. He came back from Vietnam and got a job as an assistant trainer in an aquarium in California. Worked his way up to head trainer, but got fired."

"What for?"

"He was a little too tough on the animals. He thought he was still in Vietnam, I guess. The navy trainers treated the animals like they were grunts going through boot camp. He carried over the same techniques. The aquarium just wanted the dolphins to jump through hoops. They didn't care if they got up at reveille and saluted."

"How did he end up at Oceanus?"

"He worked at a couple more marine parks and got busted each time. He started to get a reputation as a hard-ass trainer. He got results, but the wear and tear on the animals and staff wasn't worth it to most places. Then Oceanus hired him this year."

"I don't understand it. Austin must have known about his reputation."

"Almost certain, Soc, but he went and did it anyhow. You tell me why."

I thought about it. "We're looking at it the wrong way, Flagg. You know how you're always lecturing me about white man's thinking. Cause and effect, instead of stepping back and letting your feelings talk to you. Well, maybe Oceanus hired Byron not in spite of his reputation as a tough trainer, but *because* of it."

"Like I say, you may be crazy but you're not dumb," Flagg said.

Uncle Constantine had been studying a chart while Flagg and I talked. He had penciled in a series of connected *X*s to show our course. "I think we are here." He tapped the chart off Falmouth where the southerly shore of the Cape bulged into the sound.

"We'll be passing the Vineyard to the south before long," I said. "They can go either way, to the mainland or the island, or straight ahead to Point Judith, Rhode Island. There are lots of little harbors they can duck into, so we'll have to keep a close eye on them."

Flagg went over to the door and peered into the darkness behind us.

"Yeah," he said, "just like those guys are keeping a close eye on us."

Livingston followed a southwesterly course between Martha's Vineyard and the Elizabeth Islands chain. He cut through Quick's Hole between Pasque and Nashawena islands and stayed on a straight line northerly across Buzzards Bay to New Bedford.

Uncle Constantine hadn't moved from the helm. He peered into the darkness, looking for buoys. Occasionally he tapped the compass glass. I offered to take the wheel, but he shooed me away.

About two and a half hours after leaving Hyannis, we approached the lighthouse that stands on a man-made island in the middle of New Bedford Harbor. Beyond the lighthouse long breakwaters stretched from either shore, channeling passage between two massive hurricane gates that can be closed to protect the harbor from storm surge. We passed through the gates and into the Acushnet River. Livingston's boat had slowed. I urged my uncle to keep full steam.

New Bedford has the biggest fishing fleet in New England. The waterfront is a warren of fish companies, plants, warehouses, trailer-truck parking lots, docks, steel-hulled Georges Bank draggers tied up three deep, and finally the suppliers and outfitters for the fleet, the metal workers and welders and hydraulics experts. The fishery complex stretches for three or four miles along the waterfront. If we weren't careful, Livingston could dart in and lose us.

Rising on a low hill behind the waterfront was the old city. New Bedford has a down-at-the-heels look about it now, but once it was the busiest whaling port in the world. You can still see the huge mansions of the canny old Quakers who made their fortunes off whale oil and bone corset stays. A hundred and fifty years ago I would have been looking at a thick forest of masts.

I let my eye drift up to the lights on the cobblestone streets of Johnny Cake Hill and the spire of the old whaleman's bethel. The little chapel hasn't changed much since Herman Melville wrote about it in *Moby Dick*. The pulpit is still shaped like the prow of a whaleship and the walls are lined with the names of New Bedford men who lost their lives hunting whales.

Uncle Constantine jerked me back into the present.

"He goes in, there," he pointed. Livingston's boat was heading to shore. I told my uncle to slow down and to cruise by as if we were a fishing boat returning to port. Livingston was about two hundred yards away. I looked through the binoculars. The boat was headed toward a floodlit concrete dock. Behind it was a whitewashed cinder-block building. We kept going, moving at a couple of knots, looking for a place to stop.

Two fishing draggers were tied up side by side at the entrance to a narrow channel leading inland from the river. I told Uncle Constantine to turn into the channel and use the fishing boats as a screen. I stood by, ready to throw in the anchor. He maneuvered the *Artemis* in next to a dragger nearly twice our size, where we dropped the hook and killed the engine.

Flagg and I hoisted a wooden pram over the side and prepared to get in. Uncle Constantine came over. He was carrying a two-foot length of pipe.

"I'm ready," he said, whacking the pipe into his hand. "I give those bad guys a big headache. Teach them not to hurt a little girl."

Uncle Constantine's old-fashioned chivalry didn't surprise me, but I was in terror of my mother's reaction if anything happened to him.

"Look, Uncle," I said quickly, "somebody has to stay with the boat in case we have to call the cops."

He frowned in disappointment, but didn't put up a fight. "Okay, Aristotle, but they give you any trouble, call in Constantine." He handed me the pipe. I was about to put it aside but thought better of it. Flagg, who usually carries more firearms than the James brothers, checked the load in his Glock and stuffed it into a shoulder pack. He looked at the pipe.

"You going to do some plumbing?" he said.

"You heard of somebody getting the shaft?"

"Yeh," he said.

"Well, this is it."

That shut him up. I hugged Uncle Constantine and told him if we didn't report back in an hour to call on the Coast Guard for help. I slung my daypack over my shoulder and we climbed into the skiff, set the oars in the oarlocks, and rowed into the channel. About fifty feet from the *Artemis* we shipped oars and let the skiff bump into the stone rip-rap lining the channel.

"There were only two guys I know of, Livingston and his gorilla," I said, "but there could be more. The gorilla is packing a gun. I don't know about Livingston. I figure we sneak up and reconnoiter. If we think we can get Jill away without any harm, we do it. If not, we call in the troops. Okay?"

"Sounds good, Soc." There was a glint in Flagg's eye. He was spoiling for a fight.

We secured the boat with its small Danforth anchor, mucked through the grasping mud and dirty straggles of marsh grass, and climbed up the rip-rap boulders. At the top of the incline was a high chain-link fence topped with rusty barbed wire that bordered the channel.

Flagg and I split up and looked for openings, but found none. We would have to make our own. Flagg reached into his pack and pulled out a pair of wire cutters and leather work gloves. He scaled the fence, snipped the barbed wire, and pushed it out of the way, then climbed over. I followed. We were in a large, unlit parking lot with about a dozen tractor trailers in it.

We trotted across the lot to another fence. Flagg cut more barbed wire, and we climbed into still another parking area. One more fence and we were on the street side of the white cinder-block building. The loading platform and work yard were lit with two powerful floodlights. Using the shelter of a trailer truck parked next to the fence, we darted in closer and crouched in the shadow of the loading platform. All was quiet except for the constant hum of a refrigeration unit.

With Flagg keeping a lookout, I climbed onto the platform and checked the big lift-up metal door and a smaller, separate entryway next to it. Both were locked. We split up again. Flagg took one side of the building and I went around the other. A minute later we rendezvoused on the river side. There were a couple more unloading platforms, but no way to get in. We paused at a corner of the building, away from the light cast by the floods. Livingston's boat was moored alongside a concrete dock. Nobody was in sight.

Flagg shook his head. "This place is built like a frigging vault," he whispered.

We were huddled next to a stack of wooden pallets around eight feet high. I pointed toward the building's roof. Half of it was taken up by a second story that had three windows in it. "I'll climb up there. Maybe I can get in. You stand watch. If you don't hear from me in fifteen minutes, I've run into trouble."

I reached into my bag and pulled out a flashlight and the two portable CB radios I had used in Dougie's Clam Shack caper. I gave one to Flagg. "I'll call you if I need a hand," I said.

I clipped the radio onto my belt and stuffed the light in my pocket. Still carrying the lead pipe, I climbed up the stack of pallets and onto the flat roof. I peered in each window. All was dark. I tried to open them, but they were locked. I punched a hole in one with the end of my all-purpose pipe, reached in, undid the latch, and slid the window open. Then I crawled through the opening and turned on the flash.

The beam showed stacks of cardboard cartons. I peeked into a few boxes. They were filled with computer paper and old files. I was in a storeroom for office supplies. A line of yellow light shone from under the door. I went over and tried the knob. The door was unlocked. It opened onto a narrow landing and a set of metal stairs leading to a well-lit area below. Moving slowly and quietly, I descended the stairs to a large concrete-floored space that ran the entire width of the plant. Even if I hadn't recognized the filleting machinery, I would have known it was a fish-processing room by the smell.

I walked past the machinery into another section of the plant past carton-making machines, dollies, and rollers. This must be the shipping department. If I kept going, I would come to the unloading door on the street side. I started in that direction, but about halfway there, stopped at a steel door. I put my ear up against it and heard nothing. I tried the knob. The door was unlocked. I unclipped the walkie-talkie.

"I'm inside, Flagg. Mainly just fish-processing stuff so far. Haven't seen anybody yet. I'm about to go through a door into another section of the building."

"Okay," he said. "Don't forget to look over your shoulder."

I opened the door slowly, poked my head in, then passed into a lighted hallway walled in brown fake wood paneling. The floor was covered with industrial carpeting. I was in the divide between the plant and its office section. Two doors led off the corridor. The one immediately opposite me was made of steel, and there was a wooden door at the end of the hallway. I tiptoed toward that one and pressed my ear against it. A mumble came through, the voices unintelligible.

I went back and tried the steel door, stepping through onto a railless balcony overlooking a large room. I looked around and gasped. Even if I'd taken a hundred guesses about what I had expected to find, all of them would have been wrong.

30

The large windowless room was dominated by an oval pool around fifty feet in diameter. Jill sat in a wooden chair facing the water a couple of yards from the edge. She was trussed like an Italian cheese.

Whoosh.

A shiny gray back broke the water, then another, gleaming under the rows of fluorescent lights. Dolphins! For a second I thought I was looking at Huff and Puff. But that didn't make sense.

Jill saw me and wagged her head. I ran down the steps and across the room. I put the pipe down and used my Swiss army knife to cut her bindings, then unwound the gag from her mouth. It was like pulling a plug on a dam.

"That *bastard*, Livingston!" she said. I put my finger to my lips, and she nodded. She rubbed the circulation back into her wrists. She stood, as unsteady as a young foal, threw her skinny arms around my midsection, and hugged me tightly. "*God*, am I glad to see you." It was cool in the room and she was shivering. I took my windbreaker off and wrapped it around her shoulders. "I thought it was all over back in Hyannis," she whispered. "I guess you found the envelope in your locker."

"I guess you put it there."

"I wanted insurance just in case something went wrong. I followed Livingston to the Hyannis house a couple of times before. That's how I knew about it. I decided to snoop around. It was a stupid thing to do, going alone. I should have called in some help, but I thought I was being smart. The next thing I know, his ugly friend is sticking a gun in my face and tying me up."

My eyes scanned the room, taking in the dolphins and the heavyweight winches and large cloth slings hanging over the pool.

"What's this all about, Jill? Is Livingston starting his own aquarium?"

The question started her off again. "He *is* a bastard," she growled. "It's worse than that." She hugged me still tighter. "It's much worse than anything you can imagine."

"Tell me later," I said. "We've got to get out of this place."

The room had a large roll-up door. The only other exit was the way I came in. I grabbed Jill's hand and pulled her toward the stairs. Things had gone too easy for me. My winning streak was about to end. The door opened and Gordie stood at the top of the stairs. The grin on his face definitely didn't go with the Magnum clutched in his hand.

"Hold it right there, kiddies."

With Livingston following, Gordie leisurely descended the stairs and walked toward us. The muzzle of the gun pointed at my chest looked like the entrance to the Calahan Tunnel. Livingston was packing a Colt automatic. Given Livingston's academic credentials, I would have expected him to look silly with a gun in his hand. But his donnish expression was gone and in its place was a fanatical intensity. He looked entirely capable of pulling the trigger. He had his mouth open, as if he were about to say something. I beat him to the punch.

"Dr. Livingston, I presume." Okay, so it wasn't cute, but it made Livingston chuckle, and that's not a bad thing with a guy holding a gun on you.

"You presume correctly, Soc. You probably didn't know a light goes on in the office when the door here is opened," he said. "Gordie, would you check to see if Soc is carrying any firearms."

The gorilla came over and frisked me. He didn't find a gun because I don't carry one, but he discovered the walkie-talkie. He brought it back to Livingston who looked at the radio with interest. "Gordie," he said quietly, "please take a look around the grounds just in case Soc didn't come here alone."

Gordie nodded and left Livingston to cover us. I remembered Flagg's parting warning and hoped he would remember to look over *his* shoulder.

Livingston glanced at the handcuff bracelet still dangling from my wrist.

"Well, Soc," he said genially, "I give up. How did you get out of those handcuffs?"

"I once read a book on Houdini, Dr. Livingston."

"If you won't tell me that, maybe you can tell me how you found us."

"I just got a great recipe for creamed haddock and stopped by to see if you had some."

"You've come to the right place for haddock. We're quite proud of our wholesale fish division."

I jerked my head toward the pool. "What's that, the special of the day?"

"This room has nothing to do with our fish company," Livingston said. "It's an entirely different operation." The dolphins swam in close and gave us their friendly smiles. "It looks like the kids are hungry." Keeping his gun trained on us, Livingston went over to an industrial cooler and scooped some fish into a plastic bucket. Then he walked to the edge of the pool and threw fish to the dolphins, who caught them in their mouths.

While he was doing this the door at the top of the stairs opened. From all appearances, Gordie's hunting trip had been a success. Walking ahead of him, hands in the air, were Walden Schiller, his friend Ned, and the girl Sara. It was like being in a weirdly surrealistic episode of "This Is Your Life."

Gordie came over and showed Livingston a hunting knife with a blade about a foot long. He pointed to Ned, who must have felt undressed without his pigsticker, because he glowered from under his bangs.

"The shiv belongs to this creep," Gordie said, throwing the knife into a corner. He yanked a gun from his belt and gave it to Livingston. Pointing at Walden, he said, "The bearded guy was carrying this piece." The pistol was a Glock, like Flagg's.

Livingston hefted the Glock in his hand. "Who are you and why are you trespassing on private property?"

Walden shot a withering glance of contempt at Livingston. "My name is Schiller."

"Hello, Walden," I said. "I guess that was you following me from Hyannis."

"That's right, Soc. You didn't know the Sentinels have a one-boat navy. It's not very shiny or new, but it gets us where we're going. We checked out the doctor's home and didn't see anyone there, so we were keeping at eye on the Hyannis house from the harbor. We saw his boat leave, then yours. We simply followed." He turned to Livingston and said, "Your smuggling operation is finished." I had to hand it to Schiller, he was a gutsy little elf.

Livingston didn't agree. "Well, Walden Schiller. I'm honored to have the head of SOS as a visitor, but I'm afraid you're wrong about us, Mr. Schiller." He pointed to the pool. "We're holding this merchandise for an aquarium in Rhode Island. I expect it to be loaded into the holding tanks on our fishing boat and shipped out on schedule tonight." Livingston turned to me like a lawyer arguing his case before a jury. "You can blame whale huggers like Mr. Schiller here for this. Thanks to them the price of marine mammals has gone up astronomically."

"I never figured you for a guy who could get somebody a good price on a used dolphin, Dr. Livingston."

"Dolphins are small change, Soc. We'll find you a dolphin or a beluga in a way that avoids all the government permit folderol, but you can get them legally if you choose, so the price isn't the greatest. Orcas are where the money is. They are virtually impossible to acquire. You can get from five hundred thousand to a million dollars for a killer whale."

I let his answer sink in. "Rocky never did recover, did he, Dr. Livingston?"

"We tried every kind of antibiotic under the sun," he said, shaking his head sadly. "But nothing worked. It would have simplified things a great deal if they had."

"When did Rocky die?"

"About six months ago."

"That's when you brought in his replacement."

"He came from a pod off British Columbia. We transported him by boat into the coast near Seattle. He spent some time in a facility similar to this on the West Coast getting used to humans, learning the basic tricks, then we moved him across the country by truck. We didn't know if he'd survive the trauma. It was quite a tribute to the efficiency of our organization."

"With that kind of efficiency, couldn't you get a whale whose dorsal fin had one notch in it?"

"This was a rush job," he said, smiling. "We were more concerned with getting a male the same size and hoped nobody would notice the dorsal fin." He looked at Jill and shrugged. "Nothing would have gone wrong if Eddy Byron's death hadn't focused the attention of our sharp-eyed little spy over there."

"You had me fooled, too, doctor. I actually believed your soul-searching about keeping Rocky in captivity."

"I was sincere about that, Soc. I *do* believe these animals have a right to be free. But we have to be able to study them."

"That's garbage," Schiller said.

Livingston's eyes hardened behind the thick glasses. I don't know if he would have ordered Gordie to kill all five of us, but I wouldn't have put it past him. A few seconds and we would no longer be obstacles. Nobody would hear the shots behind the concrete walls, and they could dump our bodies at sea. I pointed to the fish bucket. I had just seen something that made me want all attention focused on me.

"Do you mind if I give the dolphins a fish?"

"They've already had plenty to eat," Livingston said almost absentmindedly, as if he were pondering the next dangerous step. "But go ahead," he said, in a tone that sounded too much like the warden granting the condemned his last wish. "Feed them if you want."

Jill and the others were probably wondering why the hell I wanted to feed dolphins when our lives were in the balance. That's because they had their backs to the door and hadn't seen it open a crack, then wide enough for Flagg's dark face to show through.

I picked up a couple of herring and threw a fish into the middle of the pool. It arced through the air with the dolphins in hot pursuit. I hoped the sound of their splashing would drown out Flagg's entrance.

He was out on the platform, crawling on his hands and knees.

All eyes were on the pool. It's hard for a human being to resist watching a dolphin show.

I threw another fish. Both dolphins exploded from the water.

Flagg was poised at the edge of the platform.

I tossed in more fish. Livingston had made up his mind. He stepped forward.

Flagg launched himself. He was in midair, halfway between the platform and Gordie the gorilla. He seemed to float for hours, like a Boeing 747 making a runway approach, before he crash-landed on Gordie with full landing gear deployed. Even a big boy like Gordie couldn't survive an attack like that. He flew forward onto his stomach with Flagg on his back. The Magnum skittered across the concrete floor, eyes following it, and plopped into the dolphin pool.

Ned agilely scooped up his hunting knife like a Cheyenne looking for a scalp.

Livingston took the Glock from his belt.

I grabbed Uncle Constantine's pipe from off the floor. We all moved in on him, Flagg and me, Walden, Jill and Sara.

I said, "You can't shoot all of us, Dr. Livingston. Do you really want to make the jump from whale smuggling to murder?"

He stood there, biting his lower lip, weighing the possibilities.

"No," he said with an ironic smile. He placed the pistol on the floor. Flagg picked it up and went over to check on Gordie, who was spread out like a pile of mush.

"He's alive," Flagg announced, almost ruefully. He came back and said, "Woulda been here sooner, but somebody snuck up, whacked me on the head, and stole my gun."

Walden said, "We saw him outside and thought he was one of Livingston's guys."

Flagg stared dangerously at him. "You thought wrong. You didn't know I had a hard head, either. I got up and went the same way you did over the roof, Soc. Came down here, found this party going on, so I thought I'd join in."

I put my hand on his shoulder. "You were magnificent, Flagg. I never knew you could imitate the Flying Nun."

"There's a lot you don't know about me. I was making history, Soc."

"History?"

"Sure," he said. He was stony-faced, but there was a wicked gleam in his eye. "When was the last time the Indians rescued the cavalry?"

31

It was early evening when I climbed the stairs to Dan Austin's office and opened the door without knocking. Austin was seated at his desk working on some papers. He looked over the tops of his glasses and scrunched his mouth in an annoyed pucker.

"What can I do for you, Socarides?"

I tossed the glossy photographs onto the desk and sank into a chair.

Austin glanced at the eight-by-tens. "Look," he said wearily, "I'm very busy."

"Livingston talked," was all I said.

"Dr. Livingston? Talked about *what*, Socarides?"

"He talked about you, for one thing."

He placed his pen down on the blotter, making sure it was parallel to the side. "What are you saying?"

"I'm saying Livingston's smuggling operation was busted last night. He's in the New Bedford slammer, probably looking in the Yellow Pages for a lawyer familiar with the Marine Mammal Protection Act."

He came out of his chair. "What the hell is this all about?"

"Sit down, Austin, I'm not through yet."

Austin settled like someone on a slowly deflating air cushion. He leaned back, folded his hands across his stomach, and glared at me.

"Go ahead, but make it fast, because when you're through, I'm going to call Simon Otis and tell him I want you out of Oceanus."

"I'll save you the trouble. Consider this my resignation. Before I turn in my blue jersey, let's talk about these photos you're trying so hard to avoid looking at."

He picked up the top photo, glanced at it, and put it down. "This is a picture of a whale's dorsal fin. So what?"

"It's more than that, Dan. This is a photo-ID. It's something the whale scientists came up with so they could tell one whale from another. You take pictures of the whale's markings, or scars, barnacles, their flukes, fins, stuff like that. It works pretty well. You can track their migration, births, deaths, love affairs. It's almost like fingerprints."

He smiled a cold smile. "You've become quite an authority on whales, Socarides."

"Dr. Livingston deserves the credit. We had a long talk today. I'm missing pieces of the puzzle because he saved some goodies for a plea bargain, but he told me all about photo-ID." I tapped the photo with my forefinger. "For example, this is an old publicity shot of Rocky that Jill copied. You'll have to excuse the grainy quality; it's been enlarged considerably." I ran my finger down the dorsal fin's trailing edge. "The fin in this picture has one notch. Doc Livingston says it could have been made during a fight over a female. Whales aren't too different from people that way, I guess."

I placed the second picture next to the first. "Here's where it *really* gets interesting. Jill shot this one a few days ago. I was there when she took the picture. Look at this. Rocky's got two notches in his dorsal fin. What do you think? Did Rocky get into another fight?"

"You tell me, Socarides."

"Okay, I will. The fin has two notches because it belongs to an entirely different killer whale." I looked up and grinned. A grayness had crept onto Austin's tanned face. "Am I right so far?"

We locked eyes. "Go on," he said thickly. "It's your show."

Nightfall had come. The office was dark except for the yellow circle of light cast by the desk lamp.

"Thanks, Dan. Here's my theory. We've got two different killer whales here. The first photo shows the original Rocky, the one who got sick and died. One notch. The second shot is the animal Livingston smuggled into Oceanus to take Rocky's place. Two notches. You must have been really desperate."

Austin's face flushed with anger. "I don't know what you're talking about."

He began to arrange objects and papers on the desk. I leaned back, folded my hands behind my head, put my feet up on his desk, and looked up at the ceiling.

"Your star attraction was dying just when you had enough money to buy back your interest in Oceanus. The Feds might ask embarrassing questions. So Livingston offered to get a new orca for you. The price was high, but he'd settle for a piece of the park. Atwood was fired because he had worked with Rocky and would discover the scam, but most people can't tell one orca from another. The animals were virtual twins. Both males, both the same size, both with the same saddle-patch patterns and pigmentation. Hell of a good job of matching. With the exception of the notches, the whales were identical in every way save one."

"What was that, Mr. Socarides?"

I took my feet off the desk. "Their temperament was like night and day. The original Rocky was a mellow easygoing guy who liked to please. But the second Rocky was unpredictable, a real independent cuss. He picked up the tricks in no time, but there was one thing he wouldn't tolerate. He didn't like trainers riding him like a horse. In fact he *hated* it. He'd bump people off his back and drag them down to make his point. But the whale ride was a crucial part of the show, and you wanted to keep it, so you brought in Eddy Byron because he had a reputation for dealing with difficult animals. He really knew how to crack the whip."

"It's no secret I hired Eddy because he had a reputation for being tough. It was one of his strong points." Austin's voice had lost some of its tightness and was calmer than before, as if he had resigned himself to a decision. He was sitting back, his face no longer in the pool of light. His hands had stopped their fidgeting. Austin was dangerously calm.

"But toughness doesn't cut it with a killer whale, does it?" I said. "They're big and they're fast and they're smart. Rocky was more than a match for Byron. He wasn't going to give *anyone* a pony ride for a couple of dead fish. Rocky became a challenge to Byron's reputation. He was going to break him the way a cowboy breaks a bronco. But Rocky didn't give a fig about Byron's rep. Byron was just another guy who wanted to play horsey. When Byron tried to show him who was boss, Rocky pulled him under. He let him go, just like he did with the other trainers. It scared the hell out of Byron, though. Even worse, people saw it happen. Byron was a macho dude. He didn't like being laughed at. His reputation was on the line. It became a personal thing with him. He began to hate Rocky. And that's what got him killed."

Austin leaned forward so I could see his face. His mouth was twisted in a sardonic smile. "So you think Rocky *did* kill Byron?"

"I didn't say that."

"You're not making sense. Either he killed him or he didn't."

"He didn't kill him, Dan. *You* did."

The smile evaporated. "That's ridiculous. Why the hell would I kill Eddy Byron?"

"Let's talk about that. Byron was no fool. He knew immediately that he was dealing with an untrained whale, not one who'd gotten sick and forgotten his tricks. You had to let him in on the whale switch. You knew it was a lousy idea to entrust a secret like that to a quick-tempered drunk, but you didn't have much choice."

"I suppose I fabricated the tooth marks in Byron's wet suit."

"Oh no. They were genuine. The night Byron died, he and Rocky had another go-around. This time Rocky got a little rougher. He grabbed Byron hard enough to rip his sleeve."

"You're contradicting yourself."

"Not at all. I think Rocky *grabbed* Byron, I didn't say he killed him. There's a big difference. Rocky got aggressive when he was under pressure, but he never seriously hurt anyone. That's the key. You said it yourself. I think scaring trainers became a game with him. It relieved the boredom. Maybe it was just an animal reflex the first time. Then he saw what fun it could be and kept it up. He'd drag the trainers down and let them go, then sit back and watch the reaction. Whales are fascinated by humans. Here was something totally different. They'd thrash around, yell, scream, and do all sorts of amusing things. I was in the pool with Rocky the other night. He came over and presented his back to me. He wanted me to grab onto his fin and get on his back, I'm sure of it, so he could have the fun of scaring me half to death."

Austin snorted. "That's nothing but conjecture. Every bit of evidence points to the fact Rocky killed Byron."

"I thought so, too. In fact I was about to hang Byron's murder on Rocky and be done with it, but that's before I heard about the cattle prod."

"What are you talking about?"

"Eddy Byron owned a cattle prod. I know it existed because Sally Carlin caught him once when he was thinking about using it on the dolphins. Old Ben the watchman saw Byron with the prod the night he was killed. Yet the prod wasn't found with Byron's body. It wasn't in the pool because I looked. So that introduced a third element into the equation. Somebody *else* saw Byron between the time Ben said hello to him and the next morning when the body was discovered. Somebody who didn't want the prod found."

"Why would anybody take this mythical prod?"

"Because it would raise questions. Just picture the animal-rights people getting hold of *that* one. Christ, they object to you just *having* the whale. Think of what they'd say if they found out you were shocking them. They'd charge you with inhumane treatment. They'd get Congress to investigate, revoke your permits, maybe close Oceanus forever."

"So I killed Eddy and took the prod. I had a busy night, didn't I?"

I nodded. "Here's how I figure it. Byron tried to put the muscle on Rocky, who pulled him down and ripped his suit. Eddy was a drunk. He would have gone back to his office and had a few pops. I can just see him there brooding, looking at the holes in his sleeve, knowing Rocky had beaten him, deciding he was going to punish Rocky. He wasn't thinking straight. He went out and got the electrical prod. He'd never get near Rocky again after that, but he didn't care, he had other ideas. He would get him close to the edge of the pool and shock him."

"You still haven't told me why I killed Byron."

"Stay with me. Eddy was an over-the-hill trainer with a reputation so bad nobody in the industry would hire him except you. He was going around the park grumbling that he was worth a lot more money than Oceanus was paying him. It was sort of his way of talking himself into a blackmail scheme. With Rocky putting the cap on his failure, there was nothing left for him."

"So I snuck into Oceanus and killed him. Give me a break, Socarides."

"Okay, I will. I don't think you planned to kill Byron. You stayed late that night as usual. You had a lot on your mind. Bay State wanted to sell the park. You had first refusal and it looked like the deal would be a shoo-in until the Japanese came into the picture, and Bay State started looking for a legal way to shove you aside. You had sunk a pile of dough buying the new whale—Livingston will vouch for that—and you didn't have the money to go head-to-head with Bay State. You might never get your beloved park back. You're steaming about the whole thing when you bump into Eddy at the orca stadium. He's fuming, too. You ask him about the cattle prod. He shows you the rips in his sleeve. He says he's going to teach Rocky a lesson. You argue. Maybe you threaten to fire him. That's when his blackmail intentions bubble to the surface. If you had been thinking clearly, you might have stalled him, but you were furious. You go for Byron's throat and get the best of him, which isn't too hard because he's so drunk. Then you hold him underwater. Later, you take the cattle prod, hoping the toothmarks and Rocky's past history will be enough to indict him." I paused to let the explanation sink in. "How'd I do?"

He was silent a moment. Finally he said, "You're bluffing.

You couldn't prove a thing you said unless you saw it, and you've admitted you weren't there, so you must have made it up."

"Yeah, you're right. I did make it up. I can't pin Eddy's death on you—"

Austin gave me a smug smile.

"—but I can prove you killed Hanley. It doesn't really matter to me if you do life for one murder or two."

"You're crazy. Why would I kill Hanley?"

"Blackmail again. He found out there was a payoff on your wetlands dredging permit to build this place, and he had proof from his contacts in Boston. You got scared. You hoped the Japanese buy-out would fall through. But Bay State was after top dollar and might use even the hint of a bribery scandal as an excuse to say their original deal with you was void. They could then sell the park to someone else for more money or, at the very least, tie it up in litigation you couldn't afford."

"So I killed Hanley to shut him up?"

"Uh-huh. Hanley wanted to hear you squirm, he told me that himself the night he was killed. I'll bet he called you and told you he was going to meet me and talk about the wetlands deal."

"You can't prove that."

"Don't be so sure. I remembered Hanley ran out of change when he called me from a pay phone. He had to put his next call on his credit card. I had a friend check the phone company. They have a call to Oceanus on their records. Ben remembers you working late that night. So . . ."

"So I went to his boat and killed him."

"Funny, I was thinking the same thing. You got there before me. You'd already murdered one man, so killing Hanley was a cinch. Then you called the cops. You hoped I'd get so bogged down trying to prove I didn't kill Hanley that I'd stay out of your hair. When the cops couldn't make any charges stick, you tried to get me out of the picture. You were afraid I might stumble onto something. That's why you suggested to Mike Arnold that I work the shark tank and you put fish powder in my pocket to ensure I'd have a warm welcome. And I'll bet it was you who monkeyed around with my air tank. I can't prove it, but that's okay, I've got enough to hang you when I go to the cops."

Again, Austin didn't reply. He got up and went to the closet, unlocked the door, and came back with an aluminum tube about four feet long that had a rubber handle at one end.

"Is this what you're looking for?"

I took the prod. Austin reached into the closet again and I looked up and into the muzzle of a .22 automatic.

"Actually, *that's* what I'm really looking for," I said. "It's the gun you used to kill Hanley, isn't it?"

"You tell me when I shoot you with it."

"Before you pull the trigger, grant me one last wish. Look out that window. Go ahead, it's no trick."

Keeping his eye on me, Austin glanced through the glass. Four figures were silhouetted against the dolphin-pool lights.

"Who the hell is that?"

"I wasn't quite honest with you, Dan. I've already gone to the cops. The big gentleman on the left is Mr. Flagg, who works for the navy. The others are Mr. Jones from the Department of Commerce who's interested in talking to you about transporting marine mammals against the law, and two police officers, one from the state, the other from the town."

"You son of a bitch," Austin snarled. It wasn't a nice thing to say; he didn't even know my mother. But the remark gave me a hint of his mind-set. He wasn't about to turn his pistol over and go docilely into the good night. He had killed two people and he might want to go out in a blaze of glory, turning the gun on himself after taking me with him. I switched on the cattle prod and poked his arm.

"*Yeow!*"

The gun went flying. Using the prod like a master swordsman to keep him at bay, I picked him up. Then I went over to the window and waved the boys in.

32

Austin was bundled into a cruiser and taken to the police station to make his one phone call. I went to Ben's office. He was on his cot watching a rerun of "The Fugitive." I told him I wouldn't mind a drink. He looked at me through rheumy eyes, nodded with understanding, and gave me a glass and a half bottle of rye whiskey from a desk drawer.

I strolled over to the orca stadium, turned on all the pool and bleacher lights, and sat in the approximate center of the bleacher section. I poured myself a couple of fingers of booze. The whiskey went down like double-edged razor blades. I drank it anyway.

I should have been cheering. The bad guys were in the arms of the law, my assignment at Oceanus was over, and I could go catch fish with Sam. But there was an emptiness in the pit of my stomach and I wasn't sure why. Maybe it was postpartum blues.

Rocky was swimming around the pool. His dorsal fin, wobbling a little at the tip, cut through the green water in peaceful, hypnotic patterns. With the help of the rye, I soon fell into a half-lidded trance. A voice jarred me back into the real world.

"So this is where you disappeared to," Flagg said. "Mind if I join you?"

"Naw. Have a seat. I'd offer you a swig, but I know how you feel about firewater."

"That's okay, I'm not thirsty."

For a couple of minutes we watched Rocky's graceful water ballet.

Flagg broke the silence. "What are you thinking about, man?"

I took a sip. "I'm thinking about Rocky's ancestors. They crawled out of the sea onto the land a few million years ago, then they went back into the sea, and I think I know why. The ocean's a tough place to live, but it's not half as dangerous as it is on terra firma."

Flagg grunted. After a few moments he said, "Old Maushop did it."

"How's that?" I said. Maushop was the mythical giant who lived around Flagg's hometown of Gay Head.

"He dreamed the Europeans were coming. So he changed some of his family into killer whales. That way they could go wherever they wanted to and the white man couldn't harm them."

"Hell, that sounds pretty good to me. Just think, Flagg, no cops and robbers, no car-repair bills, no taxman or wars or junk phone calls. Complete freedom from the banes of civilization."

He gestured toward the whale tank. "You call that freedom?"

I thought about it a second. "No," I said. "Guess

Maushop's children never figured the white man would follow them into the ocean and drag them back onto dry land."

"It wasn't all white men," Flagg said. "Some of my people shipped out on those New Bedford whalers."

"There's enough blame to go around. What's next for you?"

"You know the government. This case'll give me six months of paperwork. How about you?"

"Got to file a report with the guys who hired me to look into this mess."

"What are you going to tell them?" He pointed to Rocky. "Your buddy in there a murderer or not?"

"I'm sure Austin killed Eddy Byron. I just can't prove it. He'll go to the slammer for Hanley's murder; that's one consolation. I guess Rocky will go through life with a question mark over his head."

Or maybe not.

It was a funny little thought. It winged in out of nowhere, and I grabbed it with a mental butterfly net before it fluttered off.

"Or maybe not," I whispered. I got up to go.

"You going to be okay?" Flagg said. "I can give you a lift."

"No thanks. You've heard of progressive church suppers? Well, I'm a progressive drunk. The more I drink, the closer I get to home. When I'm too stiff to drive, I'm in my front yard and can crawl to the front door."

Flagg knew me. A doubtful frown crossed his face.

"I'll be fine, Flagg. I'm just kidding. Look, I'm even taking the rest of the weed killer in this bottle back to Ben. Stay in touch. And, oh yeah, please turn out the lights when you leave."

Ben's office was empty. He was probably making his first and only sober patrol. I left the booze on his desk. The bottle was still at least a quarter full. He'd appreciate that. A few minutes later I was in my pickup, heading toward Hyannis.

The night air was warm and moist at the marina. A light haze lay on the water, but the moon shone down from a cloudless sky. Tomorrow would be a hot day.

Uncle Constantine was on the deck, sitting on a folding aluminum chair and smoking a Lucky. He jumped up from his chair, grabbed me by the wrist, and yanked me on board.

"*Kalispera*, nephew! I don't believe this. I look up at the moon and stars, so beautiful, and I say to myself, 'The only thing I wish is that Aristotle is here, too.'"

He went below and returned with a tinkling glass of ouzo. The cold sweet liquor felt good going down my throat and overpowered the foul taste of Ben's whiskey.

"No backgammon tonight with Mr. Berger?"

"It's hard for me to play backgammon to lose. Harry is not a good player. Besides, Harry is busy," he said, slapping his thigh. "He finds a woman at last. Nice real-estate lady from Boston. They go out for dinner. They ask me to come, but I know better. So, Aristotle, how is the little girl, the one we rescue?"

"She's fine, Uncle."

"Good. We chase bad guys again sometime, Aristotle, but not too soon. The *Artemis* is tired, like me. She has to rest for the trip back home."

I looked up from my glass. "Home? You're going back to Florida?"

"Sure, nephew. I go back to sponging. Don't worry, no diving," he said quickly. "I just run the boat and tell the young divers what a smart fellow I am."

"What about the tin wreck?"

He wrestled with the question a moment. "I'm too old for treasure hunt," he said finally. "For me it's a way to fill my head so there is no room for sadness over Thalia. Okay, now

I'm not sad anymore. I know she is still with me. I can talk to her. She just can't talk back. No problem. She'll have lots to tell me when I see her again. Up there." He pointed to the sky.

"Won't you have to pay back the money you borrowed for this trip?"

"No problem, nephew. Harry wants to be my partner. He says the burger stores run by themselves. So he buys into the *Artemis*, I pay off my loan with the money. Harry's not a bad fellow. Lonely like me. We have many laughs. Maybe I make him a dive tender. We go back south together. It's too cold up here. What about you, Aristotle? What you going to do?"

"Go back to fishing, I guess."

"That's all? You should get married, have kids someday so I can tell them octopus stories."

I held my glass out and he filled it. "Sure, Uncle. I'll look up one day and see a pretty girl holding a white dove."

Uncle Constantine leaned over and embraced me. Then he poured himself more ouzo. I was getting buzzed, looking at two glowing cigarette butts. Ouzo is a treacherous drink. The sweet taste masks the alcohol, so its potency sneaks up on you. I tried to stand. My legs felt like sticks of butter and the deck started playing tag with the bow. I steadied myself on my chair. My uncle grabbed me by the arm and steered me below.

"Tonight you sleep in the arms of *Artemis*," he said.

I made it down the steps. The bunk came up to meet my face and all the world went black.

About a thousand years later I awakened. I was still facedown on the bunk. A blanket covered me. I could smell coffee. I pushed my chin up and called out for Uncle Constantine.

He came below, patted me on the back, and filled a mug with black coffee from the stove.

"You okay, Aristotle?"

"Yeah, I'll be fine. Thanks for the bed, Uncle." I sat up and felt better after some coffee.

"If you try to drive truck last night, they fish you out of the harbor. My fault. I give you too much to drink."

"I'm big enough to say no, Uncle."

He shrugged, unconvinced. I followed him onto the deck, blinking at the bright morning sunlight. The marina had a festive atmosphere. People were getting ready to head out for some fun time on the water. The big authority ferryboat was cruising out of the harbor on its way to Nantucket. I had another cup of coffee that woke me up by several more degrees, then thanked Uncle Constantine and told him I had some business to attend to.

"I talk to your mother," he said. "Tell her everything okay. She says you and me come up to the house Sunday for baked lamb. I say fine. Like old times, Aristotle."

I grabbed him around the shoulders. "Just like old times, Uncle."

From the marina I drove across the Cape to Jill's house. Her Volvo was in the drive, and behind it was Walden Schiller's black van and the blue Jeep. I went up and rang the front doorbell. Ned the Green Beret answered the door. I told him I wanted to see Walden Schiller. He moved out of the way, but as I stepped inside he dug his strong fingers into my biceps. I tensed.

"Heard you were in 'Nam," he said.

"Yeh," I said. "Marines."

He grunted. "You didn't handle yourself too bad in New Bedford. For a gyrene."

I looked into his hazel eyes. There was madness in them.

"You were pretty good, too. For a Green Beanie."

He opened his mouth to show a tooth missing. "Sorry about the other night here. Putting a knife to your throat."

"That's okay, pal. I probably needed a shave anyhow."

He didn't hear me. He cocked his head to listen to other voices. "It's crazy," he said.

"What is?"

"*Every*thing."

I gently removed his hand from my sleeve. Ned seemed to snap out of a daze.

"They're out back. Follow me." We walked through the house and onto a sunny flagstone patio. Walden Schiller was seated at a circular white metal table in the shade of a yellow umbrella. Next to him was Sara, the young dark-haired woman who never smiled. Beside her was Jill, sending out her usual sunbeams. She sprang from her chair and came over.

"Soc!" She threw her arms around me. "My hero."

"I may have to get sick if you keep this up."

"But you *are!* You rescued me and took care of Dan Austin, too. If that's not a hero, I don't know what is."

"Have it your way, sweetie pie." I looked over her head. "Hello, Walden."

Schiller grinned and gathered together a pile of papers on the table.

"Good to see you, Soc. Have a seat."

I sat beside sullen Sara. "Did I interrupt something?"

"Oh no," Schiller replied. "We were just going over our plans for SOS."

"What exactly are your plans?"

He took a seat across from me. "Still hashing them out. There are all sorts of possibilities. This is a great opportunity. I wouldn't be surprised if Jill got a movie offer for her story. Young woman goes undercover and busts a worldwide whale-smuggling ring. With some help, of course. No offense to you, Soc."

"None taken. I agree. Jill took all the risks. I'm glad to

hear SOS may go Hollywood. So I guess you won't have to
bomb Oceanus."

The shrewd eyes narrowed. "What do you mean, Soc?"

"I'll say it in one word. Semtex."

"I'm afraid you'll have to explain."

"Semtex. It's a plastic explosive made in Czechoslovakia.
Terrorists use it to make a big bang. They put a couple of
pounds of the stuff in a portable radio to blow Pan Am flight
103 out of the sky. I heard you've got some. With Oceanus
getting ready to open in a few days, I just wondered if you
were going to use it."

I glanced around at the others. It was hard to tell from
Ned's perpetually vacant expression what he was thinking,
but Sara looked like a kid who'd been caught with a crib note
up her sleeve.

Schiller saw the initiative drifting from him to me and
snatched it back.

"You're obsessed, Soc. Nobody can prove we made bomb
threats. I told you before, that would be against the law."

"Spare me the irony, Walden. Let's talk facts. The future
of Oceanus seems pretty shaky. Rocky, its main attraction, is
contraband. Austin is in jail. The park is on the financial
rocks. So if you did have some explosives, you really don't
need them anymore."

"I agree that Oceanus isn't looking too great. But there's
just too much money invested in the place to close it down
and make it into a gift shop. I'm being totally realistic about
the publicity. After the furor dies down, we'll be back to
square one. Oceanus could have a new owner and it'll be
business as usual. Even so, there are whales held in jails
all over the country. Our job isn't over until they're all
free."

"You may be right, Walden. But Uncle Sam is nervous
about that Semtex. He knows a few tons of plastique are

floating around the Middle East, but this would be just that
much less to worry about."

"You're trying to make a point, Soc. What are you saying?"

"I'm saying that I might give you a reason to rearrange
your thinking. In return, maybe you could see the Semtex
gets put someplace where it can't do any harm."

"I'm listening. Make me an offer I can't refuse."

"I can't right now. You and the gang look like you're having a good time here. I'd like you to relax for a day or two
until I put this deal together."

Schiller looked around at his colleagues. It was a polite
gesture. There was no doubt he called the shots for the Sentinels.

"Okay," he said. "I'm intrigued. Let's see what you can
do."

"Fair enough. Thanks for your time."

Jill said she would walk me to my truck.

"By the way," I said as we strolled around to the front,
"what made you suspect Livingston?"

"I didn't at first," she said. "I trusted him because he
seemed to be so sincere, so genuine. I started hanging around
Rocky a lot, but I didn't suspect anything until I got into the
files they keep on the animals."

"Austin mentioned them. They keep a complete dossier on
all the animals."

"That's right. Rocky's file mentioned he'd been sick and
recovered after treatment. They had a sketch in the file
showing Rocky's markings, too. It was probably drawn up
when the new whale came in because the picture showed
Rocky with two notches in his dorsal. They must have de-
stroyed as many of the old publicity shots as they could, but I
remembered seeing *one* fin notch in an old publicity photo of
Rocky I found in the box office. I had no idea of what was

going on. Who could have? But I figured if something was wrong, Livingston had to know because he was taking care of Rocky back when he was sick. My pictures would have proved it, but I wanted more evidence, that's why I went poking around his house the night they caught me. It was dumb not to tell Walden I was going there."

"Not dumb at all, Jill. Walden was right. You're really responsible for breaking the case."

"I still can't get over Dr. Livingston. Did he really think he could just smuggle in whales forever without getting caught?"

"No, he knew Rocky was pretty much a onetime shot. You couldn't just bring a new killer whale into an aquarium without the feds asking lots of questions about where it came from. He told me he planned to set up an orca-breeding facility legally in another country. Canada maybe. He'd breed whales to sell there, but more important he could use it as a cover to launder whales caught in the wild. He had big plans for Oceanus. Once he got a pair of whales there, he could start breeding them legally, then he'd open an Oceanus Two and so on."

"He was the guy who hated to see whales in prison, even for the good of science."

"You can convince yourself of the righteousness of anything. Look at Walden."

We were out of earshot. Her face was as serious as I had ever seen it. "Walden said he doesn't have any faith in the system. He says Oceanus and all the marine parks like it are abominations that should be blown off the face of the earth."

"You don't have to tell me this, Jill. They'd say you were a snitch if they ever find out."

"I *am* a snitch. I'm the one who told the newspapers about the holes in Eddy Byron's wet suit."

I looked at her anxious face and laughed. "Trouble comes

in all shapes and sizes, I suppose. Whom are you going to shake up next?"

She glanced back at the house. "My parents. They're coming home in another week. I'm going to ask my dad to bankroll me back into college. Time for me to grow up, I guess." She stood on her toes and gave me a kiss on the cheek. "Thanks again for all you've done."

"That's good news about school. I suggest you move the SOS command post before your parents come home. It might put your father in a better frame of mind." I told her to keep in touch, got into my truck, and headed out the drive. Kojak was going to be furious with me. I had left him dry food for a couple of days, but he hated the stuff, and I couldn't blame him. I'd have to stop off for a case of 9-Lives assorted flavors to get back into his good graces.

On the drive home, I thought about Ned's philosophical mutterings. He was shell-shocked, but he wasn't dumb. After the past week I'd be the first to agree with him. Everything *is* crazy.

33

Simon Otis stood with his back to me, looking out the window toward Logan Airport. His hands were clasped behind him. He had been standing rigidly in this position for at least five minutes, watching the air traffic in silence. He spoke, finally.

"Well," he said. "Seems as if things are in a bloody mess, aren't they?"

I sat at the long table doodling smiley faces in a Bay State Investments notepad. A folder with my typed report lay open nearby.

Otis continued his soliloquy. "The manager of Oceanus is in jail charged with murder. Our killer whale turns out to be contraband. And our Japanese investors have gone back to Tokyo at the first hint of scandal, taking their checkbooks with them."

He turned slowly and looked at me with his piercing gray eyes.

"It might have been better if we had never hired you, Mr. Socarides."

I put the ballpoint pen down.

"Austin would have gotten away with murder, Mr. Otis. And Livingston would still be smuggling whales and dolphins."

Otis came over and sat at the head of the table. "Yes, of course," he said. "It would never do to have criminals running around, would it? Well, you don't have any suggestions, do you?"

"Yes, sir," I replied. "As a matter of fact, I do."

He glanced up under frosty eyebrows. His question had been rhetorical. I told him what I had in mind anyway. When I was through talking, he smiled tightly and toyed with one side of his mustache.

"You told me public relations wasn't your specialty, Mr. Socarides. I think you underestimate yourself."

I shrugged and doodled some more while he thought things over. After a moment, he said, "I'll run your suggestion by the Bay State board of directors." He stood and extended his hand. "Thank you for coming. I'll have the limo run you home."

"Thank you for sending it. It beats hell out of the P-and-B bus any day."

He acknowledged my gratitude with a slight nod. His thoughts were already elsewhere.

The black stretch limo was waiting for me at the front door. I settled into the plush seat and opened the bar. There was no Bud, so I had to settle for Heineken's. I asked the chauffeur if I could use the telephone. He said it was no skin off his nose, so I played big-time executive.

I called Sam's house and left a message with Millie saying I would go fishing tomorrow, gave Dan Shaughnessy a ring to tell him I would send him a copy of my report, then called Parmenter at the state-police barracks.

"Glad you caught me," he said. "I was just cleaning the stuff off my desk. Hope to be out of here in about an hour."

"Thanks again for helping me in my case and for keeping Pacheco off my butt."

"It was worth it for the chance to see his face when he found out you got the collars in his murder investigation. He looked like he'd just been plucked out of the beet patch. He's going to have a lot of explaining to do and I don't think he'll bother you for a long time, but just the same, I'd stay under the speed limit when you go through his town."

"I will, John. And I'll give you a call the next time I'm in Boston."

"You make sure you do that. Maybe I can get another assignment down this way again. The file's still open on the Mid-Cape Flasher."

"No maybes about it. What if I call you in a couple of weeks? I'll take you out fishing."

There was a pause at the other end of the line, then Parmenter said, "I'd like that. Yeah, I'd like that fine."

Next I called Sally. I said I had a few things to explain to her and asked if she wanted to come to a family lamb dinner Sunday. She said she would. I called my mother to let her know I was bringing a friend.

"A *girl*friend?" she asked.

"A woman friend," I answered.

"Ah," she said. She was too polite to ask any more questions. "Your friends are always welcome in our house. Uncle Constantine called. He sounds very happy. He was no trouble, after all, Aristotle?"

"No, Ma, he was no trouble at all."

I said good-bye to Rocky for the last time about a month later.

He was hanging above a tractor trailer, wrapped in a nylon

sling like a stork-delivered baby. The sling was attached by a cable to a crane at the rear of the orca pool. Sally and I stood on the trailer next to a thirty-five-foot-long fiberglass tank partially filled with seawater.

I patted his side. "Say hello to the mermaids for me, pal."

Sally gave him a kiss on the nose. "Good-bye, Rocky. I'll never forget you." She reached out to touch his skin one more time. Then I signaled the crane operator and he gently lowered Rocky into the tank. A couple of workers bolted aluminum sides and a roof onto the trailer. Minutes later the truck started and drove off.

We walked around the now empty pool to the bleachers where Walden Schiller sat watching Rocky's departure. Sally lingered near the pool while I went over to talk to Walden. He got up and came over to shake my hand.

"Well, tally one for our side," he said. "How did you do it?"

"Easy, really. I told Simon Otis the truth. That Rocky was smuggled goods. That even if Bay State won the legal fight to keep him, it would raise a hell of a fuss and cost his company enormous legal expenses. And after that, they'd have a whale nobody could be sure of, an animal that may have killed once and could kill again, in public, in the middle of a show."

"Do you really believe that would have happened?"

"I just laid out the possibilities. Otis was ripe for a good suggestion. So I proposed that he take the initiative before the feds did and return Rocky to the wild. Bay State couldn't buy that kind of favorable publicity for a million bucks."

"What happens at Oceanus?"

"They'll scale down. They'll scrap their expansion plans and go more for education than entertainment. Might be a nice little place for the kids to learn about the sea."

"What about the dolphins?"

"They stay." I pointed to the whale pool. "They'll have Rocky's old pad. It'll give them more room. I know you'd like to see it otherwise, but that's just the way things are for now. Maybe you can get them set free eventually without blowing the place apart. Which reminds me. We discussed a quid pro quo for springing Rocky."

Schiller nodded. "There's a package in your truck. Don't leave it alone."

Lucky me, I now had enough plastic explosive to blow Hyannis off the map. I hoped I still had Flagg's number. "I'll take care of it," I said.

We shook hands again and Schiller left. The orca stadium was quiet. Sally was still standing by the pool, now empty, looking into the water. I went over and put my arm around her. She had a tear in her eye.

"Don't worry about Rocky," I said. "He's going first class all the way. He'll be at Logan Airport in a couple of hours. By this time tomorrow he'll be in a halfway house on the West Coast. When he's ready to go back into the wild, they'll put him into the water off British Columbia. The guys in his pod are probably planning a welcome-home party for him."

"I know it's for the best," she said, sighing, "but I'll miss him."

"I will, too. But you've still got Huff and Puff and Froggy. And you've got me."

She put a slender arm around my waist. "Yes, I've got you."

"I'm glad you agreed. My mother wants to have us to dinner again. She told me to stay home if I don't bring you."

"I accept, with one condition."

"What's that?"

"I want to see that picture of you again. The one when you were twelve, in the Greek soldier uniform with that cute little pleated skirt and pom-poms on your shoes."

"We'll talk about it," I said, taking her arm. "But first, let's get something to eat. I know a little shack near the beach that makes the best fried clams in the world."